The Lost Spyder

C.S. Michael

WALKABOUT PRODUCTION GROUP

TO MY GRANDMOTHER,
WHO TAUGHT ME TO LOVE BOOKS

PREFACE

This book was written shortly after the turn of the new century. Not unlike the mythical car at the heart of the story, the manuscript was stashed away for a few years. The advent of new e-reader technology motivated me to revive the project and bring it to publication.

For more information on this book, including original video interviews and photographs, please check out the official website: LostSpyder.com.

Although writing may appear to be a solitary endeavor, no one really does it alone. I'd like to extend special thanks to my wife Kristy for her ongoing support (including many hours of "research" that involved various Porsches). Her feedback has been invaluable.

Also thanks to my parents, especially my mother Gail, a retired English teacher who always kept my grammar straight. She insisted that I break this novel out of storage and share it with the world.

Thanks to literary agent Bob Lescher and all of my other "pre-publication" readers from Alabama to New York. Your commentary on the story and its characters helped make the book better.

Finally, thanks to you, the reader.

I hope you enjoy the ride.

C.S. Michael

"Dream as if you'll live forever.
Live as if you'll die today."

James Dean

1

A PIG TAUGHT JOHNNY life's greatest lesson. It happened when he was just a boy, maybe six years old. It's funny how life unfolds. Most people spend their lives avoiding conflict and drama. They sleepwalk safely from place to place, never bothering to step outside their comfort zone. Always avoiding drama. But a life without drama is like clay without a mold.

Johnny spent the rest of his life thinking about that simple gullible little pig. He fed it, raised it, even gave it a name like one would a pedigreed pet. Oscar was his buddy. He was healthy, pink, and plump. One day Daddy gave the word. Johnny's pet was to be slaughtered, smoked, salted, and stored in the meat house. Oscar would help feed them through the winter.

Their home was a scarcely tamed patch of undesirable Alabama red clay. To call the ramshackle, sprawling patch of land a farm would've been generous. Scattered amongst acres of kudzu was a menagerie of rugged vegetables, a scrawny milk cow, dozens of lean chickens, and the hogs. Oscar was merely one occupant, albeit the only one Johnny cared about.

Of course, when the day arrived, there was drama. Johnny cried. He struggled against the inevitable, wielding the usual childish sentimental arguments. Daddy was unsympathetic. Johnny was a reluctant participant in the killing. Oscar came to him willingly, the way obedient loving pets are apt to do. Daddy did the shooting, straight through the animal's skull. Daddy assured him that Oscar didn't feel a thing. He explained that it was right.

"That's the way of the world, son," Daddy said. "The strong eat the weak. That's the way God wants it."

Lesson learned. The boy never forgot slipping that first tender piece of pork into his mouth. He felt guilty and ashamed. There's nothing like eating your best friend to reorient one's axis. The pig became a part of him. He went through life remembering Oscar, the pet that sacrificed its life to nourish his body. Most importantly, Johnny Callahan remembered the lesson. Six decades passed for the little boy. He spent most of his time on earth eating the weak, just as God intended.

His SUV climbed the steep road, its massive heart thumping beneath champagne skin. It tugged a sleek silver trailer, a bullet connected by an umbilical mass of metal chains. Together they rolled forward with improbable synchronicity, defying the laws of gravity. Up they traveled along the misty mountain highway. Up, up, up flew the lonely caravan, up into the clouds.

A smile crept across the driver's face. It started in one corner of his mouth, and evolved into a wide-open grin.

John Christian Callahan was a happy man. He was more than happy. He was downright giddy, and laughing out loud. His SUV was painted champagne for a reason. It was time to celebrate, because he finally had the prize. At long last he had it, the one they said did not exist.

He cleared the incline and entered a stretch of thick forest. The mountain road was paved but twisty. Callahan loved twisty roads, but this cargo demanded care. He maneuvered the SUV and trailer through each successive turn like a steady pendulum.

His life was a series of acquisitions and conquests. His story was that of the strong consuming the weak. Now he was on the verge of his greatest triumph. In a lifetime of improbable stunts, this one took the prize. This time he achieved the extraordinary.

You crazy old fuck. You flew solo and found the Goddamned holy grail.

The road leveled. Even a party of one needs music. He flicked on the stereo, an intimidating mass of tiny black buttons and knobs.

He stabbed at the buttons, his glance alternating between the road and control panel. At last he was rewarded with music, a woman crooning in Spanish.

Why do they make these things so complicated? You need a PhD to figure out the damn radio.

Unsatisfied, he twisted the knob. At this moment, while struggling to find a decent radio station, the sedan pulled onto the road. He didn't notice. He was watching the radio instead of the rear view mirror. When he finally saw it, he was startled. The car, a battered four-door that had long since lost most of its weathered black paint, was close. It pulled alongside his SUV and matched speed.

The men inside wore crude masks fashioned from pantyhose. One man had a gun, and he waved it out the window in Callahan's direction. Another held a handmade sign of cardboard and ink, an incomprehensible scrawl of messy Spanish. He pressed the sign against the window of the car.

Callahan looked at the sign, heartbeat kicking into gear.

Ne hablo Español, motherfuckers.

He didn't read Spanish, but he understood. The strong eat the weak. This was decision time.

In an instant, the choice was made. John Christian Callahan was incapable of compromise, even when the alternative was deadly force.

He pressed his right foot to the floor. The turbo spooled and with a whoosh, the SUV and trailer surged forward like an elephant propelled by slingshot. As Callahan snapped back into his seat, he couldn't resist a laugh. He loved conflict, and hadn't enjoyed such an adrenaline rush in years. Conflict was Callahan's favorite indulgence, his place to snap apart the bones of life, and suck out the juicy marrow. This was how sex used to be, the euphoria of excitement, the violent thumping of his heart, the tingling in his stomach.

He had risked disaster with the holy grail, but the trailer held fast and true.

The sedan receded in his rear view mirror, beaten. Technology and hubris and audacity had triumphed. In any contest with rules, Callahan knew he would triumph.

These men did not play by rules.

The bullets came from behind. They sprayed into the SUV through the rear, at a skyward angle, shattering the window by his side. Some exited through the roof, leaving streams of sunlight. Others pelted the front windshield, creating intricate webs of broken glass.

He felt stabbing pain. One bullet passed through his body. It entered eight inches below his right shoulder blade, exited, and continued through the front windshield. It left behind a splash of blood in its wake, spattered across the leather dash like a Pollack canvas.

The blood affected Callahan. He could've handled these punks in a fair fight. The sight of his own blood wasn't fair. Seeing it smeared across the dashboard sent him into shock. Worse, his right arm didn't respond to input. It twitched unnaturally. It was all he could do to keep his rig on the road.

Finally he lost control, and swerved. The SUV brakes bit hard and brought the procession to a screeching halt. The sedan fishtailed to avoid slamming into the trailer from behind. It cut across the front of the SUV, stopping in a cloud of dust and smoke.

With his left hand, Callahan fumbled to open the glove box. He had one more card to play. If only he could reach it.

As he extended across the passenger cabin, the driver's door jerked open. Someone grabbed his legs and dragged him from the seat. He hit his head on the door sill, saw stars, and looked up into the distorted face of his assailant. Behind the man's pantyhose mask, a thick pink scar was visible. The scar ran a jagged line south, from beneath the left eye across his cheek. Above the scar, two calm eyes. They stared with the empathy of a snake sizing up its dinner.

That's the way of the world, son. The strong eat the weak.

The butt of a shotgun slammed into Callahan's jaw, dislodging two teeth. The old man saw stars again, this time in full color. He closed his eyes and braced for the end.

He was crumpled in a heap, bleeding onto a road that was now slick with the stuff. As he drifted from consciousness, he heard more Spanish.

He sank into the pavement, the scent of warm asphalt filling his nostrils, the bitter taste of blood filling his mouth. His head was on fire. He blinked and tried to open his eyes one last time. He discovered it felt better to keep them closed.

Devils. It's not supposed to end this way.

Eyes shut, John Christian Callahan saw nothing at all.

Nothing but blackness.

THE LOST SPYDER

With the gringo secured, the men sprang into action. They worked with maniacal efficiency, like piranhas stripping a bloated cow. The silence was heavy, only broken by the rhythm of rapid breathing and work being done. The sun was melting into the horizon, casting long shadows. This was the best time for work.

They had to hurry. No one, not even these hard men, could linger on the road. Inside this *piñata* were tasty treats, spoils to be inventoried but not yet enjoyed.

One man, who was really nothing but a boy, searched the SUV. His small hands moved briskly throughout the passenger cabin, with a precision that bordered upon artistry. Gringos were predictable, with valuables kept in predictable places. The glove box. Under the seat. Inside luggage. There were only so many places to hide, and wealthy gringos usually didn't try. The more they own, the less they care.

The second man, the chubby one who was fat in the body and in the head, searched the gringo's body. The old gringo was sprawled across the pavement like roadkill. He must've been lost to be traveling this road. Lost or stupid. Perhaps the gringo was fat in the head, too.

The third man, The Man with the Scar, held the gun. He stood watch halfway between the SUV and the sedan. He poised, stiff and unflinching, senses cocked at full alert, limbs frozen like a startled wild animal.

His eyes scanned the horizon. He saw nothing to inspire concern. The mountain highway was clear. Locals knew the threat of dusk, and they stayed off this road. Even the police, the smart ones who valued survival, stayed off this road at night.

A shout came from the SUV. The boy was into the glove box. He was excited, and acting like a child.

The stoic face of The Man with the Scar, rippled with pockmarks, morphed into a frown. He glanced again in each direction, then walked to the SUV to scold the boy. He was just a boy, but he knew better. The Man cursed and barked in Spanish. The boy was acting fat in the head.

In response, the child held aloft a white envelope. It was stuffed thick with green notes. Cash. American dollars. More cash than they'd seen in a year. Maybe in five. The boy bubbled with infectious joy.

"*Tranquilidad*," said The Man with the Scar, his pulse quickening. His hand rested steady on the gun. His mind reeled. The fat man had been correct about this target. He said this gringo was rich and carrying cash. He'd never seen so much cash. *Who was this gringo?*

Another shout, this time from the fat man. In the gringo's jacket he found more American greenbacks. He held the notes aloft in one fist, triumphant.

The Man with the Scar stood still, frozen in thought. He knew he should drag this gringo into the bushes, put the gun to his head, and pull the trigger. Fill his skull with bullets. Leave the carcass. Finish the job, take the cash, and get back on the road.

He knew they should not linger. But The Man with the Scar had to know more. There was the silver trailer jackknifed behind the SUV. What did it contain?

He motioned to the others, and they responded instinctively.

He jerked the door of the trailer, but it held fast. It was locked.

They stepped back from the door. A single gunshot erupted into the dusk, shattering the silence. The crisp sound echoed through the empty hills, bouncing from one to the next.

The Man grabbed the door again, the barrel of his gun still smoking. This time the door swung free.

They peered inside the trailer.

There was a large mound of fabric, stretched long and low and wide.

The boy climbed into the trailer and jerked the canvas free. There was a wooden crate beneath, long and low and wide. Next the boy pried open and lifted the crate lid. As the sun set behind them, light sparkled from the shiny metal inside the box, glinting across their masked faces. The sun was casting its final rays from the darkness within.

The Man with the Scar shielded his eyes with one hand, and studied the prize with reptilian interest. It was like another pile of cash spilling onto his feet, another glorious surprise from this *piñata*.

The fat man and boy breathlessly awaited what came next. They knew this day was different. This day was special.

Their leader's yellow eyes sparkled in the last remnants of sunset, surveying the scene without emotion. The Man was calm again, accessing the situation with his usual military efficiency. He'd made his decision, and it was momentous. This was a rare opportunity. Like a python, they would swallow and consume the whole thing.

He barked and his crew leapt into action, pulses in overdrive. They scooped up the limp body of the gringo and shoved it into the SUV.

They were predators in this ecosystem, feeding on what wandered into their midst. Usually the scene of their feast was messy, leaving bones and bodies behind. This meal was different. This time they left only tire tracks, and a sticky slick of gringo blood on the pavement.

Engines started and the motorcade slowly rolled away. The sedan and SUV lumbered together back down the mountain road.

The Man with the Scar smiled in satisfaction. This time he was going to eat the whole damned thing.

2

CHARLES MORTIMER BYRD WAS ANNOYED.

He stared at the thin piece of onion paper in his right hand and cursed. Another parking ticket, courtesy of the downtown meter maids.

Byrd checked his watch. His trip to the bursar's office had run fifteen minutes late. Now, thanks to this ticket, he was another fifteen dollars in debt.

It was going to be one of those days.

With a loud screech, Byrd pulled open the door of his aging Ford Bronco. The vehicle had once boasted a pristine coat of snow white, but over the years assumed a dull cream patina. Its fading paint was peppered with chocolate mud and red clay accents. His was the rare SUV that was actually driven off road. It had the dents, dings, and dirt to prove it. The only regular washing it received came in the form of acid rain.

Byrd liked the evolving color of his truck. He liked the fact that driving a white Ford Bronco was no longer stylish. The Bronco had gone the way of the dodo. Soccer moms had long since moved on to Lexus and Mercedes and other fashion statements. Meanwhile, Byrd's beloved stallion assumed a charisma all its own.

He slid his six-foot 200-plus pound frame into the well-worn driver's seat, slamming the door shut with another ear-piercing squeal.

Yes, he liked the color. He liked the odor. He liked the frayed cloth seats with their spongy cushions and faded fabric. He liked the squeaks and rattles that seemed to erupt from every part of the vehicle. Best of all, Byrd liked the fact that he, not the bank, owned the damn thing. The Bronco was paid for. Which was more than could be said of his legal education.

With a note of grim satisfaction, he crumpled the parking ticket into a small wad, and tossed it in the backseat. It disappeared into a sea of newspapers, textbooks, t-shirts, and food wrappers. If the exterior of the truck was dirty, the interior was chaotic. A slew of parking tickets were buried beneath the rubble.

Byrd shifted the Ford into gear, and stomped hard on the gas. He was late and needed to make up for lost time.

The truck hesitated, and then lurched away from the curb. As the aging V8 sucked down a deep drink of fuel, Byrd flipped on the radio. He was greeted by Cyrus Bergman crooning his signature country anthem, "I Love New York," which in the wake of 9/11 became an improbable local rally cry. The song remained an anchor of radio play lists, and Byrd appreciated the sappy escapism.

On a cool summer morning
That felt more like fall
The twin towers fell
But the people stood tall

Our hearts they sank
When those souls hit the ground
But our spirits rose up
When we knew what we found

I Love New York (We love it)
I Love New York (We love it)

The anthem continued to bleat and rattle from the tinny speakers of the Ford. Byrd couldn't resist a dreamy smile. He liked to imagine himself living the good life in Manhattan, far away from his routine existence deep in the heart of nowhere.

Byrd steered his Bronco onto the highway entrance ramp, and all movement ground to a halt. The road was jammed with morning commuters, most of whom were busy slurping coffee from travel mugs and doing little else. What should've been a busy highway was instead a parking lot. There'd been a wreck.

Byrd's brief flirtation with a good mood disappeared. He was annoyed again. Times like this, trapped in morning traffic, made him feel so ordinary. As if on cue, it was time for the obligatory morning zoo disc jockey.

"Good morning L.A.," the DJ cackled in a baritone radio voice that was as genuine as a three-dollar bill. "It's another beautiful morning in Lower Alabama."

It should be criminal to call Birmingham L.A., he thought. *To hell with the First Amendment.*

Charlie Byrd was in no mood to hear this sort of drivel. He clicked the radio to AM. Talk radio had its share of rambling idiots, but at least here the idiots were authentic.

The caller was in mid-sentence. " . . . and I think that boy is gonna win not one, but two, Heisman trophies while he's at Alabama. That's assuming he don't jump to the NFL. I mean, the boy's got a absolute cannon for a arm. If he goes pro, you got to play some second-string guy, and second-string ain't gonna cut it in the SEC."

Byrd shook his head and punched the radio off. In some cities, talk radio was replete with political debate about pressing local and national issues. Birmingham had the debate, but only one issue—college football, that amateur gladiatorial contest involving blood, sweat, and pigskin. Ancient Romans had bread and circuses; Alabama was content with barbeque and football. The state boasted two universities that each fielded improbably talented teams. The flagship University of Alabama Crimson Tide squad faced its fiercest rival in the nearby Auburn University Tigers. Residents of the state were forced to swear allegiances at an early age. Some joked that football was much like religion, only more important. Byrd chose the Crimson Tide and Methodism, both for reasons of expedience.

Charlie Byrd played the sport in high school. Much like military service in Israel, participation in football was expected. But he blew out his left knee in the ninth grade. The injury was a dislocated patella, doctorspeak for what happens when a kneecap pops out of joint.

Byrd never had the injury repaired. Torn cartilage and ligaments, the doctor said. Not much he could do. What he didn't say, but everyone understood, was that a bench warmer like Charlie Byrd wasn't worth the expense.

The knee never received surgery, and sometimes it decided to pop. When it popped, Byrd fell flat on his ass like a collapsing house of cards. That knee was the reason he transferred classes from athletics to health. Instead of practicing football, he practiced sucking face with a CPR doll named Annie. The bum knee kept him on the bench. It kept him second-string.

His entire existence, he thought, could be summed up in those two words. He was a second-string athlete, second-string student (the kind one might diplomatically call "beneath the curve"), second-string lover (according to his legion of ex-girlfriends). He owned a second-string truck with a shitty second-string factory stereo.

This town is second-string, he thought. Byrd didn't really believe it, but he was pissed off and lashing at the one reliable friend in sight.

Charlie Byrd was born and bred in Birmingham. It was his own thorny briar patch. Most of the world knew Birmingham from grainy black-and-white film footage, violent images of white suppression captured during the American civil rights movement of the 1960s. Tensions between the races reached a fever pitch after one of the nation's most heinous crimes was committed on 16th Street; four young black girls were murdered while attending church.

If 1963 represented the city's low point, the decades since had seen a steady recovery. Maybe that was one reason football was glorified beyond the norm. Football was a unifying force, blacks and whites working together to score touchdowns for the common good.

For all of his New York fantasies, Charlie Byrd was comfortable in a modest little fishbowl. He felt an affection for Birmingham not unlike that a mutt feels for its master. For reasons long since forgotten, residents called Birmingham *the Magic City*. Cynics—Byrd included—called it *the Ham*, a cheeky and affectionate nickname. Absolutely no one—except "morning zoo" disc jockeys—ever called it L.A.

But Birmingham traffic did resemble L.A. He edged his Bronco to the side of road, and continued moving forward along the shoulder. The traffic was bumper-to-bumper, but Byrd's Bronco rumbled past cars along the side of the road. At last he rolled down the next exit ramp, and onto the labyrinthine back roads. Like most cities, Birmingham was distinguished by neighborhoods that each boasted their own unique character.

The road less traveled would take him from Homewood (home to many a young urban professional) to Diaper Row (named in the 1940s from the clotheslines full of diapers hanging in each backyard) into the exclusive community of Mountain Brook. Winding roads, rolling hills, and thick foliage characterized Birmingham's reservoir of Old Money. Centrally located, you could get anywhere quickly if you knew the back roads. Charlie Byrd knew the back roads. His brain was a veritable Birmingham GPS, and Mountain Brook was its central map. This was an area that, despite its trappings of wealth and comfort, had seen its share of tragedy over the years. Mountain Brook was the type of place where well heeled families eschewed graduation trips to Florida in favor of the Caribbean islands. It was on the island of Aruba where one of these celebratory adventures went horrifically awry. A Mountain Brook teen named Natalee Holloway mysteriously disappeared during her graduation trip. Her disappearance set off a global media firestorm and became one of the world's most discussed missing persons cases.

As his truck snaked past acres of kudzu and colossal antebellum homes, Byrd reflected upon a morning wasted at the bursar's office. His schedule for the third year of law school was locked into place. The tuition payment loomed on the horizon like an approaching thunderstorm.

In one more year, for better or worse, he'd be a lawyer. Until that time, he needed a break. A profitable break. Legal education at Birmingham School of Law was reasonably priced, as such things go. The school was not accredited by the American Bar Association. Lack of membership, Byrd liked to say, had its privileges. Kids who were spending Daddy's money got their legal education at ABA accredited schools like Samford and the University of Alabama. BSL existed for the rest, those whose long term legal ambitions remained safely within state borders. A hearty serving of hamburger in a world of steak, BSL filled a need. But Charlie Byrd was paying his own way. "*Birmingham SOL*," he called it, for he often felt *SOL*. *Shit outta luck*.

He emerged from the hills of Mountain Brook onto a promising expanse of interstate. Traffic was thinning—he'd finally escaped the snakepit of Highway 280.

As the Bronco merged onto the freeway, Byrd pulled out a too-old-to-be-hip mobile phone. Like his truck, it was second-string technology. For all practical purposes, the financial well-being of *Byrd's Eye Investigation* rested upon these two shaky pillars.

He dialed his voice mail. He wanted to hear the message one more time. It was from an old man who didn't bother to identify himself, which wasn't altogether unusual. He promised Charlie Byrd prompt payment in cash. All Byrd had to do was show up on time, and ask for Chris Callahan.

That was all that Byrd knew. A phone call to his voice mail in the middle of the night. An elderly gent with a pot of cash, both waiting at the end of the rainbow.

He'd heard of Callahan, of course. Callahan understood one of the fundamental truths of nature—Alabamians love anything deep-fried and heavily salted. The old man made a fortune selling potato chips and other fried salty snacks in Alabama. He once played a prominent role in local affairs, but receded from public view. Now he was calling Charlie Byrd?

Byrd was intrigued. More importantly, he was broke. The word "cash" was more than enough to get his attention.

He checked at his watch. Twenty minutes past nine. He was late.

Byrd stomped on the gas, and flogged his groaning truck to go a little faster.

3

CHARLIE BYRD WAS LATE.

It was thirty minutes past nine when he arrived at Alabama's unlikeliest tourist attraction. The Park was tucked away on a massive expanse of wooded land. Surrounded by acres of rolling hills and towering pines, it felt rural, even isolated.

Byrd knew the story. The Park was the brainchild of a local entrepreneur named George Barber. For most of his life, Byrd had been wolfing down ice cream, butter, milk—and his personal nectar of the Gods, chocolate milk—bearing the Barber name.

After selling the dairy business and making a small fortune, George Barber started giving back to the community in his own special way. The man was into motorcycles, so he built a museum, stocking it with over 750 rare vintage bikes. It was the largest collection in the United States.

Barber liked cars, so he built the ultimate car playground. He bought a 740-acre tract of land, and planted a state-of-the-art racetrack upon it. After plowing more than $60 million into the ground, Barber Motorsports Park opened for business. Some called it the prettiest track in the world. It was, they said, the Augusta of race courses, a synergistic union of aesthetics and athletics.

THE LOST SPYDER

Rolling through the Park gates for his first time, Charlie Byrd wanted to stop and soak up the view. But he was late, almost forty minutes now. He wasn't supposed to be late.

He steered his Bronco through the carefully landscaped grounds, attempting to locate the correct building. When he arrived at the racing paddock, the place looked deserted. The parking lot was empty, save for a few fancy European sports cars whose names he couldn't pronounce. He pulled his Bronco into a vacant space, and bounded toward the paddock building.

The morning quiet was broken by the shrill, distant wail of an engine in full song. Somewhere on the far side of the track, a fast car was being put through its paces.

The three-story control building was a modern expression of gray concrete, shiny aluminum, and walls of tinted glass. The décor was utilitarian and functional, exuding the type of raw cleanliness only possible in new construction.

The ground floor of the paddock housed several garages. The top floors looked like office space, while the rooftop boasted an open viewing area from which to observe the track. Atop the building, a few dozen white flags fluttered in the breeze.

The impact was impressive, even to a cynic like Charlie Byrd. Standing before the paddock, Byrd was bemused by the contemporary elegance of the place. Ironic, he thought, to have this millionaire's recreational sandbox sitting in rural Alabama.

The building was three stories high, but it had an elevator. Even this was state-of-the-art expressionism, its sheets of thick glass offering full view of the action below. In a brazen display of laziness, Byrd rode the high-tech elevator to the third floor. He ducked through the first door he saw, the one that appeared to contain offices.

The receptionist was a cute Asian girl wearing a low-cut black dress. Byrd had never dated an Asian. If the opportunity arose, he wouldn't say no.

"My name's Charlie Byrd," he said. "I'm looking for Chris Callahan."

"Yes, Mr. Byrd," she replied in a heavy Southern accent. "Just one moment please."

The receptionist picked up her telephone, spoke into the receiver, and nodded.

"Mr. Byrd," she drawled, "If you'll step back outside and down to the track area, your meetin' will start in just a few moments."

No trace of flirtation from the country Asian chick, so Byrd did as he was told. This time he used the stairs, jogging down the spiral staircase to the racetrack below. He paused along the way to soak in the view. Like most of Alabama, the twisting Barber track was full of green hills. There were no grandstands, only bucolic amphitheatre seating.

Toto, he thought, *we're not in Talladega any more.*

Like most Alabama residents, Byrd had attended the famous NASCAR race. Talladega was a gigantic people magnet, improbably attracting all aspects of Southern culture. Trailer trash and high society gathered together under the Alabama sun, though one segment clearly outnumbered the other. Byrd remembered little of Talladega, except a mechanical clamor loud enough to cause permanent hearing damage. The day after the race, his sunburn complemented his hangover.

On the far side of the Barber track, a yellow blur was working its way through corners. As the race car grew closer to the paddock, the engine noise grew more shrill. The wail was different from the American muscle cars with which Byrd was familiar. Not a deep throaty roar, it was a high-pitched metallic scream, like a formula car mating with a *Transformer*.

The car entered the final straight as a yellow blur. As if for dramatic effect, the driver waited until the last moment to slam on the brakes. Tires screeching in protest, the vehicle skidded to a halt with shocking immediacy—right in front of Charlie Byrd.

The yellow blur was no longer blurry. The car sat low to the ground, like a race car. Its driver reached over and opened the passenger side door. Her voice beckoned.

"Hey *Byrd's Eye*," she said. "Hop in. Not nice to keep a girl waiting."

With a grunt of discomfort, Byrd folded his frame into the passenger seat, and inhaled the new car smell.

The interior of the vehicle was a Spartan display of stitched leather and polished aluminum.

In the driver's seat was a young woman wearing a flimsy lace shirt and the kind of denim jeans that looked so tattered and worn, they had to be not only new, but expensive. Her hands wore black driving gloves. Her face was framed by a wild mane of auburn hair. It was tangled and disheveled, either fashionable or just plain sloppy. Charlie Byrd wasn't sure which.

The woman turned to face Byrd, and his mood changed again. He felt a pang of sincere regret at being late. She was a good-looking woman, blessed with pale fair skin, high cheekbones, and striking green eyes.

"I'm Charlie Byrd," he said. "I'm here to meet with Christian Callahan."

"I know who you are," the woman replied with a genteel Southern lilt. "You're late. I was beginning to think you weren't going to show up."

Byrd flinched as if he'd just been slapped.

"Well," he said, "I'm sorry about that. Traffic was terrible. Do you mind telling me who you are and what you do?"

The woman smiled. "Kris Callahan," she said, extending a gloved hand. "I do many things, none of 'em well. No offense Charlie, but you seem awfully slow for a private investigator."

Byrd sized up the woman. She was in her early thirties, trim and fit. Her face hinted at greatness. She had an aura about her, the aura of money. Somewhere beneath that flimsy lace lurked a tattoo or two; he was sure of it.

Her ears weren't only pierced, they were decorated. Multiple piercings extended up the right ear. Tiny silver renditions of a sun, moon, and stars, all connected by a jangling silver chain. When she moved her head the resulting effect was distracting and undeniably attractive.

She was not through prodding Charlie Byrd.

"Tell me," she said. "Is that your real name? What do you call it, *Byrd's Eye Investigation*? I mean, what are the odds?"

Byrd was not amused. He was sick of answering the question.

"It's my real name," he said.

The woman laughed. "I like *Byrd's Eye*. It's cute," she replied.

Byrd again flinched, this time at the word *cute*.

"Call me Kris," she said. "Short for Kristen."

"Okay, Kris. Everybody calls me Byrd. All I know is that I was supposed to come out here for a meeting. Some older gent left the message. He said I'd be paid five-hundred dollars for my time. Cash."

"Spoken like a true goat, right down to business. You're a Capricorn, aren't you?"

He shrugged.

"I guess so."

"Well, time is money. Since your time runs about an hour behind the rest of the world, how about four-hundred?"

Byrd kept a straight face, but inside he winced at the cost of being late. She was already driving the price down. She seemed to be getting sadistic pleasure from his predicament.

"All right," he said. "Fine. Four-hundred."

"I assume cash will be okay?"

"Cash will be fine."

In truth, cash would be outstanding. Cash would be magnificent. In Charlie Byrd's business, cash was king, queen, and the whole damn court. Byrd wasn't the world's greatest law student, but he understood the basics of Federal taxation.

The woman pulled out an envelope. She removed one bill, and handed over the remainder. Byrd counted four crisp hundred-dollar notes. His heart skipped a beat. Cash was always nice.

Charlie Byrd was no longer annoyed. He was happy. Four-hundred bucks was four-hundred bucks. She could annoy him all day long for four-hundred bucks.

"Okay Kris Callahan," he said. "I'm all yours."

The woman turned her gaze forward.

"Good," she said, "I strongly suggest you buckle your seatbelt."

The seatbelt clicked into place, and Charlie Byrd placed his head against the headrest.

At that moment, Kristen Callahan pushed her right foot to the floor, and he held on for dear life.

4

CHARLIE BYRD WAS NO STRANGER TO THRILL RIDES, roller coasters and the like. To Byrd, carnival rides were as fun as carnies were disturbing. It was all about the adrenaline rush.

No carnival ride prepared him for Kristen Callahan. She pushed down her right foot and sent the Porsche hurtling through a land without speed limits. They were on the track.

She handled the car with controlled aggression, testing the limits of physics, biology, and common sense. With each successive curve, Byrd was pressed hard into the side bolsters of his seat. His stomach buckled, and he feared his morning chocolate milk might make a return appearance. Throughout the ordeal, he clenched on for dear life with a death grip, and said nothing.

After sliding through a final turn, Callahan braked and coaxed the Porsche onto the main road. She cruised out of the paddock area, past the control building, past the museum, and out the main gate. Finally beyond the boundaries of the Barber Park, she brought the car to a standstill, waiting for passing traffic to clear. Byrd felt his stomach settle back into place, and he attempted conversation.

"This car," he said. "It's a Porsche, right?" He pronounced the word

Porsche with a single syllable.

She threw a glance his way, and again her face was revealed. First impressions had been right. Kristen Callahan had naturally beautiful facial structure, the kind that could sell truckloads of mascara without ever once needing the stuff.

"No," she said. "It's a Por-shaa. Two syllables."

Byrd shot her his best *go to hell* look.

"I'm just giving you a hard time," she said with a laugh. "You're taking me far too seriously. And yes, it's a Porsche. It's a 918."

Byrd nodded. For some reason, the car was named after an area code.

"I didn't think people who owned this sort of car actually drove 'em."

Again she laughed, as if Byrd had just told a private joke.

"They usually don't."

"So what's the deal with this one?"

"It's not mine," she said. "It's my father's. He's out of town. When the cat's away . . ."

Byrd nodded, recalling a recent story in *The Birmingham News*. Germany's most prestigious auto maker had moved its high-performance driving school to Alabama. Barber Motorsports Park was home to the Porsche Sport Driving School, a high-dollar classroom for performance driving. Birmingham hosted CEOs and celebrities as they christened muscular new cars on the track. Some of the world's most accomplished racing drivers called Alabama their home, and they spent their days gamely tutoring the idle rich. It seemed there was always a media buzz about the Barber track. You never knew when Jay Leno or Dr. McDreamy might be in town, and those types weren't shy about making the papers.

The idea of Hollywood celebrities flocking to rural Alabama struck Byrd as ironic. The state never got a fair shake in the movies. Some thirty years living in Alabama, and he'd never met a single member of the Klan or witnessed a burning cross. Except in the movies, where both were as inevitable as buttered popcorn and closing credits.

"Nice track," he said. "First time I've been out there."

"Best in the world," she replied.

"Oh really? Says who?"

"Drivers like me. No expense has been spared. Entire place is just gorgeous. That surface is like glass. When the first coat of asphalt wasn't perfect, George had the whole track ripped up and redone. Cost an extra half-million, but they got it right."

The words rolled off her tongue with an intriguing Southern lilt. It wasn't an old-money lilt. There was a perceptible trace of country in this city girl's accent.

"Well, it's big enough."

"Size matters," she replied. "It's the largest philanthropic undertaking in Alabama."

Byrd cocked his head at the word philanthropic, but he let the comment drop.

"So do you work for Porsche?" he asked, placing sarcastic emphasis on the second syllable. She had clearly been trained to drive a race car.

"No," she replied. "I run with the Porsche guys sometimes, but for me it's more of a hobby."

Her statement landed in his lap like a lead balloon. To Charlie Byrd, a reasonable hobby might involve yarn or musical instruments. This was her hobby?

"It's a good time," she said.

As if to emphasize the statement, she punched the throttle of the Porsche. Byrd felt a strong shove in his back as the car sprinted ahead.

"Okay, so we're riding in your daddy's car. Excuse me, your daddy's Porsche. And you're paying me four-hundred dollars to do it."

"You're wondering why?" she asked. "You tell me, Sherlock. You're the detective."

Byrd grinned. Despite the fancy car and the model's face, this was going to be routine. Help the little rich girl bust her boyfriend. Snap a few photos at Motel 6 (or considering this class of clientele, perhaps the four-star Tutwiler downtown). He'd be well paid, so that he in turn could pay his law school. This was Charlie Byrd's *modus operandi*. He was a conduit, transferring money from jilted women to Birmingham School of Law.

"Let me guess," he said. "You think someone is cheating on you, and you want me to follow the guy. Maybe snap a few photos?"

Byrd had seen these situations before. He worked his way through law school thanks to Birmingham's legion of wandering Romeos. Girlfriends, fiancés, and wives paid princely sums to catch their men in action. Byrd thanked God that rich guys had trouble keeping their zippers zipped.

She shook her head. "If only it were that simple. Let's just say that when this glove comes off," she raised her left hand, "no ring goes back on."

"Okay, so you're not married. Or engaged. Or whatever." He paused. "You dating anyone?"

"The short answer is no. My love life, or lack thereof, has nothing to do with this. Do you always ask such questions?"

"Yeah," he said. "Helps clear the air right in the beginning."

She braked the car hard enough to snap the seat belt against his chest, then turned onto a private driveway framed by decorative wrought iron gates. She pressed a button on the dash of the vehicle, and the gates slowly swung open.

"What's next?" he asked. "The Bat Cave?"

"Not a bad guess."

"Okay, I'm done guessing. Why don't you tell me why I'm here. Not to mention where 'here' is."

"Here is my father's estate. We're on his property for several reasons. Mainly because he's an asshole. And because of what you did in Greystone."

Greystone. New money. Old news.

Byrd had been hearing the G-word every day for two months. If he had a dollar for every time someone mentioned Greystone, he'd be out of debt. It was amazing how something could generate so much news, and so little money.

"I heard what you managed to do," she continued. "That was a wonderful achievement, bringing home that little girl to her parents. You did good."

The Greystone kidnapping occupied the local media's attention for months. A young woman disappeared from her parents' home. The family lived in an exclusive Birmingham suburb called Greystone. Prestige in Greystone derived from living "behind the gates," those swinging mechanical devices that protected little except narcissists' self-esteem. If Mountain Brook was known for old money then Greystone was known for new. Everything in Greystone was freshly minted, like the money. New golf courses, country clubs, cars, swimming pools, and jumbo houses, mostly financed by jumbo mortgages. Even the wifely tits were new, and almost as hard as the fat diamond rocks on their fingers. When someone goes missing in a shiny gated community like Greystone, it makes for a good story. The media paid attention. CNN sent a crew over from Atlanta, and broadcast the news all over the globe.

As a general rule, Charlie Byrd avoided CNN and the rest of the media like the plague. He was a private detective, emphasis on the word private. He tried to maintain a low profile, to keep his name out of papers and his face off TV. He usually succeeded.

"That case got a lot of attention," he said. "That's what happens when a rich kid—" He paused, realizing that he was talking to a rich kid.

She finished his sentence.

"When a rich kid disappears?"

"Well," he replied. "That's right. Poor kids go missing every day and nobody gives a damn. We might see 'em on milk cartons, but that's about it."

"But a rich kid disappears, and the media takes notice? Yes, you're right. When a rich kid's in trouble, it makes news. It makes a lot of news. Yet you solved this high-profile missing child case, and you managed to avoid the news. How is that? Why was your face never on CNN?"

"My business depends upon confidentiality," he replied. "If my face is recognized, it gets a lot harder for me to do my job. So I stay away from it all. Don't need it. Don't want it."

"Spoken like a Southern gentleman," she replied. "That false modesty is very becoming. You just might be the man of my dreams."

Byrd shrugged off the comment. She seemed to have a knack for verbal jabs.

"Look," he said, "I'm not being modest. Fact of the matter is I run a pretty small operation. Me, my truck, and my camera. Doesn't take Sherlock Holmes to snap pictures of some cheating SOB down at the Hampton Inn. But if that SOB happened to recognize me, then my job could get pretty unpleasant. It could be dangerous."

She wasn't convinced.

"Ah, but what about Greystone? The cops searched for that girl for months. Her face was on billboards and fliers and milk cartons. Yet you're the one who found her, thanks to some—shall we say unconventional?—

investigation techniques. They say you don't mind breaking the rules."

Charlie Byrd snorted at the suggestion.

"Who says? That's an exaggeration. Sounds like you've been talking to the police. Those guys don't like me or my kind."

"Actually," she replied, "it was a cop who recommended you. When I asked for a discreet local detective, your name was the first he mentioned."

Byrd was taken aback by this revelation. He'd crossed wits with the local police more than once, and there was no love lost between the two parties. He'd been called a lot of names by the cops, and discreet wasn't one of them. The underlying reality of the Greystone case was a fairly standard case of suburban parental adultery. Through the course of his nocturnal observation, he had noticed the teen daughter sneaking out of the house at night. When she went missing, he had facts that police and family did not. These weren't the type of facts one wanted splashed all over newspapers, but they ultimately paid off.

"Okay," he said, "What's the problem here? Someone's kid missing?"

Her voice tightened.

"Well, it depends on how you look at it. You might say a rich kid is missing. An overgrown, spoiled, rich kid."

"Sorry, I still don't follow you."

As they spoke, the yellow Porsche rolled up the hillside along a well manicured driveway. The property was framed by acres of neatly trimmed turf, all nicely punctuated with mature Alabama oak and pine. Byrd had seen, and played, golf courses with far less impressive grounds. Atop the hillside was the house, looking like a mountain perched atop a mountain. It was a hulking Old South behemoth that threatened to blot out the sun. He glanced at the house, and then back at the young woman in the driver's seat.

"I already told you," she said. "My father's an asshole."

Dear God, he thought, *the maintenance.*

Callahan pulled the car to a stop at the top of the driveway. She turned off the ignition key and the humming Teutonic spaceship suddenly fell silent.

"Give me a minute," she said, "I'll explain everything."

He again turned his gaze toward the house.

5

CHARLIE BYRD UNFOLDED HIS SIX-FOOT FRAME and emerged from the Porsche. With an exaggerated limp, he staggered away from the car.

With an easy pivot motion, Kristen Callahan sprang from the driver's seat. At last, freed from the confines of the car, Byrd enjoyed an unobstructed view of the woman. She was trim, petite, and athletic.

Her outfit was hardly appropriate for performance driving, but it showcased her figure well. The thin lace shirt barely touched her low rider jeans, which revealed a rather dramatic amount of midriff. She was wearing a bra, presumably of the push-up variety. The sole nod to sport was on her feet, which were clad in red leather driving shoes. The addition of flat-soled sneakers to her otherwise hip outfit was a comical touch.

"Nice shoes," Byrd said.

"Thanks. That reminds me."

She pressed a button on the key. With a gentle click, the car's front hood popped open. Byrd stepped forward, expecting to see the engine. Instead, she reached inside and withdrew a pair of women's shoes.

"Oh yeah," he said. "The engine's in the middle."

He pointed at the yellow car. "I have to ask. How much is that piece of plastic worth?"

He was being rather blunt, he realized, by referring to the Porsche as a piece of plastic. Probably not a smart move. Sometimes Byrd spoke first, and thought about it later. But he really wanted to know the price tag.

She feigned offense. "I'm shocked. Didn't your mother teach you any manners?"

He shrugged. "Well, that car's not exactly subtle. I didn't think you'd mind. You don't seem too shy."

"This one's a prototype. A 918 goes for about eight-fifty. It's a limited production, as these things go. First electric hybrid P-car."

His jaw dropped. *Eight-fifty?* As in eight-hundred-and-fifty thousand dollars?

Byrd stared at the two-seat vehicle with a new found combination of admiration and disgust. The Porsche was worth more than one-hundred 1989 Ford Broncos. It was worth more than the house he grew up in. But he wouldn't trade his truck for this car. He wouldn't drive this alien Chiquita banana if someone gave it to him. It took the phrase *conspicuous consumption* to a whole new level.

"It costs $850,000—and you're actually driving it?"

"Like I said," she replied, as she slammed the door shut. "It's not mine. It's my father's."

"Nevertheless," Byrd said, "I'd be careful about leaving it parked outside Walmart. You'll get a door ding. Trust me, I know from experience."

"Thanks," she replied. "I'll keep that in mind."

He turned away from the Porsche and surveyed the house.

Set on a large expanse of farmland, the Callahan estate was as conservative as the Porsche was radical. A classic Southern mansion, the full-length front veranda was flanked by stately Greek columns. The plain white trim was old school, acres of paint with flat black shutters forming the sole exterior adornment.

It was impressive, but cold. Something about the house struck Byrd as too perfect, a new money version of the Old South. It was like one of those imitation Tiffany lamps, convincing replicas of the real thing except for the *Made in China* stamp on the bottom.

She opened the Kubrick-inspired front door and Byrd watched her enter. For a moment, his attention drifted from the mammoth foyer to her curvaceous rear end. He far preferred the latter view. On the small of her back was a blue tattoo, the symbol of the Chinese yin-yang.

High dollar tramp stamp, he thought. *Perfect.*

Byrd watched the yin-yang bob and weave its way into the home. His mood lightened.

The entrance to the home beckoned like a spread for *Southern Living* magazine circa 1864. Thirty-foot ceiling. Marble floor. Crystal chandelier. Red velvet staircase. Mr. Callahan covered all the bases. Yet something about the place felt antiseptic, as comfortable as a new pair of Sunday shoes.

"Nice house," he said. "Very *Gone With the Wind.*"

She raised her eyebrows.

"My father has … traditional tastes," she said, as if she'd just named a disease. "You get used to it."

An older gentleman stepped into the room. He was tall, thin, and wiry. He moved with cautious precision, but greeted them with a warm smile.

"Hello, Kristen," he said.

Byrd recognized the croaking voice. It belonged to the elderly gent who'd called his cell phone.

"Baines," she replied, embracing the man in an enthusiastic hug. "It's so nice to see you again. Did you get my message?"

"Yes, ma'am," the man said. "The library is all ready. Y'all let me know if you need anything."

She nodded.

"That will be great. Thank you, Baines."

The obligatory servant, Byrd thought. *What a nice touch.*

They made their way through the cavernous and well-appointed home. They walked past the dining room with its enormous crystal chandelier and stout English antique furniture, hand-carved tables and oversized chairs. Past the living room with its coffered ceilings and Greek columns and plush oriental rugs. Past the game room and exercise room and sunroom. Past the awkward, angular spaces that indicated the architect of this sprawling McMansion simply ran out of ideas.

At last they arrived at the library, a room which, in terms of ambiance, put Birmingham School of Law's rather utilitarian facility to shame. It was a scene more appropriate for a George Plimpton or William F. Buckley than a

Charlie Byrd. Acres of dark stained walnut, coffered molding, banker's lamps. Dominating one wall was a framed color photograph of legendary Alabama football coach Paul "Bear" Bryant, wearing his trademark houndstooth fedora. Judging from the rest of his attire, the picture was taken at the height of the Bear's 1970s prime. The old coach was shaking hands with a much younger man. It must've been Callahan. Shrines to football were a staple of homes in Alabama, though most were more modest.

Nearby bookshelves stretched from floor to ceiling and were stacked full of leather bound tomes.

Byrd studied the scene with a healthy skepticism. No paperbacks, but plenty of nice leather-bound versions. The expensive kind. He doubted any of the books had actually been read. New money types always put on a show; classic books were almost as important as lush landscaping.

"You know," Byrd said, "your Dad could free up a lot of storage space with a good e-reader."

On one side of the room was a large oak desk, looking less like a desk and more like a medieval dining table. Facing the desk was an overstuffed leather couch, complemented by a couple of matching club chairs. The room was bubbling with a crusty millionaire vibe. Byrd awaited the obligatory scotch and cigar. They never came.

The woman pulled the door shut and motioned for him to sit down.

"Please, have a seat wherever you'd like."

He viewed the expanse of cowhide. To sit in one of these chairs, a person would sink to the floor. He'd be looking up at the bottom of her chin, which under other circumstances might not be so bad. But this was business.

"If you don't mind," he said, "I'll stand. I'm still recovering from our little joyride."

"Suit yourself."

She plopped into her chair as if it were a beanbag. Then she stretched her hands across the massive oak desk and leaned forward. Her eyes narrowed and her tone again grew serious.

She's quite the drama queen, Byrd thought.

"Okay, it's time for me to tell you what's happening," she said. "Before I do, I want to stress the importance of confidentiality. What I tell you shouldn't leave this room."

"What happens in the library, stays in the library," he replied.

"I'm serious," she said, "My father's a privacy freak. I guess he deserves to be left alone, if that's what he wants. God help us all if J.C. Callahan doesn't get what he wants."

Byrd snorted.

"He's gotten what most men want. A fast car and a big-ass house. Didn't this have something to do with potato chips?"

"Only as a supplier. He started Callahan Food Group back in the 50's, right after he got out of the Army. He went from the Korean War to the war back home. That's the way he puts it, anyway."

"Right."

"To his credit, he started with nothing, and that wasn't exactly the best time to start a business in Alabama. But potato chips are color blind, and he did well. Had a big deal with Golden Flake."

Byrd remembered a scene from his youth. Bear Bryant, at one time the winningest collegiate football coach in history, endorsed Golden Flake Potato Chips. This was akin to having the Pope recommend your brand of holy water.

"It probably didn't hurt business to have Coach Bryant eating those chips every Sunday on his TV show."

"You've got a good memory," she replied. "Every time Bear grabbed another fistful of chips, sales went up."

Byrd smiled at the mental image. Life was simpler in those days, back when he was a kid watching Sunday television. There were two seasons in Alabama, football season and recruiting. There were really only three channels on TV. If the Bear Bryant Show was on, the other two didn't count.

She leaned forward in her chair. "You don't know my father," she said. "There's not much he won't do."

"He likes to stir up shit, right? Dumped all those potatoes on the Governor's lawn?"

She smiled. "Yeah. No matter what he does with the rest of his life, he'll always be known for that incident."

Byrd wasn't the political type, but he had a healthy respect for rebels. The elder Callahan was undoubtedly a cocksure son-of-a-bitch. They still ran TV footage of his most public stunt. The Alabama Potato Party. It was the stuff of which legends were born, the way flamboyant entrepreneurs earned their stripes.

"Wasn't it a tax dispute? Some vote?"

"Yeah. The Governor and my father weren't on the same page."

"So your Daddy dumps twenty tons of potatoes on the front lawn of the Governor's Mansion, in the middle of the night, right before the vote. Didn't he get arrested?"

"Yeah. He got off." She shook her head in incredulity. "Won the vote, too."

"Well, he sure doesn't sound like a private person."

"He wasn't, not in those days. But a lot's changed. He's different now. Totally different."

"How so?"

"Over the past decade, he's retired out here and kept a low profile. I think retirement's been bad for him. He's become more withdrawn. More distant. More of an asshole, frankly."

Byrd understood. In this equation, something about retirement didn't make sense. Rich guys like J.C. Callahan weren't the retiring type. Usually these super-wealthy business characters were driven by ego. They had more financial wealth than they could possibly consume. Their only reason for survival was ego. This led them to pursue idiotic indulgent fantasies like flying their own Cessna through a windstorm, or even worse, running for governor of California.

"Don't most retired people have hobbies?"

She nodded. "My father's a collector. That's a piece of his collection sitting in the driveway."

"He collects cars?"

"You might say so," she replied. "He's one of those people who can't do anything in moderation. He always goes to extremes. If he knew we were talking, he'd be extremely pissed. He wants to be left the hell alone. So I leave him the hell alone. That's why we've got to keep this quiet."

Byrd was annoyed again, this time by the lecture.

"Look, you don't have to worry about confidentiality," he said. "My bread-and-butter business concerns people's love lives. Private stuff. Birmingham's a small town and I know how to keep my mouth shut. My work depends on it."

"Well, that's why I contacted you. It's like you said before—when a rich kid disappears, it makes news. If this thing goes public, it'll make big news. It'll make Greystone look like small potatoes."

"Understood," he replied. "Y'all want this kept quiet. So what's the deal here? A rich kid in trouble?"

"You might put it that way."

She shifted in her leather chair, then slipped her legs up into the seat and crossed them.

"It's my father. He's skipped town. We're not sure where he's gone."

"How long's he been gone?"

"A couple of weeks."

Byrd was taken aback. *A couple of weeks?* Two weeks was a lengthy period of time. In two weeks, any trail could grow cold. In fact, two days was the professional rule of thumb. Police referred to "the 48-hour rule." The first 48 hours of any missing persons case are the most crucial. As time passes, evidence is lost, and memories fade.

"Skipped town? What do you mean, he's skipped town?"

"I mean just that—no word from him in two weeks. He chartered a one-way flight to Germany. We know that he took a shitload of cash, which is very unusual. No one has any idea where the hell he is."

Byrd shook his head in surprise. Two weeks? This was a job for the police, not a second-string private eye.

"Look, if you don't mind my asking, why aren't you just dealing with the cops?"

"Couple of reasons," she replied. "First of all, we have talked to the cops. They're making inquiries, dealing with the German authorities. But police have to follow rules. I want someone working full-time, someone whose hands aren't bound by procedure. Someone with a low profile. The cops sent me to you."

"I guess it's easier to ask forgiveness than permission."

"Exactly," she said. "And to answer your other question, about the length of time. It's like I said, my father is a private man. He collects rare Porsches. I leave him the hell alone."

The detective wasn't impressed.

"Okay, he collects cars. Some people collect stamps. What's it matter?"

"No, you don't understand—he doesn't collect cars—he collects rare Porsches. Most of what he buys isn't found here in Alabama."

"Yeah, that's not surprising."

"He inspects and buys these things from all over the country. The man's over sixty years old. He doesn't need permission to go somewhere. Even if he did, he wouldn't ask me."

There was something strange in the way she spoke about her father. There was sincere concern, but it was buffered by a thick layer of resentment. These familial relationships were always complex. In Byrd's experience, a more expansive estate usually meant a more cavernous relationship gap between parent and child.

The less they need, the less they need each other.

"So if it's not unusual for him to hop an airplane and skip town," Byrd asked, "why'd you call me? Why is this any different?"

"I didn't call you, remember? Baines did, and he's worried. He thinks this time's different."

"Okay," Byrd said, "what's different?"

"First of all, on the week he left, he sold some stock. Made a major withdrawal of cash. A lot of cash."

"How much?"

"Seven-figures."

Seven-figures? Holy shit.

"Who carries around that kind of cash?"

"Like I said, this time's different. He usually leaves some sort of contact information. Not this time. Baines didn't hear a word. No phone calls. No emails. Nothing. He just left."

"If he's been gone that long," he said, "you sure you don't want to just deal with the cops?"

She shrugged. "Look, we're going through all the motions. I've spoken with the Chief of Police," she replied. "They're investigating, but we're not going public."

"Because he's a privacy freak?"

"Basically. Here's what I'm thinking. If we go public, the media will have a field day. Next thing you know, CNN will have a satellite crew over here and *The Birmingham News* will be running front page headlines. We want to avoid all that. Between you and me, Baines is a worrier, and I love him to death. I'm doing this for Baines, not for J.C. Callahan. This is just like him, to go off on some stupid crusade without even bothering to think about other people. It's just so typical."

Although Byrd's specialty was photographing adulterous liasons, he knew something about missing persons. There was always a risk / reward analysis where media attention was concerned. In most cases, the upside of media attention overshadowed any negative.

"So you want me to find him?"

"You've got a proven track record. You've found missing people, and you've done so discreetly. You find him, and we don't have to go public. You get paid. Everybody's happy."

Byrd nodded as if he understood. He did not understand. This woman was as crazy as her old man.

"Here's what I have in mind," she said. "You start work immediately. If you don't find anything in the next couple of days, then I'll green light the police to go public."

Wheels began turning in Charlie Byrd's head. His upcoming tuition fee would be a financial root canal. He'd need several thousand bucks to satisfy Birmingham School of Law, and he was more than a few eggs short of a full basket.

"So," he asked, "what kind of deal do you have in mind?"

"Well," she said, "you'll be working for me and only me, all day and night until this situation is resolved. We expect your undivided attention. No more staking out motels until this job is complete."

"Okay," he said. "My undivided attention."

"What do you think is a fair price?"

"How about you give me a wheel off that yellow car?" he replied. "It's probably worth what, thirty grand?"

"Very funny. How about we give you cash. Say, a thousand dollars a day? That enough to get your attention?"

She'd said the magic word, and modified it with zeroes. This was the kind of job that Charlie Byrd fantasized about—a nutty rich chick who liked spending her father's money. Cash. With this sort of work, he could pay tuition, with extra left over for books and Ramen Noodles.

"Say yes" she said as she pulled a folded bill from her pocket, "and you get the Franklin back. Plus an additional five."

"Okay, a thousand dollars a day," he said. "Hell yes. You've got yourself a detective."

Byrd took the bill from her hands, and tried to conceal the gleam in his eyes. It was unprofessional to smile under these circumstances. But *damn*— one thousand dollars a day.

"In that case," she said, "I suggest we take a look at the barn."

6

CHARLIE BYRD STEPPED INTO THE SUNSHINE.

The air-conditioned chill of the Callahan home gave way to humid air. A merciful breeze wafted across the property, relieving the intensity of the heat. It was springtime, which meant the most relentless temperatures were kept at bay. Alabama heat was a pit bull, wagging its tail in April before chomping down for blood in August. Byrd had learned to appreciate pleasant weather while it lasted.

He turned to examine the rear view of the Callahan home. Floor-to-ceiling windows. A large entertainment patio, complete with a bubbling Italian marble fountain and well-manicured gardens. The estate was not unlike Kristen Callahan, equally impressive from the backside.

"You'll have a better understanding of my father after seeing his barn," she said. As she led Byrd along the sidewalk, he couldn't resist taking in the view. The glance confirmed his suspicion—her own backside held a mesmerizing appeal. He watched the yin-yang tattoo bounce its way along the sidewalk.

"Nice view," he muttered under his breath. He knew he shouldn't have said it. You don't risk a lucrative cash deal by being anything less than Eddie

Haskell polite. Yet something about this woman's demeanor, her general attitude, demanded it. She was a handful, and Byrd felt the urge to flirt.

She cocked her head. "Excuse me?"

"The house," he replied. "I like it back here. Backside's just as impressive as the front."

She wasn't buying it. "Uh-huh," she said, striking a tone of mock disapproval.

They walked along a red brick pathway some one-hundred yards to the barn. The structure itself looked like any other barn that might adorn a well-heeled farm. It was a substantial building, finished in white with cherry red trim. But this barn was different—the paint and finish were spotless, the grounds suspiciously free of clutter and debris. The landscaping was perfectly tailored, in a manner that could only come from pouring large heaps of money into the job.

Follow the red brick road.

They stopped at the side entrance. Next to the door was a numerical keypad. Callahan punched a four-digit code, her gold bracelet jangling like a wind chime.

The door emitted an electronic beep and unlocked.

They stepped through the door and were enveloped in cool dry air.

"A cold barn," he said. "Your cows enjoy air-conditioning?"

"You'll see," she replied.

They walked down a short corridor, following the hallway as it opened into the main chamber.

Byrd stepped into the vast room. The walls of the barn were painted white, matching the exterior. Overhead, natural wood beams crossed in a rustic designer touch. Light streamed through the beams onto the simple concrete floor below.

The main area of the barn was open space. There were several wide stalls, though none contained livestock. The floor itself was barren, and almost too clean. The concrete was smooth and white, devoid of the usual stains.

"I thought barns were supposed to have hay," he said. "Not to mention cow shit."

"Hay is for horses," she replied. "And Porsches don't shit, unless you count oil."

In one corner of the room was an antique tractor. Clearly the machine had done more than its share of farm labor. Its faded red paint was flaking in places.

"That thing a Porsche?" he asked.

"Actually, yes," she replied. "It is a Porsche."

"You're kidding."

"No. Porsche made tractors back in the 1950's. He's had that one a long time. I think it's a fifty-seven. He'll actually drive that one."

Byrd winced at the mental image. A rich old fart puttering around his kingdom on a Porsche tractor? This was too much.

"No offense," he said, "but have you considered having his head examined?"

"We ought to," she replied. "This isn't a hobby. It's an addiction."

He took a look around the otherwise barren barn.

"Well, it's hard for me to believe that his addiction consists of that tractor, and that yellow thing you're driving. Where does he keep his cars?"

"Like I said, sometimes you seem pretty slow."

She walked to a nearby wall and started jabbing a code into another numerical keypad.

"Watch your feet."

With a mechanical lurch, motors began grinding. One of the nearby stalls began sinking into the barn floor. The "stall" was actually an oversized elevator, one suitable for cars.

"Some people have doggy doors," he said. "I assume this is for cars?"

"You assume correctly. Hydraulic works extend about eighty feet beneath the ground. This thing handles everything he's got."

She opened the door of another stall, revealing a winding steel staircase to a lower level. He followed her down into the cool darkness, their metallic footsteps echoing throughout the stairwell. Byrd was suitably impressed by the turn of events. The barn had a basement.

With a loud snap, she flipped a couple of heavy-duty light switches on the wall. The entire area was flooded with light.

Byrd found himself standing in an underground parking facility. It was a massive garage. There were at least a dozen cars in sight, but only two were uncovered. The rest were encased in protective bubbles of clear plastic. The visual effect was eerie, a dead silent room full of time capsules. It looked like a hospital intensive care unit, or perhaps a mortuary. The air was dry as well as cool.

"Feels great down here," he said. "This entire area is dehumidified?"

"Yes," she replied. "About time you got something right. Dry air helps prevent rust."

"Rust must be a big problem with these old cars."

She nodded.

"Early cars were made of ungalvanized metal. It was vulnerable to rust. Most of the best cars ever made have just turned to rust."

Byrd pondered the scene. He was surrounded by dozens of vintage Porsches. Most were concealed underneath their bubbles. A few, however, were exposed to open air.

She pointed to the uncovered vehicles.

"These cars," she said, "are probably next on the maintenance schedule."

"How often are they driven?"

"Driven?," she said. "Never. My father is adamant about that point. These cars are not to be driven. Not anymore."

Byrd reacted as if he'd just smelled an unpleasant odor. The point of this hobby escaped him.

"A couple of the cars are occasionally started," she explained. "Just enough to keep the juices flowing. Most are museum pieces, and haven't been started in decades. He calls them his garage queens."

"What's the fun in that?" Byrd said. "If these cars are never driven, what were you doing this morning?"

She winked.

"The old man doesn't know about that, now does he?"

Byrd walked throughout the garage, taking stock of the sheer number of vehicles. The breadth of the collection was staggering. For a struggling third-year law student, it was too much. His disdain lurked beneath the surface, and he kept it on a tight leash. Who collected Porsches as a hobby? Did such people really exist? Apparently they did, and he was standing next to one. It made him a little uneasy, all these cars just resting in a hole in the ground. It seemed like such waste.

"As you can see," she continued, "His collection's quite extensive. It surpasses Jerry Seinfeld's in size and variety."

Byrd cocked his head. Comedian Jerry Seinfeld was a living legend, and Byrd had seen every episode of his landmark 1990s TV show. Syndicated reruns aired every night, and made for a useful study break.

"Seinfeld's into this stuff?"

"Seinfeld not only *collects* Porsches," she replied, "he built his own garage in Manhattan to house a couple dozen of them. He also keeps several dozen at an airport hanger in Los Angeles. This," she made a sweeping wave of her hand, "is my father's equivalent."

For a moment, Byrd wasn't sure whether to smile approvingly or gag. Millionaires and their hobbies. Here was hard evidence that the time-honored cliché was accurate: the rich really were different. It was bad enough that people bought luxury automobiles. This Callahan guy bought with no intention of actually using. The underground garage was one man's insane piggy bank, a bizarre investment portfolio composed of metal, leather, and German engineering.

"It's unbelievable," he finally said with a note of exasperation.

"Believe it," she said. "It's an obsession. Seinfeld says that most big money stuff is overrated. But not the cars."

Byrd stopped in front of an uncovered vehicle, a small red convertible. With a nod of approval from his companion, he carefully leaned over and gazed into the cabin.

"The key to a good Porsche collection, of course, is finding the rare cars. This one, for example, is among the last Speedsters ever built. An ordinary Speedster might be worth fifty grand. This car, given its history, is worth more. A lot more."

"Okay, I'll bite," he said. "How much more?"

"This particular car? At least three-hundred grand."

Byrd whistled as he studied the forty-year old car. He felt a tightness in his throat. He didn't know whether to be impressed or appalled. Either way, his expression didn't change. He maintained a blank stare as if to say that three-hundred grand was no big deal.

Of course, it was ridiculous to think any car could be worth that much money. Yes, the Porsche looked showroom new. The paint retained its original luster, and the interior glistened with the rich texture of well treated leather.

Not unlike Sophia Lauren, the aging Porsche maintained a dignified superficial sex appeal. But *three hundred grand*? The price tag seemed squarely in the realm of science fiction.

"Well," Byrd said, "I like this one better than the electric banana. What do you mean this car was among the last ever built? How do you know?"

"Porsche keeps detailed records. Some cars, like the 918, are only built in limited numbers."

The detective nodded. One of the fundamental truths of human nature was that a limited supply increased demand. He'd seen the principle applied to everything from football tickets to stuffed animals.

"Kind of like Beanie Babies. My mom collects those things. So this old Speedster was built in limited numbers?"

"Yeah, kind of like Beanie Babies. The story on this car is a little different," she said. "As legend has it, Porsche had six Speedster chassis left over after they'd already stopped production on the model. The six cars just sat in a German warehouse, waiting to either be scrapped or completed. Fortunately, someone made the right choice. They stuffed in a four-cam engine and sold the cars, long after they'd officially stopped selling Speedsters. That," she said, "is why this car's worth three-hundred grand."

"Okay," he said, "I get it."

He played along like a dutiful soldier, but Charlie Byrd did not get it. Not in the slightest. He strolled around the Porsche like a careful shopper at a car lot, examining every angle. On the rear fender, he spotted a flaw. The area was no more than two inches long, but it was noticeable. Globs of paint had been crudely brushed on top of the smooth factory surface.

"What's up with this paint?" he asked. "Looks sloppy."

"Everything is original, dents, touch up paint, and all. He keeps them original. They're worth more that way."

"Yeah, that's the philosophy I've adopted with my truck," Byrd replied, his voice assuming an intellectual tone normally reserved for Masterpiece Theater and law professors. "I strive to keep it original."

"So I noticed," she said.

He stopped at the rear of the car.

"Can I see the engine?"

She reached into the Porsche and pulled a latch. The rear trunk of the vehicle popped open, revealing a spotless chrome engine that shined like new.

Byrd peered inside. In the base of the engine, resting on the floorboard, he saw a blue cloth.

"There's something in here," he said.

He reached down deep into the car, and fished his fingers around until they located the cloth. Tugging at it gently, he removed an oily blue rag from the car. The rag had been resting at the bottom of the engine floorboard.

"I don't suppose it's standard procedure to leave oily rags in antique engines," he said.

She took the rag from his hand. "See, you're paying for yourself already. You probably just saved that Speedster from going up in smoke."

"If I just saved a three-hundred thousand dollar car, then I need a raise."

Byrd leaned against the wall of the facility, his hand propped against the concrete. The wall was solid and cold to the touch.

"Well," he said, "I suppose you couldn't find a safer place for these puppies. It's like a bomb shelter."

"Exactly," she replied. "Underground storage has many advantages, not the least of which is tornado protection. You know what tornadoes have been known to do in this state."

He nodded. It seemed that once a year a tornado ravaged the Alabama countryside, destroying homes and lives in the process.

"A tornado could wipe away the barn upstairs and these cars would still be fine."

"Well, it's an impressive collection," he finally offered. "Jerry Seinfeld would be proud. I guess I understand what you mean about collecting Porsches."

She looked at her watch. "It's almost one o'clock and I haven't eaten. You want to get some for lunch?"

The mere thought of food sparked hunger pangs in his stomach. Byrd was running on caffeine and little else.

"What does your father typically do?" he asked.

"Well, it depends. He's got his routine, and takes a lot of meals here at the house. But there's one place he goes every Wednesday."

"Today's Wednesday," he replied. "Let's go there. And if you don't mind, I'd rather we take something besides that yellow rocket out front."

"No problem," she said. "We'll take my car."

Byrd rolled his eyes and braced for the worst. In a Herculean feat of self-control, he held his tongue.

Play the game, he thought. *Just play the damn game.*

7

W ITH A SOLID METALLIC *THUNK*, Kristen Callahan slammed the door shut on her own hybrid. Charlie Byrd was intrigued by the car, one of the new Toyota sedan models. He thought it was ugly. He was embarrassed by the bumper stickers. One insisted WOMEN HAVE THE POWER TO STOP NUCLEAR WAR. In an apparent contradiction, another urged WAR EAGLE – the signature battle cry of Auburn University. Of course, this was actually no contradiction, since to the best of his knowledge Auburn was not yet waging nuclear war.

There were beaded necklaces swinging from the rear view mirror. Byrd immediately recognized the shiny green, purple, and gold strands. Costume jewelry, plastic beads were used as currency during the Mardi Gras festival in New Orleans. In exchange for exposing breasts and other body parts, women received strands of beads. The more provocative the act, the nicer the beads. These were nice beads.

Byrd was embarrassed, but he was also impressed. Here was yet another vehicle engineered in the new century. The Toyota probably got better gas mileage than his aging relic of the 1980s. Hell, an M1 tank got better mileage than his damned old truck. Byrd's Bronco sucked fuel like an asthmatic sucked oxygen, and it dug deep into his shallow wallet.

He motioned toward the Toyota.

"How much horsepower in that thing?"

"Enough," she replied. "It's good for the environment."

Good for the environment? Byrd was struck by the contrast. Earlier she'd scared the living daylights out of him in a screaming yellow monstrosity, one boasting at least ten cylinders that kicked out more noise pollution than the average rock festival. Now they were puttering around town in an anonymous econo box, one with environmental pretensions. Perhaps the only indulgence more irritating than flamboyant wealth was *greener than thou* environmentalism.

"How is a new car good for the environment?" he said. "I mean, wouldn't it be better for the environment just to recycle an old car?"

"This is a hybrid," she replied. "It uses a lot less fuel."

"Yeah, maybe, but think about the environmental impact of building and shipping new vehicles, especially cars with big nickel batteries like this one. It would be much better for the environment just to drive an old car instead of buying a new one."

One of the upsides of a legal education was exposure to arcane trivia of all stripes. Every law student, subjected to a daily deluge of fact heavy reading material, plows through a solid portion of environmental content. Environmental law was a hot field. Charlie Byrd's interest was primarily in annoying environmentalist posers.

"Alright Byrd, you win," she said. "Your truck is much greener than my hybrid. Happy?"

He laughed.

The parking lot was full of dirty pickup trucks, oversized SUVs, tricked-out Japanese cars, and unwieldy portly Cadillacs. There was nary a Porsche—or for that matter, another Toyota hybrid—in sight. They made their way through the ocean of metal to the front door of the restaurant.

Niki's West was located in a nondescript one-story brick building, several miles away from downtown Birmingham. In fact, it was miles away from anything, save the bustling industrial warehouse across the street. The cafeteria was a unique west Birmingham landmark, an isolated outpost of regional cooking. For some fifty years, *Niki's* served cafeteria food that matched the local palate. Alabama cuisine was decadence steeped in pragmatism. A proper midday meal was dubbed a "meat and three." One entrée was framed by three side items that began their lives as vegetables.

They stepped inside *Niki's West* and took their places in the winding cafeteria queue, making small talk and browsing the room. The internal décor was dated. Simple, faded posters had long ago been hung upon the wood panel walls, offering up random scenes of Greek life. It's likely the original founders of the restaurant once intended to create a Greek establishment. The Greek menu had long since given way to deep-fried Southern cuisine. The only thing Greek about *Niki's West* was the name, and the faded posters hanging on the wall.

"This art was probably a good idea a few decades ago," he said.

"It's all about the food," she replied. "You learn to appreciate the ambiance."

As always, the cafeteria was busy with lunchtime traffic. The clientele represented a true cross section of Birmingham. Lawyers from the stately firms downtown, dressed in their best coats and ties, stood alongside blue-collar mechanics whose arms were still peppered with machine grease. The racial mix was diverse, with an equal number of black folks and white folks shuffling past steam tables. All were united by the grand cause of Southern cooking.

At last, it was Byrd's turn to grab a plastic tray and approach the steaming cafeteria table. He worked his way down the line, choosing individual saucers of food along the way.

The cuisine was a mixture of Alabama country cooking and soul food, with the signature dish a Blue Plate Special on steroids. In addition to a meat entrée, customers chose vegetables. There was a wide variety of such staples as fried green tomatoes, fried eggplant, fried okra, fried squash, fried potatoes, and anything else that could be covered in batter and submerged in boiling fat. At least one-third of the items had been subjected to a thorough breading and deep-frying, in the local tradition.

Kristen Callahan accepted a dish of fried green tomatoes and placed it on her tray.

"Only in Alabama," Byrd said, "is the humble tomato an artery-busting food."

At the end of the cafeteria line, past the cornbread and rolls, were desserts—a plethora of homemade pies and cobblers. Chocolate, coconut, cherry, peach, and lemon meringue tempted brave souls with adequate appetite. These sugar bombs were the *coup de grace* of any complete Southern meal.

After being escorted to a seat, they unloaded the dishes of food onto their table. Byrd had attempted to assemble a healthy lunch, a pathetic menagerie of broccoli, house salad, and cole slaw. He was a good twenty pounds overweight, the result of a few too many Pabst Blue Ribbon. The social schedule at Birmingham School of Law was dominated by networking parties and ambitious students. One had to drink heavily at the former to tolerate the latter.

Callahan expressed her disapproval with Byrd's selections.

"I'm disappointed," she said. "How do you expect to ever become a man while eating nothing but green stuff?"

Byrd assessed her meal of country fried steak, fried green tomatoes, fried okra, and mashed potatoes and gravy.

"How on earth," he replied, "can a woman eat like that and look like you?"

An elderly waitress approached their table. She was well into her seventies, the kind of grandmotherly lady that even a cheapskate would generously tip. When she spoke, her voice had a melodic quality, like she was singing the words.

"How y'all doin' today?" she asked. "Kristen, where's your daddy hidin'? I haven't seen him in a while."

"Hello, Miss Dorothy. Daddy's out of town."

The waitress poured two glasses of ice water.

"What would y'all like to drink?"

"Tea," they replied simultaneously.

"Sweet or unsweet?"

"Sweet."

The waitress quickly put down two glasses of iced tea.

"You tell your daddy we miss him in here," she said. "Y'all let me know if you need anything."

She floated on to the next table, carrying a tray of water and iced tea. The restaurant bustled with the incessant lunchtime chatter of happy clientele, a constant clattering of silverware and Southern drawls. Byrd was familiar with the scene, but never suspected J.C. Callahan was a regular diner. The reclusive millionaire had blended right into the crowd.

"This is helpful," Byrd said. "Your father comes here on a regular basis?"

"Yes, every Wednesday. He likes to get out of the house."

"Must be his social life."

"Yeah," she said, "this is about all that's left."

"What else? Charity work? Church? Politics?"

"None of the above," she replied. "He keeps to himself. He talks to Baines. Quite frankly, he doesn't talk to me much. Not anymore."

"You two have a falling out?"

"You might say so. Sometimes we don't get along."

"How about his love life? Does he date? Any guy with that many Porsches should be cruising Southside and picking up chicks."

"No. To my knowledge, he hasn't dated in the past fifteen years. At least, no one he's told me about."

"What a waste of fine cars," he said.

What a waste of a life, he thought. J.C. Callahan must've been bored out of his mind. Either that, or he had a screw loose. Perhaps Callahan was just another wealthy recluse with more money than common sense. When it came to elderly human beings and large sums of money, anything was possible. The most outrageous fictions were regularly eclipsed by absurd truths.

Upon dying, one Alabama grandmother bequeathed her entire estate to 83 stray cats. Byrd sometimes cruised past the walled Mountain Brook property, which was overrun with the creatures and their offspring. The cats were expected to live in luxury for decades, until the old lady's estate was entirely drained. Compared to such examples. J.C. Callahan seemed positively normal.

"So, you think your daddy's off to Germany on a car-collecting trip?"

She took a bite of a fried green tomato, and washed it down with iced tea.

"Yes. Like I told you, I don't know where he was going beyond Stuttgart. It wasn't unusual for him to go on these trips. What's unusual is for him to be gone this long without any communication. And to pull out that much cash. It's very peculiar."

"I'm no expert," he replied, "but your father's collection looks pretty damn extensive. What's it missing?"

"Not much. He's managed to find at least one example of every Porsche that matters. But there's always the lure of the unique. Every collector dreams of discovering a perfect example hidden away in somebody's barn."

"I don't know too many folks with barns like Mr. Callahan's. Let's backtrack. Suppose he heard about one of these cars. Would he just jump on a plane and go see it?"

"Yes, he would."

"Does he have his own plane?"

"Not any more. Back in the salad days he kept a company plane. Now he'll just charter a flight. That's the deal here. The cops know he chartered a flight to Stuttgart."

"Well," Byrd said, "the obvious first step is to interview the pilot. That been done?"

She nodded.

"The Germans handled it. Apparently the pilot's German. He said the old man showed up at Birmingham-Shuttlesworth on time, and he took him to Stuttgart. But he never talked to him. He was basically just a hired hand. He was a dead end."

"He didn't know anything else?"

"No. Said he'd never seen J.C. Callahan before. Said he was quiet the whole way to Germany. Slept through most of it."

"Anything else?"

"Said he had a couple of trunks with him, suitcases on wheels."

"The cash?"

She shrugged. "Maybe."

The cash tossed an interesting variable into Byrd's mental algebra. In the modern and post 9/11 era, everything and everyone left some sort of electronic data trail. Many a missing persons case was solved thanks to the tracing of little plastic cards. Most missing persons aren't carrying a small fortune in cash. Paper currency not only allowed Callahan to cover his tracks, it also indicated one of two possibilities. Either the old man was planning to leave the country for a very long time, or he was planning to conduct a very illegal transaction. American dollars were the fuel powering the world's shadow economic engine. Wire transfers to Switzerland and the Caymans were not what they used to be. Thanks in large part to Osama Bin Laden, unmarked bank accounts were less secure than ever before. But ink and paper remained elusive to the IRS, TSA, FBI, and other three-letter governmental authorities. In other words, no one ever bought a stolen Picasso with a Mastercard.

Satisfied with this line of inquiry, Byrd turned back to the Callahan obsession.

"So out of the cars in his collection, what's the most valuable? What do you think he's looking for? What Porsche could be worth seven figures?"

She smiled at the question.

"It would probably be something historical, like one of the early race cars. Like a 550 Spyder. You what a Spyder is, right?"

"I know they scare the shit out of me. I hate spiders."

"Okay," she said, "time to go back to school. That 918 prototype? That's a Spyder. We're talking about one of the all-time great car lines. A legend. You know the 550 Spyder, right?"

She asked the question as if this should have been common knowledge, something taught in every kindergarten. It was as if Byrd hadn't known about the existence of George Washington, or San Francisco, or the Space Shuttle. He said nothing in reply, but his blank stare spoke volumes.

"I realize that I grew up around this shit, but trust me," she said, "you'd know a 550 Spyder if you saw it."

Byrd wasn't so certain. In fact, he was finding himself again annoyed by this rich woman who thought obscure German sports cars should be common knowledge. She'd apparently been raised in some sort of pampered bubble, an isolated world of trivial pursuits.

"Oh really?" he said. "Would you know a 1969 Chevy C-10 pickup if you saw it?"

"Actually, I would," she replied. "That's not the point. How about James Dean. Would you know James Dean if you saw him?"

"Yeah," he said. "I've watched the *True Hollywood Story*."

"Thank God," she replied. "It's nice to know you have a little culture."

"Okay, so James Dean had a Spyder," Byrd said. "Didn't he die in it?"

"Bingo," she replied. "James Dean owned a Porsche 550 Spyder. He called it *Little Bastard*."

"What a coincidence. My daddy used to call me the same thing."

She ignored the joke.

"Dean got his Spyder in 1955. By that time, the car had a reputation. It won major races."

"So what's the big deal about the Spyder? Why's it worth so much? Because James Dean croaked in one?"

She went on to explain that the 550 Spyder was the first Porsche race car, that the term "Spyder" referred to a two-seat mid-engined roadster, and that the originals were street legal race cars. When the 550 debuted, it put the company squarely on the radar screen for racing enthusiasts worldwide. They were hand-built, rare, expensive, and thus often purchased by wealthy celebrities like James Dean.

There's nothing like untimely violent death to cement a celebrity legend.

Dean, she explained, was driving his car to a race in California when he ran into the arms of fate—in the form of a 1950 Ford.

"Dean smashed headlong into the Ford," she said with a peculiar gleam in her eye. "He died instantly. They say he was decapitated."

"I've heard people debate Ford versus Chevy," Byrd said. "I guess Ford versus Porsche has already been settled."

"Very funny," she replied. "That was a long time ago. For such a lightweight car, the Spyder was rugged and durable. That's why it won endurance races. But no race car could withstand a collision with a 1950 Ford."

Her eyes sparkled as she spoke. Despite all of her New Age hippie protestations, her pseudo-environmentalist credentials, it was obvious that this woman enjoyed talking about cars. And dead celebrities.

"Okay, so despite the lack of factory air bags, your daddy likes old school Porsche Spyders. Surely he has one by now."

"Yes," she replied. "He owns one. It doesn't function, not anymore."

"Not anymore? Sorry, I don't follow."

"His 550 isn't drivable. It's more like half a car."

"Wrecked?" he asked.

"Yes," she said. "The car has a history. It's one of those that hasn't been started in years. It's kind of a mess, really."

"I don't get it," Byrd said. "He's got an obsession with the 550 Spyder. Why not just plunk down the money and buy a nice original? Or fix the one he's got?"

"Couple of reasons. Like I said, he's very choosy, and there aren't many originals left. He wants the type of cars that elude the Jerry Seinfelds of the world. Those are hard to find. The search can take years."

"Okay. What's the other reason?"

"It's personal," she replied.

"It's personal. Personal?"

"Yes, personal," she replied. "I'd really rather not talk about it."

"Are you serious?"

"It's about the wreck," she said. "My mother was injured in it. She later died. It's pretty depressing, really. I don't like to talk about it. Suffice to say that he hasn't touched the car since. Really, he hasn't been the same since."

"Sorry," Byrd said. "I didn't know."

"I was pretty young at the time. But I remember. That day changed everything."

Her voice trailed away, but the look on her face said that she was uncomfortable. That expression—and the underlying flush of sadness in her voice—convinced Byrd to drop the issue. For the first time since meeting Kristen Callahan, he detected an air of genuine vulnerability. Byrd could exchange verbal jabs with the best, and often did so at law school. But at times he managed to hold his tongue.

"So, your dad's in Germany for a Porsche Spyder?"

"I think so," she said. "I don't know. I don't know anything for sure."

She polished off the rest of her fried okra, and took a long drink of iced tea. Her tone had changed, and it was clear that she was no longer enjoying the conversation.

"You asked questions, and I gave you answers. I have a hunch, but I'm going to let you sniff the trail first."

She pulled out her mobile phone, one of the trendy models that had more in common with a supercomputer than a telephone. This was a sign. Lunch was over.

"Speaking of getting back into the car, I've got things to do. We should start heading back."

"Let's get out of here," he said, "while I'm still able to walk."

Byrd took one final draw of iced tea, draining his glass.

He sat the glass down, and pushed back from the table.

8

A BLACK SEDAN SLINKED INTO THE COURTYARD like a rat swimming in a sewer. The car crunched across dry gravel rocks and slowly came to a halt. A quick flash of light as the tail glowed red. Then all returned to black.

Next came the captive SUV, still towing the silver bullet trailer. Together they rolled into the small space, a unholy parade. There was another crimson glow as the procession jerked to a halt. Then they too fell silent.

Three men stepped into the cold night. Their masks were gone, and their breath drew frost in the air. Their faces, now revealed, were hard as stone. Even the boy's face was improbably hardened, weathered and mature beyond its years.

The men were surrounded on all sides by a house. The structure loomed larger than the sky overhead. Its walls stretched high toward the stars. They managed to deflect most of the moonlight, creating an eerie vacuum in the courtyard.

No one spoke. The Man with the Scar directed the others without sound. They obeyed without question. They all understood. Even the fat one understood.

First order of business was the gringo. They opened the SUV and dragged the man from the backseat. The seat was a sticky mess of dark blood on sand leather. No doubt the interior was plastered with DNA. But the SUV would remain assembled for no more than a few hours. Soon, it would be broken apart like kindling, carved to pieces and redistributed into the food chain.

The gringo was still breathing. The man had lost a substantial amount of blood, but the worst had stopped. The boy and the fat man hauled him into the house like some sort of prize fish. His body was limp, almost lifeless.

It may have been a waste to bring him, The Man with the Scar thought. The gringo was weak. But if he survived, he would be valuable. There was always risk when taking any prisoner. This risk offered clear rewards.

The gringo was rich. Anyone could see it. The SUV, the cash. His clothes and his watch. They all said he wasn't just another tourist. He was the catch of a lifetime.

With the gringo secured, the next order of business was the trailer, and the vehicle inside. The tiny old car posed a unique dilemma. The Man with the Scar knew little about such matters, but he knew the chop shop wouldn't want it. Vultures want fresh young meat. Like the gringo, this car was too damned old. It wasn't as desirable as the SUV. It would be worth shit in the City.

There was something else, something about the car that he didn't understand. It would've been waste to discard it, to simply give it away to jackals in the City. It was small enough to easily conceal. So he would keep it until he did understand.

The trailer door swung open. The silver car rolled out. The car was light, they noted. They rolled the rich man's toy into the house, where it too was swallowed by darkness.

With all treasure secured, it was time to dispose of the SUV. The boy would drive it to the City, while the fat man stayed behind to watch the gringo.

The boy was thrust into the driver's seat. He was young, no more than sixteen. His eyes opened wide and didn't dare blink. He gazed at The Man with the Scar with respect. There was fear in his eyes, too. In this land, fear and respect were frequent companions. The Man with the Scar stood outside the SUV, and returned the boy's stare.

The boy was young but he held great promise. The best always started young. He was old enough to shoot out a gringo's brains, if necessary, and he showed signs of the necessary resolve. This job was easy, no killing required. He was to drive the SUV into the City. There, he'd deliver it to those who would consume it. They'd cleanse the blood from the backseat, remove the broken glass and pieces damaged by bullets. Then they would break it apart. Once parted out, the pieces would be valuable. The SUV would feed them for months. Perhaps years.

The City was vast. Anything was possible in the City. The boy had been several times, but never alone. Never like this. Never in the chill of the night, driving a dead gringo's SUV.

He sat in the driver's seat, hands gripping the wheel with nervous enthusiasm, heart wedged in his throat. The SUV was parked, its engine idling and humming in anticipation.

The Man with the Scar stood outside with both hands on the door. He leaned toward the boy, head nearly poking inside the cabin. As he leaned forward, the boy got a close look at the scar. The Man with the Scar had a pink scar on his cheek. It ran from just below his right eye down toward the jaw. It was at least five centimeters long, pink and pale as a woman's lips. As he spoke, the boy tried not to stare at it.

Yes, the boy nodded, he had the address. Yes, he understood the responsibility. He was to take the SUV into the City, deliver it, and return before sunrise.

The Man with the Scar felt like a seasoned General sending a young recruit into battle. He wanted to impress the importance of this task. But seeing the boy's nervousness, he couldn't maintain his stern expression. A faint curl appeared at one corner of his mouth. It wasn't much of a smile, but it was there. His thoughts drifted to a time long past, when he was a boy, before the civil war, before the gangs, when he lived in the squalor of the barrios and stole scrawny chickens for survival. The Man with the Scar knew the boy's heart was skipping, that his hands were slick with perspiration, and that he would remember this night forever. He felt motivated to say a few words, to reassure the child.

Darkness covered them like a blanket, he explained. Darkness masked their return from the road, their transport of the gringo to the house. Darkness would protect the boy on his journey to the City.

The Man with the Scar patted the boy on the shoulder, then stepped back. The SUV rumbled away into the darkness, trailer in tow, tires softly crunching the gravel that lined the small courtyard. The night was quiet save these sounds. Small stones shifting, and trailer chains rattling into the night.

"*Espera*," he shouted. Wait. There was a problem. The rear door of the trailer became unfastened. The door swung wide and banged against its hinges. The boy stabbed the brakes of the SUV and it jerked to an awkward stop.

Earlier in the evening, when they stopped the gringo, they destroyed the trailer lock. One bullet shattered the mechanism. Now that door wouldn't stay closed. It was tied with rope by the fat man, but the rope had come loose.

The open door revealed a barren space inside, save for the canvas cloth that had once shrouded the car. In the moonlight, the trailer looked like an empty tomb.

The Fat Man reappeared, cursing and shaking his head in apology. He refastened the rear door of the trailer with thin rope, working in the soft crimson glow of brake light. After a moment, he jerked on the rope. This time it held. He shouted in Spanish and the SUV again lurched off into the night.

The Man with the Scar said nothing. This was why he sent the boy into the City. The boy was young, but he wasn't fat in the head.

With the SUV gone, one problem remained.

The gringo. He seemed like a stout relic, more resilient than most, but he'd been bleeding. He could die, and that would be a waste. It was dangerous to have the gringo in their possession, but he was a rare find. Such a man would have access to money. They had his possessions, his papers, his documents. They had him. So long as they kept him in the house, they'd be safe. The house was decrepit, an anonymous decaying outpost on the edge of town. The house was their own safe haven.

To kill the gringo would've been easy. The Man with the Scar had killed many times, with the army and with the gangs. He'd killed men and boys, usually with a gun, twice with a blade. He'd kill the gringo when the time came.

The gringo was rich.

First the rich gringo would pay for his life.

He would pay and then he would die.

9

THE OLD MAN WAS ALIVE.

This revelation came as a surprise.

He took a few minutes to be certain. He remained still, eyes closed, mind fading in and out of blackness.

Yes, he was definitely alive. The pain told him so. He attempted to move, and sharp bolts of pain flashed down his right side. He groaned. Then he lay still, and the blackness took hold.

His jaw was swollen and quite nearly shut. He ran his tongue across the bloody gap where two teeth used to be. The bleeding had stopped. The flavor had not.

His head pounded. There was a large welt where his skull had bounced off the door sill, and his nose was skinned raw.

More bolts of pain, this time down his spine. He felt dizzy. Spooling his energy, John Christian Callahan cracked open his eyes. He saw nothing. A crude blindfold had been stretched around his head. More blackness, and a dank musty odor.

What the hell happened?

It all came flooding back. The lonely stretch of road, pantyhose, gunfire, shattered glass. Impressionist paintings with his own blood. The final events weren't clear. Callahan had vague images, hazy memories of a nightmare. This was no dream. This was reality. He'd been damn nearly killed, and had no clue by whom.

He was warned. That was the funny part.

Don't go in the hills, he was told. In the hills are bogeymen, desperate criminals without fear or mercy. They want one thing—money—and give two shits about the rest. If you're stopped, just cooperate and live. The country really isn't so dangerous any more. It's much better now. Cooperate and live. Easy formula.

Bullshit. Cooperation was the crux of the problem. Cooperate with thugs and criminals? That's bullshit. You don't cooperate. You ram a spike through their hearts and be done with it.

He was warned. He bucked the warning, and now the barbarians did the unexpected. They didn't kill him. They did something worse. They caught him.

No way to be sure, but the whole thing felt random. It was a twist of fate, as random as a marble coming to rest on a roulette wheel. What an ironic twist. He came to this country seeking what was lost. He found it. The price was high. Damn thing already cost him one life. Now it was collecting his own.

You found what you lost, you sick bastard. And it found you.

He swallowed, and again tasted the sour paste of his own blood. His clothes and mouth and hair were saturated with the stuff. A musty odor filled his nostrils. The air was moist and cool, like a cellar. He caught a whiff of urine. His pants were still damp. He'd pissed himself, for the first time in about sixty years.

This will make the news, he thought.

He rotated his head. The surface against his back was rough. It felt like dirty concrete, perhaps cinder block. He scraped his head against the wall, saw flashes of pain, and tugged at the blindfold. The blindfold didn't come off. It did, however, loosen over his right eye. He saw a dim sliver of pale light.

He was surrounded by blackness and shades of gray. Gray floor and gray walls. Gray stairs leading up to a gray metal door. Only the bottom of the door broke the monotone. A narrow sliver of warm light afforded his sole comfort.

His head felt woozy. Vision came and went. It was hard to focus.

Through the blurry sliver of light he saw blood. A long streak of dried blood saturated his shirt, now dark and crusty. Around his shoulder they'd wrapped a crude tourniquet. The filthy towel was well soaked with his blood.

He tugged at the bonds holding his hands together. They were tied behind his back, much tighter than the blindfold. He felt weak, and a few moments of effort convinced him the bonds weren't coming off. Too much pain. Too little strength.

The watch, a gift from his wife, was gone. No way to gauge the time.

His temples throbbed. He felt lightheaded. He lay back against the cold concrete wall and listened. Nothing. No voices, no sounds. Nothing. There was silence, the kind of quiet when even the predators of the world were asleep. Were it not for the violence of his condition, the calm would've been peaceful.

J.C. Callahan was totally alone. The irony wasn't lost on the old man. The best moments of his life, his most cherished achievements, were all accomplished solo. He wasn't a team player. It somehow seemed right and appropriate that he die alone.

He was comfortable with the idea of dying. Death was an unbeatable foe. Trying to win only worsened the loss. Better to accept death with dignity. You had to know when it was time to exit the stage.

Callahan had watched other rich fools try and cheat death. They always failed. There was no fountain of youth. Generations of Cortez followers decomposed like every other foul beast on the planet.

His wealth always put Callahan in exclusive Southern circles. In the sixties, he'd known Doris Duke. She'd been among the wealthiest women in the world. When he saw the film of Duke dancing half-naked around an African campfire, chanting songs like a tribal hippie, he'd been disgusted. She spent ungodly amounts of money in pursuit of immortality. She became a joke. Now her ashes were sand in the Pacific. Doris was fish food. In Callahan's eyes, Doris Duke failed with memorable humiliation.

He resolved to face death on his own terms. He'd meet death alone, but with dignity.

Suddenly the gravity of his situation became clear. For the first time in years, he was no longer in control. He couldn't control his life. Therefore he couldn't control his death.

THE LOST SPYDER

He felt fear and weakness. The fear was forgivable. The weakness was not. Callahan despised weakness. It was the one sin he wouldn't let himself commit. Lying on the cold concrete floor in a sticky pool of his own dried blood, blindfolded and bound, he felt weaker than he'd ever felt in his adult life.

Someone will come looking for me. But who?

Callahan was alone. He orchestrated the perfect head fake, took his sweet time getting down here, then covered his tracks. No electronic trace. No e-mail. No wire transfer. No credit cards. No swipe out.

He brought a new SUV and a small fortune in cash.

He told no one.

What a colossal fuck up.

In hindsight, what he'd done was damned reckless. Perhaps even stupid. This was a crazy idea. Callahan loved crazy ideas. He'd been pursuing them for years. He built an empire with ideas, he liked to say. With ideas and potatoes. So ideas were always of interest, especially the ones tinged with insanity.

That's the funny thing about extreme wealth. Life gets boring. Most people didn't eat foie gras, but they sure as hell became foie gras. Humans were not meant to be force-fed a daily buffet of fine food and creature comforts, coddled like cattle, fattened like captive geese. Humans were meant to scratch, claw, and pursue happiness like there was no tomorrow. Callahan called it the three F's: feeding, fighting, and fucking. This particular mission encompassed all three. But it was becoming clear that this time, he was the one who was fucked.

Eventually, someone would notice he was missing. It might take a while, but someone would start asking questions. Someone would look for a trail.

But who? Certainly not his wife. His wife was gone. The marriage was long since turned to dust, and Callahan never made the same mistake twice. Mrs. Shea Callahan was nothing more than a memory.

There was Baines. He should've told Baines. The butler was getting on in years, and by now was accustomed to his employer's peculiar travel habits. But this time there were legal considerations, and it was all part of the agreement. Privacy was part of the deal. He couldn't tell Baines. Callahan kept this trip concealed from the old boy, which wasn't difficult. Baines knew nothing. He was loyal as a Labrador but not the brightest bulb in the box. Confiding in

Baines would have been a recipe for disaster.

Baines would eventually get worried. Baines would tell . . . who? The police for sure. And then his daughter.

Kristen would be informed. Unlike Baines, she no longer gave a damn. For reasons that mystified the old man, she no longer made an effort. She was bullheaded and stubborn, incapable of compromise, and she always held a grudge.

He treated her well. Gave her everything she wanted. Everything except the one sacrifice he could not possibly make. He understood that time was the most valuable gift of all. If time was a commodity, its value would be astronomical. Forget gold, silver, and copper. Coal, salt, and sugar. Rice, wheat, and even potatoes. Time outstrips them all. J.C. Callahan wouldn't freely give away his time to anyone. Not even his own flesh and blood. Time was more valuable than money. Time was life itself.

Despite his example, despite his efforts, his daughter had turned out . . . different. That was the thing about kids. What to do when they turn out completely different than you expect? Kristen seemed adrift. She wasn't grounded and focused like a son would've been. Sometimes she was scary different, and more than a little like Doris Duke. She knew exactly how to push his buttons, with her strategically placed piercings and tattoos, heavy drinking and ill advised relationships. And for God's sake, she cheered for Auburn. Kristen Callahan stood to inherit a modest fortune, yet she spent more time reading her horoscope than her financials. She was a stone's throw from dancing half-naked around a campfire, chanting some ancient African bullshit about eternal life.

Her marriage was catastrophic, the most memorable episode in which she ignored his advice. He smiled at the memory. She rode that sick pony down into the water. He loved nothing more than being right. He was usually right.

The kid she married was weak and a loser. Callahan could handle an honest loser, but his daughter's mousy husband—he never really seemed like a son-in-law—didn't fit the bill. The old man was happy to see him go. At least she never took the bastard's name. Even she wasn't committed to the deal. Kristen remained a Callahan throughout. Always a Callahan. *What a cold bitch she could be.* He secretly admired that about his daughter. In many ways, she really was the son he never wanted.

THE LOST SPYDER

He shifted against the concrete wall. He shivered in the darkness, cold damp air sinking into his bones. He was close to death, perhaps as close as he'd ever been in his adult life. But his heart was still beating. The bleeding had stopped. There was pain, but he could handle pain. He was close to death, yet he felt ... alive. In truth, this feeling was what drove multimillionaires to take stupid risks, to escape the numbing daily reality of extreme wealth. This was why Doris Duke left her Hawaiian *Shanri-La* to bust her ass for a dollar in an Egyptian canteen. This was why Sir Richard Branson attempted to circumnavigate the earth in a fucking balloon. Ordinary people would never understand; that's why they would always be ordinary. Life isn't about comfort. Life is about ambition and risk and pain.

You got yourself in deep this time, you sick bastard.

John Christian Callahan was alive, and he wasn't going to die without a fight. Not here, not alone, and not at the hands of these bastards.

Not like this.

10

CHARLIE BYRD JERKED AWAKE.

His phone rang, breaking the morning calm. He lifted the receiver and slid it to his ear without once opening his eyes. When he spoke, he tried to sound awake.

"Hello?"

"Good morning," she said. "You awake?"

"I'm awake," he said.

He cleared his throat. He was still half-asleep.

One thousand dollars, Byrd. One thousand dollars.

He staggered to his feet and shuffled to the kitchen of his studio apartment, pausing to rub the sleep from his eyes and confirm his balance. The kitchen was three steps from the bed. The apartment was one room filled with a haphazard collection of ragged furniture.

He grabbed a can of ground coffee from the kitchen counter, opened it, and raised it to his nose. After a deep inhale, he began to develop a pulse.

"You sure I didn't wake you?" she asked.

"No," he lied, "I'm always awake by now. I'm a law student, you know. What's up?"

"I've got a lead for you," she said. "There's a mechanic's shop over in Ensley. RennSport Auto. It's Stanley Griggs's place. My father went there on the day he left town."

"Sounds like a plan," he replied. "I'll check it out."

"You'll enjoy talking to Stanley," she said. "Check in with me as soon as you're finished and we'll meet downtown."

"You got it, boss."

Byrd hung up the phone. It was seven o'clock in the morning. He opened the refrigerator door and peered inside. A couple cans of Pabst, several moldy Tupperware containers, and a plastic jug of chocolate milk. *Barber's* chocolate milk. He grabbed an empty glass from the kitchen counter, rinsed it out in the sink, and filled it with chocolate milk.

Nothing like a glassful of sugary carbs to start the day.

He opened the sliding glass door and stepped onto the balcony. The best part of his Morris Avenue apartment—perhaps the only truly impressive part—was the view. On one side of his apartment building lay a nest of busy railroad tracks. Beyond the adjacent tracks, Byrd had a view of downtown.

The city's skyline had developed over the course of a century. If Birmingham was a mature city, its adolescence must have been the 1960s and 70s. Racial unrest gave way to urban growth spurts. Over the years, a few high-rise developments sprang skyward in the downtown business district. Alongside historic buildings of antique brick were contemporary towers of dark glass. The city was framed by hills thick with pine trees and other evergreen growth. Locals called these hills mountains, but most objective observers wouldn't be so gracious.

Atop one such hill stood the largest cast statue in the world, Vulcan. The pagan god of volcanoes and destructive fire was an odd choice of idols for this Bible Belt town. Odder still was the statue's attire, as Vulcan's loincloth barely covered his exposed rear. As a symbol, Vulcan made sense long ago. Once upon a time, the steel industry ruled Birmingham. This was the Pittsburgh of the South, where the mills spat plumes of smoke into the air so thick that children were not allowed to play outside.

Vulcan no longer gazed upon a city of fiery steel mills. The morning air was crisp and clean.

Byrd took another swig of chocolate milk and pondered the day ahead.

J.C. Callahan was missing. He needed information on the dinosaur, and it was time to dig.

ᦂ

A familiar white Ford Bronco cruised the streets of downtown Birmingham. Byrd steered the truck with his left hand casually propped on the wheel. His right hand held a mammoth plastic mug, filled with coffee strong enough to wake the dead. Each slurp of the dark elixir was working magic on Charlie Byrd.

Soon he was wide awake and approaching his destination, a downtrodden metropolitan neighborhood he rarely visited after dark. Ensley was once a separate industrial city in its own right, strategically positioned between the city of Birmingham and a nearby mammoth coal seam. In its heyday this was an economic boom town, where steel mills churned out tonnage in record amounts. Ensley was once the vibrant heartbeat of Alabama, famous for lively dance clubs and packed fraternal halls. It was an Ensley junction called *Tuxedo* that served as subject matter for a hit 1939 Glenn Miller song. It was also Ensley that was the front lines of integration in the 1960s. It was Ensley that was abandoned by its major employers in the 1970s. It was Ensley that boasted a murder rate guaranteeing Birmingham annual placement on the list of America's "ten most dangerous cities." If Ensley still had a heartbeat, it was beating slow.

Charlie Byrd had gone to Ensley in search of a place called *RennSport Auto*. According to the aging sign slung upon a filthy brick wall, he'd found it.

They said this was the best shop in Birmingham for Porsche service. It looked more like a junk yard, or homeless shelter, or perhaps a crack house. It was as inviting as a wounded porcupine in full alert mode. Bricks once red had assumed a dull shade of dirty brown. Windows were covered with sagging broken shutters, their sunny yellow paint flaking off in long strips. Illegible graffiti peppered the walls. The only greenery was provided by weeds, of which there was no shortage. A protective chain link fence surrounded the shop. Atop the fence was curled razor wire.

Nice. Nothing says 'safe neighborhood' like razor wire.

Byrd pulled his Bronco inside the fenced courtyard area.

Outside the garage were a couple of dingy cars.

He parked his truck alongside a Porsche. The car's dark blue paint was fighting a losing battle against the Alabama elements. Its hood, roof, and trunk had faded like a well worn pair of denim jeans.

Byrd sized up the garage. The building itself was large, as spacious as a warehouse. There were two bays, each containing at least a half-dozen cars. Porsches of all stripes, young and old, clean and dirty, bright and dull.

The vast garage was a labyrinth of shelves, tables, and assorted storage cabinets. Spare parts and tools occupied every visible space. Unidentifiable engine and suspension pieces were scattered amidst the oil-soaked concrete floor. The strong scent of automotive grease filled the air. On the wall was a well-worn sign—ABANDON ALL HOPE, YE WHO ENTER HERE.

Stepping into the building, Byrd noticed that some cars lacked engines. Conversely, some engines lacked cars. Entire motors had been plucked from their homes, and were undergoing surgery on stands. It was a mad triage unit for German machinery.

In one corner of the shop, a thin, bearded man stared intently at the engine component in front of him. He was attempting to stretch a small piece of rubber over a large piece of metal. The rubber showed no willingness to cooperate, and kept snapping back into place.

This was causing no small amount of angst. The man cursed under his breath.

Byrd walked to his side. The man never looked up.

"Can I give you a hand?" Byrd asked.

"Nah," the man replied, his gaze never moving from the stubborn piece of rubber. "Just tryin' to stretch this boot over the axle. It's an art, not a science."

He cursed again as the rubber snapped back.

"Germans," he muttered. "It's their revenge."

Byrd was amused. "Are Porsches harder to work on than other cars?"

"Nah," the man grunted, eyes still fixated on the task. "Not harder, just diff'rent."

Byrd watched the wrestling match for a moment. Once it became apparent that his presence wasn't nearly as interesting as the little piece of rubber, he raised his voice.

"I'm looking for Stanley Griggs," he said.

The man finally looked up from his work.

"Oh," he said, "Sorry. Stan's in the back."

He pointed toward the rear of the shop, and turned again to the little piece of black rubber.

Byrd found his way to the rear of the garage, dodging tools and machinery along the way. A man with a heavy Southern accent was speaking into the telephone. His voice had the gravely rasp of a longtime smoker. The man's throat had taken daily baths in tobacco smoke of unfiltered Marlboro vintage.

"Good mornin' to you, sir," the voice growled into the telephone. "How am I doin'? I'm doin' a hell of a lot better than you are today."

The man grunted, a noise that sounded almost gleeful.

"That little car's got some problems. Ball joints are bad. Outer tie rods are bad."

The man pronounced the word "bad" as if it had two syllables.

"Goddamned rack is gushin' fluid. Seal rings on the pump are leakin'. The right sway bar bushing is fuckin' gone because of the leak. That fluid has just destroyed it. And the front of the engine is leakin' oil. I can't tell where it's comin' from, because the bottom's a mess. If the oil's gotten up in her front, she's gonna need new belts."

This sounds worse than my truck, Byrd thought.

"Yeah," the man said, savoring the moment. "That little car's got some problems. Eighteen-hundred just to get started. No tellin' what else we'll find once we open her up."

There was a faint noise on the other end of the line.

"That's the kind a car that'll make you hate Porsches if you're not careful. Kinda like goin' to see a doctor for a headache, and finding out you got a fuckin' brain tumor."

Definitely worse than my truck, Byrd thought.

"All right. You think about it and tell me what you wanna do. But don't think long. We ain't runnin' a parkin' lot down here."

The man hung up the phone and emerged from the back office. He pulled out a red pack of Marlboros. As Byrd suspected, no filter. He opened the pack, and out slid a long white cigarette. He lit it.

Byrd smiled. His smile wasn't returned. The man studied him like he was some sort of exotic animal.

"I'm looking for Stanley Griggs," Byrd said.

"You found him."

Stanley Griggs was a tall, burly man in his early 50's. He was energetic in demeanor and boasted a full head of dark gray hair. His open face was clean-shaven, but framed by bushy sideburns worthy of Elvis Presley. He was wearing the standard grease-stained mechanic's uniform: blue pants and shirt with two patches upon the chest. One patch read *RennSport*, while the other simply read *Stan*.

In his right hand, Griggs held the cigarette at mouth level. He handled his cigarette with the kind of careful precision usually reserved for surgical instruments. When it was time to take a drag, he merely moved it a small distance horizontally, and inhaled. He tapped ashes directly on the garage floor, the way only the owner of the place could.

From behind came another sharp curse. A persistent optimist continued his quest to stretch an impossibly small piece of rubber over a large piece of metal. Griggs abruptly turned his attention to the younger mechanic.

"Frank," he said with a note of exasperation, "you've gotta use the fuckin' hook tool on that thing."

Griggs walked to a hulking tool cabinet. The bureau contained several drawers and shelves, upon which were piled stacks of oily tools. He yanked open a central drawer and stuck his arm inside. One deft rustle and he had procured a tool, like a magician pulling a rabbit out of a hat. The apparatus looked like a screwdriver, but the end of the metal shaft was bent into a hook shape.

"Here." Griggs grunted as he thrust the tool at the young mechanic. "Use that."

With a loud *snap*, rubber popped into place around the metal.

"Gotta use the right Goddamned tool for the job." Griggs grinned at Byrd, a newfound enthusiasm in his growl. "Now what can I do for you, sir?"

"I work for the Callahans. I'm down here to check on one of the cars."

"Oh, you're talkin' about that little bastard." Griggs pointed at an orange Porsche adorned with a gigantic rear wing. "The Great Pumpkin."

"Yeah, that must be it."

"Not ready," Griggs said. "It's been a fuckin' Chinese fire drill down here. She needs new brake discs and they're on the Airborne Express truck that didn't run yesterday. Won't be any trouble to put 'em on, but God only knows when they'll get here."

"Mind if I look at it?"

"Be my guest."

Byrd approached the orange Porsche and peered inside. With a click, he opened the driver's door and sat behind the wheel. The smell of treated leather enveloped his senses, a welcome relief from the motor oil and stale smoke of the garage.

Byrd scanned the cabin of the car and saw nothing unusual.

He popped open the glove compartment. Inside were a few automotive manuals, a ballpoint pen, a tire gauge, and a notepad. Scanning the notepad, Byrd read the following handwritten script: *antigua arana #146 acquired— conf. shipment*. The word *acquired* was underlined twice.

Byrd tore the sheet of paper off the notepad, and tucked it in his jacket. He then emerged from the car, and closed the door with an appropriate metallic thunk.

"What's the old man up to these days?" Griggs asked. "Got anything new in the barn?"

The barn. Byrd nodded with understanding.

"I was there with Kristen yesterday. Mr. Griggs, there's always something new in the barn."

The mechanic laughed. Byrd had passed the test.

"So you know about the barn. I guess you're a friend of the family after all."

"Yes, sir. Do you really service all of those cars?"

"Yeah," Griggs said, "we handle most of 'em. We don't do the Spyders or RSKs. And I told the old man we wouldn't store any of the real high-end race cars. Not worth the risk."

Byrd glanced about the garage. He'd established a bond with Griggs, and needed to seal the deal.

"So which one of these cars is yours?"

"Blue Turbo out front."

Byrd remembered the faded paint, and the look of a tired machine that was past its prime.

"What year is it?"

"Nineteen-eighty."

"Is it fast?"

Griggs grunted again. He found the question amusing, though it was the one question he most liked to answer.

"Well, it ain't stock," he said, special emphasis on the last two words, each boasting at least two syllables.

Byrd was intrigued. Like college football, excessive speed was always a viable topic amongst Southern males. A healthy fascination with speed was part of the fabric of any civilized society.

"How fast is it? What's the top speed?"

"Shit, I don't know. Fastest I've gone is 175. It wanted to go faster. When you start movin' that fast, you begin to ask yourself, *how stupid am I?*"

Their eyes gleamed with mutual understanding. It must have been biological lust, this formula of man and machine. The essential ingredient, both knew, was a man willing to push said machine beyond the reasonable— and into the realm of the stupid. On some basic level, stupidity and courage were interchangeable.

"I guess at 175," Byrd said, "you start to think about what can go wrong." His voice sparkled at the notion.

"Exactly," Griggs growled. "Blow a fuckin' tire at that speed, and things get ugly real quick."

They grinned. A rapport had been established. This was ritual communication as unique and distinctive as any in tribal Africa or the remote Amazon forest. They were finally speaking the same language.

Yes, it would be terrible to blow a tire at 175 miles per hour, just terrible. But wouldn't it be fun?

Byrd prodded the mechanic. "Did you say you don't handle Spyders? I heard old Callahan's got a thing for them."

"I can't tell you much about them fuckin' Spyders," Griggs replied. "Williams's the man when it comes to Spyders. Always has been."

"Who's Williams?"

"Blake Williams. Lives up in Cullman."

Griggs thumped his spent cigarette on the ground, and scrubbed it out with his boot.

"You want to know about Spyders, Blake Williams's your man."

"Okay, I'll keep that in mind. In case I ever have an extra million."

"You'll need more than that. Hell, you're a friend of Callahan's, he's got plenty of money. Maybe the old bastard will cut you a deal."

"Speakin' of Callahan," Byrd said, "Did he mention where he was going after he dropped the car off?"

The mechanic shook his head. "Nah, he didn't say much. Just told me about the damn brakes going bad."

Byrd nodded. "Was it typical for him to bring a car down here himself? Anything seem unusual?"

"Well, I wouldn't call it typical. Usually we go get 'em."

"Right."

"This time he brought it to us. We pulled it off the trailer, shot the shit for a couple minutes. Then he left in that Pepper he rats around in."

"He left in what?"

"The Pepper. You know, the Porsche SUV. The Cayenne."

"He still have the trailer in tow?"

"Yep."

"You talk to him for long?"

"Nah," Griggs replied. "Said he's gonna bring home a car, but he didn't say what. He said it's gonna be so good we wouldn't fuckin' believe it. No tellin' what he's got up his sleeve."

"He say where he was goin'?"

"Not exactly," Griggs replied, "but I think he mentioned Germany? He said something about the factory, so I guess he meant Stuttgart. Though they've got one in Leipzig, too. Hell, I don't know."

"Right. What color was the . . . the Pepper?"

"Beige. Or tan. Kind of a metallic tan color. Ginger Ale? Champagne? Hell, I don't know what the fuck they call it."

A shout came from inside the garage. It was the other mechanic. "Hey Stan," he said. "Dr. Johnson's on the phone. What do you want me to tell him?"

"Shit," Griggs said. "I gotta take this."

"No problem," Byrd replied. He thanked the mechanic for his time, and returned to his Bronco.

Stanley Griggs shuffled back inside the garage, shook his head and pulled a fresh cancer stick from his pocket.

THE LOST SPYDER

Byrd settled into the driver's seat and picked up his second string mobile phone.

He punched the big green button and started dialing.

11

CHARLIE BYRD BRAKED HIS FORD BRONCO to a slow halt. The brakes made an ear-splitting whine, metal grinding on metal like fingernails scraping across a chalkboard. It was time for a brake job, and if the Callahan family kept handing out cash, the long delayed repairs might actually happen.

He was stopped at a traffic light in the middle of Southside. This was Birmingham's trendy club district, if the city could be said to have one at all. In its heyday, roving packs of young residents flocked to Southside, and staggered from one watering hole to the next. Like much of Birmingham, Southside's fortunes tended to ebb and flow. The finest dining was still here, but so were the most talented thieves and beggars.

At the heart of the area lay the convergence of five roads, an intersection dubbed *Five Points*. There was a fountain, a flowing cascade of water and statues. The fountain served as a natural meeting place, and a hangout for idle minds. Much like the Vulcan statue, it was an icon of the city. Also like Vulcan, it was an oddity.

The fountain, officially named *The Storyteller*, depicted a bizarre scene from a children's book. There was a statue with a man's body and a goat's head. The man-goat creature was reading aloud from a book to other animals of the forest—turtles and frogs and rabbits and so forth. The visual impact of this scene was either charming or alarming, depending on one's worldview.

Some residents were convinced the fountain was Satanic. Anything involving a goat had to be Satanic. The Dark Lord worked in mysterious ways, especially when it came to public beautification projects. So no one called it *The Storyteller*; it was *The Satanic Fountain*.

Charlie Byrd didn't put much thought into Birmingham's steady undercurrent of old-time religion. He viewed Bible thumpers with a mixture of pity and bemusement. Birmingham was an old school Protestant town, and had more than its fair share of God-fearing folk. According to these people, the world was filled with ghosts and demons. But Byrd had little use for church, and even less for the hypocrites who populated it.

Byrd parked his Bronco next to her silver Toyota (the environmentally correct one with all the Mardi Gras beads), and joined his boss in the shadow of Satan.

He spotted her immediately. It was hard to miss Kristen Callahan. Sitting on a bench amidst a litany of homeless teenagers, she looked like she'd just left a hippie fashion show. Low rider jeans, Jesus sandals, and a ragged loose-fitting t-shirt that appeared to be held together by thin threads. Her style was all over the place, and somehow it all meshed together. Somehow she looked like she belonged.

She was carrying a substantial *Louis Vuitton* bag. Brandishing that kind of purse in this part of Birmingham was like dumping chum in a shark tank.

"Morning," he said. "Up early today, aren't we?"

Byrd knew she had no job. Not a real one, anyway. It must have been tough for a Callahan to get out of bed with something to do.

"I'm up at six every day," she replied. "That's when I get in my jog. When do you take your jog?"

"Not until after my yoga."

She was a smart ass, Byrd decided, but that wasn't necessarily a bad thing. Byrd was a smart ass himself. All too often, his banter fell flat with the females. Callahan seemed to get it.

"You have no idea, babe" he said. "Sometimes I work all night long."

Sleep was an elusive luxury for Charlie Byrd. The academic rigors of legal education were demanding in their own right, as professors piled on reading assignments with sadistic pleasure. But work as a private detective in a town like Birmingham entailed a lot of waiting. Waiting for suspects to sneak away from their home or place of employment. Waiting for the inevitable discrete adulterous rendezvous at an equally discrete location. Waiting for the right time and place to snap the right incriminating photo. Private detective work was really a form of human hunting and fishing. Instead of waiting for deer in a tree stand, Byrd waited for photo ops in a Ford. Often he found himself reading his legal casebooks after midnight, as he patiently waited for that magic moment when he would definitively earn his fee. Sleep? He hadn't slept since high school.

"What are you doing in Southside?" he said.

"I've got a condo down here. It's near where I work."

Byrd cocked his head.

"I thought you lived in that big house?"

"No," she said, "not any more."

"Well, where do you work?"

"*Flex*. Heard of it?"

"Nope."

"It's a gym. I teach *Pilates*."

"Never heard of that, either. What is it, aerobics?"

"Not exactly. I teach people how to find their core. Pilates is great. You should try it sometime."

"Maybe someday," he said, "but right now, my core needs caffeine."

They left the Satanic Fountain, crossing the street to the corner Starbucks. He got a cup of coffee, the house variety, with no cream or sugar. She got some pseudo Italian concoction of caramel, milk, and cinnamon that struck Charlie Byrd to be as unappetizing as it was unpronounceable.

They took a seat at a sidewalk table. For a moment, he was distracted by her breasts, and the question of their authenticity.

She had a habit of dressing so her breasts were on display. Cleavage peeked through the thin material on her shirt, and there was a layer of golden glitter sprinkled across her chest. That was the fashion; women were using some sort of glitter cream to attract men, although in this case it was unnecessary. Her bosom was ample and well rounded. But was it genuine? A boob job would've been pocket change for this gal. But granola chicks, even rich ones, didn't get boob jobs. Byrd finally concluded that her breasts were all natural. The New Money woman had Old Money breasts.

"How's your five-dollar coffee?" he asked.

It was ridiculous what people were paying for coffee these days. Byrd loathed Starbucks, and all the other upscale coffee shops. The places were populated by an unholy alliance of hippies and yuppies, two groups he sought to avoid.

"My five-dollar coffee is good," she replied. "So tell me how things went this morning."

"Pursuant to our conversation," he said, "I did go see Griggs."

Byrd loved peppering his speech with legal terms like *pursuant* and *arguendo*. It made him feel like he was getting his money's worth at *Birmingham SOL*.

"Right. Did Stan have anything useful to say?"

"Not really. Said your father dropped off that orange car a couple of weeks ago."

"The Great Pumpkin?"

Byrd dropped into a deadpan impression of Stanley Griggs. "Yes ma'am, the Great Goddamned Pumpkin," he said. "And it ain't fuckin' ready."

She laughed, music to his ears. Indeed, there were few things more musical in the world than a pretty woman laughing at his jokes.

"Stan's a colorful character."

"You don't say? Anyway, your father dropped off the car and left. Griggs said he didn't stay long. He left in something called a champagne . . . Pepper."

Byrd looked down at his notepad to get the name right. "Cayenne SUV. Pullin' a trailer."

"So he just dropped off the car and left."

"Right."

"Anything else?"

"Yeah. He told Griggs he's going to get a car. A car so good that no one will believe it."

"Why am I not surprised," she deadpanned. "What else?"

"Griggs thinks he mentioned Germany, but he's not sure. Either Stuttgart or ... Lip swig?

"Leipzeig."

"Right, Leipzeig. One more thing."

Byrd pulled the piece of notepad paper from his pocket, unfolded it, and placed it on the table.

"Mean anything to you?"

She studied the paper for a moment, then looked up. "Well, it's definitely my father's handwriting," she said. "No idea what *antigua arana* means. Sounds like a foreign language."

"It is," Byrd said. "If I remember my Spanish, *antigua* is Spanish for old or antique."

"See? You can be useful, after all. I was thinking about the island."

"What island?"

"Antigua. It's an island in the Caribbean. A resort community, sort of like Cannes. Very nice. But I don't know what that would have to do with anything. My father's never been to Antigua."

"We should check flight records, just in case."

"Cops already did. If he flew to Antigua, we'd know about it. But sure, check all the records you want."

"What about *arana*?"

"Spanish for—guess what?"

"What?"

"Spider."

"You're kidding."

"No," Byrd replied. "I hate spiders. That's one Spanish word I'll never forget. On that note, any reason he'd write this in Spanish?"

She shook her head. "No idea. He doesn't speak Spanish." She said it with a snort, as if the very idea of her father speaking another language was laughable.

"How about the number 146? And the word acquired?"

"That could be a racing number. Or a production number. I have no idea."

She reached inside her oversized *Louis Vuitton*, withdrew a plain white envelope, and handed it to Byrd.

"I've got something you should see," she said. "Arrived in the mail yesterday."

The envelope was addressed to John Christian Callahan. The script was barely legible, wildly scrawled in black ink. There was no return address, though the postage was German. The government seal indicated Stuttgart as place of origin.

"Well, whoever sent it, they sure got terrible handwriting," Byrd said. "Did you open it?"

"Yes," she replied. "And yes, I know that opening someone else's mail is a crime."

He opened the envelope and withdrew a single page of paper. It was weathered and yellow and appeared to be of significant age. At the top of the page were the words "serial number" and a code of seven numbers that began with 550. The rest of the page was blank, save for the Porsche logo.

"A 550 Spyder," Byrd said. "Someone sent your father a Porsche document. What's the significance?"

"I don't know. He already owns this car. This goes with the wrecked Spyder that's in his garage. Maybe he wanted additional documentation?"

"This looks original. How could he get the original paperwork? I thought the factories kept these things on file."

"They do. That's one of the things that's weird."

"This morning, Griggs mentioned some guy up in Cullman. Williams?"

"Blake," she said. "Blake Williams. He's sort of the Spyder expert in this region."

"Maybe we should give the guy a call."

"We can be there in less than an hour. Hang on a minute, I'll see what he's doing."

She stood up from her chair, pulled out the supercomputer cell phone, and stepped away from the table. Once again, Byrd couldn't refrain from taking in the view. This woman spent most of her spare time molding her body. That much was evident. She had curves that could stop traffic, and she liked to show them off.

There was something else about Kristen Callahan, something that bothered Charlie Byrd. He couldn't put his finger on it. She was obviously bright, funny, and generous when it came to paying the hired help. But something about her glib attitude, under the circumstances, was off-putting. Where was the concern of a daughter missing her father? Pilates? Had this woman ever worked a day in her life? Kids were starving in China. Hell, kids were starving in Alabama, and these people were joyriding in a bunch of German rust buckets. Her nonchalance was odd to the point of distraction. Aside from that brief moment in the library, she appeared at ease. At times she seemed to be enjoying the situation.

And what was Byrd doing on this case anyway? If she was truly worried about her father, why not call the FBI and be done with it? Why not plaster the story on the front page of *The Birmingham News*? Why not stamp the old man's face on every milk carton in America? After all, they could afford it. They could afford better than Charlie Byrd. They could afford better than second-string. Something else was happening here, but Byrd couldn't figure it out.

She finished her call, and walked back to the table with a smile on her face.

"Good news," she said, "Blake will be in his shop all afternoon, and would love to see us. Let's head that way."

Then she paused. Her eyes drew narrow.

"What?" she asked. "What's that look for?"

Words no man can stomach – *what's that look for*. She'd caught the expression on his face. This was a weakness of Charlie Byrd's. He played an awful game of poker, because when Byrd had a lousy hand he let the entire room know it. He fancied himself a master of emotional distance. Yet his feelings were broadcast for all to see.

The look of an ego bruised. The look of pious judgment. Of distaste.

"What?" she repeated for good measure. "What's wrong?"

"Nothing. Nothing's wrong."

His face went blank, as best as he could manage.

"Why do you ask?"

"That look on your face," she said. "Someone pee in your coffee?"

"Naw, no one pissed in my coffee."

She shot through his unconvincing grin.

"You don't like me, do you?"

It was his turn to act offended. "What? Of course I like you. What a thing to say."

"I'm your employer, as you remind me every two minutes. You don't have to like me. I don't have to like you."

"Look, I never said, nor would I say, that I don't like you. I barely know you. We just come from two different worlds, that's all. We're different kinds of people."

"Here we go," she said. "Different worlds."

"Well, not exactly. But yeah, we come from different backgrounds. I didn't grow up collecting rare German cars and *Louis Vuitton*. I don't read my horoscope. I don't have tattoos. And forgive me for saying so, but I don't believe women have the power to stop nuclear war."

"Poor little Charlie Byrd," she said. "You seem well-fed to me. You're a well-fed misogynist."

He held up his hands as if to surrender. Like brush fires and Santa Ana winds, this type of situation could easily get out of control. He needed to get a grip and steer the conversation back to safe territory. He needed to remember Eddie Haskell, and one thousand dollars a day. A fat wad of cash was at stake here. Eddie Haskell, he decided, was one smart motherfucker.

"Look," he said with careful precision, pondering each word before it left his mouth. "I didn't mean to upset you."

He was now convinced that she was crazy. The Callahans were nut jobs. Then the words slipped out again.

"Hell, lady, you brought this up, not me."

"No, you brought it up," she replied. "You brought it up with that look on your face."

Byrd wanted to fire back, but visions danced in his head. He saw a thousand dollars floating out the window. Kristen Callahan may have been a nut job, but she was a nut job with deep pockets.

"This is silly," he said. "Can we just drop it?"

"Why should we drop it?"

"Look, all I'm saying is this."

Byrd paused. It was his nature to speak his mind, especially when dealing with high-maintenance females. In this instance, he'd choose his words carefully. He found himself in an argument, and he wasn't sure why. He lowered his voice in a shameless attempt to defuse the situation.

"Your father is MIA," he said. "To Germany, or wherever. Sure, he does this sort of thing all the time. Sure, he's an eccentric guy and he'll probably show up any minute now with some car in tow. But what if he doesn't? What if this time's different? I'm sorry if I offended you or whatever. But that worries me. "

He stopped, pleased with himself. Best to quit while ahead. He'd managed to speak without worsening the situation. He said he was sorry. Who doesn't like a good apology? Charlie Byrd sounded respectable, almost . . . thoughtful.

"You think I haven't considered that possibility?" she replied. "Like I told you yesterday, I've already talked to the police. Wheels are in motion. If we strike out, this whole thing will change."

"Okay. Sorry I asked."

He raised his hands again in a gesture of helplessness. Poor thoughtful little Charlie Byrd.

"Don't be," she replied. "I'd rather you shoot straight than try to dance around issues. We'll never get anywhere if you're not completely up front with me. I mean completely. I always want to know what you're thinking."

He nodded.

No, you really don't, he thought. *There's no way in hell you want to know what I'm thinking.*

He nodded and kept his mouth shut.

"And another thing," she said. "About money."

Byrd braced for the diatribe. Was she already renegotiating?

"My father has money. I make no apologies for it."

"No apologies necessary."

"Don't give me any sob story about your life as a struggling student. There are a number of schools you could have attended, any number of financing programs. You made your choices. Deal with it."

"I'm dealing with it just fine," he said, turning away from her icy gaze. Then he lost control of his tongue. "It's dealing with you that's the problem. Maybe you should slip a little Prozac in your five-dollar coffee."

She laughed, this time a hearty laugh.

"Well, that's certainly being up front," she said. "Now grab your stuff and let's go see Williams."

Charlie Byrd exhaled. Feeling like he had just dodged a bullet, he stood up.

12

THE FAT MAN SAT THE BOWL ON THE GROUND, and quickly backed away. His body language was tense, and the dogs could smell his fear.

He stood back a safe distance, eyes wide, bracing for the dogs. He'd been through this routine a hundred times, and yet each time he was afraid.

The Man with the Scar smiled. The Fat Man was amusing, like a child.

Behind the closed door, the dogs whimpered in anticipation. They, too, knew what was about to happen. They clawed at the base of the door, digging deep grooves into the unpainted wood. Drool rolled from their tongues like molasses. Their paws clicked on the concrete floor, which was now slick with saliva.

Then the door was open. The whimpering and growling stopped as the hounds ran free through the courtyard. Their target was a cavernous metal bowl, wide and low and filled to the brim with scraps of raw meat and fat and gristle.

This was a predictable drama, but it never failed to entertain. The beasts raced to the food together, like a flock of blackbirds crossing the sky. They were one mind, one collective mind focused on one goal.

They'd attack the bowl, fighting for the largest pieces of meat. One dog would anger the next, and they'd snap at one another. The leader, a speckled mutt with traces of hound and wolf, would take command. The animal snatched the largest piece of flesh from the bowl. He turned to face the pack, snarling, the meat gripped in his jaws. There were no challengers. Satisfied, he walked away to devour it in private. The rest of the pack descended upon what remained.

These dogs paid for themselves many times over. They were the ideal security system—loyal, cheap, and vicious.

The drama was over. The Man with the Scar turned away from the courtyard, leaving the mongrels behind.

The next order of business was the gringo. He had to know more about the gringo. He had to know more about the bounty.

The Man with the Scar walked up the creaking flight of wooden stairs that connected the courtyard to the house. Once inside, he was enveloped by darkness. He navigated through the house from memory, feeling his way around corners. He stopped in the hallway and lit a candle. Then he continued down the hall to the kitchen, guided by candlelight, his heavy boots thumping on the bare wooden floor.

The kitchen was warm. From the ceiling hung a single bulb suspended by a long wire. The pale electric light was supplemented by candlelight. Candles were scattered throughout the room, resting on ceramic plates. The kitchen table, a raw and splintered chunk of wood, also glowed with warm candlelight.

The Man with the Scar sat in the shaky chair at the head of the table. It felt good to rest. For a moment he watched hot wax ooze from the candles onto the table. In the flickering light, it resembled blood.

He felt like a king about to enjoy a royal feast. There was no food or drink here. Instead, there was property. The bounty of the gringo.

It was late and The Man with the Scar was tired. He pulled a cigarette from his pocket and, leaning forward, lit it in candle flame. The tip of the cigarette glowed orange as he inhaled. He let the smoke fill his lungs and clear his mind. Exhaling, he watched clouds billow across the table. The smoke mixed with the flickering light, and shadows danced throughout the room. Simple pleasures.

Now it was time for the money.

He set a leather pouch onto the table. From the pouch The Man with the

THE LOST SPYDER

Scar pulled money, stacks of American cash recovered from the gringo's SUV.

It was quiet in the room. Outside in the courtyard, the dogs were fed and happy. The boy was in the City, selling the SUV. The Fat Man was probably already asleep, or at least pretending to be asleep. The world was asleep.

The Man with the Scar smoked his cigarette and eyed the cash, accompanied only by amber flame and dancing shadows. Then he began counting. It took a long time. There was more money than he thought.

Next he looked at documents. There were papers, most of which were written in English. They were impossible to understand. The Man with the Scar couldn't read English, nor did he know anyone who could, at least no one who could be trusted.

He pulled out a blue passport. *The United States of America.* This was easy enough to understand. The gringo was American.

He flipped open the document. It was written in Spanish as well as English. Finally, something he could read.

In the candlelight The Man with the Scar studied the face on the passport. The face of a man named John Christian Callahan, a man whose battered body lay in the basement.

Above Callahan's signature was scrawled a request in three languages. One of the languages was Spanish.

"The Secretary of State of the United States of America hereby requests all whom it may concern to permit the citizen/national of the United States named herein to pass without delay or hindrance and in case of need to give all lawful aid and protection."

The Man with the Scar smiled thinly.

"Ayuda y proteccion."

John Christian Callahan would receive no aid.

He had no protection.

He wouldn't pass without delay.

It made sense to kill the gringo. They could've killed him on the road. That would've been the clean way, the safe way, the usual way.

But there was too much here. Too much money to just kill the gringo and be done with it. John Christian Callahan was a rich man. The catch of a lifetime. When fate grants opportunity, it must be exploited to the full. The Man with the Scar would extract more from the gringo before killing him.

It was necessary, like with the dogs. The cosmos tossed him a pile of fresh meat; it was his duty to consume it. All of it.

A noise at the back door. It was the boy. He walked into the room, tired but beaming. His slick face glistened in the candlelight. It was chilly outside, but his clothes were soaked with sweat. He grinned a wide smile. He still had all of his teeth, and his smile said more than words.

The boy was followed by the Fat Man, who'd accomplished little more than feeding the dogs, but didn't want to miss anything.

From his jacket, the boy pulled an envelope. More cash. He'd already returned from the City. He'd delivered the SUV and was paid in cash, and he'd returned before dawn. His rite of passage was complete.

The Man with the Scar was impressed. If he'd sent the Fat Man, anything could've happened. The boy had done the job quickly.

He accepted the envelope of cash, and set it on the table next to the rest of John Christian Callahan's property.

This gringo had so much. If he died now, all would be in vain. They needed to keep the gringo alive in order to extract more. They should call the woman. She would help keep him alive.

The woman would nurse the gringo.

The Man with the Scar would extract the money.

Then the gringo would die.

13

FROM THE DRIVER'S SEAT, Charlie Byrd reached across the passenger cabin of his Ford Bronco.

The door swung open with a shrill squeal. Byrd raked the contents of the seat—a menagerie of old newspapers, fast food wrappers, legal journals, and empty aluminum cans—into the floorboard. With the seat cleared of refuse, he swept away a final layer of crumbs with a few brisk strokes of his palm.

"Hop in," he said.

Hands on her hips, Kristen Callahan refused to budge.

"You've got to be kidding."

"Naw, I'm not kidding," he replied. "We rode in your car yesterday. Not sure my knees can handle it today. Besides," he said, "your fee includes transportation."

Callahan groaned as she slid into the passenger seat, where she was greeted by the telltale odor. Wintergreen tobacco juice was perhaps the most disgusting substance on the planet.

"I just took a shower," she said.

"Don't worry," he replied. "It won't bite."

He raised his eyebrows and spoke with mock sincerity.

"Please be gentle when you close that door. This truck is one-hundred percent original."

She slammed the door shut, and Byrd mashed down his right foot. With a lurch, the Bronco bolted forward, rattling away from Southside.

"Buckle your seatbelt," he said over the braying engine. "Please keep your arms and legs inside the vehicle at all times."

"No problem," she muttered as she clicked her seat belt into place. "Assuming the door doesn't fall off. How many miles you got on this thing?"

"Two-twenty when the odo stopped working."

"When did the odometer stop working?"

"Couple years ago."

Byrd maneuvered his trusty steed back on Interstate 65, heading north. After a few minutes, they were outside of Birmingham and driving past the Callahan estate.

The highway passed a mere half-mile in front of the millionaire's compound, providing a dramatic view of the property. In fact, the estate was so prominently visible that authorities built a parking area for passersby. The private home was considered a scenic viewpoint, a juxtaposition that Byrd always found odd.

Almost as odd as having a Callahan right there in his truck. He'd seen that house a thousand times before, always from his Ford Bronco and I-65. Now a former resident was seated by his side.

Kristen Callahan gazed upon her father's home in silence.

"Gotta be nice to have the highway so close to your house," Byrd said. It was, he knew, a dumb thing to say. But it broke the silence.

"Yes, we enjoy the sound of interstate traffic," she replied. "It was a fun day in the Callahan household when they announced the new highway."

"Huh?"

"Ever hear about the law of *eminent domain*, Perry Mason? The state can do whatever it wants, even run a highway through your front yard. Daddy pissed off so many people in the government, I wasn't surprised."

"Yeah, I recall reading something about that."

"He'd already built the storage facility and all, so he didn't want to move. He got used to it. Probably the one time J.C. Callahan didn't get his way."

Byrd cleared his throat and shifted uncomfortably in his seat.

Dumb remark. Again. Change the subject.

THE LOST SPYDER

"So, you know Blake Williams, right?"

"Yes, of course I know Blake Williams."

She looked out the window, and Byrd looked straight ahead. At times, talking to this woman was like pulling teeth.

"How'd you meet?"

"He's known my father since the 50s. I think they went to driving school together. Long as I can remember, he's been a part of my life."

Byrd nodded. "He just takes care of your Dad's Spyder?"

"Not really, not any more. But you might say he's the local expert."

The conversation died a quick death, and they rode on in silence. Byrd welcomed the reprieve. Awkward silence, perhaps, but less awkward than the conversation.

He listened to his Bronco drone, and watched the Alabama countryside roll past. Despite many centuries of occupation, first by the natives and then their conquerors, Alabama remained raw. Wild pine, oak, and maple blanketed the landscape. Tufts of white dogwood in bloom, patches of pink azalea. In some places, kudzu took control, choking out all other greenery. A Japanese vine, Kudzu grew faster than weeds. It had become a staple of the Deep South, like it or not. Byrd liked it. It all made for a scenic drive.

Charlie Byrd was familiar with Alabama's small towns. More than once he'd followed a cheating husband to some rinky-dink rural motel. They always thought they were anonymous out there in *Bum-Fuck Egypt*. But in *BFE* they were more obvious than ever.

Success in a small town depended on one's ability to adapt. Once you left the Birmingham city limits, things changed. The "Magic City" was an oasis of New South in a state dominated by the Old. Areas of Birmingham were indistinguishable from Atlanta or New York or Los Angeles. No one would ever say the same of Arab or Bug Tussle or Opp, which were to urban development what moonshine was to fine wine.

Rural Alabama had a character all its own. The key, Byrd knew, was to appreciate customs, rituals, and mores. Stretching out vowels worked wonders. Folks in the country took life at a different pace. Better to go slow, ask questions indirectly, and season one's speech with the appropriate *y'alls* and *ma'ams*. Eddie Haskell with a drawl.

Within minutes, they were maneuvering through the streets of Cullman, a quiet farming community of German heritage. Cullman was noted for producing plenty of chicken and sweet potatoes—and no alcohol whatsoever. Byrd thought he'd make another attempt at conversation.

"Cullman's dry, right?" he said.

"Dry as a bone," she replied. "Town and county. No booze allowed. Since the area was settled by Germans, they still have Oktoberfest every year. A dry Oktoberfest."

He laughed. "Isn't Oktoberfest a beer festival?"

"Everywhere else, yeah. Not here. Cullman's got the world's only dry Oktoberfest. If they got beer, it's non-alcoholic. You know, *near beer*."

"Only in Alabama," he said. "Land of the oxymoron."

If Alabama was the heart of the Bible Belt, Cullman was its left aorta. Many mysteries of government and politics befuddled Charlie Byrd. Perhaps nothing was more bizarre than the state's myriad alcohol policies. Despite the well documented fact that Christ's first miracle involved the production of wine, the beverage was not welcome in God's Country. Had Jesus turned water into wine here, he would've faced a swift incarceration.

"This was a great place to attend high school," she said with mock sincerity. "A real highlight of my life."

"You went to high school in Cullman?"

She nodded.

"I started out at Altamont. After a couple of years, my father decided it wasn't the place for me. Spent my last two years up here in *Dullman*. That's what we used to call it. Graduated from Saint Bernard."

Byrd understood. Altamont was the kind of blueblood private school that served as launching pad from Birmingham to the Ivy League. Altamont graduates went on to Brown and Harvard, married well, and set about the business of governing their peers. That is, if they didn't succumb to recreational drugs and rebellion first. St. Bernard, on the other hand, was a small Catholic school, operated by nuns and monks in the isolated rural gulag of Cullman County. It was the sort of school where every student had a backstory. Usually they came from wealthy families. Often misbehavior was involved. Parents sent wayward kids to St. Bernard so the monks would straighten them out.

"What about you?" she asked. "Where'd you go to high school?"

"Minor," he replied.

"Purple Tigers?"

"Right," he said flatly. "Purple Tigers. I'm trying to forget about it."

Minor High was the type of Alabama public school where a few graduates went on to become local police officers, who then proceeded to arrest their fellow classmates.

❧

Byrd had spent time in Cullman before, parked outside a quaint motel that was popular amongst the Birmingham adulterous set. The city was much as he remembered it. A typical small Alabama town, it boasted an aging downtown district, several fast food chains, and a Walmart the size of Rhode Island. He cruised his truck through downtown, noting mom-and-pop businesses surviving in the shadow of Sam Walton. Thanks to a hardy breed of antique stores and barber shops and southern cafes, Cullman retained a healthy dose of its original charm.

As his Bronco pulled into the parking lot of Blake Williams's garage, the detective once again felt underwhelmed. The garage was located in the downtown section of Cullman amidst scores of empty buildings. None were taller than two stories. None had received fresh paint in decades.

Williams's shop was particularly colorless—a gray cinder block cube, with a parking lot of gray gravel. No signage. The main door of the garage bay was open, but there was no car inside. The odd passerby might be excused for thinking this was a vacant storage facility. Only the persistent odor of motor oil revealed otherwise.

Byrd's passenger, however, felt at home. As soon as he stopped his truck, she bounded from the vehicle. Walking toward the garage, she dusted off her curvaceous rear end—as if she'd been sitting in dirt for the past half-hour.

"Hey, Patch," she said. "Guess who's here?"

An elderly man emerged from the garage, walking with a slight limp. Wearing a pair of denim overalls and work boots, the man smiled in recognition.

"Great to see you," the man said. He held his arms open, and received a hug from the young lady.

Byrd hopped out of his vehicle and extended his hand.

"I'm Charlie Byrd," he said.

"Blake Williams," the man replied with a broad smile. He grabbed Byrd's hand in a beefy paw. "Nice to meet you."

Although clearly in his seventies, Williams moved with an energetic gait. His weathered skin looked every bit its age. But his eyes, teeth, and attitude seemed thirty years younger. He was the kind of man who somehow stood taller than his actual height. As he gripped Byrd's hand, the detective noted the man's strength. The body was deteriorating. The spirit was not.

"It's nice to meet you . . . Patch? Everybody just calls me Byrd."

Williams laughed. "Okay, Byrd. But she's the only one who calls me Patch."

Byrd looked the man squarely in his smiling blue eyes, and noticed something amiss.

Kristen Callahan grinned. "Blake used to wear a patch over that glass eye of his," she said. "When I was a little girl, I thought he looked like a pirate."

Byrd nodded. "Sorry, Mr. Williams. I didn't realize you have a glass eye."

"No apology necessary, son. Had it almost fifty years. Back when I was younger than you, I was hammerin' a piece a steel. It shattered and a shard got into my left eye. Hurt like hell. Never slowed me down, though."

"That's amazing."

"It's not so amazing. You just do what you got to do. Now y'all come on inside and tell me what's going on."

They stepped inside the garage. The bay stood empty. Not a car in sight, although pieces were everywhere. An engine here, fenders there, wheels there. Piles of parts stacked on tables. The place reeked of some indefinable scent, the odor that permeates every garage.

"My office is back here."

Williams led them to the rear of the garage. His simple office was constructed by a glass and wood partition. Walls were adorned with photographs, many lacking frames. Most were black-and-white. Several of the pictures displayed a youthful Blake Williams either driving or standing next to Porsches. In some of the photos, he was wearing an eye patch.

In one photo, Byrd recognized the young man sitting in the passenger seat.

"That's Mr. Callahan, isn't it?"

Williams nodded. "Yeah, that's ol' J.C. That was Daytona back in, I don't know, sixty-three."

Byrd was curious about the patch.

"Kris mentioned that you owned a 550 Spyder. So you were able to race a car with one eye?"

"Like I said, son, sometimes you do what you got to do. Hell yes I raced these cars. I'm 73-years-old. Got an artificial knee, hip replacement, and a glass eye. And I'm *still* racin' these cars."

"Is depth perception a problem?"

"Not really. All my cars had a modified rear view mirror. Extra wide, so I see everything with my good eye."

He smiled. "'Course back in the early days, only one man would let me drive his cars on a track. That man was John Callahan."

Williams opened a desk drawer, pulled out a business card, and handed it to Charlie Byrd.

Byrd studied the plain white card. In one corner was a small Porsche logo. The center of the card said Blake Williams in blue ink, and beneath was the simple inscription Porsche Specialist.

"Me and Callahan have had some good times. Like the card says, I'm a specialist. I've got experience no book can match. Over the past five decades I've seen just about everything. I can take 'em apart and put 'em back together. If something's not right or original, I can usually spot it. If I can't spot it, I'll drive it—and then I can *feel* it. So when I'm not fishin', I'm doin' work for buyers."

Byrd was impressed. He'd heard of niche expertise, but he'd never met a Porsche Spyder expert. This fellow had to be a member of a dying breed, master of a niche within a niche.

"I've flown all over the country to look at cars. California, Texas, New York, you name it. One time a fellow from Quebec flew me up to inspect an RSK. Between all that stuff," he said, "I manage to stay pretty busy."

"I bet you do," Byrd replied with newfound respect. At an age when some people were picking out their burial plots, Williams was driving race cars.

Byrd peered at a tattered black-and-white photo of the man standing next to a 550 Spyder. In the image, Williams appeared in the physical prime of his life, a robust man full of spit and vinegar.

"Was that your car?"

"Yep, it sure was."

"So if you don't mind my asking, how did a kid your age go about getting a 550 Spyder? What's the story of your car?"

"Two different questions, son. I'll tackle the second one first."

"Okay."

"Porsche built ninety 550 Spyders. Then fifty-five of the 550A. So the cars were always rare."

"Right. If you don't mind my asking, how much was a car like that worth?"

The old man smiled. "I paid $4000 for it back in 1958. If you're lookin' for one nowadays, they'll run ya a little more. Hell, mine was full of dents and scratches. When I sold it, it was still worth a couple hundred grand."

"Best $4000 you ever spent, huh?"

"Yes son, as a matter of fact it was. Even back in the fifties these things were hard to find. And $4000 was a fair amount of cash in those days."

It's a fair amount of cash these days, Byrd thought.

"Like I said, my car was an original. It had a history. First buyer was some fellow from Central America. It was supposed to run in the *Panamericana*."

"A race?"

Williams grinned and launched into what Byrd later referred to as *Spyder Education 101*. It all began with the story of the *Carrera Panamericana*, the Mexican Road Race. From 1950 to 1955 the Mexican government sponsored an open road race to promote the newly completed Pan-American highway. The *Panamericana* stretched from the northern border of Mexico all the way south to Guatemala. It was at the *Panamericana*, Williams said, that the Porsche Spyder debuted and earned its nickname of *Giant Killer*. But automobile racing in those days was sheer brutality, with little consideration given to safety. The level of danger to participants was so severe, it made modern extreme sports seem like knitting or shuffleboard by comparison.

"They stopped the *Panamericana* in '55," Williams explained. "You have to understand, in those days racing was deadly. There weren't no safety equipment. People were already getting killed. Then in '55 they had the disaster over in France at *Le Mans*, more than 80 spectators died. Mexican government shut the whole *Panamericana* thing down and I guess you can't blame 'em."

His voice trailed away for a moment, and then he regained his train of thought.

"Well, anyway," he said, "My car started out just bein' packed in a crate and shipped down to Central America for some crew down there. But a funny thing happened. A military coup or somethin' or other. All hell broke loose, and the original buyer of my car just disappeared, never took delivery. For weeks, no one even knew where the car was. It was misplaced."

"Misplaced? Where was it? Stolen?"

"Well, after all the trouble died down, Porsche sent some guys down to Central America to look for it. They went to the loadin' dock where the Spyder should've been delivered. They asked if anybody had seen a car. Well, no one had seen it. So these Germans were about to leave, but first they went into the warehouse and snooped around. They didn't see no cars, but they saw an awful lot of boxes. Over in one corner, there was a real big box. Sure enough, the Spyder was inside."

Byrd cocked his head at the the prospect of squeezing a car inside a wooden box.

"You see, Porsche removed the wheels and windshield for shippin'. You know how small these cars really are, especially when you take off that stuff. People saw the box, but no one figured there was a car inside."

"Form follows function," Kristen said, and Williams nodded in agreement.

Form follows function. It was true. Of all the exotic cars Byrd had viewed in recent days, the 550 Spyder was the smallest. It was a relic of another era, a time before safety concerns and comfort demands had expanded the girth of sporting automobiles. It was drop dead simple, two seats and a knee-high aluminum chassis that hugged the earth. Its design reflected a distinctively German sentiment that *form* should follow *function*. The Spyder was beautiful, but its beauty was an afterthought. All elements all served a purpose. Remove the wheels and windshield and you could squeeze these things into a shoebox.

"Do you know *where* all this happened?"

"Not exactly," Williams said. "Just that it happened in Central America. I heard all this stuff second hand, from the fellas who sold me the car."

"So how'd you end up with the Spyder?"

"Like I said, that's a whole 'nother story. If you want to hear it."

Byrd nodded his assent. Williams was a natural storyteller, and he brought a unique enthusiasm to these autobiographical tales. And besides, Byrd was on the clock. There's nothing better than to be paid and entertained at the same time.

"Well," he continued, "Porsche brought the Spyder back from Central America to Germany. Then they sold it to a couple of doctors down in St. Augustine, Florida. Now at that time, I was just a kid working down at the Daytona track. You know, I was in heaven. Then one day, I seen these local doctors show up with their brand new Porsche."

The old man grinned. "They wanted to race the thing. So the first doctor takes the Spyder onto the track. After two laps, he pulls back into the pit stop and jumps out of the cockpit screamin' that the car's a killer. He won't drive another inch in it."

"So the other doctor gets in the Spyder, takes it out a couple of laps, and he does the same thing. Jumps out a cussin' and a screamin'. He swears the car's a killer. So neither of these doctors will drive the Spyder. They swear there's somethin' wrong with the suspension and it's dangerous. So I asked if I could take the car out for a lap. They said sure, if I didn't mind the risk."

"So was the Spyder dangerous?"

"Not really, son. I drove the car and figured out what was botherin' these doctors. There's a turn in Daytona that really plays with the suspension. The whole car shifts one entire width to the right. If you ain't comfortable with how these things handle, it'll scare you. Me, I've always liked drivin' Porsches. It was no problem."

Kristen Callahan was intrigued by the anecdote.

"I've always wondered how you got that car, but for some reason never asked. You bought the Spyder from the doctors?"

"Well, to make a long story short, yes. Got a good deal because those guys were so damned scared of it. They just wanted to get rid of it."

Byrd was impressed. Blake Williams didn't disappoint.

"So when was the last time you drove your Spyder?"

"It's not really mine any more son," he said. "Well, maybe half of it is. I sold half to Callahan back in, oh, guess it was 1980 or so. Then a few years later I sold the other half. It's sittin' in his garage."

His eyes grew dark. "You know son, that car has a history to it. No one drives it now."

"Yeah," Byrd said, "Kris told me something about what happened."

Williams threw a quick glance at Kristen Callahan and stiffened. He looked uncomfortable, as if they were broaching a forbidden subject.

"It was damaged in a wreck," he said. "Not too bad, but J.C. chose not to fix it. It's been sittin' in his garage ever since."

Kristen Callahan broke the tension. Yesterday she'd snapped at Byrd, but today she seemed more amenable to talking about the Spyder. Perhaps the presence of a comforting family friend like Williams made the topic easier to discuss.

"It's because of my mother," she said. "When I was a little girl, she had an accident in the Spyder. She was driving the car on a track, Sebring. She had a wreck."

"A wreck?"

Byrd almost held his tongue, but he needed to know.

"Bad wreck?" he asked.

"Not too bad," she replied. "Car wasn't totaled by any means, and Mom walked away. Just got shaken up, and a laceration on her arm. There were complications later. She went to the hospital for minor treatment. Hospital botched the job. Malpractice. She died."

The mother was out of the picture. Now Charlie Byrd understood why. It was an awkward moment. What to say upon discovering that someone's mother died in such a manner? Some personal tragedies are not lightened by the passage of time.

"I'm sorry," Byrd said. It was all he knew to say.

She shrugged.

"I was three-years-old at the time. I barely remember a thing. The Spyder didn't cause my mother's death. But Daddy didn't want the car touched. He just left it the same. It's stayed the same all these years. The same as the day she died."

Williams put his arm around her shoulder. "That was an awful thing to happen," he said. "Awful hardship. Things were never the same. Your momma was a beautiful woman. I know your daddy loved her."

She smiled thinly at the gesture, but wasn't convinced. She knew no such thing—it was questionable whether her father truly loved anyone—but the words provided some comfort.

"I'm not sure what my father loves now," she said.

Williams deftly changed the subject. "You kids are awful kind to sit and listen to an old man's stories. But surely you didn't come up here for that. What brings y'all to my neighborhood?"

The whisper of a smile disappeared from her face.

"It's about my father," she said. "And the 550 Spyder."

14

IT WAS WARM IN BLAKE WILLIAMS'S GARAGE. Spring sunshine was turning into summer heat. Most Alabama establishments employed gargantuan cooling units that cranked out arctic temperatures year round. Along with food, water, and shelter, proper air-conditioning was considered a necessity of life. But the cinder block garage was woefully underpowered. A window-mounted air-conditioning unit attempted to chill the area. Other than making a terrible racket, it accomplished little.

Kristen Callahan shifted in her seat, a folding metal chair. One of the chair legs was shorter than the rest, so the entire thing wobbled. After recanting the story of her father's disappearance, after confiding in Blake Williams, she had fallen silent. Her demeanor changed. For the first time, Charlie Byrd detected a hint of vulnerability.

Twenty-four hours had passed since she first contacted Byrd. In that time, no one had heard from J.C. Callahan. The man had been gone for two weeks. With each passing moment, the odds of his absence being innocent grew more remote.

Blake Williams offered the obligatory Southern elixir.

"Hon' can I get you a cold drink? How about a co-cola?"

Kristen Callahan's head of disheveled auburn hair sagged into her hands.

"No, thank you. I'm fine," she replied. "I haven't been sleeping well lately."

Williams's tone was reassuring, confident, and fatherly.

"Now honey, don't you fret," he said. "I've known your daddy for forty years. We both know he's got a wild streak. He'll probably show up any minute now, and we'll all get a good laugh out of it."

She grunted her assent.

"When he does," she said, "I'm going to give him a kick in the ass. God, I can't believe him sometimes. This is a ridiculous way to live."

Williams turned to Charlie Byrd.

"You're well-versed in this matter. From your questions, I assume you have an interest in this situation?"

Byrd looked to his employer for approval. They had skirted the issue of his role. Was it okay to tell this guy everything? He assumed so, but approval from the boss would be nice. She offered a silent nod.

"That's right," he said. "I'm a private investigator in Birmingham. Byrd's Eye Investigation. I usually handle cases on the QT."

"Byrd's Eye?"

"Yes, sir."

Charlie Byrd dug into his pocket and offered a business card. Williams appeared bemused.

"Now that is something," he said.

Byrd said nothing. He'd learned to expect such comments, and ignoring them was the best way to advance the conversation.

Williams took the hint. "So Mister Byrd," he said, "how can I help? I haven't seen J.C. in quite a while. But if there's anything, and I mean anything, that I can do to help y'all, then just let me know."

"Well, there are a couple things we'd like you to see. So far we've not found much. We know he pulled out a lot of cash, and chartered a one-way flight to Germany. Police are checking credit card records and so forth."

Byrd pulled a scrap of paper from his shirt pocket—the paper he'd taken from the garish orange Porsche at Stanley Griggs's shop. He handed it to Williams.

"I'd like you to take a look at this paper. Tell me what you think."

The old man accepted the paper and raised it to his good eye. He closed his glass eye and squinted, staring at the note.

"It's definitely Daddy's handwriting," Callahan offered.

The old man furrowed his brow and stared at the note.

"We know *antigua* is Spanish for old or antique," Byrd said. "And *arana* is Spanish for spider. So what do you make of it? Antique spider. Mean anything to you?"

"That son-of-a-gun . . . Where'd y'all find this?"

"I pulled it from a notepad," Byrd replied. "In one of Mr. Callahan's cars, the one he was driving on the day he left."

"Well," Williams replied, "what this note says is pretty plain. But it's not possible. Unless you believe in ghosts."

"Explain."

Williams cleared his throat and squinted at the paper. "It reads *antigua arana* #146 acquired. Now from *arana*, you've got to assume this refers to a car."

"That much we figured out." Byrd said. "We're here for a reason."

"Well, I suspect the number 146 would refer to the chassis production number. As in the one-hundred and forty-sixth 550 Spyder. But there's one problem," Williams said, "Only 145 of these cars were built. You can bank on that."

"So, besides the cars that were destroyed through wrecks or whatever, those 145 are the only 550 Spyders ever made?"

Williams nodded. "That's right. The only real ones."

"What about replicas? Could someone forge an exact replica?"

"Exact? No," he replied. "Not possible. Now there are Spyder replicas, but the engines are usually Volkswagen not Porsche, bodies are fiberglass not aluminum. No way a trained eye would get the two confused. No way at all."

"What about this note? Do you think it refers to a replica?"

"No," he said. "I do not. No way John Callahan is goin' to acquire a replica. I know exactly what this note is about. But it don't exist."

"What do you mean?"

"There's a story that makes the rounds amongst Porsche collectors," he said. "Hell, it's not just a story. More of a myth really. It involves the 550 Spyder."

As he spoke, Kristen Callahan's mood visibly changed. A hint of optimism returned to her face. The sound of Williams speaking with confidence was enough to rejuvenate her spirits. Her vulnerability passed. The little girl receded, and the headstrong woman returned.

"Go on," she said. "You're talking about the lost Spyder, right?"

"Well," the old man said, "as I told you, Spyders have always been rare. Every one ever made is now worth six, maybe seven, figures."

"Right."

"Over the years, people told me about a Spyder bein' built. Built but never sold. They say it was stolen from the factory and hidden away somewhere in Germany. Then it was lost, you know, never seen again. Now if those rumors were true, and that car was found, then it'd be worth a hell of a lot of money."

It would be worth more than money to some people, Byrd thought.

If he had learned anything in his brief but headstrong introduction to the magical world of Porsche collection, it regarded money. Charlie Byrd understood. Money was a secondary consideration. Yes, these *wealthier than God* collectors liked to make money. Yes, they found creative ways to deduct expenses, and used their race cars as a shallow means to dodge taxes. But these people were motivated by more than money. Porsche collection was about ego, a bunch of small dicks with fat wallets trying to compensate for their shortcomings. "Son, you never know how these things get started," Williams said. "Old farts like to tell tall tales. Some people tell fishin' stories. Other people tell car stories. We call 'em barn yarns."

Williams smiled, and his face brightened.

"Every collector dreams of findin' that perfect car hidden away in a barn somewhere. You know, some jewel that's been tucked away and forgotten, and spent decades in storage. Looks like new. Well, it happens sometimes. People get lucky."

"Why is the lost Spyder a barn yarn?"

Williams stiffened.

"It's a myth, son. Since I inspects these things for a living, people always tell me that bunk. They call it the lost Spyder, number 146."

"You don't believe it?"

"Only one problem with this old yarn. It's a bunch of horse manure. I talked to Porsche. There is no Spyder one-four-six. It doesn't exist. Never did. Factory says that 145 Spyders were built and sold. All documented and accounted for, including mine that was temporarily misplaced. Ain't never been one lost. Ever. So there you have it. Straight from Porsche."

He turned to Callahan.

"This note worries me. You know I love your daddy, but he always bought into this sort of foolishness. Now please don't take this the wrong way. John Callahan is a dreamer. He's always searching for the Holy Grail. The lost Spyder would be it, if it existed. That's for sure. But it doesn't. Your daddy," he concluded, "Is the kind of man who won't take no for an answer. He wants to believe it. The wrong sort of person . . . "

He paused, contemplating a diplomatic end to the sentence.

"The wrong sort of person could take advantage of that."

He sat the paper down on his desk and jabbed at it with his finger.

"Says here that number 146 has been acquired." He looked at Byrd. "You know what I think?"

"Someone's sold J.C. Callahan the legendary lost Spyder," Byrd replied, "Only there is no lost Spyder. Maybe they built an exact replica? Kind of like a fake Picasso?"

Williams shook his head. "No way someone could replicate the real thing. J.C. Callahan could tell the difference once he saw it up close."

Byrd arched his eyebrows in doubt. Diamonds could be faked. *Louis Vuitton* could be faked. Hell, with the right sunglasses, a white jumpsuit, and some pork chop sideburns, even Elvis Presley could be faked. Why not a Porsche Spyder?

"Lots of reasons," Williams continued. "Too complex. A four-cam engine. Too many parts that are damn near impossible to find. Parts with ID numbers. Physical stuff aside, they'd need papers—documentation. Since Porsche never built such a car, the factory never documented it. Hell," he said with a snort, "it'd be easier to forge a Picasso."

"Either way," Byrd said, "we know he went to Germany with a fortune in cash. We're talking seven figures."

Kristen Callahan leaned forward in her chair. "So if this means what you think it means," she said, "then he's in danger."

Silence enveloped the room as they contemplated this turn of events. To Byrd, the news wasn't unexpected. But once apparent, it was unsettling. If the note was legitimate, then J.C. Callahan might have been kidnapped. Or worse. Kidnappers, especially when dealing with moneyed families, usually offered some communication to the other side. To date they had received nothing of the sort.

Williams spoke with a newfound sense of urgency.

"Honey," he said, "I know the old boy likes his privacy. But you need the police, the FBI, and the newspapers workin' for you. Y'all don't need to waste any time."

She nodded, but made no eye contact.

"That's what I wanted to avoid," she said, staring intently at the floor. "But I know you're right. God, have we wasted too much time already?"

Williams put his hand on her shoulder.

"Honey, what's past is past. Y'all have done everythin' just like J.C. would want. Now it's time to go public. You can blame me for it. And no offense to you Mr. Byrd," he said, "because you've done some good work. But if we're right about this note, then every minute counts. We need the police gettin' to the bottom of this thing. Maybe I'm wrong. I hope so. But if I am, I'd feel better if the police told me so."

Byrd didn't protest. He spent most of his time gently paddling in the kiddy pool of detective work. This Callahan job was a belly flop into the Gulf of Mexico. He was in over his head, and caught in a wicked riptide.

"Mr. Williams," he said, "I agree with you one-hundred percent."

As the words slipped past his lips, he saw visions of hundred dollar bills going up in smoke. It was true. Good jobs never lasted.

As his mind clicked through the day's events, he suddenly realized there was a key piece of the puzzle that Williams hadn't yet seen.

"There's one thing I can't figure out," he said. "We've got something else to show you. Arrived by mail yesterday afternoon. From Germany."

Accepting the envelope with both hands, Williams furrowed his brow. His good eye narrowed as he closely studied the address, a wild cacophony of loops and scrolls, rendered in sloppy black ink.

"Recognize the handwriting?" Byrd asked. "It sure is unusual."

Williams shook his head.

"Naw," he said. "I can barely even read it. I don't see how the post office can deliver this sort of thing."

He opened the envelope and removed its contents. After examining the document in the same meticulous fashion, he sat it on his desk.

"Well, I'll be damned," he said. "Let me show y'all something."

Next to the desk was a modest safe, the cheap kind sold over the counter at Walmart. With a mild groan, he lowered himself to one knee in front of the safe. He gingerly spun out the combination code, clicking each tumbler into place. With a solid jerk, he opened the door.

Inside were a few envelopes, some keys, a folder, and a money pouch. Williams removed the manila folder and—with support from Byrd—stood back up.

"Thanks," he said. "That gets a little tougher every day."

He opened the folder and removed a solitary piece of paper. The paper was wrinkled, brown, and brittle. It had the texture of parchment. The ink had faded, but remained clearly legible.

"This," he said," is the only document I have that pertains to my 550 Spyder. Your daddy lets me keep it here. It's a copy of the build sheet. Porsche filed it in Germany when my car was made. Came with the car. Most of these build sheets are long gone. Just like the cars, and the people who made 'em."

He sat the paper on his desk, next to the recently arrived document from Germany. The two pages were identical. But the paper from Germany had a crisp, clean appearance. It looked equally authentic, but the ink and general appearance were fresh. It was as if one document had aged, while the other had been preserved in a time capsule.

Williams shook his head.

"Don't know why someone would send this to your daddy."

"Is it legit?" Byrd asked. "Maybe the document's a fake."

Williams shook his head.

"It looks original," he said. "It's got the seal and everything. But they keep originals on file over in Germany. Don't make no sense."

Williams put his hand back on Callahan's shoulder.

"Honey, every minute counts. Let's call the police."

15

W ITH A SUDDEN START, John Christian Callahan was awake.

He took a deep breath and inhaled a dollop of damp air. His tongue and mouth were bathed in a sour paste, like milk gone bad.

He peered through the swollen slit that was his right eye. He was still in the dark, lying on a cold and gritty floor, wearing stinking clothes that were stained with his own dried blood. He turned his gaze upward. Blackness. Nothing had changed.

There was a rattling outside. Keys jangling. Lock tumblers clicking. A door crept open, and light invaded his skull. It penetrated the blindfold, and his eyes struggled to adjust. He saw shades of red and black.

A man walked into the room. The musty aroma was seasoned with more body odor, this time of the local variety. Through the blindfold, it was impossible to gauge the intruder's age. He was a dark impressionist blur, a vague outline surrounded by a halo of light.

Another person entered the room, perhaps a woman. Yes, it was a woman. He caught a glimpse of a billowy skirt floating above her feet.

The man whispered something, a string of unintelligible gibberish.

Callahan didn't speak Spanish, or any other foreign language. Why learn to speak it when you can hire a translator? Spanish had never been of interest. Never until now.

He decided to make nice with his abductors. Talk to them. Get some information. Knowledge was power, and Callahan was powerless.

"Who are you?" he said with as much authority as he could muster. "You're making a mistake. Why do you have me here?"

There was no use in trying to hide his identity. The kidnappers, whoever they were, could see the obvious. By now they'd rifled his wallet. They'd taken his credit cards—but would they be stupid enough to use them? They had his licenses, membership cards, and passport. They'd pilfered his SUV and found the cash.

Oh God, the cash. Callahan brought Fort Knox on the trip. Took his time along the way, meandering across the continent. Thousands of dollars in clean American cash. It was probably the mother lode of cash, he noted, that kept him alive. Once they found that cash sitting in a glove box, they wondered who the hell they'd clubbed into submission. You don't kill the golden goose after finding a few eggs.

There was another possibility. The kidnappers could've been working for someone. The whole thing could've been orchestrated. He could've been followed, and set up. He considered this a very real, but remote, possibility. He'd taken extreme measures to cover his tracks back home. The attack felt random, one of those wild cards of shit luck. Nothing happened to J.C. Callahan in moderation.

Either way, they kept him alive for a reason.

"*Tranquilidad,*" the man said. He said nothing else. Callahan didn't speak Spanish, but the tone told him enough. This was the man in charge.

"You don't know who you've got," he replied. "You don't know *what* you've got. Do you speak English? Bring me someone who speaks English."

If one of these devils spoke English, Callahan could talk his way out. He'd let his money do the talking. He had a favorite saying. *If money will solve the problem, then I don't have a problem.*

"*Tranquilidad,*" the man said, this time with authority. Callahan heard a threat in the voice. It sent chills down his spine. There was that feeling again, that familiar tingle.

You wanted to feel alive, you son-of-a-bitch? You got it.

He heard additional whispers of Spanish.

The man bent over and examined the wounded shoulder. Again, Callahan caught a whiff of body odor, this time as gale force 10. He grimaced.

He no longer felt fear. They kept him alive for a reason, he told himself. They could've killed him on the road. They had no incentive to kill him now. He was of value alive. He was worthless dead.

The woman entered the room and crouched in front of him, her arrival announced by a whiff of perfume. It was the only respite, the only nod to civilization, that he'd experienced since the abduction.

She put a glass to his lips. "*Bebida*," she said. "*Agua*."

He refused the drink. He was thirsty, but there was no telling what these devils put in the glass. He knew better than to drink. Even if it was water, he wouldn't drink it. Probably laced with drugs. Probably came from some filthy tap teeming with *Montezuma's Revenge*. Callahans didn't drink tap water, especially not in this foul place. Drinking the water was a quick ticket to dysentery.

"*Bebida*," the woman said.

She was kneeling in front of Callahan. His mind reeled with possibilities. He could fight back right here, right now. She was vulnerable. Perhaps he could overpower the woman, and use her incapacity to fight back.

But he was powerless. Feet and hands bound, he had no control over the situation. He wanted to resist, to fight. But he had no way to fight. He was still weak.

He desperately wanted to feel water on his tongue. He wanted to ingest the water, to feel it replenishing his ravaged body. He wanted to rinse the blood from his mouth.

But he had to resist. He did the one thing he could. He refused. She pressed the glass against his lips. He could smell the liquid in the glass, his leathery tongue ached to touch it. But he refused. He turned his head.

"*Idiota*," the man said. He pulled the woman away. They withdrew and the door slammed shut. Darkness was restored. Tumblers clicked as the door was locked.

Once again, he was alone.

He took a quick inventory of the facts. Although plunged back into darkness, his mind was active and seeking answers.

THE LOST SPYDER

He'd caught a glimpse of his abductors, even though it was fleeting and distorted through the prism of a sloppy blindfold. No faces yet, but he knew the smells. The woman's perfume. The man's foul stench. He wouldn't forget either.

Think about it, Callahan. Relish these memories because they may be your last.

They wanted to keep him alive. They had checked his bandages. The drinking glass probably contained water. If it had been poison, they would've forced it down his throat. In his present condition, half-dead, bound hand-and-foot, stretched on the cold floor, he could've offered little resistance.

He swallowed. His mouth was dry. The taste of the blood was disgusting. He'd need water soon. Next time it would be hard to resist a drink. Next time he wouldn't resist. A man can't survive without water.

He shifted his weight against the wall. It was still quiet in the room, but something was different. He heard a steady rumbling noise upstairs. It was faint and barely definable. Perhaps it was an airplane. Perhaps a delivery truck. It told him nothing except there was life outside this dank hole.

His mind began to drift.

He relaxed, his breathing grew more rhythmic, and his mind began to wander. It traveled far away, back in time. It arrived in an unlikely place.

His daughter. He saw his daughter. His only child, and for all practical purposes his only family.

To his wandering mind, Kristen was still a young child. She was standing there in the doorway, bawling her eyes out. Her bushy orange hair, a gift from her mother, was disheveled. Her left kneecap was bloody. She'd busted her knee. She was learning to ride her new bike.

She was learning alone. *All real learning,* he told her, *happens when you're alone.* There are some things you have to teach yourself. His parental techniques were not adopted from the Dr. Spock baby boomer mold. What he was doing was by no means illegal, even if it could be labeled cruel.

She stood in the doorway, a faint trickle of blood streaming from her knee. John Callahan had never worn kneepads, and by God neither would his daughter. He'd suffered more than a few skinned knees. Non-fatal wounds built character. To hell with the Girl Scouts. They were selling cookies while his daughter was busting her knees. He'd take a dose of spilt blood over thin mint cookies any day.

"Where you going?" he said. "You tryin' to quit?"

"I hurt my knee," she replied and wiped tears from her face. "I hate this."

"Callahans don't quit," he replied. "You're a Callahan. Get back on the bike."

"My knee's bleedin'."

He examined the child's knee. She'd scraped a nice quarter-sized wound in her soft skin. It was bloody, yes. But the blood was oozing, not flowing. The sight of a little girl's blood always brought drama.

But it didn't bring sympathy, not this time. It wouldn't require stitches. She was going back on the bike.

"It's only a strawberry," he said.

He wouldn't give her the satisfaction of sympathy. That would only encourage weakness.

He pulled a monogrammed handkerchief from his pocket, and mopped the blood. He pressed hard against the wound, forcing it into submission. The little girl winced.

"You're a Callahan," he said. "You almost had it. Get back on the bike." His voice left no room for dissent. He never left room for dissent.

The girl sagged with resignation. She stopped crying, turned around and walked back outside.

He stepped to the front porch and watched her go. She was in the driveway, alone, struggling to lift the bike. Then she was back in the saddle. The bike moved forward, and success was in doubt. It wobbled from side-to-side, the front tire making awkward swooping motions like a drunken reveler just before the fall. She somehow regained her balance, and the bike straightened. It picked up speed as it rolled down the long driveway. She disappeared down the street and into the sun. He smiled at the memory.

Atta girl, Kristen. Now you've got it.

A loud noise at the door, and his mind snapped back to the present. He was lying in the dark on a cold concrete floor. He had a bullet wound, and had lost a couple of teeth. He'd pissed his pants. He was alone. What was that mantra? All real learning happens when you're alone.

It's only a strawberry, he thought. *You're a Callahan. Get back on the fucking bike.*

16

CHARLIE BYRD'S FORD BRONCO RUMBLED ALONG A COUNTRY ROAD. It was Saturday morning. Three days since a wealthy client with nice breasts and a great ass fell into his lap. Already it was time to pass the baton. Police, FBI, and ravenous newshounds were now on the case. Time for Byrd to step aside and let the professionals take over. He understood reality. A thousand dollars a day for his limited services was excessive, even extravagant. Nothing good lasts forever.

So long as men got married, Byrd would be able to make money. Sin wasn't going out of style.

Alabama was replete with churches, and they exerted a profound influence over local culture. The Bible Belt tightened in mysterious ways, like beerless beer festivals. In some parts of the state, one couldn't even buy tomato juice on Sundays. After all, people might make Bloody Marys out of tomato juice. Yet despite all God-fearing folk, there was no shortage of sex scandals. There was no escaping biological inevitability. Why did grown adults risk everything for a few moments of pleasure? Sex was like that British fellow said: fleeting pleasures, ridiculous positions, and exorbitant prices.

Byrd went to a strip club once. One of his buddies dragged him to *Sammy's*, or as his friend called it, *the Valley Avenue Ballet*. The drinks were strong, the girls were hard, and the clientele shady. He awoke the next morning with a wicked hangover, a fresh dent in his truck, and an empty wallet. He hadn't been back since.

It was amusing from a distance, this bizarre behavior by Alabama's married men. It kept Charlie Byrd in business. If a few fine men of Birmingham wanted to roam the city like stray dogs, he'd gladly follow, camera and notepad in hand.

Byrd cursed. He was again stuck in a morning traffic jam. And this time, the traffic sandwich was in front of John Christian Callahan's estate. An assortment of cars, trucks, and vans were haphazardly parked next to the front gates in what could only be called a clusterfuck.

Approaching the mass of motionless vehicles, he eased his truck to a halt. Every TV news crew in town was setting up camp. As so often happens in these situations, everyone arrived at once. There were dozens of press milling about—reporters in their formal television attire, shaggy cameramen and sound guys who looked like they just rolled out of bed.

In addition to the usual suspects, CNN descended upon the scene. It was a rarity for these national news types to make an appearance. National stories emanating from Alabama typically involved a tornado or racial crisis—and sometimes both. But there they were, crew vans, satellite dishes, and all.

Alongside the TV media were the print media. Watching over the media were local police, state troopers, and a sheriff's deputy. There were some other guys in blue; perhaps they were FBI.

To cap it all off, some Bubbas parked their pickup trucks on the outskirts of the property. They brought lawn chairs, coolers, and binoculars, and were apparently planning to make a day of it. This was an official "scenic view," after all.

Byrd was impressed and saddened by the unfolding fiasco. He pulled his Bronco to the side of the road and slammed it into park. He bounded toward the front gate, dodging equipment and camera crews along the way.

Byrd was ignored by most of the assembled media. One reporter, however, recognized him and said so.

"Charlie Byrd," said the balding forty-something man, "Fancy meeting you here."

Byrd grimaced at the sound.

THE LOST SPYDER

Brett Lancaster was a local crime reporter for *The Birmingham News*. He was the type who relished his role, especially when it created public embarrassment for private citizens. On a couple of occasions, he'd crossed paths with Charlie Byrd. There was no love lost between the parties.

"What brings you out here?" he asked. "Was Callahan having an affair? He screwing a married woman?"

"This case is like your life," Byrd replied. "It's got nothing to do with sex."

He shoved his way past the reporter and proceeded to the iron gates. A couple of private security cops were on hand, purporting to be in charge. One held a clipboard.

"All right, people, we need to keep this entrance clear," a rent-a-cop shouted. "This is a private residence, not a ballpark."

A general murmur of concession passed through the crowd. One by one, the vehicles began backing up and realigning themselves along the side of the road. Still a clusterfuck, but a more orderly clusterfuck.

Byrd approached one of the rent-a-cops, who was clearly pleased with himself for sorting out the traffic.

"Excuse me, sir? I'm Charlie Byrd," he said. "I'm here to see Kris Callahan."

The rent-a-cop offered Byrd his best *who the hell are you and why should I care?* expression. Then he scanned his clipboard. As always, Byrd braced for rejection.

"Here it is," the guard replied. "Charles Mortimer Byrd."

Like many Southern males, Byrd been saddled with an inexplicable family name.

"We're not allowing vehicles up to the house," the rent-a-cop said.

Byrd looked over his shoulder at the assorted media. Brett Lancaster was still watching, as if Byrd himself was a criminal suspect.

"Hang on," the rent-a-cop continued. "We'll page the shuttle."

The shuttle. Byrd almost expected to be whisked up the driveway at warp speed in some exotic piece of German machinery. To his disappointment, the shuttle was a blue Chevy minivan that had rental car stamped all over it. It lumbered down the driveway with little sense of style.

Byrd contemplated the irony. A couple of days ago, he'd passed without resistance through this same gate. Now he had to undergo an anal exam to get back inside.

The young man driving the minivan wore a navy blue suit with a matching cap tucked low over his eyes. He was a kid, not more than eighteen-years-old. Byrd climbed in the backseat, wondering who pays for a shuttle at a private crime scene. If Kris Callahan had anything to do with it, the kid was probably making a thousand bucks a day. She clearly loved spending Daddy's money.

As the minivan cruised up the lengthy driveway, Byrd found himself looking forward to the visit. He felt a sense of anticipation, and it involved more than just getting paid.

Maybe it was the exclusivity. The media was locked outside, and he was ushered through the gates. For once in his life, he was a member of the cool kids club. He was allowed beyond the iron gates, to see the inner sanctum. Maybe that was it.

Maybe there was more to Kris Callahan than he realized. Sure, she was a physical knockout. But she didn't seem to be Charlie Byrd's type of knockout. She was wealthy, she was probably a snob, and she almost certainly had never truly worked a day in her life. She struck Byrd as a limousine liberal, sporting the latest fashionable political beliefs like high-dollar handbags. Byrd had more in common with the girls at good ole Birmingham SOL, fellow law students who were dealing with the same daily grind. He had little use for people whose politics could be neatly summarized on bumper stickers. Dating a Callahan would be like owning a Porsche. A thrill to tame and master— but dear God, the maintenance.

Charlie Byrd was a bachelor at heart. He'd never been caught in the typical Southern rush to the altar. He saw it happen every day, college kids scrambling like lemmings to see who could get married first. In Byrd's view, marriage brought nothing but downside risk. In exchange for blowing a giant wad of cash on a wedding, the groom gave up freedom and his bank account. For what? Unlimited access to one vagina?

Byrd could never be a romantic. In his professional role as "adultery documentarian," he'd seen too many marriages fail to have any faith in the institution. Besides, he liked living life his own way.

According to his mother, the Byrd family had a few influential drops of Native American blood in its German and Norwegian tree. He'd combined the best qualities in his mutt DNA. He was intelligent. According to his Law

THE LOST SPYDER

School Admissions Test, he possessed an instinctive grasp of abstract problem solving techniques. He was tall, dark, and despite the self-inflicted beer jiggle across his midsection, handsome enough to land dates without much effort.

If he got married, he knew his life would change. It would start with a house. He'd swap the apartment for a house and a mortgage. Then he'd trade the Bronco for something more sensible, like a minivan. He'd get a respectable job to make the monthly debt payments. After a couple of years, he'd be just another poor sap holding bags of useless crap at the Galleria shopping mall, wondering what the hell happened and why he never had fun anymore. At that point, he'd probably start sneaking out of the suburbs and into the strip clubs.

Better to be single, independent, and emotionally distant. His girlfriends all hated his emotional distance. One by one, the women in his life fell by the wayside. Some lasted longer than others, but six months appeared to be the limit. With no exception, each dumped Charlie Byrd. After a few months of futility, each surrendered and cut her losses, exactly as he wanted. It was a brilliant strategy. He never had to do the dumping. Eventually, each realized that he wouldn't change. He'd never become an obedient lapdog. Sooner or later, they got the message. Meanwhile, Byrd got what he wanted.

Kristen Callahan was just another woman. A wealthy woman, to be sure. A great looking woman, no doubt. But the maintenance wouldn't be worth the upside. Better to collect the cash, say thank you, and hit the road.

These thoughts coursed through Charlie Byrd's mind as he walked away from the shuttle, was ushered into the house, and delivered at the private library. These thoughts disappeared once he opened the massive library door, and stepped inside the room. The lights were dim, and the air was cold—very cold.

She was seated behind her father's monstrous oak desk. When he entered the room, their eyes locked. Byrd saw the strain on her face. But it wasn't just her face. It was her body. As she stood to greet him, she looked tired and beaten, her nest of hair even more wild than usual. The hipster outfit was replaced by jeans and a black sweatshirt.

"Byrd . . ."

One word. The sound of Kristen Callahan uttering his name was enough. With one word, much of his vaunted bachelor philosophy and machismo simply melted away. To hell with independence and emotional distance. To hell, even, with a thousand dollars a day. Here was a beautiful woman who needed help. And he found himself wanting to help.

What drove Byrd wasn't love. It wasn't sex and it wasn't money. Was it pity? No, you don't feel pity for flighty rich liberals who live a carefree existence. But he sensed her vulnerability. She needed help, and she was alone. Perhaps more than anything else, it was the loneliness that struck Charlie Byrd. Despite their extravagant surroundings, the Callahans appeared to be lonely people. They had constructed a million dollar moat between isolation and normalcy. That was sad, even pitiable.

"Hey there, boss," Byrd said. In the dimly lit library, it seemed appropriate to speak with a whisper. "You hanging in there?"

She offered a weak smile.

"I'm okay. Thank you for coming," she said. Byrd perceived a subtle but clear transformation in body language. She put her guard back up. Her game face returned. The confident Callahan, or at least some semblance of her, resumed control.

"Hey, you told me to pick up my final payment, remember?"

She managed a chuckle.

"Oh yeah," she replied. "A thousand bucks. Cash. I'm glad to see your values remain intact."

The switch had been flipped. Now the confident Callahan was back in charge, despite the circumstances.

"This is a new look for you," he said. "You dress up just for me?"

"If you're going to sleep in your clothes, they better be comfortable."

"Sorry to see the mess outside," he said.

"It's been worse than I feared. Word got out yesterday afternoon. The local TV choppers were buzzing overhead about an hour later. It's amazing how fast news spreads these days."

"It's amazing you were able to keep it quiet for so long."

"Maybe. Although I'm not sure that I should have. I may have jeopardized my father's life by keeping quiet."

He knew that she was right. Any delay certainly didn't help. Solving a missing persons case was usually a matter of speed. Callahans were not exempt from the 48-hour rule. But in truth, the fault for this situation rested with the old man.

"Don't think that way. You did what he'd want you to do."

She rolled her eyes.

"Thanks, Dr. Phil. Did you come here to counsel me? Should I lie down on the couch?"

"I really just came by to see how you were doing," he said. "Oh, and to pick up the cash."

"Yeah," she replied. "With regards to that final payment, I've been thinking."

"Yeah?"

He could sense it coming, and was eager to hear it.

"I think we were a little hasty yesterday when we agreed to end your involvement. I don't care what the cops say. I'd rather have you working on this thing."

His face brightened at the notion. Of course there was the matter of the money. But this was now about more than money.

'You know," he replied, "I was thinking the same. Only I wasn't sure how to say it. I thought it might not be polite."

"Since when did you care about being polite? I'd rather you speak your mind."

"Next steps?" he asked.

"Next step for me," she said, "is a shower."

She marched to the door and turned up the lights.

"Give me a half-hour," she said. "Baines will bring coffee. Make yourself useful. Remember, you're still on the clock."

As she left the room, Byrd walked to the doorway and ratcheted the lights back down low. He settled into one of the overstuffed leather chairs. It was still freezing, and the cowhide was cold. So he stretched a fleece blanket over his chest and closed his eyes. While she got ready for the day, he would steal a little shuteye.

Byrd still had a client. This pleased him for more reasons, he realized, than a thousand dollars a day.

17

SOMEONE SLAPPED A ROLLED NEWSPAPER DOWN ON A DESK.

"Sleeping on the job?"

Charlie Byrd snapped awake. It seemed he'd just disappeared into the leather chair a moment ago. A half-hour had passed, long enough to endure another bad dream about law school. His professors taught using the traditional Socratic method, a form of teaching that relied upon public humiliation to motivate students. Law school was often the stuff of nightmares, and it even haunted Byrd in his sleep.

He cleared his throat, but could only manage one word.

"Coffee?" he said.

"On the desk. Baines brought it fifteen minutes ago. But he thought better than to wake you."

The detective rubbed his eyes and took a deep breath. "That was nice. Guess I didn't sleep too well last night, either."

Byrd threw a groggy glance at Kristen Callahan. It all came flooding back. He was in the library, and he was still getting paid. That was the good news.

In just thirty minutes, his companion had transformed. Gone were the ragged blue jeans and sweatshirt. In their place was another trendy outfit showcasing her curves. The rat's nest of hair was washed and styled, and fell attractively across her shoulders.

"You just had an extreme makeover," Byrd said.

"You could use one," she replied.

On a silver tray was a carafe of coffee, accompanied by the usual accoutrements. They filled their cups with hot coffee, and began nursing the steaming beverages with concentration. She went for cream and sugar, while Byrd opted for his usual undiluted prescription.

"Caffeine," he said, "It does a body good."

She nodded, blowing her coffee cool. He noticed this about her at Starbucks. She was the type of person who orders a hot drink then waits for it to cool.

As he spoke, they heard the steady *thump thump thump* of a helicopter in flight. The media was offering the outside world an aerial tour of the Callahan world.

If they only knew what's sitting beneath that barn.

"So," he said, "You wanted to discuss the agenda."

She nodded. "This is making me sick. I feel like a prisoner in this house. Did you see this morning's *Birmingham News*?"

She tossed the paper into Byrd's lap.

"Take a look."

The front page bore the headline. J.C. CALLAHAN MISSING; FOUL PLAY SUSPECTED. A rather unflattering photo of Kristen Callahan, sweatshirt and all, accompanied the story.

"Yeah," he said. "Cat's out of the bag. When was this picture taken?"

"Yesterday afternoon," she replied. "I made the mistake of stepping onto the front porch. Bastards have powerful lenses."

Byrd sympathized with her plight. Yet he also considered the Natalee Holloway case. The case was a mystery, and the American public loves nothing more than a genuine mystery. The Holloway girl had gone missing on a Caribbean island. Her family, led by her brilliant and attractive mother Beth, had gone on the offensive. Beth Holloway used the media to create a constant drumbeat of talk show chatter, making the name "Natalee Holloway" internationally recognized. She kept the case in the headlines for weeks, months, and years after her daughter went missing. She viewed the media as an ally, not an enemy.

"Look on the bright side," he said. "At least this'll drum up a lot of public interest. We'll get new leads."

"Maybe. But this is making me feel claustrophobic. I need to get out of here, get away from these people. But once they see me go, they'll follow."

He smiled. "That's correctable. But once you get out, where do you go?"

"Anywhere would be an improvement. Being back here is making me crazy."

"Well, you've been working with the police. Have they found anything? The SUV? Credit card trace? Anything more from the flight records?"

"Nope. The trail ends in Germany."

"What have the Germans found?"

"Not a damn thing," she said. "I don't even know what they're doing over there . . ."

Her voice trailed away and silence returned, a silence punctuated by the steady drumbeat of another helicopter. Kristen Callahan was lost in thought, seemingly perplexed by the situation. The police were going through the motions, but the motions weren't enough.

"So they found nothing at all?"

She shook her head.

"I've been thinking about something Williams told us," he said. "About the Spyder."

She regained her train of thought.

"What?"

"He said 145 Spyders were built."

"Right. 145."

"Well, we're assuming this *antigua arana* is a ruse. But how would Williams know that? I mean, he said the factory told him so, but where would he get that information?"

"Like he told us," she replied. "Straight from the source. Porsche itself."

"Where is Porsche located?"

"Atlanta."

"Since when? I thought it was a German company."

"Well, it is. Porsche is based in Stuttgart. But the North American headquarters, PCNA, is in Atlanta."

"You follow what I'm thinking? That's only two-and-a-half hours from here."

"Two if you let me drive."

"No thanks," he replied. The notion of being her passenger again made his stomach queasy. "I'm driving. But if you want to get out of the house . . . Know anyone who works at Porsche?"

She nodded. "We've got friends there. I can call in some favors."

"Do it. But before we go anywhere, I'd like to see your father's Spyder. That is, if you don't mind."

"Easy enough," she said. "Let's go."

❧

Byrd stepped off the metal staircase, and was enveloped in chilly dehumidified air. He looked upon rows of vehicles, each covered by translucent bubbles of plastic. The visual effect was eerie.

When she spoke, Kristen Callahan's voice echoed throughout the garage.

"Let's see," she said. "The 550 is kept in the back."

They walked to the far corner, where a small vehicle was encased in a plastic bubble.

"Can you give me a hand?" she asked.

She reached down beneath the vehicle and unfastened a strap. Together, they peeled away the plastic to reveal the car underneath.

Byrd stepped back to absorb the entire picture. He emitted a low whistle.

"So that's what all the fuss is about."

"This is the real deal. An original Porsche 550 Spyder."

She nodded her head. "This is it. As we discussed, Porsche has made other cars called Spyders, like Type 718 and Type 918. But this car started it all. The 550 is a legend."

Byrd studied the car as if he were trying to memorize every detail. The color was a dull shade of aluminum. The surface bore more than a few battle scars, but they somehow enhanced its sense of purposeful beauty.

The Spyder was small—strikingly small to Charlie Byrd—-sitting no more than a few feet off the ground.

He leaned over the cockpit. The interior was spartan, streamlined, even barren. Two small seats were finished in red leather that was worn and cracked. In the driver's seat were dark stains.

Blood?

The car was simple. Two seats sat flush against the engine compartment. No rear seat. No carpet. The floor was bare aluminum. On the dash, three gauges and a couple of switches. That was it. Simple.

From the front, it was obvious the car had been in an accident. One headlight was shattered. Tires were deflated. The car rested on a jack stand like a wounded soldier on a crutch. Byrd was briefly reminded of James Dean. He remembered a photo he once saw of the legendary actor. In the picture, Dean was standing at a gas station with his pride and joy, the same car in which he would later lose his life.

He leaned over and again studied the cockpit of the car.

"James Dean," he said. "No roll bar, no air bags, no shoulder belts. The thing is made of aluminum. I can't imagine anyone surviving a head-on collision."

As soon as the words escaped his mouth, he wanted to take them back. Her mother had been the last person to drive this car. He suddenly realized what he'd said, and that recognition was plastered on his face.

"I'm sorry," he said.

She didn't skip a beat.

"It's okay," she said. "The wreck wasn't so bad. Here, you can see it on this side."

He walked to the opposite side of the Porsche, squatted and examined its surface. Deep abrasions extended along the side. The metal was pockmarked and dented. The front fender was smashed. The rear right fender bore a noticeable dent.

"What a shame," he said.

"Like I told you," she replied. "The accident didn't really cause my mother's death. Not directly, anyway."

Byrd ran his hand along the contours of the intact rear fender, gently caressing its lines.

"Well, I've got to say, there's something about this car. It's got charisma. She's got curves in all the right places."

"Sounds like you're talking about a woman."

"A woman would've slapped me by now. One thing I don't get though."

"Shoot."

"Authenticity. Let's say you find a car like this. How do you know it's legit? I saw the build sheet. But what about title?"

She shook her head. "For many of these cars no title was ever issued. When they were built, states didn't require titles. Before 1975, Alabama didn't require car titles."

"So without a title, how do you know it's the real deal?"

"Different ways. The vehicle identification number is one. Engines are numbered in various places. Transmissions are numbered. Too many numbers to fake 'em all. And Porsches are registered in the Kardex."

"What's a Kardex?"

"Porsche keeps records of every car they've ever built. When you buy a rare Porsche, you can check the numbers and make sure they match. Make sure it's all original. Porsche will issue a certificate of authenticity for the car."

Byrd was curious about the power plant. The engine was concealed beneath an aluminum rear cover held shut by two brown leather straps. Each strap, left and right, was behind the seats. They unbuckled the belts and raised the engine cover like a clam shell into its vertical position.

Byrd peered into the engine compartment. The motor sat in front of the rear axle, flush against the cockpit.

"So the engine is numbered?"

"Yes," she replied. "Engine numbers are one measure of authenticity. You also want documentation—the more the better, and preferably from Porsche. All of these cars are well documented. Many go back to the original MSO."

"MSO?"

"Manufacturer's Statement of Origin. The first document ever put on a car."

"That's like what Williams showed us, right? Like what was mailed from Germany?"

"Right."

"Where do y'all store this paperwork? I'd like to see it."

⋐⋑

The office was small, perhaps ten by fifteen feet. Florescent lights flickered and hummed to life. The interior was unremarkable, a cheap wall calendar serving as the sole decoration. There was a utilitarian desk and swivel chair. Along the wall stood a series of locked filing cabinets.

"Here's the deal," Byrd said. "If your father has been duped into buying a replica, then some of that evidence could be here. Let's take a look at the Spyder files."

She pulled a key ring from her pocket and held it aloft. "Keys to the kingdom," she said.

She unlocked the cabinet drawers and pulled out files. There was one manilla folder for the 550 Spyder.

Byrd flipped through the folder, looking for anything out of the ordinary. The file was about a half inch thick, and contained a variety of documents. Most of the paperwork seemed to reference vehicle maintenance, oil changes and engine work. There were receipts and service reports and part order forms. All were decades old.

"No mention of a #146," he finally said. "Your father has one Spyder, and we've got one folder here."

"As expected," she replied. "Although I suppose it never hurts to look."

"What about Porsche itself? You really think we can learn anything different in Atlanta?"

"I spoke with my friend at PCNA. He's going to do some digging, and get back to me by mid-afternoon."

"That's pretty fast," Byrd said. "Can he really get what we need in such short order?"

"I've known this guy for years. He's great. If he can find it, we'll get it."

"You think he's worth a trip to Atlanta?"

"Anything's worth getting away from this zoo."

She tapped her cell phone. "The cops know how to reach me. I just hope we can get out of here without making the papers."

"Don't worry," Byrd said. "It'll be a cinch."

❧

A half-hour later, the blue Chevy minivan plodded down the Callahan driveway, pausing at the iron front gates as they opened wide. With a nod from the rent-a-cops, the shuttle driver piloted the van through the gates.

Reporters scrambled at the photo op. Their enthusiasm quickly faded once they recognized the slovenly young man riding solo in the backseat. The van stopped next to a filthy Ford Bronco, and out stepped Charlie Byrd. The media turned away.

The driver of the van, still wearing the blue suit and matching cap pulled low over the eyes, escorted Byrd to his vehicle. Two doors slammed shut, and the Ford Bronco pulled quickly away from Chateau Callahan.

One reporter, however, maintained his interest. As Byrd's SUV rumbled away from the scene, Brett Lancaster jumped into his silver Volvo station wagon. Within a moment, the turbo-charged wagon was riding Byrd's rear bumper, tailing the SUV closely.

Byrd glanced into his rear view mirror, and saw the reporter grinning from ear to ear.

"Lancaster's onto us," he said. "That asshole's not as dumb as he looks."

Byrd stomped on the gas. His truck surged forward down the narrow country road. But the old Bronco didn't have enough juice to lose the Volvo. It remained a few feet from his rear bumper.

Now Lancaster cackled with glee, laughing out loud at the game.

He began snapping pictures of the Bronco.

By and large, the local media of Birmingham were a good group of guys. There were always a few sour apples in every bunch, and Lancaster was among the worst. He was one of those who seemed to relish bad news, and had special skills in the annoyance department.

"Stay down," Byrd said. "Grab hold of something. This could get hairy."

They hurtled down a small country road that ran parallel to the Interstate highway. Byrd spun the steering wheel and tossed the Bronco hard left around a corner. The tires howled as they slung gravel and tested the limits of the aging chassis. Byrd's truck shot underneath the Interstate, bypassing the obvious entrance ramp.

A female voice came from the backseat.

"Jesus, take it easy Byrd. You're going to tip the damn thing over."

"Nah, I'm not," he replied as he gunned the gas. "Just hang on. Couple more to go."

He knew where he was going. Alabama back roads were second nature to Charlie Byrd, and he lived for this sort of chase. From time to time, these situations would arise. He loved the rush, and he had previously tested the limits of the top heavy Bronco. No rollovers yet.

Sometimes he found himself the hunter. But more often the reverse was true, and Byrd found himself being chased. Being caught by a pissed off adulterer could be hazardous to one's health. Byrd knew the abilities of his truck, and that was one more reason that he loved it.

He slung the Bronco through a sharp right turn. With each successive slide, the tires grew noisier and the complaints in the backseat louder. The contents of the truck, namely a collection of empty cans, parking tickets, textbooks, and one of Birmingham's wealthiest young women, sloshed from side to side.

For all the commotion, Byrd's driving maneuvers gained little ground. The silver Volvo continued in hot pursuit, only a short distance behind. There were no more turns in sight, the stretch of unpaved road being unmolested by intersecting streets. To the left was a thick patch of Alabama forest. On the right, a steep and grassy hillside.

Byrd took his foot off the throttle. He checked his rear view mirror. In a matter of seconds the Volvo was back on his rear bumper. Byrd eased off the throttle and let the truck slow down. They went slower, and slower, and slower . . .

Finally he tapped his brakes, skidding the Bronco to a halt.

Brett Lancaster laughed and raised his camera.

"Say cheese . . ." he said.

"What the hell are you doing, Byrd?" Callahan hissed. "Why have we stopped?"

Byrd looked into the mirror. His eyes met Lancaster's. He smiled.

"Just stay down and hang on. We're going to Atlanta."

Byrd clicked his Bronco into four-wheel drive. He twirled the steering wheel hard to the right, rotating his truck perpendicular to face the thirty-foot incline. He stomped the accelerator and the Bronco charged forward, assuming an improbable sixty-degree angle as it conquered the vertical challenge. A hurricane of soil and turf spewed from behind the rear tires. More commotion from the backseat, this time peppered with profanity.

Brett Lancaster cursed, dropped his camera and—after a brief hesitation—directed his Volvo to follow. Tires spinning, the station wagon ripped through the grass and into the mud. Within a moment, it was stuck. Lodged on the incline at a ridiculous angle, it was going nowhere fast.

At the top of the hillside, the Bronco rested on the shoulder of the highway. Byrd lowered his window and looked down upon the reporter below.

As he merged onto the highway, he smiled and said, "Cheese."

Then he glanced into the rear view mirror.

"Okay, coast is clear."

Kristen Callahan popped up from the backseat, and removed the blue driver's cap from her head. As her auburn locks fell back into place she laughed.

"I'm impressed," she said. "That's the most fun I've had since high school."

Byrd grinned. He loved this sort of thing.

"Never underestimate a man and his four-wheel drive," he said.

"I won't. But this seat is disgusting. Let me up front."

Byrd looked into the mirror at the woman in his truck.

This job is a good one, he thought. *Too good to last.*

18

CHARLIE BYRD'S BATTERED FORD BRONCO SNAKED TOWARD ATLANTA, looking like a creature from the swamp. Long streaks of mud were caked along its side panels. Occasionally chunks of soil dropped and exploded on the highway.

The truck's speakers rattled with the rhythmic pulse of hip hop music. Kristen Callahan bobbed her head to the music, lost in thought. Byrd had reluctantly allowed her to select the radio station, but he had reached his limit of tolerance. He didn't like to dance, and he didn't like dance music. Neither belonged in his truck.

"This is giving me a headache," he said. "How about we change stations?"

She said nothing, but her head continued bouncing to the beat. He made another attempt.

"We're getting close to Atlanta," he said. "How about we listen to something else?"

She feigned shock.

"You don't like hip hop? What do you like?"

"I like quiet," he said, turning off the radio.

With silence restored, Byrd refocused his attention on the road. The Atlanta skyline loomed on the horizon. As they approached the city, surrounding traffic began to reach claustrophobic levels. Byrd felt his stress level rise. It was another heavy dose of bumper-to-bumper, only this time delievered at 80 miles per hour.

The actual distance between Birmingham and Atlanta couldn't be measured in miles. The two were very different cities. Only a generation ago, they'd been roughly the same size. But somewhere along the line, their respective paths diverged. Byrd's hometown grew selectively—and sometimes not at all.

While Birmingham merely accepted change, Atlanta pursued it, embraced it, and nurtured it. In a couple of short decades, the crown city of Georgia underwent a metamorphosis, blossoming into the economic capital of the New South. In the process, Charlie Byrd believed, Atlanta sold its Southern soul. In Byrd's view, Atlanta could have its international airport and Cable News Network and Olympics—and all the problems that went hand-in-hand with growth.

The traffic was the worst. Atlanta was one giant snarling mass of shiny metal hurtling through space. Rush hour never ended. As he drove into the city, Byrd made his opinions known.

"This is like Highway 280," he said. "Times ten. No way I could live over here."

"Atlanta's a great city. There's traffic because people actually want to live here."

"I suppose," he said, as if the notion of enjoying life in Atlanta was incredulous.

Soon the Bronco was leaving the crowded freeway and approaching the headquarters of Porsche Cars North America. As he pulled his truck into the quiet suburban office park, he spied a silver Porsche sitting on a pedestal. It was displayed in front of the office building like a work of marble sculpture.

Other than the unique art display, the Porsche building looked like any other office complex, an attractive but generic fifteen-story structure of tinted glass and flat concrete. But for the Porsche logo and the silver car sitting out front, and it would be indistinguishable from the law firm next door.

Byrd slowly rolled his truck into the parking deck.

"This looks like a nice building and all," he said. "But I expected something different."

"What did you expect? The Indy 500?"

"Nah. I guess I expected to see a test track or something. Something different."

"This is just the company headquarters. Not the place where the cars are built or tested. Nothing but office space."

"No tourist stuff?"

"All that stuff's in Germany. Here they have some art on the walls, and a couple of engines. But nothing nearly as interesting as, say, Stanley Griggs's shop."

Byrd dropped into his best impersonation of Stanley Griggs.

"Nothing's as interesting as that fucking shop."

She indulged in a laugh. Given the circumstances, it was impressive that she could still do so. Kristen Callahan was a mass of contradictory impulses. Byrd was never sure which direction she might go. She clearly had the intelligence and fortitude to cope with this situation. But she wasn't a Beth Holloway. She didn't seem capable of using the media to her advantage, of exploiting those who sought to exploit her situation. Instead she was running away.

Byrd parked his truck in the far corner of the parking deck. The garage was unremarkable, except for one aspect. Half the cars were Porsches of the daily driving variety.

"Reminds me of your father's barn," he said.

"Except all of these cars are new. Working for PCNA has its benefits."

"That's what I need at Byrd's Eye. An employee lease program."

She laughed.

"Twenty bucks a month toward the piece-of-shit truck of your choice. You'll have prospective employees beating down your door."

They sat in the parking garage for ten minutes, running the air conditioning to stay cool. At last, a man approached holding a manila folder.

She sprang from the truck, her face beaming.

"Dirk," she said. "Great to see you again. Thank you for doing this."

The man smiled. He was trim, blond, and fit. Not a hair out of place. Not an ounce of fat. His suntan looked like it had been painted on by a professional. When he smiled, his teeth were pearls.

Looks like he gargles with Clorox, Byrd thought.

Although he must've been in his late thirties, his physique was that of someone ten years younger. Guys like this made Charlie Byrd feel even more out of shape, even more inadequate. It seemed his own beer gut suddenly expanded another inch.

Even worse, the guy was named Dirk. What kind of name was Dirk?

"Kris, it's great to see you too," the man said.

His voice carried the slight trace of a European accent. It could've been German, but Byrd wasn't sure. Whatever the origin, it was much more civilized than Byrd's own Southern drawl.

"You know that we're always here for you," said the annoyingly attractive Porsche employee.

In response, she embraced the man in a hug. Not a handshake. A hug. One that seemed to linger.

Stepping out of his truck, Byrd arrived at a conclusion. He didn't like this fellow named Dirk. He didn't like him at all.

Charlie Byrd couldn't be feeling jealousy. That would be impossible, thanks to his twin pillars of independence and emotional distance. But whatever his shortcomings, Byrd was blessed with a healthy supply of testosterone. This damn sure felt like jealousy.

Although he couldn't manage a genuine smile, Byrd extended his right hand with courtesy.

"Charlie Byrd," he said. "Nice to meet you . . . Dirk?"

The man gripped and squeezed hard—very hard.

Figures, he thought. *Dirk is a hand squeezer.*

She interrupted. "Oh, I'm sorry. Dirk Heinricht, this is a friend of mine."

"Nice to meet you," Byrd lied through his teeth.

Dirk offered a smile and went on appearing to be genuinely nice. That would make matters worse—if this asshole was nice. He cleared his throat and spoke.

"Kris," he said. "I'm so sorry about what happened. It's all over the news here."

Of course it was all over the news there. CNN was based in Atlanta, and CNN was camped on Callahan's front doorstep. Thanks to CNN, for better or for worse, it was all over the news everywhere.

The mention of her father brought the younger Callahan back down to earth. Her smile melted away. This was not a field trip. It was a temporary escape from the grim reality back home.

"It's all so confusing," she said. "Every day I expect to hear from him. Every day we've been disappointed. Finally we had to go public."

"And you think the Spyder," he raised the manila folder, "has something to do with your father?"

"We're acting on a hunch, but yes. We think the information could be relevant. What did you find?"

"As we discussed this morning, I've pulled all the data from our computers here on the 550 series."

He glanced over his shoulder at the PCNA building.

"I know I don't have to tell you, but this is a rather sensitive matter for me. For most people, there's no way I can release such information. Company policy, you know. But given the situation, and the fact that you're such wonderful customers, I wanted to help."

Dirk handed over the envelope, and pulled a pack of Marlboros out of his jacket.

His first blunder, Byrd thought. *Smoking in front of this fine grass fed piece of Callahan ass? Ol' Dirk must've be European for sure.*

Whereas Americans viewed smoking as comparable to porn addiction on the personal habit respect scale, Europeans had no such qualms. Byrd smiled as the man lit his cigarette and took a long drag.

"So you think you've found what we need?"

"I don't know. First of all, we don't have original production records here in Atlanta. Those are in Germany. So all my information is tainted by that fact. The 550 Spyders were built over fifty years ago. If you want original documents, you need to go to Germany. They have things that are not in the computer."

"Okay. What did you find here in Atlanta?"

"Well, it's strange. I've checked multiple sources. First our own databanks, which weren't as helpful as you might think. Then I looked at several registry books. The upshot is this. You want to know how many Spyders were built? Depends on who you ask."

"Suppose we ask *you*," Byrd said. He didn't want this Dirk character beating around the bush and acting cute.

"I'm serious," Heinricht replied. "The 550 series is unique amongst Porsches. Different sources cite different production numbers. For every other model of Porsche we know exactly how many were produced. Exactly. But not with the Spyder."

"You're kidding."

He shook his head. "No. According to my internal sources, there were a total of 145 Spyders produced. The first twenty-three were prototypes. Then eighty-five were built for racing customers. Finally, thirty-seven were made of Type 550A."

"So is that number definitive? Our friend in Alabama told us the same thing."

"Definitive? Not quite. Most of the early cars were made for racing. If a car was crashed, it wasn't uncommon to reconstruct a new car using old parts. Frankly, our own records appear to be incomplete."

Heinricht crossed his arms, and his eyes drew narrow.

"Forgive me, but may I ask an obvious question? What does the 550 Spyder have to do with Mr. Callahan? I don't mean to pry, but more information might be helpful."

"We have reason to believe he left town to get a Spyder," Byrd explained. "They say there's a lost Spyder somewhere in Germany—an unspoiled, perfect car. Kind of the holy grail of Porsches."

Heinricht nodded as he contemplated the possibility.

"Such a car would be extremely valuable," he said. "The factory itself would be interested in this car."

Callahan nodded.

"Exactly why my father would chase such a dream," she said. "It would be the crown jewel in his collection. His legacy."

Heinricht lowered his voice.

"Well," he said, "unfortunately my research shows nothing about a stolen Spyder. However, I too have heard these rumors. That one car was removed the factory, and hidden in Germany."

Callahan's jaw dropped.

"You're the first Porsche employee I've ever heard acknowledge it."

"Many years ago, your father asked about this car."

"What did you find out? What did you tell him?"

"I told him what I told you. My resources here in America are limited. Our data on the early cars is scarce. The only way to find the truth is to go to the source—Stuttgart."

"So that's it?"

"Well, not entirely. As you might imagine, I travel to Germany quite often. I've inquired about the existence of this car. Most people either have no clue what I'm talking about, or they deny it altogether. But some of the old guard in Stuttgart—men who've been with the company for decades, since the time of Professor Porsche--believe the lost Spyder exists. What evidence of this car remains, I don't know."

He again threw a glance over his shoulder.

"Besides, I'm not supposed to even be here right now. If you'll forgive me," he said, "my little smoke break must come to a conclusion."

He dropped his cigarette to the ground, and scrubbed it out with his shoe.

Strike two, Byrd thought. *He's not only a smoker, he's a litterbug.*

"This is everything I know. If you want more," he said, "go to Germany. I will make arrangements. I have friends there who'll help."

He tucked the manila folder inside her jacket.

She sighed as she again embraced the man in another lingering hug.

"Thanks," she said. "You're the best."

ॐॐ

Charlie Byrd's white Ford Bronco drove away from the acres of shiny new Porsches, back onto Hammond Drive, and headed west on the crowded Atlanta freeway.

Byrd broke the silence. His voice was stern and deliberate, almost a growl. He sounded like a parent disciplining a small child. In truth, he was just upset with the situation. He had already lost this case once. He could feel it slipping away again. He could feel her slipping away again. If Dirk had done anything, he'd kicked Byrd's testosterone into gear and clarified the situation. Charlie Byrd liked spending time with Kristen Callahan.

"You're not going to Germany," he said.

"You know it makes sense. He's somewhere in Germany."

"Don't be ridiculous," he replied. "You're not going to Germany. You need to stay here. With the cops."

"The cops." She spoke the word like an epithet. "The cops can reach me anytime they want. You saw what's happening in Birmingham. I don't want to go back. My father is searching for the lost 550 Spyder, and there's only one way to find it. You heard what the man said. We've got to go to Germany. Someone over there knows what's going on. Someone who sent my father that build sheet."

Byrd could sense her tone changing. She now seemed downright excited about the idea. How to talk her out of it? He could make the case about the media. She should be using the media to her advantage. Again, the Natalee Holloway case came to mind. Beth Holloway used the media to brilliant effect.

But this line of reasoning ran shallow. Beth Holloway's first course of action when she learned her daughter was missing was to book an international flight. She conducted her first key interviews on the island of Aruba. Her actions made intuitive sense. When a family member goes missing, the natural instinct is to retrace their steps.

"It would take forever," he said.

"It's an nine-hour flight. We leave tonight, sleep on the plane, and arrive tomorrow morning. That's hardly forever. I've done it several times. You got a passport?"

He nodded reluctantly.

We?

"Yeah, I've got a passport," he said.

He had a passport that contained exactly one stamp, his souvenir from an ill advised trip to a Cancun all-inclusive resort, one boasting all the bad food you could eat. Byrd's sole experience with international travel had been steeped in alcoholic mediocrity. Given the usual costs and demands on his time, Europe seemed about as reasonable a travel destination for Charlie Byrd as the far side of the moon. To his surprise, it sounded like she wanted to include him on the trip.

"I don't know," he offered one final protest. "The arrangements alone . . ."

She held her trendy mobile phone aloft, and waved it like a magic wand.

"One phone call to Baines. He'll handle it all. Probably within the hour."

He shook his head in annoyance. She had an answer for everything.

"You have any idea how much this'll cost?"

She smiled. "You think I care?"

Byrd was giving ground, albeit reluctantly. She always had an answer, but this still seemed a stretch.

"What have the cops in Germany come up with?" he asked.

"Not much," she replied. "We know he chartered a flight to Stuttgart. We know he checked in at the airport. And we know he brought seven figures in cash."

Byrd said nothing in reply, and instead turned to look out his window at the thick forest of Georgia countryside. They were outside Atlanta now, and urban development had surrendered to a landscape of towering pines. The Bronco's engine churned. Byrd stared straight ahead, his right hand resting casually on the steering wheel. They rode for several minutes like this, surrounded only by the rumbling noises of interstate travel.

Finally she spoke.

"It may not make sense. But nothing in this world makes sense. I believe my father is searching for the lost Spyder. I can feel it in my bones. And the only way we'll find him is to go to the source, to where the thing was built—we'll go to Germany."

Byrd made one final effort. "We've got no proof the car even exists," he said. "Just a bunch of tall tales and bullshit. The responsible thing to do would be to wait it out in Alabama, work with the media. See what the cops find."

Callahan looked offended.

"The *responsible* thing? You lawyer types are so conservative. I thought you were different. Haven't you ever done anything a little different in your life?"

He shifted in his seat. "Yeah," he said. "I've done plenty of different things. Like taking this job."

Her gaze burned holes in him. Maybe she was right. Birmingham SOL was like every other law school, beating down students daily with heavy-handed discussions of downside risk and liability exposure. The notion of a "risk taking attorney" was a true oxymoron. Attorneys never took risks. Byrd didn't want to turn out like one of those cookie cutter lawyers in a $500 suit, afraid to interact with the world with honesty because someone somewhere might be offended. Usually he was the risk taker in a relationship. She was the first person with the ability to throw him off his game.

"You of all people should know," she said. "Sometimes you've got to follow your instincts. Sometimes you've got to take a leap of faith."

A leap of faith. She uttered the phrase with an almost demented zeal. At that moment, Charlie Byrd realized the discussion was over, the decision made. She was right, after all.

They were going to Germany.

19

JOHN CHRISTIAN CALLAHAN DIDN'T LIKE SOCIAL GAMES.

He tried golf as a youth. It once seemed a pathway to the blue blood society he longed to join, a necessary step in the march of upward mobility. Perhaps if he mastered golf, if he wore the right clothes and shoes and attitude, then he too could join the Birmingham Country Club. He could inhabit a stately Tudor in Mountain Brook. He could drive a respectable European sedan, perhaps a Bentley or Rolls, and it would be black. He could send his kids to the finest schools to be properly indoctrinated in the ways of wealth. He could socialize on weekends with old money. And finally, he could become old money.

It never happened. He was new money and that never changed. He never mastered the game of golf. Never, in fact, came close to doing so. His sole visit to the Birmingham Country Club, when he was 36-years-old and petitioning for membership, was an exercise in humiliation. The brash multimillionaire lost both the game and his cool in spectacular public fashion. His application for membership was subsequently refused in a more private, but no less spectacular, fashion. Callahan was new money, and was viewed with appropriate skepticism. This was an unspoken rule of the Deep South, an axiom that permeated the Mountain Brook worldview. Wealth and culture didn't always go hand-in-hand. Money, like bourbon, needed age to become palatable.

Callahan was new bourbon, and treated as such by the Mountain Brook elite. His bank account hadn't acquired the preferred bouquet, so they turned up their noses. He was burned by the rejection. It was the last time he subordinated himself to trust fund babies. He spent the rest of his life making them pay. Old money, despite its bullshit trappings of pretension, was incestuous and weak. He swore to never again play their game.

Fuck golf. He'd never become an old fart doddering around the hills of Alabama in a golf cart, sipping cans of Budweiser on the sly, sweltering in the sun.

Instead, Callahan took refuge behind the controls of a race car. While his peers, if one could even call them such, were pissing away their lives in dainty white shorts and polo shirts, he was donning fireproof race suits and helmets. He drove competitively, but not professionally. In his world, the only prize that mattered was ego.

Club racing was Little League for millionaires. Here a man with money held a clear advantage. Old money or new, it made no difference. Callahan was a competent driver, but not a natural talent. He compensated with the finest in equipment. He took new racing machines straight from the factory, their seats still pungent with the scent of fresh unspoiled leather. He wrung the cars without mercy, treating them like magnificent beasts of burden. Callahan loved nothing more than flogging such a machine into crazed submission, taking it to redline until either the engine or his skill-set blew up. He was a weekend warrior, and despite the small army of a pit crew, his victories were solo affairs. It was called *Callahan Racing* for a reason.

He preferred racing to golf, he liked to say, because success required more than one ball. No one would ever out-bluff the man. He had the necessary equipment, and loved nothing more than proving it.

Second, he loved racing because money mattered. Cash was the lifeblood of the sport. The guys who lost their shirts were the ones who lost their nerve. With a bottomless bank account, Callahan had plenty of nerve.

He tossed around money with reckless abandon because he had more than enough. Some people thought it was gauche. They didn't understand. He didn't give a shit about the money. He loved the winning, the heady boost to his ego.

He had a gift. Some people had an aptitude for music or sports or sex. His gift was human weakness. He could smell weakness in other people, on the racetrack and in the boardroom. He was a shark. Sweat on opponents was blood in the water. Once he caught the scent, he had no reservations about exploiting it.

This gift served him well. It brought him more than fleeting success on the weekends. It allowed him to build a small empire. He started with a bucket of potatoes, and parlayed them into *Callahan Food Group*. In his worldview, there was only one scent more welcome than that of frying potatoes and burning rubber. That scent was weakness. Once he caught a whiff, he went for the jugular.

This was why, lying on a cold floor in the darkness, beaten to within an inch of his life, he decided to change strategy. He smelled no weakness. He smelled, in no particular order, urine, blood, sweat, mold, rat feces, and body odor. But he didn't smell weakness, at least not on his captors. For the first time in decades, he was the weak one.

He had no choice. To resist would only worsen the situation. His captors were holding all the cards. They were making the rules. He had to keep his composure. Find the weakness. Find it, and exploit it.

There was a rattle at the door.

Callahan's feet were bound. He couldn't run.

Mr. Body Odor was back. The ogre walked directly to him. Without hesitation, he bent over and scooped up the old man.

"*El bano,*" he said.

More Spanish, but even Callahan recognized the word for toilet. The man said something else, and it sounded like a curse. No one, not even a soulless thug with excessive body odor, likes the smell of fresh urine.

Callahan was carried up a flight of stairs. Pressed against the man's sweating body, he could feel his fat. The man was heavy, and his breath grew short. The wooden stairs creaked under their combined weight.

They were on the main level of a house now. It was hot. What should've been a miserable environment was instead a relief. Gone were the smells and the cold and the darkness. He was surrounded by light and heat, and the steady roar of industrial fans. Large fans were blowing throughout the house. They stirred the hot air, and masked any sound from the outside.

His bones ached like never before. He was tired. He needed to cooperate, to bide his time, to gain knowledge and somehow regenerate strength.

They arrived at the toilet. Mr. Body Odor plopped Callahan onto the floor. Using a knife, he severed the rope around his ankles and wrists. The blade nicked his wrists. Callahan felt pain, and suspected he was bleeding again.

"*Banos*," the man said again.

Callahan felt his face turn scarlet. It was absurd to be on the verge of death and yet experience embarrassment at bodily functions. But the alternative was even less dignified. This was his chance. He sat on the toilet and relieved himself.

How low the mighty have fallen.

After he was finished, Mr. Body Odor led the still blindfolded millionaire to a sink.

Running water, a laudable nod to civilization. His thirst was getting the better of him. At the sink, he was tempted to scoop water into his mouth. He thought again of dysentery, and resisted the temptation.

Mr. Body Odor walked Callahan down a hallway, and into a different room. It was warm, much warmer than the dungeon below. He was grateful for the warmth.

The room contained a small bed. It was a simple thin mattress on a squeaky metal frame. The mattress was bare, with rough fabric stretched over the metal coils. It was devoid of linen. Ordinarily, Callahan wouldn't have touched the filthy thing. But under the circumstances, he thought it was the finest he'd ever experienced. He moaned with pleasure at its very touch. He would do anything to stay on this bed.

Mr. Body Odor spoke.

"*Espera*," he said.

Callahan had no idea what the devil was saying. But he got the gist. He wanted to cooperate. He lay on the bed, quiet and submissive, listening to the steady hypnotic hum of an industrial fan.

A few moments passed. The hand restraints were reapplied. This time his hands weren't fastened behind his back. Instead, each wrist was tied to a bedpost. He was stretched on the bed, his arms extended. The bed was his crucifix, and he accepted it. His wrists were blistered and chapped by the rope. Again he felt sharp stings of pain as the binds were fastened to his wrists. He absorbed the pain in silence. He wouldn't give this thug the satisfaction of anything else.

And then he smelled the perfume.

He caught the scent in the waves of billowing air, a welcome change from body odor and urine and other sensory assaults. She was standing by the bed.

"*Coma*," she said. She held a piece of bread to his mouth. "*Coma*," she repeated.

Her voice was open and earnest. It beckoned.

He considered refusing the food. It would've been a gargantuan act of willpower. His stomach was already clenched in knots. He'd reached a stage beyond hunger. The pangs that plagued him through the night had passed. He thought the problem was under control.

The scent of the bread changed everything. His hunger returned, and it was overwhelming. He wanted the bread more than he'd ever wanted anything in his life.

He relented, and accepted the bread into his mouth.

She held the glass to his lips. This time, he couldn't resist. He tasted the water, and was refreshed. It washed bits of bread and dried blood down his throat. He went to the glass again and again, swallowing great gulps of the water. *Don't drink the water*, he'd been told. He was drinking the water, and it tasted like blood. His own blood.

In a matter of moments, he'd consumed his simple meal. The impact was immediate. He felt rejuvenated, recharged. He felt a faint glimmer of hope.

The woman stood from his bedside, and through the slit of his blindfold he caught a glimpse of her wispy white skirt. She left the room silently, like an angel, leaving him lying there on the bed.

They're fattening me up, he thought. *Just like Oscar. Just like a little pink pig*.

Callahan was back. He felt the change inside, the return of willpower to his wretched spine.

He wouldn't give up the fight. Not yet. Not like this.

Lying on the bed, he descended into unconsciousness.

20

CHARLIE BYRD STEPPED OUT OF THE BATHTUB, and his feet sank into the damp floor mat. The floor was drenched with hot water. The tiled bathroom walls were soaking wet.

Byrd's first encounter with a European shower had been a success. Not only had he cleaned his body, but—thanks to the handheld attachment that squirted water in every conceivable direction—he'd cleaned most of the room too.

He grabbed a towel, which was about half the size he needed. Scrubbing his head with the damp rag, Byrd walked into the main room.

This wasn't just any hotel; it was a five-star German hotel. Byrd had spent a great deal of time at hotels, usually parked outside, just down the block, with a large telephoto lens at the ready. But this German place was a different breed. The *Steigenberger Graf Zeppelin* was only distantly related to the sordid economical love dens of Birmingham that Byrd knew so well. This was a lion; those were stray cats. They may have shared some ancestral genealogy, but the DNA had taken two very different paths of development.

Everything here was different, from the light switches to the doorknobs. And then there was the toilet. He'd spent a good five minutes figuring out how to flush the toilet. Thank goodness there was no "European toilet section" on the LSAT.

His freshly scrubbed eyes confirmed the truth. Last night hadn't been a dream. He was in Germany, of all places. His first trip to Europe, and he was traveling first-class.

The *Graf Zeppelin* was an eight-story hotel, each level packed with floor-to-ceiling opulence. This was a J.C. Callahan kind of place, the authentic equivalent of his New Money McMansion. Adorned with traditional furniture and décor, Byrd's room radiated old world charm. He even had a mini-bar, one stocked with rare European delicacies like *Pringle's* and *Toblerone*.

But the real appeal of the *Graf Zeppelin* was location. The hotel sat in the heart of Stuttgart, across from the main train station, adjacent to the wealthiest shopping district. It was a natural meeting place for the well-to-do, a place to see and be seen. Not the kind of place frequented by Charlie Byrd.

After a quick change of clothes, he went downstairs to the lobby. He stepped off the elevator and was immediately greeted by the usual suspects. A couple of valets, a bellman or two, and some staff milling behind the main desk. His curvaceous employer nowhere in sight, he sank into a leather couch. After a glance at his watch, he began to gloat. He wasn't on time; he was early. He was handling the time change of trans-Atlantic travel with aplomb. Perhaps this was one advantage of his usual work. He'd scrambled his biorhythms so many times that his brain had come to expect it.

When she arrived, looking harried and disheveled, the smug look on his face said everything.

"*Guten tag*," she said. "For once, you're ahead of me. Of course, you should be. You slept the whole damn flight."

"I can sleep anywhere, anytime," he said. "It's a necessary skill in my profession."

Byrd often spent the night in his Ford Bronco, sometimes sitting straight up. Vertical sleeping was an acquired talent.

She rolled her eyes.

Her gorgeous eyes.

Callahan looked fine to Charlie Byrd, showered and dressed per her usual motif. By now, the yin-yang tattoo in the small of her back had seared its image into his brain. He looked forward to seeing that artwork almost as much as her face.

She'd clipped her auburn hair back on her head, revealing her temples.

Byrd loved the look. Nothing more attractive than a fresh scrubbed naturally beautiful face. She was, as the guys at Birmingham SOL would say, talent. But beneath the polished exterior, she was suffering. There was weariness in her eyes.

"Everyone has a gift," Byrd said. "Mine just happens to be sleeping."

"God, I hate jet lag," she replied. "Always takes me a couple of days to adjust."

Byrd pulled himself up from the leather couch.

"So you've been to Europe a lot?"

"Enough," she replied. "My father thought it'd be a good idea for me to see the old world. You know, take the Grand Tour and get cultured and all that jazz. Of course, he never bothered to do so himself."

She took a look around the lobby, scanning the valet area in front.

"Any luck getting a car?"

He nodded.

"I took care of it. Should be here any minute."

"What did you get?"

"Mercedes."

"What kind of Mercedes?"

"A black one. They were out of sedans. This is a coupe, but it wasn't cheap. The lady said they're good."

The bellman motioned, and they stepped out the front door of the *Graf Zeppelin*. Their rental car was parked in front of the hotel. The Mercedes was black. It was also small. The entire vehicle, according to Byrd's best estimate, was five feet long—perhaps the smallest vehicle he'd ever seen outside a three-ring circus.

Callahan squealed with delight.

"A Smart Car," she said. "It's cute."

Byrd winced at the word. *Cute* was perhaps the highest praise in the Southern female lexicon. The word was usually reserved for fuzzy white poodles and dainty pink shoes. No respectable Southern male would ever aspire to be seen in a "cute" vehicle.

Nevertheless, the Mercedes certainly qualified. It was as if someone had taken a pair of bucket seats and neatly wrapped the shell of a car around them. It was, Byrd reluctantly conceded, *cute*.

"I've seen bigger golf carts," he said.

She glanced at her watch. "We've got twenty minutes," she said. "Let's go."

Byrd bent over and folded his six-foot frame into the passenger seat. He buckled his seat belt as she pushed the car into action.

"Actually," she said over the whine of the engine, "Smart Cars have their uses in the city. I wouldn't get near the *autobahn* in one, but you can park these things anywhere."

৩৯৫২

She drove the tiny car aggressively through the streets of Stuttgart, weaving in and out of the thick traffic with ease. Although Byrd would never admit it, the woman's driving skills were remarkable. As she'd demonstrated multiple times, she had professional training and an inherent understanding of a vehicle's limits. She seemed to wring more performance out of a car than it could possibly deliver, plowing through curves with enough G-force to snap Byrd's seatbelt tight. What's more, she seemed to adapt to Germany without skipping a beat. She didn't drive tentatively, like a tourist. She drove like she owned the place.

As they sped through town, Byrd gazed out the window in fascination. This was a surreal experience, the adjustment from America to Europe. Life passed though a filter, and things came out different on the other side. The streets were bustling with activity, and the vehicles, traffic lights, buildings, streets, sidewalks, and even the demeanor of the people were all somehow shuffled like playing cards. He'd been dealt a fresh hand, one forged from familiar elements that was nevertheless truly foreign.

"Fish out of water," Byrd said.

"What?"

"I feel like a fish out of water here. Everything's different."

He narrowed his eyes and studied a bright yellow traffic sign. It was flashing a message in German.

"What's that sign mean?" he asked.

She shrugged.

"I have no idea."

"That's comforting."

"Europe's confusing at first," she said. "But you get used to it. At least they drive on the right side of the road. You can usually find what you need in

English. Just use common sense and you'll be fine."

Confronted with a stall in traffic, she whipped the Mercedes over an adjacent curb. Once on the narrow sidewalk, she deftly steered the car across a street corner into entered a cobblestone alleyway. For a moment they were alone in the alley, weaving through a maze of discarded boxes and garbage dumpsters. Then they emerged onto a less trafficked cobblestone street.

"You seem to know your way around," he said, grabbing the dash for support as they scrabbled across cobblestone. "Need the GPS?"

"Sure," she replied. "Might as well see where we are. We take the twenty-seven towards *Ludwigsberg*, then off in *Zuffenhausen*. Fifteen minutes, tops."

Byrd gingerly activated the car's GPS unit, and attempted to determine which end was up.

True to her word, they arrived at *Porsche Strasse* with time to spare. Parking, however, was limited. After prowling the street for an empty space, none were to be found.

"To hell with it," she said.

She jerked the vehicle to a halt. With a hop, the rear tires jumped the curb. Soon the entire car was resting on the sidewalk, wedged improbably between two much larger vehicles. It was a tight fit, and quite possibly illegal. But it was a fit.

"See?" she said. "You really can park these things anywhere."

Byrd looked across the street. The Porsche factory beckoned.

21

THE DOOR OPENED, AND IN STROLLED A WAVE OF BODY ODOR.

J.C. Callahan felt his bonds being loosened. His hands came free. With a violent jerk, he was lifted from the bed and wrestled out of the room.

He offered no resistance. But still the Fat Man treated him like a rag doll. He pushed and pulled and wrenched in a display of needless violence.

Callahan tried to peer through the blindfold. But this time it was tight. It cut into his face, and he saw nothing.

A sweaty hand clamped down on each shoulder. The Fat Man was squeezing hard. Each hand was a vice, and the vices closed tight—tight enough to inflict pain.

Callahan was loose and supple but the stinking ogre was playing rough. He could feel the Fat Man's stomach pressed against his back, the stench of hot breath wheezing on his neck. Then he was shoved forward, down into a creaking wooden chair. The chair sagged but held his weight.

The Fat Man uttered something in Spanish, probably an epithet. A door slammed. The room fell silent, except for the Fat Man panting behind him like a dog. The industrial fans were still churning and crating their own unique brand of white noise.

Callahan felt his own strength was slowly returning. His captors kept him alive this long. They'd fed and watered him like a houseplant, if not a pig.

They'd kept him alive . . . *why?*

What did they want?

Stupid question. What did everyone want from John Christian Callahan? The answer was obvious; it was the answer to all questions that haunted his existence. Money—they wanted money. Of course they wanted money. Money would solve the problem, and he had money. No problem.

Now it was time. Give them what they want. Buy a passage out of this hell. He decided to speak. His voice broke the silence.

He was startled that his throat and brain could still produce coherent words.

"Look, if it's money you fellas want, I'll get you money," he said in his measured Southern drawl.

The Fat Man barked a reply. Another Spanish epithet.

"Really," he said. "I don't care about the money. I'll get you the money. More than you could spend."

Another epithet, this one with conviction.

"Can anyone here speak English?"

The Fat Man lashed out with an open fist. It struck the back of the Callahan's skull hard enough to spark mental fireworks. His head snapped forward, and sank down to the table. Amidst the blackness filling his mind's eye, he saw colors. Brilliant colors. He was transported away from the hellish room and the Fat Man who spoke only Spanish.

Then with what dignity he could muster, he lifted his head off the table.

I'll take that as a no. You can't speak fucking English.

If anyone could speak English, they weren't letting on. But why would they hide something like that? There was no reason to do so, no advantage to be gained. This language issue was going to be a problem. A serious problem. Possibly one that money wouldn't solve.

If they couldn't speak English, what could they understand? Did they know what they had in their possession? Did they have any idea?

Time passed. Minutes ticked by. He sat erect in his wooden chair, blindfolded and silent. His nostrils filled with the body odor of the sweaty fat brute, an odor that seemed to be increasing by the minute. His mind was still seeing colors . . .

The room became a spinning kaleidoscope, and the colors rushed past his bound eyes. The dark shadowy images of the Fat Man, the translucent glass of the sand and grit covering the floor, the brilliant flashes of white and red and gold that followed the blow to his head. He saw burgundy through his eyelids, and it reminded him of wine. Blood? Was he hallucinating? His head swayed. He was on the verge of losing consciousness. He had to focus . . . to beat the devils.

He heard the labored breathing of the Fat Man, and it pulled him back to earth.

He focused on the incessant droning of the fans. The fan blades beat the air and moved it through the stagnant house.

The air was dead, but it was moving.

Dead . . . but still moving.

Then a new sound. Footsteps echoing throughout the hall. Heavy boots pounding the dry wooden floors. They started down the hall, miles away, and drew closer . . . and closer . . . and closer.

Finally the boots stopped. They were outside the door. The door opened again, its hinges squealing their long low song of resistance.

The boots entered. The boots were in the room.

The door slammed shut with finality, echoing like a vault. He snapped back into reality, one dominated by black. Was black a color or was it the absence of color? Could he see or were his eyes as useless as his ears?

More words he didn't understand. Epithets? He caught his breath, and braced for impact. It never came.

He felt the rolls of human fat behind him again, pressed against his back. Chubby hands peeled away his blindfold. Cloth pulled over his head, and his deep blue eyes were liberated.

Bright light, like the sun. The room was a blur. From the ceiling dangled a lone source of light. The table was fuzzy. He couldn't see details.

He struggled to focus on the face that was peering into his own. Finally his eyes cooperated, and a chill passed through his body. His skin turned to gooseflesh. He wished for the blindfold, but like everything else he cherished, it had been taken away.

Looking at the Man with the Scar, he was afraid. He instinctively recoiled. It finally dawned on him. He was a mouse in a cage of snakes, frozen and powerless.

THE LOST SPYDER

The face was weathered and leathery, pockmarked by the untreated acne of a brutal youth. The face had once been handsome. But those days were a lifetime ago. Now it was rough and haggard, a haunted landscape of unyielding anger, molded in the furnace of civil war. The eyes were lifeless pools, offering no window into the soul.

The face was dominated by one imperfection—a thick pink scar that snaked from beneath the man's eye to his jawbone. The scar dominated his appearance, like some sort of demonic birthmark, a knotted river winding its way through the desert. Along its body were individual strands. But it wasn't a birthmark or tattoo; it was the result of violence.

Just like The Man with the Scar himself.

❧

The Man with the Scar looked at the gringo.

John Christian Callahan was a rich man, so rich it made him angry.

This was typical of the gringos. Mercy was wasted on these people. They lived lives of comfort, with no knowledge of the *barrios* or the war or what it took to survive in this land. They came like tourists to some exotic nature preserve, and they viewed him like an animal. So The Man with the Scar had become an animal.

We're not so different, thought the Man with the Scar.

You're a man. I'm a man.

You had power. I have power.

Callahan looked into the face of his captor. The Man towered over him, a column of serene rage. He was an animal, and somehow Callahan could hear his thoughts.

We're not so different, the animal said. *We're one and the same.*

"I'm nothing like you," Callahan said. "What do you people want?"

Want? The Man with the Scar brandished the knife. It was a cheap knife, the kind that might be found in any kitchen drawer, the kind that should've been discarded years ago but somehow survived. The thin blade was still sharp. The plastic handle was distorted. It had been left too near a fire or hot stove and nearly melted away. But the blade was still sharp.

The Man with the Scar looked at John Christian Callahan. His lips never moved but his eyes spoke.

We're not so different, his eyes said. *We're one and the same.*

He leaned forward, staring down his prey with cold black eyes.

I will become you, said the eyes. *I will eat you alive and then you will not exist. There will be no you and me. There will only be the Man.*

The Man with the Scar put the knife against Callahan's face.

The blade was cold. It pressed flat against the face. It stroked delicately against his cheek, almost lovingly.

Callahan recoiled. He couldn't move; he couldn't breathe. The knife caressed his cheek like a woman's fingernail. It stroked one cheek, and then the other.

He wanted to close his eyes, but his eyes wouldn't close.

He felt the chilled blade of the knife suck warmth from his cheek. He heard the eyes speaking again.

We're not so different, you and I. See?

The knife pressed deeper.

The incision started just below his left eye socket. With surgical precision, the blade dragged south. It snaked down the Callahan's face, riding just beneath the surface of the skin. The incision was thin and clean, but the cut wasn't straight. It curved towards the jawbone, and finally withdrew.

Blood pooled in its wake. It left an oozing crimson trail down the left cheek. An open wound.

The knife pulled away. The Man with the Scar stood back and reviewed his work.

See? We're not so different. We're not different at all.

We're the same, you and I. We're one and the same.

The wound was fresh and shallow, enough to disfigure the old man. It was enough to make him cry.

John Christian Callahan leaned forward and looked down, his eyes clouding with tears.

He again saw color, the now familiar color of his own blood. It ran down his face and fell into the table. The blood dropped in three-dimensions, then disappeared in only two. He watched it sink into the thirsty wood. It was always a shock, the sight of one's own blood. Instead of bringing oxygen to an old man's brain, it simply stained a wooden table. Blood and tears mixed together on a bare pine table.

He raised his head.

22

WALKING ACROSS THE STREET, Charlie Byrd felt a whisper of moisture greet his face. Dark clouds swirled in the sky above. On this spring morning in *Zuffenhausen*, the air was thick and damp. Byrd was already breaking a sweat. But this wasn't like being in the heat of Alabama. This was different—a clammy feeling, laced with an undercurrent of chill.

Given that Porsche was the world's most profitable car company, Byrd expected a grandiose monument to yuppie wealth. He was not disappointed.

After decades of successful business operation on historic *Porscheplatz*, the firm finally decided to construct a proper monument to its success. The Porsche Museum was billed as the most spectacular building project ever undertaken by the company. Flush with cash, the company peeled off $130 million and created this sleek alien spaceship of a building. It officially opened its doors in 2009, a towering contemporary structure of concrete, steel, and glass.

The building's spacious interior was finished in white. About 80 vehicles were scattered throughout, some sitting on standalone pedestals, others stacked in neat rows. Each vehicle was accompanied by an information display with key facts such as construction date and performance history.

Only a few days ago, Byrd had been awestruck at the Callahan's Alabama collection of vintage Porsches. But upon viewing the German museum, he gained new perspective.

The factory collection made Callahan's private display seem comparably modest.

The Porsche Museum was positioned at the entrance to the factory, perched at the perimeter like a futuristic airport terminal. It served not only as storage space for some remarkably valuable pieces of German engineering, but also as a natural meeting place for company employees and the public. American buyers could even take delivery of their cars here, and depart on whatever European destination suited their fancy. Most important for Charlie Byrd was the existence of the Porsche Archive, a massive library of information concerning everything Porsche. It was kind of like the Library of Congress but tailored to the world of Porsche, an endless database of knowledge on one niche topic.

Along one wall was a glass-encased row of golden trophies, presumably racing cups. Several people milled about, browsing the cars and snapping photos. It was almost amusing to Byrd—people treating cars like serious works of art. There was a sense of almost unnatural quiet in the room. He lowered his voice, although he had no reason to do so.

"What's the point of taking delivery at the factory?" he asked. "Just a yuppie wet dream?"

"Well," she replied, "there's really no point other than fun. Imagine how you'd feel if you ordered a new Porsche, waited months for it to be built, and then came to Germany to take delivery."

Her suggestion, of course, was preposterous. Charlie Byrd could no more imagine ordering a new Porsche than he could buying a diamond-encrusted belt buckle or a solid gold water faucet. These were equally reckless purchases in his eyes. He snorted at the very idea.

"Wait here while I check us in," she said, clucking her tongue. "Don't wander out of my sight."

With Callahan occupied, Byrd browsed the display floor. The first car was a small race car from the 1920s. Its white paint was adorned with red spades—like a playing card. To Byrd it looked more like a lawnmower than a car. Across the front grill he saw the word *Sascha* scrawled in silver script. This was one of the cars she had told him about on the plane. It was a simplistic early effort built by the godfather of this empire, Ferdinand Porsche. What impressed Byrd was not so much the car, but a rumor related to the car. Renowned comedian and confirmed Porsche addict Jerry Seinfeld had named his first child *Sascha*. Was it pure coincidence?

Callahan returned to his side, paperwork in hand.

"So Seinfeld named his kid after this car?"

"It would seem so," she said, handing him his plastic nametag. "Here you go, Mr. Callahan."

Byrd looked at the name tag. Printed across the front of his badge was the name Charles Mortimer Callahan.

"You've got to be kidding," he said.

His mind flashed back to Atlanta and a man named Dirk. The man who arranged their trip, who briefed them on every inch of the Porsche factory, and whose friends coordinated every minute of their trip.

The asshole who somehow managed to smoke and maintain a million dollar smile. He must've done this on purpose.

"Sorry Charlie," she said, "I told them this was incorrect, but they said it's too late to change. We got on the English language tour, and we're Mr. and Mrs. Charles Mortimer Callahan."

"Guess we know who wears the pants in this relationship," he said, attaching the name tag to his lapel.

"Come on now. Would being married to me be so terrible?"

"Being married to anyone would be terrible," he replied. "Being married to you would be intolerable."

As the words left his mouth, he knew they were a lie. They were delivered with a wry smile. Even insults had become flirtation. He liked this Kristen Callahan, but the twin pillars of independence and emotional distance compelled him to profess otherwise.

"Well, this tour lasts ninety minutes," she said. "About like my first marriage. You'll survive."

First marriage? Byrd took the comment in stride. That she had been previously married wasn't particularly surprising. In addition to maintenance issues, this woman came with enough baggage to fill a Greyhound bus.

Byrd wanted to say something about consummating their marital relationship. But he held his tongue. To hell with sexual chemistry. This was still a job. They had meetings planned, but she had been insistent about taking this tour. She said it would be educational and relevant. He wasn't convinced. But he knew that understanding the Callahan's world could help find the old man. So he went along. If it was all about a car, and there really was a Spyder, then the formula was simple: *find the car, find the man.*

Their guide was a short and rotund German man who spoke English with an accent that Byrd found highly amusing.

"Porsche has sold over one million cars since 1948," he said with the canned enthusiasm of someone paid to utter the words. "So if someone tries to sell you a Porsche older than 1948, don't buy it."

The group chuckled politely at the joke.

Byrd took hold of Callahan's arm and lowered his voice. "German humor," he said. "This is going to be a long ninety minutes."

ᔇᔐ

The delivery area was clean and antiseptic, like a hospital. Spread throughout were gleaming new cars.

This was the moment for which the expectant yuppies had been waiting. Within a matter of seconds, each made a beeline to his or her baby. One by one, they opened doors and glove compartments and trunks, examining the cars top to bottom.

"So which one is ours?" Byrd asked.

As if on cue, the guide handed Charles Mortimer Callahan a set of keys. All the vehicles in the room, with one notable exception, were either silver or black in color. The notable exception was parked in front of Charlie Byrd, and he was holding the keys. The car was yellow. Color aside, its curves and design were reminiscent of the 550 Spyder. Two seats and a drop top. It was a roadster.

"Of course," Byrd said as he slid behind the steering wheel. "Matches the one back in Birmingham. It's even got matching seatbelts."

She settled into the passenger's seat. "You try arranging a factory delivery in under forty-eight hours."

Byrd knew she was right. She'd expedited a process that takes months. Their very presence on the tour was an achievement. Somewhere in Atlanta, a man named Dirk was responsible. He'd called in more than a few favors. Customers like Callahan and Seinfeld warranted special favors.

"Look familiar?" she asked.

"Same formula, different decade?"

"You might say so. Fifty years have passed, but this car shares the same DNA."

"Do we get to keep it?"

"No, it's not really our car. We just get to see it. Experience it."

They lingered a few more moments in the delivery area, Byrd studying the reactions of the new car owners. He found the scene fascinating. To Charlie Byrd, vehicles were functional objects that delivered him from point A to point B. If they didn't break down or blow up along the way, he was satisfied. His truck was a tool, a mode of somewhat reliable transportation. Nothing more.

This was a different world. These people viewed their cars as what? Entertainment? Status symbols? Compensation for small penises? Steroids for undersized egos? It was a perspective Byrd couldn't comprehend. As he watched the new owners scour their cars, he wondered what kind of person would spend so much hard-earned money on an appliance.

"I don't get it," he said.

"You don't get what?"

"I don't get it. All of this . . ." he replied, and made a sweeping gesture toward the gleaming new cars.

"What's there to get?"

"Look," he said. "You and I won't see eye-to-eye on this issue. I've never been much of a car guy."

"Your point?"

"I don't get it. Why do you people do this stuff? There are kids starving in Bangladesh, and we've got our yellow seat belts here in Germany."

He shook his head. "Sorry, I just don't get it."

"The belts should be red to match your bleeding heart," she said. "You've had no trouble collecting your exorbitant *per diem* salary. Who are you to say what's appropriate?"

"Nothing to do with a bleeding heart. I admit these things make people happy."

"So what don't you get?"

He held his tongue. He could feel the conversation veering into dangerous territory, and he wanted to pull back. But she wouldn't let him do so. And in many respects this was the point. This was the point of his employment. It was the point, if there was one at all, of touring a fucking car museum while a wealthy man remained missing. Someone had to ask uncomfortable questions.

"Go ahead," she insisted. "Say it."

"You sure?"

"Say it."

He took a deep breath.

Choose your words carefully, Byrd. Think like a lawyer.

"Well," he said. "It's about your father. Something I can't figure out. Why would J.C. Callahan risk everything he has for a car? Vanity? Prestige? Surely he's got all the prestige he could want. Sorry, I just don't get it."

She withdrew, stung by the words. Once again, Byrd sprinkled verbal salt into an open wound.

"Why don't you ask him?" she snapped. "When we find him."

Byrd realized he was treading sensitive emotional ground. The woman's father was missing, and here he was questioning the man's motives. Or worse, his sanity.

"Fair enough," he said. "Sorry."

"Don't be sorry for speaking your mind. I can't tell you what motivates my father now. He's his own man."

He nodded, and resolved to shut his mouth and follow the factory tour like an obedient dog. She was on edge, and it was dangerous of him to push. His thoughts returned to the woman in Alabama who willed her entire estate to cats. This was a similar case here, a wealthy narcissist with his own absurd obsessions. Truth was always stranger than fiction. How many times had Byrd read news of some random rich dude steering his own Cessna into the ground? The rich are different, and they indulge in their own ridiculous fantasies. No more cynicism, no more sarcasm, no more questioning the motives or sanity of John Christian Callahan and his merry band of extreme car collectors.

They left the shiny yellow car behind and proceeded on their factory tour. Adopting his new code of silence, Byrd found the experience interesting, even educational.

It was the engine, he learned, that was crucial to Porsche construction in

THE LOST SPYDER

Zuffenhausen. In most auto plants, robots had replaced humans with regard to most tasks. Porsche was different. The assembly lines were gleaming and modern but devoid of robots. Instead, actual German workers used actual hands and actual tools to construct each engine.

By hand. Byrd watched German workers hunched over individual Porsche engines. A conveyor system crawled through the room, carrying each engine past assembly stations. Workers walked along with their engines, plugging necessary parts into place.

"Porsche is unique," the tour guide said. "Every worker assembles a complete engine from start to finish. Every worker is responsible for one engine at a time, and must sign for it. Exact records are kept. This means that after many years, we can always look and find exactly who constructed the engine. Not only when—but who."

Exact records.

The words rang in Byrd's ears.

Not only when . . . but who.

He turned to Callahan.

"Do you think the original cars were made with this level of craftsmanship?"

"Craftsmanship? Sure," she replied. "Arguably more. The modern methods are an evolution from the early days. Think about it. The Spyder was built by hand. No computers, no robots. The records may be incomplete, but the cars were hand-crafted."

Byrd nodded but said nothing. The majority of the factory, it seemed to him, was like other car manufacturing plants. Porsche, like other companies, streamlined and computerized its production methods. Conveyer belts, elevators, LCD screens and technology—all looked state of the art.

But some things, like individual workers who personally signed for engines, remained different.

And the grounds in Stuttgart were small. Instead of building out, Porsche had built up. The construction facility wasn't an expansive structure capable of holding football fields. It was compact, even intimate. It was the ultimate high tech garage.

"Pretty cool," he said.

She threw him a knowing glance.

"You ain't seen nothing yet."

At that moment, their tour took a turn for the unexpected.

The group stepped outside into the mist and, it seemed to Charlie Byrd, turned back the clock some fifty years.

23

CHARLIE BYRD SCANNED THE SKY above *Zuffenhausen*.

"*Achtung*, boss. Looks like rain."

Early morning humidity had given way to a fine mist. Moisture hung in the air, made all the more unpleasant by a thin layer of winter's last chill. The gray sky grew darker, obscuring the sun.

"Feels like rain," Kristen Callahan replied, wiping the first drops from her forehead. "Let's go."

As they walked across the street, Byrd's focus was interrupted by the raucous snort of a sports car exhaust. He stopped and saw a new Porsche, its body panels clad in white protective coating, crawl past the factory and continue down the street. He watched the car exit the factory grounds, and merge into street traffic. The car barked as it turned a corner and disappeared down the street. It was an arresting sight—a newborn car on its maiden voyage.

Byrd regained his composure and rejoined the group. The factory tour had taken a detour, away from the comfortable facilities of the production plant. They stood before a wooden garage that boasted a fresh coat of gray paint. It reminded Charlie Byrd of the simple mechanic's workshops he'd encountered in rural Alabama. It might even have been at home in Ensley, but for the conspicuous lack of razor wire. Yet it was planted squarely in the middle of the Porsche production complex. It was so small and primitive that its placement seemed odd.

Their tour guide spoke, his pace hurried by the threat of an imminent downpour.

"You're looking at the first Porsche factory, *Werks I*," he said. "This garage is listed on the registry of protected German historic sites. The architecture may not be modified. It's preserved, and looks the same today as it did fifty years ago."

Thunder rolled, and the heavy mist turned to sprinkles of rain. Despite the elements, the guide was determined to complete his speech.

"*Werks I* is still being used to make Porsches today," he said. "It houses our exclusive options program, where we customize special order cars."

A sharp clap of thunder punctuated the sky, this time much closer. The guide finally ceded authority to the elements, and began herding the group inside the building. Everyone got wet as they fled the street.

Stepping inside the chilly building, Byrd was struck by its familiarity. The place was littered with a random assortment of metal car parts, the floor saturated with decades of grease and motor oil. There were the usual noises of mechanical work in session. It bore a striking contrast to the modern facility he'd just left. It was unorganized, and boasted the time-honored scars and stains of a historic building. As with antebellum Southern homes, the building had an ambiance gifted not by architectural design, but by many generations of inhabitants. The air itself tasted thick with history.

Outside, rain fell in heavy sheets. The downpour roared, pounding the roof like machine gun fire, overwhelming every other noise in the shop. Even the tour guide relented; he smiled and waited for the noise to soften. For a moment, all attention went to the sounds of Mother Nature.

The room was populated by an assortment of workers, all clad in gray jumpsuits. Most appeared to be German. Byrd noted that most were young, in their thirties and forties.

Byrd saw no computer monitors or assembly lines. Instead, individual workers tinkered away on their own, like elves in some elaborate wizard's workshop. There was little order amidst the chaos.

He turned to Callahan and his gaze lingered. She'd caught a good dose of rainfall and her white shirt was damp. It clung to her curves in a manner he found extremely entertaining. He arched his eyebrows in amusement.

"You look cold," he said. "Want my jacket?"

"I'll be fine," she replied, rubbing her arms for warmth. "Keep your eyes on the tour."

He smiled and reluctantly pulled his gaze away from her nipples. The garage scene was far less compelling. Each worker appeared to be piecing together different projects. An engine here, a dashboard there, a seat there.

Nearby, a young man stitched initials into a piece of purple leather. The tour guide seized upon the opportunity.

"This is an example of our customization program," he said. "A customer from Texas in America wants ostrich leather in his car. He wants his brand stitched on it. For the seats, you understand."

Byrd rolled his eyes.

"Monogrammed ostrich leather?"he whispered to his companion. "Sorry, I still don't get it."

"Vanity," she smiled. "All is vanity."

He nodded in agreement, knowing she was quoting something, but not sure exactly what.

With rain still thundering, no one was in any hurry to leave the building. They browsed the room at leisure.

In a far corner of the garage sat an elderly German. Like the other workers, the thin man wore a simple gray jumpsuit and cap. But unlike the rest, he was clearly older than the garage. The skin on his face was wrinkled and weathered, reminiscent of leather. He sat on a small wooden stool, looking more like a crafty elf than an autoworker. Hunched over the work, his face a mask of concentration, he was oblivious to the tour group.

As he worked, the man's right hand shook uncontrollably—a slight but noticeable tremor. Byrd's thoughts went to his grandmother. For the last decade of her life, she'd suffered from Parkinson's disease. This man was exhibiting the same symptoms—the same uncontrollable shaking.

From his mouth dangled a lit cigarette. After each shaky drag, he dropped ashes on the floor. The man looked up at Byrd, his steady gaze straddling the line between curiosity and contempt.

Byrd again lowered his voice.

"I shudder to think how many European Community laws he's breaking," he said. "Feels like we're in Ensley."

Callahan got the reference. In some 30 years, she'd never seen Stanley Griggs without a cigarette in his mouth.

"Kindred goddamned spirits," she replied in a growl.

Despite lowered voices, their tour guide overheard their laughter. Even in tobacco friendly Europe, smoking in a work environment was taboo. Motioning toward the man, the guide smiled.

"He's been here so long," he said. "We let him do what he wants."

Outside, the rainfall had subsided. Gone was the thunderous roll of water off the garage roof. In its place was the mechanical music of the shop. Sensing a momentary break in the weather, the guide was eager to leave.

"If you'll all please follow me," he said, "we'll visit the *Gästekasino* for lunch."

"You'll love the canteen," she said.

"Cafeteria food," Byrd replied. "What a treat."

"Trust me. The food rocks, and they even have a beer machine. No Pabst, but they have the German stuff."

His eyes fixated on the guide, who'd already jogged to the promise of dry land across the street.

He lowered his voice to a whisper.

"Wait for me," he said. "I'll meet you. Twenty minutes."

"Okay," she said. "This is probably our best chance."

"If anyone asks, I've gone to the toilet. Time for me to start earning my keep."

One by one, the tour group shuffled outside the protective confines of *Werks I*. Although rain had subsided, the dark sky continued to spit drops. It was enough to prod the lingering stragglers into jogging across the street.

The threat of rainfall provided an ideal diversion for Charlie Byrd. Lurking behind, he feigned joining the group, then veered off to the side. He looped around the corner of the building and stepped through a doorway. He stood in a carpeted hallway devoid of any distinguishing art or markings. But at the end of the hall was a metal door.

Charlie Byrd, professional risk taker.

THE LOST SPYDER

This felt a hell of a lot better than being a lawyer.

Byrd walked to the metal door and grabbed the silver handle. It was ice cold. He gently turned it to gauge resistance. As promised, unlocked. He slipped inside. All was as described. Some well placed phone calls from a Callahan, and they practically had blueprints to the place.

He found himself in a room notable for two characteristics. First, tall ceilings. It appeared to have once been a part of the main garage area. But the space was converted to a new purpose, a special kind of storage. Second, the room was cold. It was more than cold; it was damned cold. It felt more like a meat locker than a garage. Byrd shivered as the chilled air hit his damp body.

He stood in the center aisle of the room. On either side, a series of tall shelves were stacked together in tight rows. The shelves were constructed to the room's dimensions. Equipped with wheels, in places they compressed together to conserve space. Here were documents that never made the trip to the public archive across the street.

He ran his finger across the identification plaques affixed to each shelf. The storage files were arranged in chronological order. The 1990s, the 1980s, the 1970s . . . With each row of documents he was traveling father back in time. In a matter of moments, he located the appropriate shelf for 1955—the year in which the final 550 Spyders were built. The shelf was amongst the last in the room, and it possessed the earliest records pertaining to Porsche. As promised, everything was served upon a silver platter.

Exactly seventeen minutes later, Charlie Byrd smiled and nodded to their tour guide as he took his seat in the *Gästekasino*.

Kristen Callahan was already working her way through a plate of German cuisine.

"That looks good," he said.

"It's goose fat," she replied. "And it is good."

Byrd winced.

"Thanks but I'll pass."

Her voice dropped to a whisper.

"That was fast," she said. "Everything okay?"

"It was easy," he said. "Really easy. You owe your buddy Dirk on this one. Big time. He really rolled out the red carpet."

"Good," she said. "Did you find what we need?"

He nodded and spoke under his breath. "I saw the records," he said. "Got pictures. They even had duplicates in Spanish and English."

"That makes sense," she said. "Even back in the early days, America was the key market. So what did you learn?"

"Well," he said. "You may be right about this trip, after all. Looks like the Spyder is here in Germany."

"I knew it," she said. "Where?"

"Our tour continues tonight—in the factory storage grounds of Ludwigsberg. I think it's out there."

"That's a town about fifteen minutes outside Stuttgart. Anything else?"

"Yeah," he said. "Did you hear that part earlier about workers signing for engines?"

"Yeah."

"Well, back in Alabama, do you have all the numbers for your father's Spyder?"

"You saw the file."

"Yeah, but at the time I didn't know what to look for. What time is it back home?"

She checked her watch.

"Early morning, around seven."

"Well, do you think we can get the numbers for the engine?"

"Sure, they're in the records. I'll put in a call to Baines. He'll take care of it."

The reconnaissance mission had been a success.

The elusive lost Spyder, Byrd believed, wasn't only in Germany—it was within their reach.

Find the car, find the man.

24

KRISTEN CALLAHAN SAT ON THE BED. She cradled the telephone receiver with one hand, and scribbled notes with the other. She was using a hotel notepad and pen, but the pen was low on ink. She waved the pen in the air, and Charlie Byrd handed her a fresh one.

"Hoffman," she said, and resumed writing. "Karl Hoffman. Yeah. I got it. Okay. Thanks, Dirk. I really appreciate it. You are amazing."

She smiled and laughed, as if shrugging off a flattery.

"Right. I look forward to seeing you back in the States. Okay. Bye."

She hung up the phone, and turned her gaze to Byrd. He was standing across the room, leaning against the desk, arms crossed. *Amazing* was another one of his least favorite words. It was almost as bad as *cute*.

"Amazing?" he said. "Am I amazing?"

"I don't know what you are," she said, "but that guy's amazing. He's been working on this all day. He found a match."

"Okay. Let's hear it."

"Good news and bad news."

"Good news first."

"The good news is they found a name. Hoffman. Apparently a guy named Karl Hoffman built the engine in my father's car. Right here in the

Stuttgart-Zuffenhausen plant."

"Could be useful. The bad news?"

"Hoffman's retired. He hasn't worked for Porsche in over a decade. But we've got his last known contact info, and it's also here in Stuttgart."

"Let's call him."

She shook her head.

"No need. Since my German isn't the greatest, Dirk is making the call for us. He's going to explain the situation, so we can set up a meeting."

"Anything new from the cops?"

"No," she said. "They haven't found anything."

German authorities were pursuing the Callahan investigation like they pursued about everything else —in an orderly and efficient manner that was absolutely by the book. Byrd held out little hope that they would actually produce results. The Callahan name was front page news in Birmingham, Alabama, but it didn't even register on the radar screen here. This case was just another missing American, a problem best handled by the embassies and diplomatic crops.

"Alright," Byrd said, "we've done all we can on that front. You ready?"

She stood from the bed.

"I'm ready," she said. "As ready as I'll ever be."

ை

The chain link fence was trimmed with razor wire. It was looped along the top *Ensley-style,* in the usual thick curls that promised bloody death, or at least severe maiming. So Charlie Byrd decided to go through instead of over. With deft precision, he sliced into the rusty metal.

"Wire cutters," he said. "Don't leave home without 'em."

With concentrated effort, he pulled the severed metal apart to create a small opening.

"Ladies first," he said. "Move your ass, please."

Kristen Callahan snaked through the hole. Together they darted into the compound: down a grassy embankment and across the gravel road, making a beeline for nearby foliage. From a place of relative safety, they stopped to confer in hushed tones.

"If they have cameras, we're toast," she said.

"It's not cameras that worry me," Byrd replied. "It's guns. In Alabama, they'll shoot you for this sort of thing."

He scanned the surroundings. It was a cloudy night, and the moon was obscured by layers of heavy mist. Peering into fog, he could make out several small buildings. None appeared to be occupied. The sparse landscape was punctuated by an occasional thrust of tall weeds. Artificial lighting was nonexistent. This was a storage facility, a sad collection of faded metal sheds. The *Ludwigsberg* area seemed out of character for the otherwise immaculate Porsche operations.

"These sheds look pretty damn original," he said. "Judging by the weeds, this isn't the most popular part of town. Just keep quiet and stick to my side."

They worked their way past storage sheds, creeping from one building to the next, two shadows in the night. As they progressed, Byrd felt his stress level rise. He was sopping wet. Humidity and perspiration conspired to soak his black clothing. Streams of sweat rolled down his face. It rained earlier in the day, was threatening to rain again, and in places the ground was soft. Night crawling, as he called it, was always a slippery business—especially in the rain.

Breaking and entering could never be taken lightly. Byrd had no intention of touring the German penal system. Nor did he intend to test the pistol aim of some local Barney Fife. These guys carried real guns with real bullets—and Germans weren't known for their sense of humor. Anything could happen on a job like this one. Anything usually did.

Byrd's adrenal glands kicked into overdrive. His heart thumped in his ears and pounded against his ribcage. No matter how many times he went night crawling, it was a head rush. Dry mouth, sweaty palms, shortness of breath, and dizziness—all came with the territory. All were part of the job.

For Byrd, this natural intoxication was the essence of his work. Money aside, this was what it was about. There were lots of ways to make money, some of them even respectable. But none delivered the same rush. Byrd would never admit it, but it was the rush, not the money, that kept him coming back.

He had a simple philosophy. *It's easier to ask forgiveness than permission.*

"Here it is," he said. "Storage facility number 1229-A. This is our baby."

He examined the door of the storage unit. Given the abandoned appearance of the area, he began to feel more comfortable. His pulse rate dropped and the cotton left his mouth. Like the grounds themselves, the unit's protective mechanisms were showing their age. A rusted chain and padlock secured the simple steel door in place. This shed was too damned messy to be important—too neglected to be the promised land. He began to doubt his own judgment.

"You really think we'll find it in here?" he said. "This place looks like hell."

"You'd be surprised what companies do with their own past. They throw out treasure every day. You just never know."

"Suppose we came all this way for a pile of rust?"

"Spyders are aluminum. They don't rust."

Byrd grunted in reply. She had an answer for everything.

He reached into his jacket, pulled out a tool, and once again felt the urge to mimic a certain Birmingham mechanic.

"Gotta use the right fucking tool for the job," he said.

He drove the wire-cutter into the chain, exhaling as his weight pushed into the task. The chain snapped.

"I don't want to know where you learned to do this stuff," she said. "You're starting to scare me."

"*Moon Winx Lodge* in Tuscaloosa, Alabama" he replied. "And until the statute of limitations runs out, that's all I'm going to say."

He pulled open the door of the shed just enough to allow entrance. She ducked low and slipped through, and he quickly followed suit.

From the moment he entered, he knew something was wrong. In the darkness, he felt his face break a large web. It wasn't a dry cobweb. It was a spider web, thick and sticky and fresh.

"Jesus," he said, "I've got web all over my face."

His heart began racing again. He arched his back and felt his spine tingle. This was the bad kind of rush. Webs meant spiders. For reasons that defied logic, Charlie Byrd hated spiders. The mere sight of a spider ignited primal fear. And the thought that a live one might be somewhere on his body . . .

He pulled the creaking door shut, and whisked around in the darkness.

"Light, light, LIGHT," he said, sweeping his hands over his face and head.

She flicked on her flashlight, revealing a panicked private detective writhing in the darkness. With his frantic efforts, most traces of the gooey web had been removed.

"Anything on me?" he asked. The panic in his voice was palpable.

She cackled out loud, and then muffled the noise with her hand.

"Oh my God. All this excitement over a spider? You're quite the manly man."

This was an entertaining spectacle—a grown Southern man, a detective no less, being sent into a visible panic over a spider.

"Some people hate snakes. Some people hate heights. I hate spiders," he replied. "They really bother me."

"Then you've taken the wrong job," she laughed.

Finally convinced he was arachnid-free, Byrd scanned the crowded room with his own flickering flashlight. The disheveled appearance of the container was matched by its stagnant odor. Inside the storage unit, it was moist and dirty. Years of collected sediment covered every inch. In addition to grease and grime, Byrd swore he could smell the age.

"Looks like the maid is on vacation," he said.

"Reminds me of your truck," she replied.

The room was small, no more than fifteen by thirty feet. Along one wall extended a latticework of sagging, rusted shelves stacked full of rusting metal. Upon the floor lay boxes of similar artifacts—discarded gears, and a rat's nest of wiring and tubing. Some pieces were rusted. Others were green with age. The scene was eerie to Byrd, like a tomb. Or worse, a spider-infested tomb.

"We're standing in the whale's belly," he said. "And the whale's got a case of indigestion."

He picked up a small wooden box, and rifled his hand through the assortment of metal parts. He pulled out a heavy chunk of metal that was rusted beyond recognition. No doubt the metal had once been something important, some crucial organ of a healthy functioning machine. Now it was slowly decaying, and returning to the earth, bit by bit.

"Rust," he said. "No Spyder here."

His flashlight revealing nothing else of significance, he dropped the box back in place.

"Looks like a load of junk," he said.

"Are you sure this is the right building?"

"Yeah. According to the documents, this is the place."

"Well, it may be junk," she said. "But there's certainly a lot of it. Let's check the back."

They worked their way beyond the piles of wooden crates and boxes, some of which were stacked to the ceiling, and arrived at the rear of the storage unit. A withered plastic tarp covered the entire section like a ghostly shroud.

Byrd grabbed one corner of the yellowing tarp and pulled. With a slight tug, it came free. He withdrew the tarp from its resting place, the dusty plastic crackling in the darkness.

He unveiled a massive rectangular box, at least ten feet in length. It lay flat against the back wall. It was made of thick wooden planks, and was suffering from rot. What remained of the container was hollow and decayed and splintered.

Byrd squatted and peered at the box. Along the length of one side, the word PORSCHE was barely discernible in faded black script.

"This could've contained a car," he said. "It's certainly big enough. But those days are long gone."

With a firm tug, he lifted one corner of the lid. The wood resisted, and then broke free. He slid it a few inches to the side.

Inside, the container was empty, save for one piece of metal. Byrd sat down his flashlight, reached into the box, and carefully pulled out the relic. Although cloudy and discolored, there was no rust. Aluminum. The years hadn't been kind, but it was clearly an automobile door.

He flipped the curved piece of metal over in his hands, and examined the other side. The door was designed so there was only one latch, and it was tucked inside the frame.

"So the only way to open the door . . ." he said, "is to flip this lever."

He reached inside to find the door lever. That was when he felt it. He pulled his hand away from the door. Looking down through the flickering beams of light, he saw what was quite possibly the hairiest spider he'd ever seen outside the Birmingham Zoo. And it was crawling across his left hand.

"Holy shit," he exclaimed, as he jerked his hand back, flinging the spider against the wall of the shed. In one fluid and quite unprofessional motion, Byrd tossed the door back to the ground, and jumped back five feet. His leap to safety, however, was interrupted by a tall stack of wooden boxes. With a thunderous crash, the boxes tumbled down, their contents clattering across the concrete floor of the storage unit. Byrd lay sprawled across the wreckage, convulsing in an involuntary shiver.

"Jesus Christ," he said, scrambling to his feet. "Did you see the size of that thing?"

She laughed at the spectacle. "Charlie Byrd," she said, "far be it from me to criticize your technique. But they heard that racket all the way to Stuttgart."

"Look," he said. "It bit me."

On top of his hand was a red welt that was just beginning to swell.

"That was a mean one," she agreed, turning back to the box. "Here rests the lost Spyder. Or what's left of it."

Byrd wanted to say something witty. No words came. He felt more than a little embarrassed by the scene. He stood staring at the decaying ancient container, which was looking more and more like some gigantic coffin from a vampire movie. Despite the need for levity, for some glint of optimism, he fell silent. He digested reality, and it wasn't pleasant. They'd followed their instincts. They'd flown to Germany. They'd broken the law. And they had precious little to show for it.

It was a sobering realization, one that sucked away optimism and humor from the situation. Here were two Alabamians, standing in a steamy storage shed in rural Germany, clothes soaked with sweat, rummaging through decades-old pieces of junk in search of the Holy Grail. *Find the car, find the man?* They'd come up empty, and Byrd was beginning to doubt his instincts.

Welcome to Stuttgart SOL, he thought. *Shit Outta Luck.*

A raindrop smacked against the metal roof of the storage shed. Then another. And another. This wasn't a downpour, but a random smattering of droplets, as if the sky was threatening to spill its contents. Together, they stood and absorbed the music of the rain. Other than this rhythmic drumbeat, the night was calm.

৩-৶

The calm was shattered. The barks were deep, coarse, and loud. First one dog, then a companion. When Charlie Byrd went night crawling, dogs were to be avoided.

As the sound of the bellowing grew louder, it was joined by the voices of men. Byrd cursed. Something had alerted the security goons. Judging by the racket, they were getting close.

"Not good," he whispered. "Not good at all."

"Well?" she shot back. "What do you usually do in this situation?"

"Two choices. Choice A, we stay put and hope they don't find us. If they see the broken chain on the door, or the damaged fence, or find our car, we're going to jail."

"Choice B?"

"Run like hell. And whatever you do, don't get caught."

They darted to the front of the shed and cracked open the door. The noise of dogs was growing louder, but was coming from the opposite direction—away from the car.

"They're coming from the other side," Byrd said. "At least we'll have a head start."

They stepped outside the shed, and carefully restored the door to its original position. Then they jogged past the storage units, raindrops pelting their faces, back toward the original point of entry.

As the sound of barking dogs echoed amongst the buildings, Byrd felt the signs . . . Sweaty palms, pounding heart, cotton mouth—all returned with a vengeance. Night crawling was a rush, one made more intense when German Shepherds entered the equation.

He led the way. Straight ahead was the perimeter fence, and through its center was their route of escape. At the sight, both joggers switched into full sprint mode. They crunched across a gravel pathway, and splashed through the soft muddy ground.

Any sprint for Charlie Byrd was always a roll of the dice. Since high school, the bum knee was always there, lurking. All it took was one wrong step, and that knee would collapse.

But Byrd was sprinting at a healthy clip when he suddenly realized he was alone—Kristen Callahan was no longer by his side.

He turned just as she fell. With a slight yelp, her right foot twisted in the soft earth. Her body crumbled and she landed flat on her chest, hitting the ground hard.

"My ankle," she moaned, attempting to get back on her feet. "Shit. I can't stand on it."

The sound of dogs grew louder. They were getting close.

He scooped her up into his arms.

"Thank God for Pilates," he said.

Then Charlie Byrd proceeded to sprint toward the fence. Only he couldn't sprint. He slogged up the muddy turf, feet sinking into the mud, lungs struggling to keep up. His knee held.

As they reached the exit point, three dogs broke into plain view. They were running free, unleashed to expedite the hunt.

Byrd lowered his head and pushed through the fence. They emerged on the opposite side with a clatter, as the metal slapped back into place.

Behind him, the dogs arrived, howling with frustration. The dogs were stopped—one pawed at the fence, while the others snapped their jaws and made a terrific noise.

Byrd turned to their escape vehicle. The tiny Mercedes was neatly tucked between two tall bushes, concealed from view.

He staggered the last few feet to the car, opened the passenger door, and dumped her inside. Then he slid behind the steering wheel and stated the obvious.

"I'll drive," he said. "I've got a bad feeling about this."

He turned the ignition, and the car started. Then his face was bathed in the bright glare of floodlights. The lights were approaching fast, and were focused on the little Mercedes.

"Shit," he said.

25

CHARLIE BYRD STOMPED HIS RIGHT FOOT ON THE GAS, but the Mercedes went nowhere. Instead, the car spun its wheels deeper into the mud. They were stuck.

"This is not good," he said. He jammed his foot to the floor, and the tires made that disgusting sound again, slinging loose mud everywhere.

In the distance, the glaring headlights narrowed the gap. The truck was closing fast. It charged through the fog with speed that bordered on reckless.

Kristen Callahan was rubbing her ankle.

"Not so hard on the gas," she said. "You're just digging us in deeper."

The car budged a grand total of two inches, both in the wrong direction—down. Byrd's heart thumped in his throat. This sort of job was either great for his health, or it would kill him. He wasn't sure which.

"Here goes nothing," he said.

With a grunt, he jumped out into the rain. At the front of the car, he dropped into a three-point football stance, like they taught him back in high school. His feet sank into the muck, and he felt the glare of floodlights bearing down on his back. Then he exploded, slamming against the front bumper of the car with all of his 220 pounds.

Callahan remained in her seat, her right ankle now swollen like a blow fish.

"You want me to get out?" she shouted. "I think I can stand."

He didn't reply. Instead, he slammed his body against the car. The Mercedes was no match for the former second-string offensive lineman. It lifted out of the mud and rolled gently backward.

At the fence, the German Shepherds finally squeezed through the metal and sprinted toward Byrd. The truck was also upon them. From its windows came the shouts of men. They were speaking German, but it wasn't hard to translate.

Byrd darted back to the driver's seat and slammed the door.

"Not bad for a second-string lineman," he said.

The truck slid to a halt in front of the car, blocking their path. Out jumped a guard. He had a gun.

"Drive," she said. "Or this is going to get ugly."

"It's already ugly."

Byrd shifted into reverse. With an abrupt lurch, the vehicle squirted backward. It barreled down the muddy incline, taking them away from the dogs and truck, but closer to the storage compound. It finally came to a halt on the unpaved road. Shifting into gear, Byrd sent the car surging forward, slinging a hailstorm of gravel.

His sudden maneuver bought a few precious seconds. The dogs were left behind, but the truck quickly returned. The two vehicles barreled down the road, past the storage grounds. The truck loomed a few inches behind, its blinding lights as bright as the sun. Again came shouts of German profanity.

Then they felt it. The truck thumped the Mercedes from behind, crunching its rear. Byrd struggled to keep the car on the road.

"Jesus, did you feel that?" he said. "They just hit us."

Byrd was stunned. He'd played this game before, cat-and-mouse with private security, but he'd never felt his life threatened.

The truck pulled alongside. Sensing opportunity, Byrd veered off the gravel road and pointed the Mercedes directly toward the chain link fence.

"I've got an idea," he said. "Hang on."

He drove straight into the fence. With a piercing screech, his car slid beneath, and the mangled links slapped back into place. They were back inside the storage grounds. He drove down a row of sheds, and waited for the arrival of the truck. It smashed through the fence and roared down the gravel pathway in pursuit.

There was palpable panic in Callahan's voice.

"What the hell are you doing?" she said. "This is a dead end."

They were trapped between the truck and a concrete wall. There was only one solution. Byrd noticed it earlier during their jaunt through the grounds. He'd filed it away, and now it was time to play the card. The Mercedes was small—and size mattered.

"Abstract problem solving," he said.

As truck grew closer, Byrd punched the car forward—through the narrow gap between storage sheds. It was no more than a few feet wide. Even for the tiny Mercedes, clearance was tight. But it was possible, at the expense of two side mirrors, some black paint, and a noise that made skin crawl. The pursuing truck had no chance. Trapped by its size and girth, it couldn't possibly follow.

Byrd turned up a parallel pathway, and drove his car right back through the fence. The dark, unlit and unmarked Mercedes was a mile away by the time security maneuvered its way out.

ॐ

The drive back to Stuttgart was tense. Rainfall, which threatened to return all evening, finally arrived. It fell in thick sheets, clouding visibility on an already murky night.

"This rain's good luck," Byrd said. "It'll provide some extra cover."

The downfall pounded at the car, while its wipers whisked back and forth with hypnotic rhythm. Byrd strained to read German street signs, and felt more than ever like a fish out of water. The thrill of the chase gave way to sobering reality. Find the car, find the man? They'd traveled to Germany, broken innumerable laws, and found nothing. No Holy Grail. No Callahan. And it would be a minor miracle if they spent the night in their hotel instead of the local prison.

"You think they've called the police?"

There was fear in her voice. She was a rich kid who, Byrd assumed, never spent a night in her life without 500-thread count silk sheets. The looming possibility of a German jail cell must've taken hold.

"Maybe," he replied. "But I bet they wait a while out of sheer embarrassment. That's happened to me a couple of times back home. We should be fine."

He leaned forward and concentrated on the foggy road.

"Just help me navigate. I don't care what you say—driving over here is nerve-wracking."

"You're doing fine," she said. "It's a straight shot back to the hotel."

He grunted assent, but still felt the tension coursing through his body. He was tired, sore, and jet-lagged. Worse, he felt foolish. The entire trip had been for naught.

"What went wrong back there?" she asked. "And please don't say you told me so."

He shook his head in disgust.

"Well, you might want to have a talk with your friend Dirk when we get home. I don't know. We went to the right place. I'm sure that was it. But there's no way your father's been out there. That shed hadn't been touched in years."

The Smart Car, looking dramatically less smart than it had earlier in the evening, pulled to a stop under a protective awning. It was shielded from the rain.

The hour being late, only one valet was on duty. He was a kid, no more than eighteen-years-old. His eyes opened wide when he saw the car.

Callahan furrowed her brow.

"You sure it's a good idea to valet?" she asked.

"If Stuttgart's anything like Birmingham, this swanky hotel's the last place they'll look. And besides, you can't walk on that ankle."

The valet opened the driver's door first.

"Excuse me," he said in a thick German accent. "Something wrong with your car?"

Byrd conjured up the most earnest expression he could muster.

"Nothing's wrong," he replied. "Why do you ask?"

Stepping into the night, Byrd walked around the Mercedes, surveying the damage. It was hard to keep a straight face. The hood and roof were badly clawed by the chain link fence. The side mirrors were cracked and sagged pathetically from their sockets. The rear bumper was mashed inward, and drooped at a sad angle. The rental company would not be pleased. But J.C. Callahan had money to burn, and whatever rental penalty the company might invoke would be a joke.

"This car looks like hell," Byrd whispered as he helped her out of the car.

"You look worse than the car," she replied.

"At least I can walk."

He lifted her out, and her right leg dangled. The ankle was swollen, puffy and red.

"I think it's just a sprain," she said. "But I'd rather not put pressure on it."

"You ready?"

"Wait a minute," she said, digging one hand into her purse. She pulled out some cash, and held a finger to her lips.

"Shhhhhhhhh," she hissed and handed a fistful of bills to the valet. The kid's attention went from the sad excuse of a car to the thick stack of colorful Monopoly money in his hand. Then he understood.

"Yes, of course," he said. "Not a problem."

Byrd wrapped his arm around her waist, and the valet whisked the car into an underground garage, safely out of sight.

"I guess money does solve problems," he said. "That was a fat wad of cash. How much did you tip him?"

"More than enough," she replied.

They lumbered into the lobby like some sort of alien three-legged creature. They were, Byrd realized, quite the odd couple. Their clothes were splattered with mud and grass, and they looked as though they'd spent the entire evening in the rainstorm.

The lobby was empty, save for a few curious employees working the night shift. Byrd felt eyes descend upon him.

"Jet lag," he said to the desk clerk with a polite nod.

He lowered his voice.

"You need anything for your ankle? Now's the time to ask."

"I do need something," she replied. "A drink."

"We got beer in the room."

"No," she replied. "I need a real drink."

❦

It was after midnight, yet the hotel pub *Zeppelinos* remained open. The room was empty, but the litany of bottles on the back shelf looked promising. After dumping his employer into an oversized leather booth, Charlie Byrd stormed the bar. He returned bearing two crystal glasses of ice and a tall bottle of Tennessee sunshine. He plopped the lot on the table, and sidled into the booth next to Callahan. He'd just carried this woman a great distance in his arms, and was growing accustomed to how she felt by his side.

"I assume this'll do," he said.

Byrd opened the Jack Daniels and poured two glasses full of amber liquid. He watched the bourbon melt the ice, the crystal glass boasting an almost hypnotic attraction. He stared into the cubes, hoping to find some hidden message.

"A whole bottle?" she said. "Not that I'm disapproving."

"Last call," he replied. "Bartender's billing it to my room."

"Your best decision of the night. You can expense it as medicinal supplies."

Their glasses clinked and they each took a deep draw of bourbon.

There were times when Jack Daniels burned the palate with a harshness that made Byrd shudder. This wasn't one of those times. The highball graced his system with a beguiling subtlety. He felt it go down, all the way down. It felt smooth and right, like some sort of high-octane molasses, sweet and sour and warm and cold, all at the same time. He didn't shudder. He sighed.

"Just what the doctor ordered," he said, his muscles relaxing for the first time in hours. "A taste of home. Sorry, but I don't think I was meant for Europe."

He closed his eyes, and allowed the bourbon to settle into his system. It was almost unnatural for such a simple concoction to taste so good. The stress and tension of the evening began to drain away.

As he reopened his eyes and took another drink, it dawned on Charlie Byrd that they weren't the only patrons in the bar. They were being watched. By the time the second draw of whiskey hit his stomach, the watcher stood by their table.

"Have you found what you are seeking?" the man asked in a thick German accent. He took a drag from his cigarette. Then he smiled, bringing a new series of wrinkles across his weathered face, and smoke billowed across the table.

"I suspect not," he said, answering his own question.

Byrd looked at the man with recognition.

This was, he realized, a face that he'd seen before.

26

CHARLIE BYRD SLID AN ASHTRAY across the glossy black table.

The man acknowledged the gesture, and rested his cigarette. As he did so, his trembling hands were revealed in the light. Pale skin was peppered with brown spots and purple veins. It stretched thin over the bones, giving his wiry hands a translucent quality.

This was, Byrd realized, the same man he'd seen in the Porsche factory, casually smoking in the middle of the garage. Were it not for the Jack Daniels coursing through his veins, he might've recalled the German's name.

"Gunter," the man offered, extending a hand across the table. "Gunter Swofford. I hope you please forgive the intrusion."

"Not at all, Mr. Swofford," Byrd replied. The handshake was firm but rough, revealing the calluses of a lifetime of manual labor. "I'm Charlie Byrd."

"And you must be Fraulein Callahan."

"I must be," she said with a weary smile, "because no one else wants to be."

He picked up his cigarette.

"Forgive me, my vice," he said. "To smoke is terrible habit, I know."

He smiled toward the bottle of Jack Daniels.

"Of course, we all have our vice."

THE LOST SPYDER

The man was neatly dressed, projecting a quaint formality that was charming and eccentric. He wore a simple pinstripe shirt and blue evening jacket. Judging from the lapel and collar, both went out of fashion about the time Byrd was born. The shirt bore faint tobacco stains around the cuffs. Otherwise, the man's clothes were clean and well maintained, vintage and dapper.

The man was trim. His profile lacked the paunch that marked so many American male midsections—including Charlie Byrd's. He still had his hair, thin white strands of which were combed straight back. Even his yellowing teeth appeared intact. The man had aged, but he'd done so gracefully.

Callahan raised her glass. "Drink?"

Despite her best efforts, her voice projected weariness. The combination of a missing father, jet lag, bad dreams, a busted ankle, and Jack Daniels was taking its toll. She was tired, frustrated, and uncharacteristically skeptical.

"No," he replied. "I've been waiting for you all night. I was about to go."

"We're glad you didn't," Byrd said.

The German took a shaky drag from his cigarette and smiled. "If you'll forgive me for saying so, you two look rather - how shall I say? Fatigued? I trust your visit to *Ludwigsberg* was, how you say, fruitful?"

"I don't know what you're talking about," Byrd replied.

Swofford raised his hands in a disarming gesture.

"No need for games. I know what you seek. And therefore," he said, "I know you could not possibly find it in *Ludwigsberg*."

Byrd kept a straight face.

"How could you know?" he asked.

The German leaned forward. As he did so, Byrd noticed the eyes. His brilliant blue eyes twinkled in the light—sharp, alert, and youthful. They sparkled with intelligence and wit.

"I know," he said quietly. "Because I built it."

He tugged back the left sleeve of his shirt, and pointed to the inside of his arm, a couple of inches above the wrist. Amidst veins and age spots there was a visible scar, about a half-inch in length.

"If memory is good, it gave me this. A little accident with the weld, you understand. Yes," he said, "I know all about this Spyder."

At this remark, Kristen Callahan shifted upright in her seat. She was alert.

A fire was rekindled. This unassuming German fellow, she realized, could change everything. If what he said was true . . . if he'd really laid hands on the Spyder.

"You built the lost Spyder?" she asked. "What can you tell us about it? Porsche won't say a word. They deny it exists."

The German chuckled. "The lost Spyder exists. Or should I say, it did exist."

The man took another wobbly drag from his cigarette, tapped it into the ashtray, and continued.

"But Porsche wouldn't know about it. They tell you nothing because they know nothing. Porsche has no file on this car. You'll find nothing in the Kardex. Nothing in the Archive."

"Come again? Please explain."

"Fraulein, I've been made aware of your situation. I know about the phone calls made to Mr. Hoffman's residence. I don't know your father, but he has friends here in Stuttgart. Powerful friends. And his friends are my friends."

"How did you know we were staying here?"

"At the factory, not much happens that I don't know. And when the factory called Karl Hoffman, I was alerted."

"Look, have you seen J.C. Callahan?" Byrd asked. "We know he chartered a flight to Stuttgart. We know he's here somewhere."

The man took a furtive glance about the empty bar.

"All you know," he replied, "is that Callahan chartered a flight here. That doesn't mean he was on the plane."

"What? Customs has the records. Callahan entered Germany, and he hasn't left."

"A man carrying his passport entered Germany," Swofford replied. "This was all diversion, you understand? The passport was real. The man was not."

"No," Byrd said, "we don't understand."

"Tonight I tell you something I've told no one else," the German said. "No one in fifty years."

Byrd put down his glass of Jack Daniels. This was too important to muddle with bourbon. It was becoming clear that this business of the lost Spyder went beyond a car. It went beyond an obsession. It was something else entirely. A deception?

"I'm an old man," the German continued. "I've spent my life in *Zuffenhausen* building cars for Porsche. My entire life, you understand? But my days at Porsche are numbered. Let's be honest," he said, "My days on this earth are also numbered. I am, shall we say, yesterday's news. So now I will tell you some, how you say, things that may help you. Perhaps you find the Spyder. And your father."

The German took another long pull on his cigarette, exhaled, and let the smoke settle.

"So," he said, "you know about the lost Spyder? Tell me. Tell me what you know."

"We know the legend. My father owns a Type 550."

"Yes. Was your father the original owner?"

"No. His car came from Central America somewhere, then to Sebring. He bought it from a man named Blake Williams."

The man's eyes opened wide. "I do not know this Williams," he said. "But I know this car. Callahan has this Spyder, correct? It still exists?"

"It exists," she said. "Right now it's sitting in Alabama in his garage."

The man's eyes grew wistful as he remembered his youth.

"Remarkable. I can't tell you the satisfaction that gives to me. You see, in the early days of Porsche, we put our soul into those cars. It was not a job. It was a passion."

His hands trembled as he spoke.

"Excellence," he said, "was expected. And after all these years, this car has survived."

Sounds like he's discussing a long-lost child, Byrd thought. *I'm not sure he's playing with a full set of marbles.* But this guy was par for the course.

Swofford took another deep pull from his cigarette.

"I was a young man and had just begun working for Porsche. We were a small company, only a few years old. Always on the edge, always on the edge. Ferry Porsche had his hands in everything. We were growing fast. Too fast, some people said. Do you know how much the world has changed?"

Byrd recalled the scene in the simple wooden workshop, where it appeared time stood still.

"You started in that *Zuffenhausen* shop?" he asked.

"Yes. Because of the time, Porsche gave me responsibilities that were, how you say, beyond my years. I was a young man, but I did much. This was unusual for a German firm. At that time, only with experience and age came responsibility. I was young, but I was involved at every stage of the build, start to finish."

"So you built the Spyders yourself?"

"Many people were involved in building the car. Not just me. But the Spyder you seek, the lost one, it was my doing. The Spyder was Wilhem Hild's design. I worked for Herr Hild on these cars. Type 550 was beginning its life. Not unlike myself."

The man tapped his cigarette into the ashtray.

"The car you call lost, I remember this car. Tell me . . . what do you know about your father's 550? The history?"

She shrugged.

"Like I said, it went to Central America, and was brought back to Germany by Porsche. Then it was sold to some doctors in Florida, and worked its way up to Alabama."

"The car was retrieved from Central America?" he said with a dry laugh. "There you are mistaken."

"I don't understand."

"Simple. The car we sent to Central America stayed there. This is the car you call lost."

Byrd shook his head. He'd already seen the car. In fact, he had the paperwork for it. Callahan's car was documented.

"I don't understand. That car is now in Alabama. In Callahan's garage."

The German cleared his throat. "Allow me to explain. The car was built to race in the *Carrera Panamericana*. In Mexico, you understand?"

Byrd turned to Callahan.

"That's the race Williams mentioned, right?"

"Right," she replied. "*Carrera Panamericana*. Five days across Mexico. Remember, the last year was 1954."

"It was dangerous," said the German. "Too dangerous. The Mexican government made it to stop."

Byrd nodded. "So I've been told. Well, you're saying there's another Spyder down there? A car built for the *Panamericana*?"

"Yes. Study your history. The first examples of Type 550 we built—

numbers 550-02 and 550-03—were cabriolet cars. Open top, you understand?"

"Right. Roadsters. Like James Dean's car."

The German snorted a laugh.

"I love Americans. You gave us the name Spyder, and you turn tragedy into myth. Yes, like James Dean's car. But Porsche took these cabriolet cars, made them coupes, and sold them to wealthy gentlemen in Guatemala. The cars did well in the *Panamericana*."

Byrd nodded. "Okay, I got that part."

"The next year Porsche sent a new Spyder to Mexico. This car—550-04—was driven by Hans Hermann in November 1954. It won its class, so the Guatemalan wanted another 550. Porsche sent this new Type 550 to Guatemala in 1955."

The man smiled. "And that car never left."

"Never left Guatemala?"

He nodded.

"The *Carrera Panamericana* came and went. This Spyder was sent to Guatemala, to a wealthy man living there. But it sat at the dock for weeks. Just sitting in its box. No one realizing what was inside."

"Why?"

"Because the politician who bought it was, shall we say, removed from authority. This was a violent time in that part of the world, you understand. His body was never found."

Never found. The words fell onto the table like lead.

Find the car, find the man. They were searching for J.C. Callahan, and he hadn't been found. But the German was oblivious.

"So the Spyder was sitting in its container," he said. "No one realizing. Until I saw it."

"You went to Guatemala?"

"Yes, of course. When he learned the Spyder wasn't delivered, Ferry Porsche sent us to Guatemala to bring it back.

"Us? Who's us?"

"Porsche sent me. And he sent Hoffman, my supervisor."

"We've heard about Hoffman. He built the engine in Callahan's car."

"Yes. Hoffman did many things at Porsche. Now this is what I will tell you, what I have told no one at the factory. You have heard the rumors. I will tell you the truth. We brought home an empty box."

Byrd stared directly into the German's laughing blue eyes. This confession, he realized, was a turning point.

"An empty box? You left the car in Guatemala?"

"It was not my decision. But yes, the Spyder stayed in the country, still in the original container."

Byrd shook his head.

"I don't get it," he said.

"It was Hoffman's idea. Karl Hoffman was my mentor, he was my friend, and he had many ideas. Crazy ideas. I was young and he had influence over me. We did something terrible and foolish. We knew the Spyder was valuable, and it was missing. So Hoffman convinced me. We shipped an empty box back to Germany."

"If you brought back nothing, then what car's in Alabama?"

"An exact replica. Once back in *Zuffenhausen*, we built a new Type 550 with the identical chassis number. It was made in *Werks I*."

He tapped his wrist.

"This car gave me my scar. I would say this is the car in Alabama. The original Spyder stayed in Guatemala, in the hands of those who would protect it."

"So the original car was . . . stolen?"

"In a manner of speaking, yes. I did not do the actual stealing, but . . . my hands are not clean."

With each revelation, Kristen Callahan was experiencing an energy revival.

"So Porsche thought the car was retrieved," she said. "But it stayed in Guatemala. Stolen. Porsche wouldn't have the documents because they thought they had the car. Nothing changed in the *Kardex*. Is this correct?"

"Yes. For Porsche, one Spyder was sent to Guatemala, and one came back. What came back was a replica built here in Stuttgart from factory parts. A genuine forgery, if you will. Porsche sold the replica, not knowing it was a replica. This is the car sitting in Alabama. You ask Porsche today, and they tell you 145 Spyders were built. But the true number is 146."

Antigua arana 146, Byrd thought. *Find the car, find the man.*

"How could you build a replica?" he asked. "I thought that wasn't possible."

THE LOST SPYDER

"It was possible in those days—because of the racing program. There were parts available to us, and the company records were not good. No computers, no robots. Only craftsmen and tools."

Byrd's mind reeled. If this German was telling the truth, they were sitting on the wrong continent. J.C. Callahan and the lost Spyder were a hemisphere away. Byrd wasn't a fish out of water, he was a fish in the wrong ocean.

"So what happened to the Spyder in Guatemala?" he asked.

"I do not know the owner, but I believe it is still there. I know it was hidden for many years. Then traded as stolen goods. Money changed hands. As I said, my own hands are not clean."

The German dropped his eyes to the table, in his first display of contrition. He took another draw from his cigarette, and exhaled.

Byrd didn't know what to make of the man, or his story. He was barely on the right side of the dirt, so maybe he no longer gave a damn about consequences. Maybe he was being paid by Callahan's powerful friends. Or maybe the crime was so ancient that it no longer mattered, was no longer even punishable. Statute of limitations and adverse possession. It was time for Charlie Byrd to think like a lawyer.

When Swofford started talking again, his voice assumed a tone of wonder.

"The Spyder changed hands many times," he said. "Never driven. It was perfect. Virgin, if you will."

Byrd reached inside his coat, and pulled out the envelope containing the Spyder build sheet. The source of the illegible scrawl across its face was now all too clear.

"Look familiar?"

"Of course. I mailed the papers to America. The numbers match the car in Mr. Callahan's garage, do they not?"

"They do," Byrd replied. "But here's what I don't understand. The Spyder was stolen when, in 1955? You replaced it with a reproduction, so Porsche never knew the difference. But the original car—who was its owner? Who had legal title? Porsche or the dead Guatemalan?"

A smirk came across the German's face.

"There was no title in those days. Anyway, after so much time passed, original title was irrelevant."

Now Kristen Callahan was confused, and borderline angry.

"What do you mean, title is irrelevant?" she said.

"Adverse possession," Byrd replied. "He's talking about the law of adverse possession."

Byrd indulged in a moment of smugness. He enjoyed explaining legal concepts to novices. Within the context of law school, he was an average—perhaps below average—student. But in the real world, he could wield a little clout. Maybe law school hadn't been a complete waste of money.

"Simply stated," he said, "Adverse possession means that after the passage of time—assuming certain conditions are met—the possessor of property becomes the rightful owner. Title automatically passes to the possessor, regardless of how the property was acquired."

"Now I don't get it. You're saying the law rewards stealing?"

"Yes," he replied. "Not exactly. There are strings attached. Like I said, conditions must be met. But adverse possession is recognized in every American state, and nations throughout the world."

"Okay, Perry Mason, explain to me why the law rewards stealing. That makes zero sense."

"The idea," he said, "is that the law wants to encourage the best use of property. If someone uses a piece of land for a long time, for example, the law will grant title to the person making best use of the land. You know, they call it squatter's rights. In Alabama it's eleven years. And no paperwork or legal filings are required. It just happens."

"This applies to cars?"

"Yeah. Adverse possession applies to works of art. Why do you think people buy stolen paintings by *Van Gogh* or *O'Keeffe* on the black market, when everybody knows they're hot? Over time, the possessor can become the rightful owner."

She swallowed the information, but not without a grimace.

"That's a pretty fucked up law. But I guess it explains why he's been so secretive. The car's been stolen?"

Byrd knew that there were strings attached. But if what the gentleman said was true and accurate, anything was possible. Proper legal title to the lost Spyder would rest with whoever possessed the car and satisfied the law of adverse possession. That person could transfer title however he or she saw fit.

The German was impressed with Byrd's knee jerk analysis.

"That is correct. As I told you, I was a young man. It was shameful to hide the car. But Hoffman knew it was valuable and there were people willing to take the risk. What can I say? I am not proud of what was done."

Byrd could smell the opportunity to think like a lawyer.

"So Hoffman possessed the car?"

"Yes. He did for a time. But he sold it once legal conditions were satisfied. The money was . . . substantial. It was helpful for both of us."

"Where is Hoffman? Can we talk to him?"

"No," the German replied. "You may not."

"Why? It sounds like he's the one who orchestrated this plan. We need to speak with him."

"I am afraid that is no longer possible."

"No longer possible? Why?"

"Because Karl Hoffman is dead. I took care of many final matters. My instructions were clear. I was to send original papers to the United States, to Mr. John Christian Callahan of Birmingham, Alabama."

Byrd looked down at the paper in his hands, and then turned his gaze back to the German. Now it all made sense. The mysterious paperwork arriving in Alabama, and Callahan's covert exit. Sure, there was an element of millionaire thrill-seeking here. But given the legal and historical considerations, it made sense. Callahan had done more than cover his tracks. He'd created a false trail.

"So here's the million dollar question," he said. "Where's this Spyder today?"

The German laughed. "It is lost, no? But I would start in the Guatemala City area. That is what I hear."

Swofford leaned forward.

"Are you going to look?" he asked.

When he heard the question, Byrd turned his eyes to Kristen Callahan's. *Guatemala?* It became apparent that his passport would be accepting a new stamp.

"Yeah," Byrd muttered. "I suppose we are."

"Then I will tell you something else. There was a special practice in the early days. We would sign our name in the cars. I remember very clearly these cars."

"Sign your name? What do you mean?"

"We would write our names into the metal. Into the car itself, you understand. Suppose you find this Spyder . . . If you look under the front hood, you'll see my initials. My initials will tell you this is the lost car."

Byrd nodded.

"One more question," he said. "Does the phrase *antigua arana* mean anything to you?"

"I do not know what it means *arana*," Swofford replied. "But of course I know Antigua. The original capital of Guatemala. It is what, only an hour from Guatemala City? Surrounded by volcanoes. Yes, I remember it well. A beautiful place."

Thus it dawned on Charlie Byrd that Antigua was a *place*—an ancient place in Guatemala.

This connection made, their next course of action became clear. Byrd took a final draw of whiskey, and sat his glass on the table.

"I know what we have to do," he said.

27

THEY SAID GOODBYE TO THE GERMAN AND STOOD IN SILENCE, Kristen Callahan clinging to Byrd's arm for support. Together they watched him walk out of the *Steigenberger Graf Zeppelin* into the night. The rain had ceased, but the air was still thick with swirling mist. Standing on the front sidewalk, Swofford turned, flattened the creases in his jacket, and gazed toward them one final time. His eyes narrowed. A barely perceptible smile lifted one corner of his mouth.

"I wish you luck," he said with a curt nod. Then he walked into the haze with short shuffling steps. They watched him go until he just seemed to disappear all at once, like a ghost.

"He's got Parkinson's," Byrd said.

She nodded, and tried again to stand on her ankle. It wouldn't hold the weight, so Byrd walked her to the elevator. She was clinging to his side. She needed his support. At least that's what he told himself.

They stood in the empty elevator, side by side, lost in thought. She leaned her weight against his body. The bottle of Jack Daniels dangled by her side like an afterthought, now only half-full. Her arm snaked around his waist. She squeezed, perhaps more than necessary. As the elevator rose, his pulse quickened. His body was responding to the stimulus.

"What about the Mercedes?" he asked. "It's in pretty bad shape."

"Everything's on old Callahan's tab," she replied. "Next question."

Byrd conceded the point. She had an answer for everything.

The elevator doors slid open with smooth precision. Her ankle began to balk, so he lifted her in his arms. He carried her down the hall to her room. He felt her warmth and her softness, caught the lingering fragrance of her perfume. His body, despite a few lingering notions of common sense and wise business practice, was shifting into overdrive. No red-blooded American male could have reacted in any other way.

Still holding her in his arms, he leaned, opened the door, and stepped inside her room. The rooms of the *Graf Zeppelin* were soundproof and utterly devoid of noise, in a manner that defied explanation. They were across the street from the *Hauptbahnhof*, the main station, and trains were passing through Stuttgart all night long. But the only sound in the room was that of silence—the soothing hum of the ventilation system, the gentle whoosh of fresh air being pumped throughout the building. The room was utterly private. They were sealed off from the outside world. They were far from Birmingham, Alabama, far from the prying eyes of the media, far from the pressure of tuition and the long shadow of a father's vulgar success. They were two adults, alone in a bedroom, heads spinning like tops, thousands of miles removed from reality. Byrd felt like a fish out of water, but he was learning to live with the sensation.

She'd booked some sort of *avant garde* suite, one more spacious than his studio apartment back home. The room was furnished with contemporary stuff that seemed totally inappropriate for the *Graf Zeppelin*, but totally in tune with this woman. The art deco bed sat low to the floor.

"Your room's different from mine," he said.

"Yeah," she replied. "I told you Baines was good."

With some effort, he lay her down on the bed. And then he felt it. His right knee, the injured one that conspired to make him a second-string offensive lineman, the same knee that survived an evening of unlikely athletic pounding in *Ludwigsberg*, finally buckled. He lost his grip, and she flopped onto the bed. He tumbled down beside her, grabbing his knee and groaning.

"My knee," he said. "Old football injury."

She laughed. He followed suit. Their eyes met, and he felt the kiss coming.

THE LOST SPYDER

He'd felt it coming all night. It percolated, simmered beneath the surface, and now, like an idea whose time had come, it wouldn't be denied.

They were drawn together in a slow magnetic harmony. Byrd couldn't turn back from his body's impulses, and he couldn't turn away from her beautiful face.

It was as if he'd never kissed a woman before, and he couldn't get enough. He felt her soft lips press against his own, tasted the hint of bourbon and salt in her mouth, inhaled the scent of her perfume. She was like fine wine, a woman to be savored and enjoyed.

He ran his hands through her tangled mass of auburn hair. It was speckled with traces of dry mud, souvenirs from their adventure in *Ludwigsberg*, but it was soft and full and delicate to the touch, and still carried a scent as sweet as her perfume. He caressed the curves of her ear, glancing his finger along the glittering silver earring that started on top and worked its way down—sun, moon, and stars, all the way down to the lobe.

They kissed again, softly, slowly, and quietly, and he felt his body respond. She ran her hands around his back, and through his hair. Her touch ignited a fire inside him, the passion that had long slumbered inside like glowing coals. Only now the coals were stoked and lit with flame.

Charlie Byrd felt . . . *alive*.

Perhaps more alive than he'd ever felt at any moment of his adult life. He was sinking into the bed, into the embrace of a woman more intriguing than any he'd ever met. A woman who despite her eccentricities, beliefs, and financial status—or perhaps because of them—aroused him more thoroughly, more completely than any he'd ever known. The realization came crashing down like a tidal wave, stoking the flames of his passion.

This time was different. *She* was different.

He looked into her eyes, shimmering pools of emerald, and he saw his own reflection.

Somewhere, deep in the recesses of his conscious mind, he realized that his twin pillars of independence and emotional distance were snapping in two like dry twigs. He was willfully, eagerly breaking his own rules. He was emotionally and physically involved.

Their entire relationship, Byrd realized, had been an exercise in foreplay. From the time he first saw Kristen Callahan, he had secretly yearned for this moment. He could no more stop this coupling than he could hold back the tide. Whether it happened in Alabama or Germany or even Guatemala, it was going to happen. He surrendered to inevitability.

Their bodies were on autopilot. They were moving and reacting, not thinking. They were acting on instinct and impulse, an alchemy of biology and bourbon-fueled passion that was liberated from reason. They were taking a leap of faith, and it felt right.

He helped her remove her shirt. Then, her bra. Her breasts were finally revealed and they did not disappoint.

The pace accelerated. They tore away the remainder of their clothing with lusty enthusiasm, tossing garments on the floor.

Within moments they were naked, and he was inside her.

Her suite at the *Steigenberger Graf Zeppelin* fell silent.

The world fell silent, but for the sounds of their lovemaking.

28

J.C. CALLAHAN OPENED HIS EYES.

He was back in familiar territory. They had brutalized him and strapped him on the bed. He was blindfolded, and relying on a small sliver of vision. His arms were outstretched, hands tied to the bedposts. His blindfold ensured darkness. He could see nothing.

His ears told him more than his eyes. Beyond the incessant hum of industrial fans, he heard nothing. No trucks rumbling in the distance, no planes flying overhead, no trace of movement outside the door. The world was silent.

He was drenched with sweat, but there was a reprieve in the air. A touch of cool, the kind that comes before dawn. It had to be the middle of the night. It was time to fight.

He'd regained a portion of strength. He was prepared to die alone, but not here. Not yet. For hours, he wrenched and twisted his wrists against the rope. Callahan was a wiry bird, and the combination of narrow wrists and slippery sweat loosened his bonds.

The bullet wound in his right side was painful, so he focused on the left hand. He twisted it back and forth, working against the rope, rubbing his skin raw. At last, in a single painful thrust, his left hand came free. He winced as the rope passed his hand.

First thing to go was the blindfold. He tugged at the cloth with his free hand. It came off easily, slipping over his head.

Finally his prison came into focus, illuminated by one lonely bare bulb hanging from the ceiling by a thin wire. In the dim light, he saw a barren room. A simple wooden table, a chair. A mirror on the wall, looking more like a jagged shard of glass.

A sliver of light bounced from the mirror onto the dusty hardwood floor. Behind the bed was a large window shrouded by thick cloth drapes.

Now the right hand. He shifted his weight on the flimsy bed. Every move brought a retort from the metal frame. He had to be quiet.

The bond was stubborn. When the right hand at last came free, it sent more stabbing sharp bolts of pain down his side. His body finally relented. He gave it permission to feel the pain.

Now the feet. He sat up in bed and went to work on the ankles. The stinking Fat Man was no Eagle Scout. The knots came loose. Callahan was free.

His mind and pulse raced. He had to think fast. Freedom felt good, too good to ever give up.

He touched one bare foot to the floor. The other followed. His shoes were gone.

He stood, slowly. The wooden floor creaked. The sound quickly faded into the night without incident.

His first instinct was the mirror. He was drawn to the mirror. Perhaps it was hubris. Perhaps it was morbid curiosity. But he had to see.

He walked across the room, his feet barely touching the ground. The wooden flooring was dry and cracked. He felt a thick splinter penetrate his right toe. He flinched and wanted to curse. He reached down, yanked out the splinter, and kept moving.

The mirror was broken. It wasn't cracked, it was a broken shard pasted on the wall, like some worthless relic from a landfill.

He looked into the mirror. What he saw took his breath away. He didn't curse or cry or look away. Rather, he found the image fascinating. Was that pale apparition actually John Christian Callahan, the renowned entrepreneur? He studied the face like a car wreck that was still ablaze.

THE LOST SPYDER

Dear God, Callahan, what on earth happened to you.

His face was a haunting interpretation of what it once had been. One eye was dark, a shiner that gleamed purple in the dim light. There were specks of dried blood throughout his face. His nose was skinned and possibly broken. His hair, usually a brilliant white, was caked with blood.

Then there was the cheek. Now he had a scar of his own. The slash in his cheek was caked with crusted blood. It wouldn't turn keloid and pink like the Man's. But it would be there so long as Callahan drew breath. When he flexed the muscles of his face, the scab stretched and threatened to break. It looked and felt like hell.

Behind that dreadful mask of a face were his eyes. Brilliant chunks of sapphire looked back, the same vibrant intelligent eyes he'd always known. The same eyes that watched his pet pig die, burned holes in Alabama businessmen, and chased young girls on the soft sand beaches of the Gulf Coast. The same eyes that watched more than six decades unfold on this earth. If eyes were windows to the soul, Callahan's soul ran deep.

Truth be told, his eyes were a chief conceit. He was proud of his eyes, and so long as they were unscathed, he could live with the rest. Money could solve the rest. The rest could be healed, either naturally or artificially. The eyes could not. He could never be like Williams; no glass eyeballs for John Christian Callahan.

He examined his torso. The wound was on his right ribcage. The bullet had grazed his body, drawing a mess of blood but not much else. Another inch to the center and he'd be dead. He'd dodged death by an inch.

He found the mirror fascinating. It was hard to turn away. He stared until he finally accepted that this was indeed his body and face. He'd survived his own private dose of torture porn. He was a walking splatter film. Someone had beaten the living shit out of John Christian Callahan.

He turned to the door. If these devils had any sense, someone would be outside. To even rotate the knob would invite discovery. It was too risky without a weapon. There was the chair . . .

He shuffled to the bed, every movement accompanied by a fireworks display of pain. He sat on the bed, rubbing the wound the splinter left behind. He'd left a few more drops of blood on the floor.

He reached underneath the bed. The mattress was soiled and dirty, and long since past its prime. His hands fished about until he pulled a sliver of wire from beneath the bed, part of a mattress coil. Perhaps an inch long, it was thin and sharp. He tucked it in his pocket.

He walked to the window. Pulling aside the heavy drapes revealed a mass of duct tape. The glass windowpanes were completely covered in opaque tape. The window was nailed shut.

Callahan peeled away a sticky strip of tape. Once again his eyes saw moonlight. The moon was bright and full, working its way across the sky. The world was still and quiet.

He peeled away more tape. The window stood on the second floor of the house. The roof below appeared to be metal. Like the rest of the house, it was cheap construction. Below the roof was a barren courtyard in the center of the compound. It was surrounded on all sides by the building.

There were two options. He could try to get the door open, risking discovery by his captors. Or he could take the chair, fling it through the window, and escape onto the roof. From the roof he might be able to reach the street. Descending into the courtyard would be no good. There he'd be trapped. Things would get ugly in a hurry.

He picked up the chair and walked to the window. He stood there for a moment, contemplating his next move. The wooden chair would shatter the glass, but that was also the problem. Glass would be everywhere. The thought of leaping barefoot through a portal of broken glass wasn't appealing.

He backed away from the window, walked to the door, and knelt. He pulled out the piece of mattress wire. He stuck the wire into the door's keyhole, and began scratching for tumblers.

He was no good at this sort of thing. He knelt there on the floor for what seemed an eternity, fumbling at the keyhole. The faint scratch of metal on metal seemed positively earsplitting.

He cursed. It wasn't working. So he gently tried the knob, and heard a click. It was a good click. The door, much to his astonishment, was unlocked.

He made one final search for a weapon. It was like going back to an empty cupboard looking for food. Maybe if he kept looking, the stuff would magically appear.

The chair. He turned the chair upside-down, and unscrewed one of the wooden legs. It was lightweight, something he could carry. He felt like a damned Neanderthal, clutching that club. He was prepared for the worst. A sentry was probably waiting outside.

He nudged open the door . . .

Nothing happened. Outside there was a silence dominated by the droning of industrial fans. The fans were still doing their work, pushing waves of stale air throughout the house.

An empty chair stood in the hall outside his door, a sibling to the one in the room. He was in a short hallway, one framed by walls of barren wood and sheet rock.

Along one side there was a wooden shelf. The shelf contained remnants—a few black candles in glass votives, a brass candlestick. The candles had burned to the core, leaving a dead forest of blackened stumps. Next to the candles was a pack of cigarettes, an ashtray filled with butts, and a few scattered wooden matchsticks. He scooped up a few matches and tucked them into his pocket.

He walked along the hallway, the floor creaking under his weight. Finally he reached a door. He paused. Was it a bedroom? Or a path to escape?

He cracked open the door. He smelled bleach and a dirty mop bucket. It was a closet, filled with cleaning supplies.

He turned and shuffled down the hall in the opposite direction. The passage forked, and he walked along the hallway away from the courtyard, away from the center of the house.

He arrived at a small foyer. Before him was the front door.

He grabbed the handle and turned. It was locked. He turned the deadbolt, freeing the mechanism. The door cracked open. One more step and he was outside.

Then came the growl. A low guttural sound, laced with menace.

A half-dozen dogs gathered on the front doorstep. They were mutts, wolf-like mongrels that fed on whatever bloody garbage they could muster.

The leader of the pack bristled. Like J.C. Callahan, the dog could smell fear. When the door cracked open, its growl burst into full song. The dog howled with venom, snapping at Callahan's leg.

The rest of the pack followed suit. They were vicious, and their relentless howling shattered the silence.

Shit. Dead end, Callahan.

He slammed the door shut. To step outside and confront these hounds of hell would have been suicide.

From inside the house came noises. Men were awake, and they were coming. He heard a door slam and footsteps in the hall. He had nowhere to run. He was trapped between the hounds and the devils. He clutched his weapon and prepared for battle.

When the man rounded the corner, he entered like a bucking bull, full of anger. Callahan had the element of surprise.

Greetings from Fort Rucker, Alabama.

He swung the makeshift club. It bounced off the devil's head with a hollow thump, like a baseball hitting a wooden bat. This was, Callahan's nose told him, Mr. Body Odor. He slumped to the floor in an unconscious heap.

Callahan attempted to move past, to work his way to the other side of the house. Perhaps there was another exit.

He stepped into the hallway and froze. The Man with the Scar was there, a menacing black shape in the darkness. He stood blocking the hallway like a stone golem. Callahan's steely blue eyes met the yellow orbs of his captor.

Callahan lashed out, swinging the club in a crisp arc. He caught air, and was overextended. His captor lunged forward. His fist glanced off Callahan's skull and the old man lost his balance. He fell hard, chin bouncing on the floor. His makeshift club clattered to the ground.

He attempted to raise his head. He couldn't.

Just before he blacked out, John Christian Callahan turned his gaze upward. It was met by the yellow eyes of The Man with the Scar, glowing in the darkness, alive with smoke and flame, towering overhead like a Godly apparition. Then he brought down his fist one more time.

It crashed down like a thunderclap. Callahan saw a flash of light, and then blackness.

৵৶

He awoke to the familiar musty smell, cold concrete floor, cinder block walls, and unrelenting darkness.

He was beneath the earth.

He was bound, hands and feet.

This time, the bonds were tight.

I've lost, he thought. *For once in my life, I've truly lost.*

29

FOR MOST OF CHARLIE BYRD'S LIFE, Guatemala was as meaningful a destination as Antarctica, Madagascar, or Swaziland. It was one more distant spot on a map, one of those mysterious countries south of the American border, beyond Mexico, completely off his radar screen. It had directly affected Byrd's existence exactly one time, and that was when his hometown hosted a World Cup qualifying match between Guatemala and the United States.

The Americans had scheduled the game for Birmingham's Legion Field, the sadly aging stadium once hailed as "football capital of the South," in the hopes of gaining a substantial home field advantage. Soccer being far less popular amongst Alabamians than old fashioned American football, the local fan turnout was modest. But amongst the crowd of 31,624 were thousands of Birmingham's working class Guatemalans, on hand in force to cheer the visiting team. It ruffled more than a few feathers to see Americans outnumbered in their own home stadium, as boisterous blue-clad Guatemalans proudly waved sky blue Guatemalan flags and filled the arena with the song of their national anthem. The Americans ultimately won the contest on the field by a score of 2-0. But the soccer game in Birmingham served as wake-up call to the city, vivid evidence of Guatemala's daily impact on Alabama's productive farms, busy restaurants, and well manicured lawns.

Now Charlie Byrd found himself in Guatemala. He was, once again, in bed with Kristen Callahan. The chemistry between them had moved fast, too fast. After Byrd's personal levee of professionalism collapsed in Stuttgart, their relationship had quickly rushed to the next level of intimacy. In Guatemala, they hadn't even bothered to book a second room.

But this woman was all about moving fast. With almost no advance warning, no time for mental preparation, Charlie Byrd found himself waking up on his third continent in a matter of days. His time with Kristen Callahan had been a heady indoctrination into the problem-solving power of deep pockets. Byrd thought he understood wealth, but this was different. The Callahans had real money, in amounts that could move mountains. She could make one phone call, and in a matter of minutes, flights were chartered, hotels were secured, and actions were pursued. Their roller-coaster itinerary kept taking wild swings in unexpected directions, yet money was never an impediment to progress. In hindsight, Byrd's thousand dollar daily fee seemed modest, even naive.

He looked again at the woman lying by his side.

Kristen Callahan was asleep.

She was curled in the fetal position, wrapped in a colorful cotton cocoon. Her face peeked out from beneath the quilt. She was in bed—the only bed in the room.

Charlie Byrd couldn't sleep.

Ordinarily, Byrd could sleep anywhere. This was a source of personal pride, and one reason he was so good at his work.

But under the circumstances, with that woman resting beside him, Byrd couldn't sleep. He sat on the edge of the bed and stared out the window. The glass was lined with thick iron bars.

The sun was rising. Soft light began to stream into the room through the flimsy orange gauze that served as curtains.

Byrd turned again to study her face, bathed in the first rays of sunlight. Everything looked better in morning light, and her already gorgeous face was no exception. She looked angelic. But he knew she was no angel.

She was a bundle of contradictions. Wealthy and trashy. Intelligent and scatterbrained. Irreverent and devout. Sometimes she was intimidating. Sometimes he wondered how she managed to tie her shoes. Byrd skirted issues of politics, but she was probably a limousine liberal. How many conservatives sport yin-yang tattoos?

They were so different, and yet they had come together like it was meant to be. Watching her lying in bed asleep, curled up like an innocent, he saw none of her feisty personality. He saw her not as an heiress. He saw her as a woman, and a beautiful one.

She was exhausted. The grind of nonstop travel was finally taking its toll. First-class flights were no substitute for sleep. Skipping from continent to continent will wreak havoc on anyone's biorhythms. The unfolding timeline was dizzying. From the instant they decided to embark on the Spyder quest, they had been moving constantly, like sharks sniffing an oceanic blood trail. Only they didn't have an actual trail, they had clues and rumors and a leap of faith.

For Byrd, being a low rent Birmingham PI meant keeping odd hours. But he was no longer low rent, nor was he in Alabama. He was a thousand miles to the south and a world away. And on this morning, he wanted something other than sleep.

His mind jumped back across the ocean, back to the bourbon-soaked revelation in Germany. The *antigua arana*. Antigua did mean ancient. But Antigua wasn't a description. Antigua was a place, an ancient place in Guatemala. Byrd went to Antigua with no expectations, for he'd never once thought of visiting Guatemala.

But Antigua was a remarkable surprise. Thanks to the conquistadors who designed it, Antigua felt European. The city was, he noted with irony, more European than Europe. Whereas Stuttgart offered a gleaming example of modern post-war Germany, Antigua was a time capsule. The town was a faded postcard from a vanished civilization. The Spaniards were gone, but their legacy remained. With much of its original colonial architecture intact, the town was a dusty jewel nestled in the wilderness. The spirit of the dead infused the cobblestone streets and decaying ruins that lay in the shadow of three volcanoes.

Antigua was populated by ghosts. Ghosts of Spanish conquistadors, and of their subjects. If Byrd was correct, Antigua also held the ghost of a sad old man's dream. *Find the car, find the man.*

Byrd gazed upon her sleeping face. She unconsciously shifted in bed to escape the morning sun, revealing more of her upper body. She was wearing some sort of fancy nightgown, the kind he'd only seen in *Victoria's Secret* catalogs. He'd never bought such clothing for a woman. To do so would be an impractical waste. But he felt a change in philosophy was underway.

He was sharing a bed with her. Kristen Callahan was no longer just an attractive client. She was now a lover. He was caught in a relationship with this wildcat, and it made him nervous. She was accustomed to having things her way. So was Byrd. They had chemistry, but their chemistry was volatile. The sex had been manic, intense, and raw. Those few moments in Germany had changed everything. The most addictive sensation was not the sex itself, but the moments immediately thereafter. For a few fleeting seconds they were able to lie together in bed, naked in every sense of the word, stripped free of tension and pretension, focused not on a missing man but rather on each other.

With most relationships, especially with his assorted Birmingham SOL girlfriends, Charlie Byrd dictated the flow of events. But with Callahan, he felt out of control. He found himself simply reacting to the roller-coaster ride. She was wild, and could be unpredictable. Perhaps that was her allure.

Charlie Byrd enjoyed being alone. A bachelor by choice, he understood the many personal and professional benefits of emotional distance. Yet here he was in a Guatemalan hotel, gazing at her sleeping face.

What the hell happened? Business was business. He'd done work for plenty of sexy young wifeys in Birmingham, many of whom would've embraced a revenge romance. It would've been easy to cross the line. It would've been easy for a handsome no-strings-attached young buck to take advantage of those wives. To use their vulnerability.

It never happened. He never crossed that line.

But damn. He really did like this woman. The line was now squarely in his rear view mirror.

He had to get away from the temptation for a moment. To stop staring at her face. He had to leave.

He slipped on his boots and walked to the door. He turned the deadbolt, gently rotated the knob, and stepped out of the room.

The air was chilly. Outside the door was a shallow water fountain, framed by candles that burned to their core. He locked the door behind him, and stepped across the stone path into the adjacent lobby.

Casa de Mayor was a quiet bed and breakfast located a few blocks from the heart of Antigua.

This was the *Semana Santa*, the Holy Week, the desk clerk said. Rooms were scarce. They paid top dollar to secure the last.

It was true. Thousands of Guatemalans crowded Antigua for the famous Easter celebration. All the hotels were booked. They were lucky to get a room at all, much less one in a comfortable place like *Casa de Mayor*. Under normal circumstances, Byrd would've enjoyed sharing a bed in this place. But these weren't normal circumstances, and she wasn't a normal woman.

Byrd nodded to the desk clerk.

"Message? We have message?"

"No *señor*, no message," he replied. "You want breakfast?"

"*Si*. But later. I wait for friend."

Byrd realized that he was speaking broken English. He sometimes fell into such habits when talking to foreigners. There was no need to distort his own English just because the other person was bilingual.

Venturing outside the protective confines of *Casa de Mayor*, he stepped onto the sidewalk. The sunlight was now pervasive, and he watched morning dew glisten.

No message. Their efforts thus far in Antigua had fallen flat. But they were here for good reason. The old German had insisted that Antigua was the place.

A large school bus rumbled past. It spewed clouds of noxious exhaust, black as ink. It seemed every old Bluebird bus from the 1960's was being used for public transportation. They were called chicken buses, and were painted every color of the rainbow—purple, pink, blue, yellow—all at the same time. Cheerful religious slogans exhorting passengers to find Jesus were scrawled across their sides.

This bus was packed full of morning commuters, hard-faced Guatemalan men and women. Their expressionless faces stared out the windows at Charlie Byrd. To them he was another rich *Semana Santa* tourist, browsing Antigua at leisure while they faced another day of labor in the fields.

Byrd ducked into a corner store and grabbed a bottle of Evian. He hated paying for water. Why pay for something that was free? He considered bottled water the biggest scam of the 21st Century, comparable to toll roads and Wall Street bailouts.

But Guatemala was no place to drink the water. He'd gladly pay to avoid a monster case of the shits. *Montezuma's Revenge* wasn't to be tempted.

At the counter, Byrd realized he had no Guatemalan money.

"You take dollar? Dollar okay?" he asked the teenage shopkeeper, again dumbing down his own English.

"Sure, dollars are fine, *señor*" the young man replied with a bemused expression.

Byrd handed over a ten-dollar bill and collected his change. He thought he'd better get back to the room.

༶⚬༃

At the *Casa de Mayor*, he fished the key out of his pocket, clicked open the door, and stepped inside. Their room was brighter now, as the burgeoning sunlight outside grew more confident.

Yet she was still asleep.

He gently closed the door, and her eyes sprang open. She was startled, and struggled to focus on the figure in the doorway. Once his identity was clear, she relaxed back into her quilt cocoon.

"Byrd," she said. "What time is it? Where have you been?"

"It's seven o'clock," he replied. "Central Standard Time."

One of the upsides of Antigua was the time zone. They were back in the same time zone as Birmingham, just shifted 1300 miles to the south.

He held aloft the bottle of water.

"Got some water," he said. "I'm gonna brush my teeth."

He stepped into the bathroom. It was a narrow space, one replete with authentic colonial and Mayan details. At some point in time, *Casa de Mayor* hired a fine decorator, probably a high-priced American. The stuff was too authentic to be authentic.

After pouring a dash of bottled water over his toothbrush, he brushed his teeth. He turned on the sink faucet and spat, careful to avoid the running water.

He stepped back into the room. She was fully awake now, although still horizontal. Her eyes opened wide and studied Charlie Byrd.

"Sleep well?" he asked.

"Not really. I keep having the same dream," she replied. "Like my mind is a record that keeps skipping. What about you? You didn't sleep much. I thought you could sleep anywhere, any place. "

"So did I," he replied. "But this situation is a little unusual."

"I know," she said. "Sharing a bed with me isn't easy."

For a moment, he was without words. Sharing a bed with this woman was easy. Too easy. That was the problem. If he woke up every morning and saw her face, well—there were worse fates.

"They're serving breakfast now," he said. "I'm going to go get some coffee. I assume the coffee is safe to drink."

"Changing the subject? Yeah, the coffee's safe. Hang on a minute. I'll go with you."

As she swiveled her legs from beneath the covers, he caught a glimpse of her pale pink panties beneath.

She pulled on a pair of denim jeans right over the gown. Slipping on a t-shirt and ball cap, she took a glance in the mirror and was ready to go.

"See, I'm not so high maintenance," she said.

ᔑᓍ

Breakfast was on the rooftop patio. The roof afforded an expansive view of the city. Antigua Guatemala was compact, the entire town covering not more than a few square miles. The city was nestled in a valley, squarely in the middle of three volcanoes. These green mountains—*Volcan Aqua, Volcan Acatenango*, and *Volcan Fuego*—had famously remained active over the years, with *Fuego* issuing smoke from its peak on a daily basis. They dominated the horizon, like silent sentinels from the past.

Unlike the modest hills of Birmingham, these were legitimate mountains. Charlie Byrd thought of his hometown, and the bizarre journey that brought him to Guatemala.

"They need a Vulcan down here," he said.

"What?"

"You know. Vulcan. The big statue in Birmingham? He's the God of volcanoes."

"Oh. Right."

Her voice was flat, uninterested. She wasn't in the mood to discuss the eccentricities of Alabama.

So they nursed their fatigue. Morning sunshine streamed upon the roof. The air was chilly, but the sun was bright. They sat beneath a large umbrella, drinking coffee and inhaling the standard breakfast fare. Omelet, bacon, toast, jelly—the hotel covered all the bases, everything to satisfy Americans willing to pay top dollar.

Byrd cradled a mug of Guatemalan coffee, a far cry from his usual fare. The coffee was damned good. They served it the proper way, black.

"How's the ankle?" he asked.

"Ankle's fine," she replied. "How's the knee?"

"Fine."

The knee was second-string, he thought, but it was fine.

"What's the word from the States?" he asked.

"Same as last night. Cops don't know a damn thing. Their trail ends in Germany. They think I'm a nut job."

"You are a nut job. So is your father, for that matter."

"You joined the club in Germany, remember?"

He shrugged off the comment. He didn't want to talk about Germany, especially what happened at the *Graf Zeppelin*. Yes, he had joined the club. He was more than just involved. But he wanted to sidestep the perplexing issue of sex and focus on the task at hand.

Find the car, find the man.

"What about the investigation?"

"Other than the chartered flight to Stuttgart, they got nothing. No electronic traces. Wherever he went, he covered all his bases, and he was spending cash."

Outside, another chicken bus rumbled past. The streets were alive with the sounds of people and horses and psychedelic buses. The ancient town of Antigua was awake.

"No ransom demands, either," he said. "If this was a case of kidnapping, we would've heard something by now."

She nodded. "That scares me too. He could be in a hospital, incapacitated. I'd feel better if we heard something. Speaking of, have you checked with the front desk?"

"Yeah. No messages," he said. "If he's here, or if anyone knows he's here, they're keeping quiet."

"I think he's been here. I can feel it. Besides, it would make sense."

"It would?"

"It's classic Callahan," she said. "He's the master of head games. That whole chartered flight to Germany—from what Swofford said, the whole thing was faked."

"Maybe the lost Spyder is still illegal," Byrd said. "It wouldn't be beyond your father to break the law?"

"Nothing he does surprises me any more," she replied. "Think about it. If the car's in Antigua, he could've driven down here to get it. He even had the trailer on the day he left."

"Driven through Mexico?"

"It's not as far as you think. Have you looked around Birmingham lately?"

Byrd nodded. Like most Southern states, Alabama received a healthy influx of cheap labor from Guatemala and Mexico. They came to Alabama seeking opportunity, and found it in agricultural fields, construction sites, and restaurants. Instead of earning two-dollars a day in Guatemala City, they made ten-dollars an hour in Birmingham. The road between Alabama and Guatemala, while lengthy, was well traveled.

Byrd took another swig of coffee. The caffeine was kicking in.

"Okay, so let's say he drove down here. He could've stayed for the *Semana Santa* festival. I think we should make one more sweep of the hotels."

"Sounds like you've planned our morning. Just let me grab a shower before we go."

She stood from the table.

"Be careful in the shower," he said. "Don't drink the water."

"Don't worry," she replied. "Contrary to popular belief, I'm not an idiot."

She bounded down the stairs. Byrd was alone on the rooftop, save the Mayan waitress. She hovered near the table, her alert brown eyes focused on his coffee cup.

"More coffee *señor*?"

"Yes, that would be nice. *Gracias*."

He barely slept last night, and it was going to be a long day in Antigua. If John Christian Callahan was here, they were close.

But they needed a break.

And Charlie Byrd needed all the coffee he could get.

30

T HE WOMAN LEANED FORWARD, EYES CLOSED. She was topless. In each hand she cupped one of her breasts. Her skin was smooth and glassy. Her face, neither Spanish nor Mayan, was expressionless and serene. She graced the busy park with a sense of calm.

Charlie Byrd stared at the woman. It was hard not to stare. She was, after all, more than two centuries old. From her nipples trickled delicate streams of water, sparkling like crystal in the afternoon sun. She was a centerpiece of Antigua's *Parque Central*, and Byrd was mesmerized.

"What's she got that I haven't got?" Kristen Callahan said. "I mean, besides a nice pair of tits."

He looked at Callahan. She had a nice pair herself, he wanted to say. But he kept the thought to himself.

"We need a fountain like this in Birmingham," he replied. "I'd much rather look at a topless woman than a Satanic goat."

"Someone would protest," she said, wagging her finger. "Nipples are naughty."

A young Mayan girl approached. No more than ten-years-old, she wore a traditional woven skirt. The skirt was colorful, boasting brilliant hues of indigo and jade. Resting on the her head was a wide shallow basket filled with trinkets. There were simple woven bracelets, and a selection of handmade dolls.

"Señor," she said, tilting the basket ever so slightly. She smiled, but there was urgency in her voice. "I give you good price, señor. Everything one dollar."

Byrd's stomach clenched into knots. Back home in Alabama, it was easy to send street people packing. His downtown neighborhood had its fair share of beggars and scam artists. Byrd had heard every random unverifiable sob story from these types, and had long since grown cold to their pleas.

But it was hard to say no to these girls. They lived in poverty, and tried to make an honest living selling to tourists. They weren't begging per se. They were selling. The problem at the moment was one of supply and demand. Excessive supply and minimal demand.

To buy something only encouraged the others. Parque Central was crowded with women, young and old, selling such crafts. They hovered throughout the square in a strange sort of orbit, balancing baskets of crafts on their heads, and gauging the gravitational pull of tourists. If one tourist was buying, an optimistic crowd of baskets and smiling ladies would soon follow. This was a law of physics in Antigua Guatemala.

Callahan watched the scene unfold.

"Don't do it," she said. "We'll never get out of here."

Byrd reached into his pants pocket, pulled out a wad of cash, and peeled off a five-dollar bill. Picking up a single doll, he quietly handed the money to the girl.

"No change," he said.

"Gracias, señor." This time her voice matched her beaming smile. She lowered her head, and put the basket back in place.

Byrd pulled a folded sheet of yellow paper from his pocket.

"Wait," he said, thrusting the paper to the girl. "Take a look at this, *por favor*."

The girl accepted the paper but didn't appear to understand. She turned and went back to work. Byrd saw the basket rejoin its natural orbit, gravitating toward the next American with clean clothes and an honest face.

The fliers were largely inspired by the Natalee Holloway case. When the girl went missing in Aruba, her mother blanketed the Caribbean island with small informational posters. The images, plastered upon light poles and newspaper dispensers and everything else available, became icons of the search. Such posters, Byrd realized, were not only useful on the ground but also across the airwaves. Both print and televised media liked visual icons, easy dramatic summations of a case.

They got a little creative with the fliers. The color choice was an eye-catching yellow. In addition to the bilingual headline that shouted "LOST" and its Spanish equivalent "PERDIDO" from the top of the page, there were a couple of photos. The first was of J.C. Callahan's face, in what appeared to be a standard corporate head shot. The second, upon Byrd's insistence, was of a Porsche 550 Spyder. The poster was completed with the usual height, weight, age, and police contact information in both languages.

The inclusion of the Spyder was unorthodox to say the least, but that was part of Byrd's prevailing strategy. He kept returned to the reassuring catchphrase that clicked through his brain: *find the car, find the man.*

"You gave her a flyer?" Callahan asked.

"Yeah. You never know."

"That was a generous gratuity."

"It was more than enough."

"You're a softie."

"I can't say no to a pretty face."

"Should I be insulted?" she asked. "You've said no to me on several occasions."

"I'm standing with you in Central America," he replied. "Looking for the Holy Grail. This hardly counts as refusal."

More aspiring young salesgirls approached, and soon Byrd was afloat in a sea of shallow baskets. They encircled him, beckoning like sirens. They would, he was assured, give him good price.

He was suddenly ready to leave the park. He wouldn't solve the problems of Guatemala today.

"Let's get out of here," he said.

She nodded. "By the way, you better watch what you keep in your pants. Every pickpocket in the country is here."

"I can take care of my pants," he replied.

She was flirting again. He smiled at the irony. Who would have believed it? Charlie Byrd was sleeping with a blue blood. He was playing hard to get.

THE LOST SPYDER

They walked away from Parque Central, away from the hordes of hovering baskets beckoning "*Señor*," away from the thieves lurking in the crowd. It was the middle of the day and Antigua was alive. The city burbled with the enthusiasm of *Semana Santa*. The energy of Holy Week was everywhere.

Seeking to escape the dense crowds, they walked down a side street. But the crowds didn't thin. People gathered along the street in anticipation.

"A *procession* is coming," she said. "Let's stop."

The crowd gave them little choice, so they stood along the side of the road and waited. Byrd took off his backpack and clutched it to his chest.

A colorful carpet stretched some twenty feet along the center of the road. Composed of dyed sawdust and fresh flowers, the carpet was a handmade, fragile work of art.

The procession walked down the street like a parade. There was a band marching, playing all the way. The music reminded Byrd of the blues, something he'd heard in New Orleans. It was somehow cheerful and sorrowful at the same time.

Leading the parade was a wooden float bearing the image of Christ. The float depicted Christ carrying the cross, his face a mask of pain.

"Looks like Jesus drank the water," Byrd said.

As the float approached, he realized it was being carried. The shoulders of young women supported the load. Mayan girls, their faces straining with discomfort, marched steadily forward like pallbearers carrying a giant casket.

At times, the float wobbled, and the procession slowed. But it always marched forward, inching closer and closer to the beautiful carpet of sawdust and flowers.

"The carpet is called an *alfombra*," she said. "Enjoy it while it lasts."

The procession finally reached the carpet. Without hesitation, the girls marched over the beautiful work of art. With each staggering step, Christ dragged his cross forward, and the carpet collapsed into a morass of sawdust and crushed flowers. In seconds, it was destroyed. The procession continued down the road, and the music receded.

Byrd watched with bemused interest.

"People spend all day creating this thing," he said, "only to trash it?"

"In so many words, yes," she replied.

"I don't get it," he said. "Why create this great work of art and then just wipe it out?"

"Maybe once you get out of law school," she said, "you should go back to Sunday School."

The procession had passed. Its time upon the ceremonial carpet was brief, no more than a minute. It was enough. The beautiful carpet was nothing more than a memory. A few onlookers grabbed the remnants of crushed flowers. A cleaning crew swept the scattered sawdust into garbage bags. People surged into the streets, and life along this block of Antigua resumed its normal pace.

Byrd motioned to a nearby coffee shop.

"How about this place? I don't think we've been there yet."

They stepped inside and found themselves in a bookstore. The shelves were lined with typical tourist fare. Books about the city, maps, and postcards. At the back of the store, a hallway led to the adjacent courtyard.

"Cafe must be out back," he said.

They walked onto the back patio. A handful of wrought iron tables and chairs were scattered throughout. On the wall was a cork bulletin board crowded with handwritten ads. Rooms for rent, Spanish lessons, furniture for sale—the usual expatriate student fare.

Antigua had a thriving community of Western students. They crowded its cheap restaurants and seedy bars, bringing dollars to the local economy. Many claimed to be studying a language, but Byrd was dubious. He'd seen this type of student before, always in exotic locales, usually during happy hour. Their commitment to education was debatable. Their commitment to escape was not. Antigua was a fine place to escape.

Perhaps one of these students had seen the missing man from Alabama. It was worth a shot.

"How many do we have left?"

"At least a dozen."

Byrd unzipped his backpack and pulled out a stack of yellow paper. If he'd learned one thing from Callahan and his cars, it was that yellow was guaranteed to turn heads.

He approached the bulletin board, pulled out a couple of tacks, and stuck the yellow sheet in the center. It made sense to blanket Antigua with these things, and he felt some small measure of satisfaction with each one posted.

"Until we can get him on a milk carton," she said, "these will have to do."

Kristen Callahan had a sense of humor. Byrd had to concede that much. Not many people could find humor in this situation. Comedy equals tragedy plus time, the formula went. She was rewriting the formula.

They each got a cup of coffee. It cost thirty cents, Byrd noted with delight, a far cry from the trendy price-gouging back home. This society was not without its charms. Despite the underbelly, Guatemala maintained an affordable elegance.

"We're going to need more sheets," he said. "Let's go make some copies."

They left the cafe and walked through town. The sidewalks remained crowded with tourists and street vendors. They finally arrived at the post office, a poorly marked building with faded white paint flaking off its walls. Directly across the street was *Mercado Central*, a sprawling open air marketplace.

"While you make copies," she said, "I'm going to the market."

"You want to go shopping?" he asked. It was just like a woman to want to go shopping.

"It's the middle of the day," she replied. "You're being overprotective."

"That's impossible in this country. It's too dangerous. Wait five minutes, and we'll go together."

She relented, and they walked inside the post office. She sat down on a wooden bench and began retying her shoe.

No wonder her father is missing, Byrd thought. *If he's anything like his daughter.*

Antigua, he realized, was not as it seemed. On the surface, the town was quaint and charming and full of Godly intent. But despite every appearance to the contrary, Antigua wasn't a safe place. Far worse than pickpockets walked the streets.

He came back from the counter with fresh copies of the poster. "White will have to do," he said, showing her the papers. "They don't have yellow."

He stuffed the posters into his backpack. They walked outside and across the street into Mercado Central. The central marketplace of Antigua was thick with people. Elderly Mayan women sat on the ground, fanning themselves in the sun. At their feet were large baskets of fruit and vegetables. Other baskets were filled with common household items like toothpaste and soap. Such items, Byrd realized, weren't so common in parts of Guatemala.

They strolled past piles of produce and entered the crafts area of the market. Instead of spreading their wares on the ground, the Mayan art merchants occupied a large tent. For sale were traditional masks, woven fabrics, hammocks, pottery and candles. All would've been of no interest whatsoever to Charlie Byrd, but the prices were favorable. Everything was cheap, and that was enough to sustain his attention.

He stopped in front of a booth. To stop, he realized, was a mistake. The proprietor of the booth, a Mayan boy, was immediately upon him. The boy was no more than ten years old.

"*Señor*," the boy said, "what do you like? For you I give good price."

Byrd was both amused and impressed. The boy wore no shirt. His face was unclean, but his brown eyes sparkled with intelligence. At an age when most American children would be playing video games, this kid was running a store.

Byrd scanned the collection of masks and artistic trinkets before his eye found one of interest.

"I like the monkey mask," he said. "How much for the monkey?"

The boy raised a wooden staff. At the end of the staff was a hook. Using the staff, he lifted the monkey mask off the top shelf, and lowered it down to Byrd's outstretched hands.

"Eighty *quetzales*," the boy replied. "Eighty *quetzales* for monkey."

Byrd paused while he did the math. The boy wanted about twelve dollars. Sensing Byrd's hesitation, the boy didn't delay.

"Seventy quetzales for you," he said. "For you, I give very good price."

"You take dollar? Dollar okay?"

The boy nodded eagerly. "Si señor, dollar okay. Ten dollar for monkey. Ten dollar is good price."

Byrd nodded. "Ten dollars it is," he said.

He took off his backpack and reached inside. Then he pulled out a ten-dollar bill and handed it over. He had a pocketful of Callahan cash, and it felt right to spread it around.

The boy smiled and wrapped the monkey mask in a piece of brown paper.

"You want another señor?" he asked. "I give you very good price for two.

For two, sixty quetzales each."

Byrd shook his head. "One monkey is enough."

He placed the mask in his backpack and zipped it shut. He put the backpack on and walked away from the booth.

Kristen Callahan smiled.

"You could have gotten it for five bucks," she said. "You didn't bargain much."

"That kid needs the money more than I do," he replied. "Imagine being his age and working."

"Like I said, Byrd. You're a softie."

He grunted. Charlie Byrd didn't like being called soft. But in this case, he was willing to accept the charge.

"It's been a long day," he said. "How about we head back to the room and get some rest. We've covered the town with flyers."

"Okay," she said. "Back to the room."

He knew that they needed some sort of media strategy. If J.C. Callahan was in the area, then establishing some sort of media presence would help on several levels. They needed to find a good interpreter, and coordinate with the authorities. They'd need to budget for bribes.

At that moment he felt a slight tug on his backpack. His wallet was inside the backpack, and a small hand was tugging at it.

To foil the pickpocket, he spun hard.

The pickpocket was not what he expected.

Not at all.

31

FOR A MOMENT, CHARLIE BYRD DIDN'T RECOGNIZE THE GIRL.

She looked different. Her basket of Mayan trinkets was gone. More importantly, so was her smile. It was replaced by an expression that he couldn't identify. Anxiety, perhaps?

Expecting to see a man, or men, Byrd had whipped around violently. The girl was startled. He'd caught her off-guard.

"Sorry, honey," he said once her identity became clear. "I thought you were a pickpocket."

"*Señor*," the girl said quietly. "*Calle de los Pasos.*"

High school Spanish left Byrd ill-equipped for actual conversation. He didn't understand.

"*Calle de los Pasos*," she said. She looked over her shoulder, then handed Byrd a piece of scarlet cloth. It was a woven placemat, handmade in the traditional fashion.

Byrd shook his head and tried to give it back.

"Sorry, no more shopping for me today," he said.

"*Maria y Isabella*," she said. "*Calle de los Pasos.*"

The girl refused the cloth, and Byrd watched her disappear back into the crowded marketplace. She ran away and didn't look back.

Byrd still held the folded cloth in his hand.

Kristen Callahan watched the girl disappear into the crowd. "What was that all about? Was that the girl from the park?"

"I think so," he replied. "She must've followed us. I have no clue what she just said."

He unfolded the cloth, and a yellow piece of paper fluttered to the ground.

"This is just a placemat," he said. "Nothing special."

Callahan bent over and picked up the paper.

"This looks familiar," she said. "It's our poster. Return to sender."

She flipped over the paper. On the back were the following handwritten words: *Maria y Isabella. Calle de los Pasos—9a Calle Oriente.*

"We stand out here like a sore thumb," he said. "What does it say?"

She handed the paper over and he examined the writing.

"*Calle* means street," he said. "She's given us a couple of street names. Can you grab the map?"

"Yeah."

He turned so that his back was facing Callahan. She unzipped his pack and removed a tourist brochure. The map was simple, but Antigua was a simple town, consisting of only a few dozen intersecting streets. It was easily navigated.

"*Calle de los Pasos* is across town. Actually, these two streets are a couple of blocks from our hotel. We're going that direction anyway. Let's check it out on the way back."

"And the children shall lead," she replied. "Do you think this is her name? Maria Isabella? Maybe this is her house. Maybe she's selling over there. That's what you get for being a softie and handing out fat tips."

"*Maria y Isabella*," he said. "*y* means and. Maria and Isabella are two people."

They wound their way back through the dusty streets of Antigua, past the elegant decaying Spanish ruins. The streets were bustling with the energy of Semana Santa.

The pubs were open for business, and already stocked with Western students. The beer, Byrd noted, was especially cheap between five and seven o'clock.

"Want something cold?" he asked. "A beer sounds good right now."

"You seem to alternate between caffeine and alcohol," she replied. "I guess it's time for alcohol."

"One beer won't hurt," he said. "Indulge me."

They stepped through the open doorway, past the chalkboard cheerfully announcing that happy hour was in session. The pub was like so many others in Antigua. The room was dominated by a rustic wooden bar, one lined with young Americans and Europeans wearing scruffy beards and fraternity t-shirts. Along the opposite wall was the obligatory billboard of handwritten ads, each fastened with thumbtacks and staples. Byrd noted that their own yellow sheet was still posted. The flier was partially covered by someone seeking a roommate for his two-bedroom apartment—furniture and utilities included, $225 a month.

Byrd went to the bar, and came back with two bottles of *Gallo* beer, the local favorite. He took a seat next to Callahan—despite the presence of nubile young coeds, he noted, she was the prettiest woman in the room. They sat in flimsy plastic chairs at a small wooden table, away from the chattering crowds of drinking students.

"Two dollars, two beers," he said. "I wonder if they have a law school in Antigua. Maybe I could finish my degree here."

"What's wrong with Birmingham School of Law?"

"What's wrong is they charge for tuition," he replied. "I hate debt. It's always lurking in the back of my mind."

"You pay it back over thirty years, right? Isn't it basically a finance type of deal?"

He took a long drink of the Gallo. A finance type of deal? She clearly had no clue what it meant to be in debt.

"That's what most people do," he said.

"You don't?"

"We'll see. If it takes thirty years I'll be pissed. Everything I own is paid for. Everything except law school." He took another swig of the cold beer and continued.

"I just hate the feeling of debt, of owing somebody money. Even if that somebody is a bank. Drives me nuts."

"I know what you mean," she said.

But how could she? For some reason, the tone of her voice rubbed him the wrong way. A couple swallows of beer and he was already speaking his mind.

"You know what I mean?" he said. "How could you possibly know what I mean?"

She rolled her eyes.

"Here we go," she said. "Believe it or not, I've had problems in my life. You aren't the only person with issues."

"You may have problems," he replied. "Hell, I won't dispute that. That's why we're here."

He got control of his tongue again. She'd been through hell, and he wasn't being very thoughtful. Something in her tone pissed him off, but he got it under control. If they were going to maintain some sort of ongoing romantic relationship, he needed to compromise.

"You've got problems," he said after some consideration. "But your problems aren't financial. Having a scratch on your Porsche is not a real problem."

"Have I worried about tuition payments? No. I'll give you that one. But my life isn't some fantasy land."

"Yes, actually, it is."

"You have no idea. News flash, lawyer boy. The toughest problems in life have nothing to do with finance."

"Tell that to the kids down here in Guatemala."

"Different matter entirely," she replied. "In fact, you just made my point."

"Really? How so?"

"Some people have this chip on their shoulder because my father made a lot of money and lives in a big house."

"With a few hundred cars."

"A few dozen."

"Okay, a few dozen exceedingly rare, outrageously valuable, cars." Byrd was enjoying this conversation, perhaps a little too much. "But I don't have a chip on my shoulder. I'm just saying that you can't possibly relate to my situation. My family's a little different."

She perked up at the mention of family.

"Where's your family from?" she asked. "I mean, where in Europe? Have you researched it?"

"The short answer is no," he replied. "I've got a little German, a little Norwegian. My great grandmother was a full-blooded Cherokee Indian."

"Wow. I had no idea."

"Basically I'm an American mutt. Don't have much information. How about you?"

"Same sort of deal," she said. "We've called ourselves Irish Catholic, but don't have much to prove it. That seems common in the South. Sometimes I think it's what drives my father. He doesn't know his own roots, so he's determined to build some of his own."

"I'd say he's made a name for himself. He's pretty well off."

"It's all relative. We're all pretty well off compared to most of the world. Take a look around. In the barrios of Central America, people are living in shacks. No running water, no sanitation—no nothing."

"No disputing that."

"Your piece-of-shit truck is worth more than some homes down here."

"Now I would dispute that."

"Don't, because you'd be wasting your time."

"So wealth is relative. That's your point?"

"If you don't have food, you've got financial problems. People in America have more food than they can eat. Half the country is obese. Looked in a mirror lately?"

Byrd raised his glass in a cheerful toast and took another swig of the Gallo. "Beer is good for you."

"Once you get beyond food, shelter, and clothing, the rest is bullshit."

"Interesting words coming from someone who drives a $630,000 yellow car. Or electric prototype or whatever the hell it is. Made of plastic, no less."

"Not plastic. Carbon fiber."

She was clearly enjoying the conversation, too. Byrd suspected that this sort of banter was constructive. In some ways, laughter worked on the same level as sex. For a few blessed moments, the absurd reality of the situation receded. While sex stripped away their clothing, laughter stripped away their defenses. It helped to reveal the truth.

"You have no idea what I've been through," she said. "There are times when I'd love a more normal life."

He shrugged. "What's happened between you and your Dad? I mean, you must have had some relationship. You've come all this way for him."

"Yeah, but I wonder why. I guess I've been looking for him my whole life."

He took another pull from his beer. It was, as he'd expected, going down very smooth.

"Look, I don't mean to pry."

She stared into her beer glass, watching a cascade of tiny bubbles rise to the surface.

"You talk about different worlds. My father and I are different people. Very different. Our relationship isn't normal. Never has been. Growing up the way I did fucks with a kid's mind. Especially after my mother died. Everything changed after she died. It was just weird."

Byrd nodded. "I guess so. How is your father different?"

"He's impulsive, stubborn. He gets an idea in his head and just charges forward. He doesn't think through the consequences, or how it'll affect other people."

"Sounds like someone else I know," Byrd said with a laugh. "Maybe you two aren't so different."

"No, I'm serious. My father has a saying. If money will solve the problem, then we don't have a problem. I think that with my mother gone, he saw me as just another problem. So he threw money at it. But he was never really there for me."

"What do you mean?"

"I got the private schools, the cars, the clothes. But I never really got him. I tried for years to reach him. I even got into the racing stuff, learned how to drive. Tried to bond with him, to find some connection. But it never seemed to work. Who knows, maybe he really wanted a son. He can be incredibly self-centered. And judgmental."

She took another long draw of the Gallo.

"I've often thought about that wreck in the Spyder. Things would've been different if Mom hadn't died. When it happened, he was at his peak. His business was kicking ass, he was getting into politics. That was probably the high point of his life, you know? Then the wreck happened, and he changed. Turned hard."

Byrd nodded. The high point of his life? It was a provocative statement but he knew what she meant. At some point in the Callahan historical arc, the man had fired on all cylinders. His legend was created in his the prime of his youth. It wasn't just business success. It was panache, a flair for the daring. It was having the ability and the gonads to dump a truckload of potatoes on the governor's front lawn.

"He's hard on everyone," she continued. "Especially me. He's one of those ex-military guys who never really left the Army, you know? After my marriage failed, I said to hell with it. Finally stopped trying to please him. I started being myself. Moved downtown, got my first tattoo--oh, he loved that—and stopped making the effort. To hell with him."

Byrd nodded. "Sounds like a tough man."

"You have no idea," she replied with a sigh. "And yet, here I am again, making the effort."

"Yep, here we are," he said. His eyes wandered to the bar behind her, and the assortment of coed rear ends propped against it. Charlie Byrd was an ass man.

She glanced over her shoulder and saw the source of his distraction.

"Byrd," she said. "Do you think I'm still competitive? I mean, am I good looking?"

His attention snapped back to their conversation. He leaned back in his plastic chair. What a question.

"Absolutely," he replied. "I mean, if we had met under other circumstances, say in a bar on Southside, we might hit it off."

She shook her head.

"If we met under other circumstances, someone would've told you I was J.C. Callahan's daughter. You would've wilted like a flower. I've seen it a thousand times. Men are pathetic."

Byrd was unconvinced. While no doubt some men would be intimidated by the prospect of dating a Callahan, others would've jumped at the opportunity. For Byrd, she represented a thrilling departure.

"But you did get married. How was your divorce his fault?"

"I told you: he's a control freak. My marriage was a disaster. I thought I'd finally found someone who could tolerate his daily wrath and judgment. But Frank was gone in three years, and I didn't blame him. Jesus, that's pathetic."

She took a deep draw from her bottle of Gallo as if the beer would somehow serve as salve for her marital failure.

"I'm not easily run off," he said. But look, in the last two years of law school, I've had five girlfriends. Do the math. I'm not into emotional commitments. Never have been. I don't know why."

"I know why," she replied. "Men are pigs."

"We're not pigs," he replied. "Dogs maybe, but not pigs. The way I figure, just about every relationship ends in a breakup. I mean, 99 percent end in a breakup. The other percent get married, and half the marriages get divorced. So what's the point?"

A look of dismay crawled across her face.

"The man of my dreams," she sighed, "is a pig."

Now the beer was going to work on Charlie Byrd.

"You've said that more than once. What is this man of my dreams bullshit? I never claimed to be the man of your dreams."

She took another deep draw of beer.

"You're going to think it's stupid,"

"Tell me anyway."

"I've been having a dream for the past few days. Starts differently each time. But the same thing always happens. In my dream, I see my mother. She tells me that a bird will lead me to Daddy. A bird will lead me through the snow to find my father."

Charlie Byrd didn't know how to react. He resisted a laugh, but his eyebrows arched and his eyes began to roll. This would've been funny were it not so pathetic. He'd been hired by this woman not because of his success in the Greystone case, not because she thought he was especially qualified—he was hired because she liked his business card? He'd heard of people making important decisions for the most random of reasons. But this one was special.

He spoke slowly and softly, as if addressing a young child.

"So, you had this dream about a bird and some snow. And you were looking for someone to help you find your father."

She nodded.

"You're the only man named Byrd I know. The only one who's a detective in Birmingham, anyway. So I went for it."

She went for it? She went for what? He had to make sure he got this right. He had to ask one more time.

"You hired me because my last name is Byrd?"

"Right."

They sat in silence for a moment, staring at empty glasses, Byrd digesting her revelation along with his beer. He felt some internal conflict over the matter. There was a side of Charlie Byrd, the healthy Native American chunk of his mutt DNA, that wanted to believe in dreams and visions and leaps of faith. There was another side, the one that suffered through several semesters of *lawyer-like thinking* at Birmingham SOL, that wanted to toss her out of court, or declare her guilty by reason of insanity. Following a hunch would be one thing. She had followed an unconscious whim.

Kristen Callahan seemed to read his mind.

"Look," she said, "I know you're an aspiring lawyer. You're not a person of faith. You probably think I'm crazy. Maybe I am. But I kept having these dreams and when I saw a place called Byrd's Eye or whatever the hell you call it . . . Well, it made sense to me. It might not make sense to you or anyone else, but it did to me. That's all that matters."

"What about the snow?" he replied. "Do I need to worry about dandruff?"

"I don't know about the snow," she said, looking back at her empty glass. "I know how it sounds. But that's what my dream says."

Byrd looked at his own glass. It was easier than facing the eyes of his client and lover. He wanted another drink. He wanted to guzzle another one-dollar Guatemalan beer and expose this dream for being a total absurdity, a joke of ridiculous proportions.

But for what? Why rock the boat? Maybe this was the one instance in his life where Charlie Byrd got lucky. For once, he was being overpaid instead of underpaid. Better to let the dream rest, and end the discussion before it became a full-blown argument.

Besides, he felt sorry for her. Here he was—a starving law student without two pennies to rub together—and yet he felt sorry for her. She was obviously weak, and Byrd felt pity. So his Cherokee lineage won the internal debate.

"Okay," he said with an empathetic smile. "I'd like to drink another, but that would be a bad idea."

"Let's go, little bird," she said. "Let's find our Calle and head back to the room before nightfall."

Charlie Byrd stood.

He turned his gaze toward the open door.

32

THE FAT MAN SAT AT THE KITCHEN TABLE, holding a rag to his chin. He slid the rag to his eyes, his thick hands trembling beneath the cloth. His head sank and he sobbed. As he cried, rolls of fat rippled beneath his stained shirt. His body balanced improbably upon the small wooden chair. The chair strained under his weight, but held.

He pulled the rag away. The crude bandage beneath was soaked with blood. Seeing the blood, he returned the rag to his chin.

Eyes lowered, he looked not so much like a large stinking hulk of a man, but rather like a child. A clumsy, stupid, careless child. He allowed the gringo to get loose, and like a child, he would be punished.

But there were other matters at hand. Yes, there would be punishment coming for the Fat Man. But the gringo would be punished first. The gringo would suffer for this outrage.

The gringo would die.

The Man with the Scar stood at the kitchen window and looked into the courtyard. The dogs were sleeping again, inside the compound, scattered to and fro like piles of leaves.

The gringo had almost escaped. But for the dogs, the gringo would be free. But for the dogs . . .

The Man with the Scar cursed. It had been a mistake to keep the gringo, to try and extract more money. They should've put a bullet in his skull on the first day. They should've dumped his body in tall grass and been satisfied with the American cash and property. Instead he'd been greedy; he tried to get more. In all of his years, he had never made this mistake. This time was different. He didn't understand why.

It wasn't worth the effort. Communication was impossible. Electronics were traceable. If they'd been working in the City, he could've found help. But not here, not in this small town crowded with camera-toting tourists.

It was almost time.

Time for *Semana Santa* to grow quiet. Time to put a bullet in his head and be done with it.

Outside, long shadows were stretching across the courtyard. Soon the sun would dip behind the mountains, and darkness would be restored. Soon the streets would be silent. Soon they would be able to stalk the night with impunity.

They would kill the gringo tonight, The Man with the Scar announced. They would kill him after the parades finished and the sun went down. Once the streets were quiet, they'd kill him and dump his body on the mountain.

As for the car, the rich man's toy . . . It was dangerous to keep intact. The car could be melted for the aluminum. But first the gringo. He would focus on the car once the gringo was gone.

The Man with the Scar relaxed, having reached this decision. He pulled a cigarette from his pocket and placed it in his mouth.

He walked to the table. He picked up a wooden match, scraped it against the table, and it came alive. The cigarette glowed orange and smoke rolled across the table. It billowed into the face of the Fat Man, his wet eyes blinking with stupid innocence.

The Man with the Scar walked back to the window and looked again into the courtyard.

Send the woman and boy away, he said. Send them to the City, for this is a job for men.

Tonight the gringo dies, he said.

The Man with the Scar took a deep drag from his cigarette, and exhaled.

THE LOST SPYDER

John Christian Callahan writhed on the floor.

His body twisted and turned and tried to find comfort. But no comfort was found. He was trapped in a crucible of darkness and pain. So he escaped the only way he could, to the only place he could—into hallucination, into the deep recesses of his mind. He left his body resting on the floor. The corporal shell was trapped, but the mind was flying free.

He was no longer alone in the darkness, hands bound, carved like a side of beef, withered and waiting for death like an animal. He was warm again. He was young. He was in control. And he wasn't alone.

His wife. He saw his wife. Shea Callahan was standing tall in the Alabama sun, wiping sweat from her brow. She was wearing her favorite outfit, those damn denim jeans that were too tight, like they'd been painted on her body, the ones he specifically told her never to wear at the track. She wore those pants like peacocks wore feathers. She loved nothing more than strutting her stuff for the boys. Her breasts defied scientific explanation, appearing to gain a couple of cup sizes on track day. He saw the men leering at her; the mechanics, the other drivers, every swinging dick within half a mile. They tried to act coy, to look the other way, to stare anonymously from behind dark sunglasses. But men were so damned simple. So damned obvious. Their tongues practically dragged the ground.

Callahan loved it. He loved watching the other track hounds wag their tails at his trophy wife. He'd never admit it to anyone—not even to himself—but he loved their jabbering like a fat dog loved a belly rub. What was the point of having a trophy wife, if not to brandish the trophy? Shea Callahan was made of gold, and her husband loved to flash the shiny stuff.

In addition to jeans that probably should've been illegal in any God-fearing Southern town, she wore the shirt. The wispy low-cut white shirt that looked like it was made of surgical gauze, with about a dollar's worth of fabric that cost a hundred times what it was worth. The one he specifically told her never to wear at the track. The shirt might've been useful as a lace curtain, or a table dolly, or lining a breadbasket, but it failed miserably at hiding Shea Callahan's assets from public view.

The left hand rested on her hip. The right ran through her long auburn hair, stretching strands toward the sky. As she raised her arm, a nipple threatened to poke through that pathetic excuse of a shirt. It threatened to poke through the flimsy fabric and rip the gauze to shreds. But to the dismay of every male onlooker, the shirt held. Modesty was preserved.

She flipped a curl of hair away from jade eyes that locked onto her husband. Then she flashed a smile.

God help him when he saw that smile. Shea Callahan parted her lips and revealed a glistening set of pearls. They were the stuff of dreams, those eyes and that smile. They sparkled with erotic charm, the proper sort that expressed the most shameful of thoughts in the most innocent of ways.

When she turned on the charm, she could talk him into anything. Even . .

.

The Spyder. He saw the Porsche 550 Spyder. Silver and red and black. Power and agility and grace. Antique, yet timeless. There was something about the Spyder. Like his best ideas, it was so damned simple. Pure. A distillation of all that was right with the world. Two seats, one engine, one man behind the wheel. Like his wife, the Spyder was full of curves. If sex could be rendered in aluminum and leather, this is what it would look like. The Spyder not only turned heads, it made grown men act like giddy little boys. It was the one they all wanted.

There was more to this car than grace or growl or rarity. There was magic. Like a wizard, Callahan harnessed the magic. He wielded it on . . .

The track. He saw the Spyder ripping through the track. Once again, Callahan was where he was meant to be—in control.

To own a Spyder was remarkable. But to actually drive it on the track? That was the stuff of legend. The track was the very definition of risk, a place so inherently dangerous that insurance companies feared to tread. The financial, physical, and emotional downsides were as extreme as the upsides were modest. A win guaranteed little more than a cheap plastic trophy. But a loss? That could mean anything from a bruised ego to being burned alive. The risk was devastating. Perhaps more than anything, that risk attracted the thrill seekers.

The track was filled with lesser men wielding lesser machines. Doctors and lawyers and accountants, men who played life by the rules. BMW and Mercedes, Jaguar and Ferrari, Ford and Chevrolet, cars as common as Vice-Presidents at a bank. All surrendered to the will of Callahan and the Porsche 550 Spyder. *That car was a shark*, they said. *A shark swimming with goldfish.*

In the Spyder, he was a man in full. His leather-gloved hands handled the wheel not only with confidence, but with deftness and precision. He caressed the machine like a lover, and the machine responded. The Spyder was a part of him, a mechanical extension of John Christian Callahan. Man and machine united in flawless symphony.

On the track, it wasn't about ego. It wasn't about trophy wives or trophy cars, or petty squabbles in the Little League for millionaires. It was something greater.

It was about beauty. To call this a sport was wrong. Rugby was a sport. Boxing was a sport. There was too much beauty in this dance of machine and man. This wasn't sport. This was art.

Callahan and the Spyder carved the track like ice skaters, clipping each apex with grace and accuracy, then hurtling down straights with wild abandon.

This was more than art; this was life. Racing was life—a tale told by an idiot, perhaps, but one full of drama and bluster and glory and defeat.

The Spyder's windshield was low, and wind ripped through the cabin. His steely blue eyes peered from behind clear goggles. With each press of his right foot, the visceral bark of the engine and shove in the back told him that he was alive. That roar shook him to the bone, shook his heart and his spine and he felt alive.

He rode the Spyder like a thoroughbred, whipping its flanks as he entered the final turn. This was the heart of the track, the corner that separated real men from posers.

He felt the Spyder respond. The steed bucked and the car shifted to the left, suspension flexing like mad. Too much flex—too much for anyone not acquainted with its eccentricities. Words echoed in his mind. *This car's a killer, Callahan. This car's a killer . . .*

Callahan knew differently. The Spyder wasn't a killer. He relaxed and let the car settle. As quickly as the drama had appeared, it was gone, and she was again roaring down the main straight. The car was happy, and he could feel it purr as their dance continued in beautiful unison. He felt the eyes of everyone upon him, and he felt alive.

He accelerated down the straight. Faster, faster, faster. The hood of the car transformed from dull aluminum into something as smooth and glossy as Lake Martin at sunset. It became a mirror, a reflection of truth. He looked into the mirror and saw . . .

The sky. He saw simple reflections of the azure heavens, as blue as his own eyes, and small puffs of wispy cotton. Then the sky and the clouds turned dark, and lightning flashed. But it wasn't lightning. It was her smile.

Shea Callahan parted her lips to reveal those pearly gems. They sparkled like lightning. She could talk him into anything. Even . . .

The Spyder. He was in the Spyder. And this time, Shea was behind the wheel. She was driving the car, and he was her passenger. He was her coach, her mentor, her lover, and her husband. He wasn't in control.

She laughed at his discomfort. For once in his life, all he could do was hold on for the ride.

She coaxed the Spyder gingerly through the turns. There was respect, but no unity. She wasn't one with the machine. She was fighting the machine. She was fighting for attention, fighting for control, fighting for her life.

She entered the final turn and the car bucked. The steed bucked and shifted to the left, just as it always did. Her smile was replaced by a mask of terror as she whipped the steering wheel in panic.

The Porsche shifted, and its tires ripped free from the pavement. Then they lost traction and went spinning like a top, like a child's toy thrown insanely out of control. Spinning, spinning, spinning . . . The world in slow motion, spinning past in a haze of screaming rubber and burning smoke. Spinning, twisting, flying into eternity. The track was a roulette wheel, and it was grinding to an abrupt halt.

The crash was sudden, violent, and decisive. A spray of hot sparks, the grating sound of crunching metal. With the acrid fragrance of burnt rubber filling his nostrils, the Spyder faded away. Then he *saw* . . .

The cemetery. He was standing in Elmwood Cemetery at his young wife's grave. The gravesite was covered with fresh dirt, Alabama red clay that broke apart in large chunks. The sky was raven black again, and waves of purple clouds boiled and billowed across the sky.

Ashes to ashes, rust to rust.

He looked up, held one fist in the air, and cursed the sky and its creator. He cursed this cruel twist of fate.

He sank down to his knees and sobbed.

John Christian Callahan would never relinquish control again.

He'd go through life alone.

He'd be alone forever.

33

CHARLIE BYRD STOOD ON THE NARROW SIDEWALK, squinting in the light. The late afternoon rays cast long shadows. The sun had dropped near one of the volcanoes overlooking Antigua, but hadn't yet crawled behind it.

Byrd faced the intersection of two roads. He looked at the piece of yellow paper in his hands, then back to the street signs. To his left was *Calle de los Pasos*. To his right was *9a Calle Oriente*.

A pickup truck rumbled past, its tires making loud noise on the uneven stone pavement. The rear of the truck was filled to capacity with Mayan workers. There were more than a dozen men, and many were forced to stand. Tired and sweaty, they swayed back and forth along with the truck.

To Byrd's left, the road was quiet. There was no traffic along *Calle de los Pasos*. Instead, the street was closed to make way for yet another Holy Week procession.

He stood looking at an *alfombra*. The ceremonial carpet was similar to others he'd seen scattered throughout Antigua's dusty streets like floral kaleidoscopes. But this *alfombra* was different from the rest. It was a work-in-progress. Several Mayan men and women were busy constructing the carpet.

Alongside the carpet were white plastic buckets. They contained heaping piles of crimson rose petals, snowy carnations, and bold yellow sunflowers. Some fifty feet in length, the carpet already boasted an exceptional amount of flowers. Small children laid flowers onto the *alfombra* with quiet concentration.

"This must have been what she wanted us to see," Byrd said. "It's nice. Best we've seen all day."

Kristen Callahan stood watching, hands on her hips.

"*Alfombras* are privately sponsored," she replied. "Paid for by the houses along the street."

"In that case, someone on this street has money."

She nodded. "I'd say so."

They watched the *alfombra* take shape. It was an intricate design, with shades of floral colors layered upon a thick scarlet blanket of dyed sawdust. At certain points throughout the carpet, artists had created images of golden wine goblets.

Callahan stepped onto the street. She bent over, picked up a handful of white carnations, and began laying them onto the *alfombra*.

The Mayan girls smiled and continued their work. No words were spoken, but they were visibly pleased to be joined in the effort.

Byrd stood on the sidewalk, one hand shading his eyes, waiting for the sun to drop.

After a few minutes, Callahan brushed her hands on her jeans, and looked at Byrd. He was still standing on the sidewalk, brow furrowed in concentration.

"You're not going to help?" she asked.

"I've been thinking," he said, staring at the *alfombra*. "I finally got the message."

"Okay," she replied. "Let me have it."

"Nothing lasts."

Silence. She didn't reply, but for a moment she stopped laying flowers. She looked intently at Charlie Byrd.

"Think about it," he said. "Every romance comes to an end. Youth fades. Beauty fades. Eventually, life fades. Empires rise and fall. Everything dies, sooner or later. Everything is eventually forgotten. Nothing lasts."

She said nothing.

"Everything's temporary. Take Antigua. This was once the capital of an empire. Today it's a bunch of ruins."

He paused, still staring at the *alfombra* and stroking the scraggly whiskers on his chin. The carpet was nearing completion. Soon would be gone.

"I'd say Antigua is more alive than ever," she said.

"You'd say so," he replied, "because you never saw it in its prime. At one time this place ruled an empire. Today, ruins. Hell, someday there'll be no Antigua. One more earthquake and this place is history."

"So, Confucius, you're not going to help?"

He indulged in a playful smile. Byrd enjoyed these philosophical exchanges with Callahan. She had a bright mind that was worthy of the challenge. She also brought a fresh perspective to Byrd's world, one far removed from the "think like a lawyer" mantra of Birmingham SOL.

"I'll pass," he said. "Besides, what's the point? It'll all be gone in an hour."

"That's the point," she said.

"Well, I don't get it."

"You're a cynic, Charlie Byrd."

"I'm not a cynic," he replied. "I'm a realist."

"Well, realistically," she said, "I believe some things do last. You're only getting half the message. The purpose of the procession is to remind us. Some things do last."

"Really? And they are?"

"Keep thinking," she replied. "You're making progress."

She stepped back out into the street, away from the dime store philosopher on the sidewalk, and resumed work on the carpet.

Charlie Byrd wasn't a religious man. He'd resisted repeated attempts at recruitment by the Bible-thumping legions back home. He never had much use for church. He liked his Sunday mornings free from interruption, and his neck free from ties.

Most of all, he liked his life free from hypocrisy. The religious men of Alabama had paid his way through law school. He'd caught many a church deacon making regular stops at Motel 6. If they treated adultery like alcohol, Byrd sometimes said, he'd be out of a job.

The sun finally decided it was time to retire. It slipped behind the volcano and the street of *Calle de los Pasos* was bathed in a soft radiant glow. In the dimming light, the colors of the alfombra grew all the more vibrant.

Byrd was intrigued by the alfombras and Semana Santa. This was quite different from the Easter celebrations back home. No Sunday clothes. No Bibles. No sermonizing against the evils of alcohol and state lotteries and video poker. Standing in Guatemala, in the shadow of three volcanoes, surrounded by Spanish ruins, watching young women construct a doomed work of art—he had to acknowledge the appeal of it all. The revelation was subtle and quiet, but he got the point. There was a theme to this life. At least there was a theme.

Callahan stood back and viewed the complete alfombra.

"Best looking rug in the city," she said.

There was little time to admire the work. Music from the approaching procession wafted through the air, with signature echoes of sadness and celebration. Crowds on the sidewalk began to thicken. The procession was a block away on *Calle de los Pasos*. They worked on the carpet until the last minute. Now that it was finished, it was time for its destruction.

The ceremony only took moments. A dozen men clad in purple robes were the first to trod upon the alfombra. Burning incense and torches in the twilight, they hailed the arrival of the procession. Then came the musicians. Then the staggering float of the Virgin Mary. Then the float of Jesus Christ carrying the cross, still looking like he drank the water. In a few moments it was over. The procession passed, and the beautiful *alfombra* was ground out of existence.

Once the procession passed, Kristen Callahan stepped back out into the street. She picked up a discarded sunflower, and tucked it into her jacket.

"This one's a keeper," she said.

Byrd said nothing. He understood her point. But he didn't pick up a flower.

From across the street came the sound of a woman's voice. She spoke with an American accent.

"Maria," she shouted. "Isabella. Come here."

Two Mayan girls were picking up the remnants of crushed flowers. Only a few moments before, these same children had been carefully building the alfombra. They darted across the street with the buoyant energy of children at play.

"Maria and Isabella," Byrd said. "I think we've found our friends."

He followed the girls across the crowded street. At first, he didn't see the American. He saw a gathering of Mayan locals, all in traditional dress. Then he noticed the shoes protruding from beneath one woman's skirt. Mayans weren't known for wearing Nike.

"Excuse me," he said. "Are you American?"

The woman smiled.

"Yes," she replied. "And with that accent, I suppose you are too."

"Charlie Byrd," he said, extending his right hand.

"Anna Rodriguez. And who might this be?"

"Kristen Callahan," she said.

The woman's eyes narrowed.

"Did you say Christian Callahan?" she asked. "I know a man who goes by that name."

At that moment, Byrd realized that the alfombra, for all its beauty, had nothing to do with the reason he was standing on *Calle de los Pasos*.

34

T HEY FOLLOWED ANNA RODRIGUEZ THROUGH THE
TOWERING WOODEN ARCH that shielded her home from the street.
She pulled the massive doors shut, iron hinges grinding in protest. With an
authoritative slam, the burbling song of Semana Santa receded.

Processions continued throughout Antigua, but were far removed from
this quiet sanctum. Behind the ivy-covered walls of the Rodriguez home, there
was calm. Long amber shafts of sunlight streamed into the open courtyard,
where they joined the flickering radiance of gas lamps. It was earthy and
serene and Charlie Byrd was amazed at the transition. He'd traveled twenty
feet, yet it felt like twenty miles.

They continued through the courtyard, their footsteps echoing on stone
tiles, and entered the kitchen.

"Have a seat," the Mayan said. "Make yourselves at home, and please
excuse me for a minute."

The kitchen table was covered with textbooks, scattered papers, and the
remnants of that day's lunch—bread crusts and potato chips and half-filled
glasses of milk.

"Maria, Isabella," the woman said. "Take your things from the table, and
go to the study. It's time for homework."

Without complaint, the girls gathered together their belongings and left the room. The woman followed.

Byrd removed his backpack and set it on the table. The late afternoon beer hadn't been a good idea, after all. He rubbed his eyes and refocused on the task at hand. At last they'd found Callahan's contact. After leaping from continent to continent, following a vaporous trail of disenfranchised advice and unsupported rumor, they'd hit a promising vein. Callahan's trail was warm. This woman held answers, and Byrd had to shake off the sluggishness and fatigue.

Rodriguez burst back into the kitchen.

"I'm sorry," she said, "I had to get the girls situated. Please forgive the mess. It's hard to keep things in order during *Semana Santa*. It gets kind of crazy around here."

"Reminds me of home," Byrd replied. Although it didn't.

"So Alabama is home for both of you?"

"Yes."

"Never been there, but I'd spot those accents anywhere."

Kristen Callahan picked up a small photo frame from the table. "These girls are adorable," she said. "Are they yours?"

"Not mine exactly," she said with a smile. "No relation, anyway. But I do pay for their schooling."

"What do you mean?"

"The girls are sisters," she explained. "I came across them in the park a couple of years ago. At the time, they didn't go to school. Like most other children in this town, they were working. I asked whether they'd go to school if money weren't an issue. They said they would, and their parents agreed. So here we are."

"Where is the school?"

"Guatemala City. Every morning, they get up at five o'clock to ride the bus. Five o'clock, mind you. When they started, I doubted it would last a month. It's been almost three years."

Byrd noted the observation about Guatemala City. Antigua itself was a small town, but it rested in the shadow of a teeming metropolis. It was close enough for children to hop the bus on a daily basis. In Guatemala City, the rule of law was questionable. It was the sort of place where two dozen murders occurred every week. Ambush was a technique increasingly employed by brazen local gangs. Guatemala City was, quite simply, one of the most dangerous places in Latin America. Yet every day, despite the ongoing assault on civility, innocent schoolkids rode the bus.

"It feels nice to do something good for them," she replied. "Speaking of, it's nice to meet you Kristen. Your father never told me he had a daughter."

"No surprise," she replied.

"Did he stay for *Semana Santa*? He told me that he took his sweet time coming down here but he was driving straight back. I assumed he'd be back in Alabama by now."

"That's why we're here," Byrd said. "He never came back to Alabama."

"What? It's been more than a week since our . . ."

She paused.

"Since we saw each other. He surely should be home by now."

Kristen Callahan shook her head.

"He never even told me where he was going," she said. "In fact, all clues pointed to Germany. It's a small miracle we've made it this far."

"Speaking of small miracles," Byrd said. He dug into his pocket, pulled out the yellow paper, and handed it to the woman. Rodriguez reviewed the note, digesting the import of their visit.

"My God. Have you been posting these in town?"

"Yes, we've hit all the usual tourist spots. But we've heard nothing so far. At least not until we went to the marketplace. A girl handed me one with your address written on the back. She must have known about the connection."

"A girl gave you our address? What girl?"

Byrd shrugged. "We don't know her name. Just some girl who was selling stuff in the park."

Rodriguez uttered something in Spanish they didn't understand, and shook her head.

"Olivia," she said. "It must've been Olivia. She sells in the park. She was here the day your father came."

"Who's Olivia?" Byrd asked.

"A friend of my girls. Antigua's a small town. Young girls talk."

Byrd nodded. If he had learned anything in his brief career of detective work, it was that someone, somewhere, was always watching. Often the most promising information is gathered by the most random of sources.

Rodriguez turned her gaze to Callahan.

"Have you contacted the authorities?"

"Of course. Police in Alabama and Germany are working on the case. Here in Guatemala, we've filed with the police and the U.S. Embassy. We're trying to get connected with the media down here. We've gone through all the channels. But until we met you, we had no confirmation he was even in Guatemala. He left no trail. Everything pointed to Germany. Hell, we've been following the car as much the man."

"So you know about the car?"

Rodriguez turned to Byrd, eyes loaded with suspicion. While Kristen Callahan was a known quantity, Charlie Byrd was not. But the mythical car, being plastered on sunny "LOST" posters all over Antigua, was not exactly a trade secret. If anything, it was the car that brought them to Guatemala.

"What's your role in all of this?" she asked. "Are you with the police?"

"I'm not a cop," he replied with a dry laugh. "I'm a private investigator. I work independently for the Callahans, no government affiliation."

Callahan agreed. "He's not a cop. He's barely a detective."

Byrd absorbed the insult in silence.

"I see," Rodriguez said. "So you know why your father was here in Antigua? You know about the arana."

"You mean the Spyder? Yes, we know about the Spyder. At least, we think we know. Do you know the truth?"

"Yes," she said. "I've called it the arana for so long, anything else seems unnatural. But I know the truth."

"Some people told us the lost Spyder is a bullshit legend. That it doesn't exist."

"The arana exists. It's not legend. Definitely not bullshit."

"So the most valuable of Porsches was here in Guatemala?" Byrd said. "If you don't mind my asking, how does something like that happen?"

"You're here, so you must have some idea."

"Give us the Cliff's Notes version," he said. "We've earned that much."

"It's funny. I've gone years without discussing the arana. Now that it's sold, I suppose there's no harm in talking. However," she turned to Callahan, "I did execute an NDA with your father."

"An NDA?"

"Non-disclosure agreement," Byrd said. "She's not supposed to discuss the deal."

"In fact," Rodriguez said, "neither was your father. For the security of my family, this transaction had to be private. Do you know what it's like to have a car like the arana in Guatemala? J.C. promised that no one would trace his steps. He told me about the chartered flight to Germany, the avoidance of traceable electronics, the border bribery, the cash. This was all slight of hand. He seems rather good at it."

"Fooled by the master," Kristen Callahan replied. "It's not the first time he's pulled the wool over everyone's eyes."

Byrd paused as the reality of the situation hit home. For years, people had viewed J.C. Callahan as an eccentric with few outside interests. Now it was becoming clear that he had a rich private life. Revelations of that life were both fascinating and unsettling. An NDA meant that a major deal had gone down. What else had he kept hidden? Now Kristen Callahan spoke with renewed urgency.

"If he's still in Guatemala," she said, "every minute counts."

"No doubt," Rodriguez agreed. "If you're comfortable with Mr. Byrd hearing about our transaction, then I'll talk. Everything's settled now. But if you'll forgive me, I need to see some identification. I mean, we've just met."

Byrd unzipped his backpack, pulled out two American passports, and handed them over. Rodriguez examined the documents and, satisfied, handed them back.

"Byrd knows everything," Callahan said. "And like I said, he's not a cop."

Rodriguez nodded. "Yes, I understand. Actually, to answer the question, the Spyder changed hands more than once over the years. For years, I was afraid to tell anyone we had it. If the wrong people found out about that car, our lives could've been in danger."

Byrd leaned forward. He realized that this was a tangible artifact they were discussing, that the German in Stuttgart had told them some version of the truth. Mythical folklore had been confirmed with physical evidence, then verified with cold cash. It was like someone had just caught a *chupacabra* and sold it to the local zoo.

"So this is the lost Porsche 550 Spyder?" he asked. "The legendary missing car? The car that's not supposed to exist?"

"It is, indeed. The arana is the car that originally, shall we say, disappeared back in the 1950's. Its original owner was a Guatemalan gentleman who was a casualty of politics."

"We've heard the car was stolen in the 1950's," he said. "But how did you come into possession of it? Why all the secrecy?"

"Well, I'm an American citizen, but my parents were from here. I first visited Guatemala with my husband in 1973. I guess we heard of the arana not long afterwards. I'll never forget the day I learned the tales were true. I was incredibly pissed that Paul got involved with it."

"So who was telling this tale?"

"Collectors. Dealers. There's an underground network of people down here who trade illegal goods. Even in the 70s, the arana was a hot property. Stolen goods, you understand. Rightful ownership was questionable."

"Wasn't the original guy the rightful owner?"

"Perhaps, but he was dead. Who knows what a Guatemalan court would have decided. Given the state of affairs down here, it would've gone to the highest bidder. That's politics in Central America, you understand?"

"That's politics everywhere."

"Exactly. So the Spyder wasn't openly viewed or discussed. But a fellow from Germany—a Porsche employee, I believe—originally had possession."

Byrd nodded. One of the fundamental classes taught in the first semester of any American law school was property. It was the foundation of any solid legal education, and Birmingham SOL had left him well covered. Legal ownership of property is often not as obvious as it seems. The subtle nuances of title and possession fueled many a high-priced law firm.

"Possession," Byrd said, "is nine-tenths of the law."

"In Guatemala, ten-tenths."

"So the German sold it?"

"Yes. He sold it on the black market to a man from Guatemala City. Now this fellow did something remarkable. Most people would've exported the Spyder to the United States for resale. But this man didn't. He didn't drive it. He treated it like an investment. He left the arana in its box—in its original box, mind you——and placed it into storage. Like a fine wine. It sat there for God knows how many years."

She laughed and shook her head.

"When we bought it, it had already appreciated in value. So my husband did the same. The car just sat there, untouched. It's a goddamned time capsule. I'm not a car person, but I understand the rarity of this situation."

"So your husband bought it? Did he do so legally?"

"Yes, in a manner of speaking. My husband bought this house and all of its contents. For decades, the Spyder was stored here."

In this house.

"So you became the legal owners?"

"Yes. But like I said, it depends on what legal system you consult, and who's signing the checks. We kept the car here in Antigua. We came down from California for Semana Santa every year, too. The car was always here. It's been sitting in our cellar, still in its original box, for decades."

"In the cellar?" Byrd asked. "How does a car get into a cellar?"

"You'll see," she said. "It was a safe place. No one knew we kept it here."

"But you just sold it. After all that time, why did you sell it?"

"Well, Paul's goal was to keep the car long term. But after he died, he sure as hell didn't take it with him. Frankly, I got tired of this thing just sitting in our cellar, doing nothing. It was time to cash out, time to do something good."

"If you don't mind my asking," Byrd interrupted, "what is it that you do?"

Rodriguez smiled, revealing a host of fresh wrinkles around her eyes. The Mayan American was plain spoken and folksy, yet her sharp brown eyes revealed a sparkling intelligence.

"I've done a lot of things," she said. "Some called me a venture capitalist. Others called me a merchant banker. A few just called me a bitch."

"How did you meet my father?"

"I've known J.C. Callahan for many years," she replied. "We met back in the 1970s, in Atlanta, I believe. What a character. My husband financed Callahan Food Group, at least the part west of the Mississippi."

"Has my father always known the truth about the Spyder?"

"J.C.'s known the truth for several years," she replied. "We've been planning the transaction for, I don't know, at least the past three."

"Three years?" Byrd asked. The notion was incredulous. Byrd didn't plan three days in advance, much less three years.

"With a property like the *arana*, you'll have interest coming from all sides. Porsche. IRS. Guatemalan police. Local gangs. It wouldn't surprise me to see the UN get involved. There's too much money and publicity at stake for them to ignore it. Owning a car like that Spyder can be more of a curse than a blessing. Best to keep it quiet."

"I'm confused," Byrd said. "Does J.C. Callahan own the car or not?"

"Of course," she replied. "We finalized the transaction last week. One hundred percent cash. He was smart in the way he constructed this deal. That's one of the reasons it took so long. He's covered all his bases legally. According to the best legal minds in Guatemala City," she said. "This is a textbook case of adverse possession. There's no paper title for a car this old, of course. Actual title transferred to my husband and me in the 1970s. I've now sold it. John Christian Callahan of Birmingham, Alabama owns the Spyder now. That much is certain."

Byrd's mind reeled. A cash deal. That explained why the old man was living off cash. He had enough on hand to buy Manhattan. Or at least a pristine original Porsche 550 Spyder. The doctrine of adverse possession meant that title had been legally transferred without a single piece of paper being filed.

"For me," she said, "this car was an investment, like a bank account. It was time to cash out. Now I have some liberty to reinvest in other things."

"Yeah, I guess it was a garage queen," Byrd said.

Rodriguez smiled. "The arana was the ultimate garage queen. I decided it was time for that car to do something."

"What is the Spyder going to do?"

"Something good," she said with conviction. "That car is going to do something good."

"I don't follow."

"You've already met the reasons. Maria and Isabella."

A pause.

"You sold the car for the girls?"

"I'm starting a school with the proceeds. The Spyder will pay for textbooks, uniforms—even teachers. Local Mayan children are going to get an education. Yes," she said, "the lost Spyder is going to do something good."

Byrd nodded. It was hard to argue with her conclusion. Maybe some benefit would emerge from Callahan's insane behavior, his obsessive collection of millionaire tokens, his reckless subterfuge.

Find the car, find the man.

"You said the car was kept here in the house. Can we see where it was stored?"

"Sure," she replied. "Let's go."

35

ANNA RODRIGUEZ LED THEM DOWN A LONG HALLWAY, and into an adjacent room. It was a living area of sorts, containing a couple of overstuffed chairs and a cinnamon leather couch. The space was dominated by a large woven rug, completed in the traditional Guatemalan style. Upon the rug sat a mahogany cocktail table, a mass of twisting, gnarled arms that supported an elaborate marble top.

"I'll need some help with the table," she said. "It's quite heavy."

Charlie Byrd grabbed one end of the table and lifted. He grunted, and the slab didn't budge. So all three took hold, and were barely able to move it aside. They dragged it to rest next to the couch.

"Jesus Christ, that's heavy," he said.

Rodriguez rolled back the rug, revealing a faded hardwood floor beneath. Looking down at the floor, Byrd saw nothing.

"We bought the house furnished," she said. "For many years this door was covered. It was built for the purpose."

She crouched over the floor and ran her fingers across the planks of wood. One small plank, no longer than four inches wide and one foot long, lifted free from the floor. Two brass handles were revealed.

With a grunt, she pulled the handles.

Suddenly the faint outline of a doorway became clear. Under ordinary circumstances, the passage would be impossible to detect. The doors were horizontal, part of the flooring, and opened into the earth itself.

The massive doors swung vertical, up from the floor, and rotated wide. They revealed a concrete stairway leading into the ground, descending into darkness.

They walked down the stairs. The passage was wide—as wide as the length of the doors, wide enough to walk three persons across. Byrd felt the temperature drop with each step downward. It was cold beneath the floor, like a cellar. In a moment, he was standing in a darkened room.

Rodriguez reached overhead and clicked a switch. A single light bulb sprang to life, dangling from the ceiling on the end of a thin wire. The room was full of boxes, some wooden and some cardboard. Some were labeled, but most weren't. There was a latticework of shelving along one wall, the type used to hold bottles of wine. The shelves were about half-full with dusty wine bottles, but most of the bottles were empty.

She led them to the rear of the room. The floor itself was concrete, and Byrd could feel a chill emanating from it. The natural chill of the earth.

"If you'd help me move these boxes," she said.

They slid a half-dozen or so empty cases across the floor, away from the wall, revealing a separate wooden floor beneath.

She crouched down upon the floor. She then grasped a small brass handle, a match to the handles on the doors upstairs. She lifted the handle and the flooring lifted along with it.

"I'm going to need a hand with this," she said.

Together they pushed. Up, up, up went a wide section of the floor itself.

It rose with a cloud of lingering sediment and finally came to rest against the wall on the other side. The floor leaned at an angle, revealing a massive empty cavity.

They stood looking at a rectangular hole. It was perhaps twelve feet long and eight feet wide. It was shallow, but deep enough to conceal a large object. It was, Byrd realized, of perfect proportions to store a Porsche 550 Spyder.

Rodriguez leaned against the wall.

"For decades, this was the resting place of the arana. It sat here in the darkness of this cellar. A buried treasure, if you will. When we acquired it, my husband had the cellar modified to reduce humidity. The car stayed here for all of his life, and most of my own."

A silence enveloped the room. Byrd felt like he was staring at an empty tomb.

"The car is perfect," she repeated. "No mold, no rust, not a single scratch. Still in its original shipping crate. Hasn't aged a day. It's bizarre. Almost unnatural."

Byrd looked around at the wine cellar, at the scattered boxes and decayed wooden shelving. He felt an eerie quiet. They were below ground, and all sound had evaporated. His mind flashed back to Callahan's garage in Alabama, and then the storage shed in Germany. Once more he had entered the belly of the whale.

John Christian Callahan was close. So close, Byrd could almost smell the man. He'd been here, standing in this very room, breathing this same stale air, only days before. If there was a chance to find him alive, Byrd needed to absorb everything. He needed to do so quickly. A man's life hung in the balance.

Byrd looked back up the steep stairwell, and the shaft of light that poured down from above.

"How the hell did the car get in here?" he asked.

"That I cannot tell you," she replied. "Like I said, it was all here when we bought the house."

She laughed. "I can tell you that getting it out wasn't easy. But the arana doesn't weigh much more than a thousand pounds. With enough strong men, anything is possible."

Byrd looked at Rodriguez in the dim light. She was an odd sight, this traditionally dressed Mayan in her Nike shoes and California accent. She looked like she could be selling crafts in the market, but spoke with the glib precision of an American attorney.

"So Callahan waited until he had the legalities worked out—the adverse possession—and then he came down here himself to handle the acquisition?"

"He was explicit," she replied. "He wanted to personally retrieve the car. I believe it had something to do with the legal issues, and the need for absolute privacy."

"Here's what I'm trying to figure out," Byrd said. "Callahan picks up the

Spyder. A bunch of local guys load the damn thing. They put it in what?"

"He was driving an SUV, one of the new ones. He was pulling an enclosed trailer. The Spyder was secured in the trailer."

"Did he have private security?"

She shook her head. "Not to my knowledge."

Byrd was stunned at the revelation. He said nothing, but his mind reeled at the arrogance. Callahan must be insane. Either insane or reckless or just plain stupid. He picks up the most valuable of Porsches in one of the world's most dangerous places and transports the damn thing himself. One of the wealthiest men in Alabama was lost on an egotistical crusade.

Byrd's facial expression said it all. He was standing next to Kristen Callahan, the only daughter of the missing man. He was thinking that her father was an idiot.

"I told you," she said. "He's ex-military. He's always taken care of himself."

Rodriguez spoke in a guarded tone.

"Guatemala is not as dangerous as it once was," she said. "But there still are incidents. I don't mean to cause alarm, but tourists are sometimes targeted. Antigua itself is a peaceful town, but there's always an element beneath the surface."

"What kind of element?"

"Thugs, gangs. People who care about nothing but money. I told Mr. Callahan—the key is to cooperate. They only want money. Kidnapping is rare here. Violence not so rare."

The words rang in Byrd's ears. *Violence not so rare.* Guatemala was a dangerous country, and the arrogance of wealth could be deadly. J.C. Callahan was not known for cooperation.

"Look, this is important," he said. "And I want to clarify. The day Callahan picked up the Spyder. Where was he going?"

Her face paled as she recounted the last conversation.

"He was going out through Guatemala City. But he mentioned *Cerro de la Cruz*—the Hill of the Cross. He was going in that direction, and I told him to check with the Tourist Police. There have been some ugly incidents in recent years. Now the Tourist Police provide protection."

Byrd cursed under his breath. J.C. Callahan wouldn't consult any Tourist

Police. The old man was an egomaniac, and egomaniacs think they're invincible.

"One more question," he said. "The men who helped to move the car out of the cellar. Where did you find them?"

"There were maybe half a dozen men in total," she said. "Just local guys. A couple of them came down from that run-down house at the end of our street. There's always a few hanging out there."

It was a significant lead. Every hired hand who had any contact with Callahan would need to be interviewed. Workers, Byrd knew, would talk. He'd seen the scenario dozens of times in Alabama, when hired labor witnessed what residents had missed. This was especially true when an employer like Callahan was involved, flashing a thick roll of cash. These workers had something juicy to talk about. And if one of the workers turned out to be guilty of criminal involvement? It certainly wouldn't be the first time.

Byrd felt his knees buckle. The sensation was slight, so slight as to almost be unnoticeable.

His eyes met Callahan's. She felt it, too.

They looked up at the ceiling of the Spyder burial chamber. The dirty yellow bulb was still dangling at the end of its flimsy wire. It was moving. The motion was slight, but it was moving, gently swaying to the left and right.

"Rundown house at the end of the street," he said. "I want to go to that house. I want to go now."

His eyes shot back to the light bulb.

It was still in motion.

36

J.C. CALLAHAN WAS AWAKE.

He was cold. He was thirsty. One of Alabama's most successful businessmen, one of its least successful fathers, was lying on a concrete floor in Antigua Guatemala. Hands and feet bound, he was prepared for the end. He was beyond prepared; he *wanted* the end.

Time melted and blurred. How long was he trapped in this hell? Three days, three nights? He wasn't certain. Time lost its meaning. The old man was ready to die. But he wasn't ready to die alone.

He opened his eyes. Although his hands and feet were still bound with rope, the blindfold was gone. Perhaps after the struggle, his captors forgot to replace it. Perhaps they no longer cared what he saw. Perhaps they kept him alive for no reason at all.

He caught a lingering scent of perfume. It reminded him of his daughter. If only he'd been able to see Kristen before the end. He had so much to tell her. If he ever escaped this hell, things would be different. He'd make it up to her.

He'd frittered away his life in pursuit of the wrong goals. Only now did he realize what he'd done. Only now did he realize the true tragedy of this affair. He chased and caught a dream, planted his phallic flag one more time, won one final Pyrrhic victory.

I've failed, he thought. *I've failed as a man.*

For Callahan, failure was poison. This failure stung worst of all.

The lost Spyder.

This was not about a car. To say this was about a car would be to miss the point entirely. This was no more about a car than sex was about bodily fluids. This had nothing to do with aluminum, steel, leather, and wood.

The Spyder was more than the sum of its parts. This was about time. The distilled essence of the past, a life-sized snapshot rendered in three dimensions. The Spyder was about the people who created it, skilled German craftsmen who labored for both wages and passion, who infested every element with ingenuity, sweat, blood, and passion. This was about savoring life, about capturing lightning in a bottle. This was about growing up poor and going to bed hungry, working his ass off for three dollars a week. It was about forging documents so he could join the Army young, just to get away from his drunk of a father and start a new life.

Memories.

This was about memories. Memories of the past were dying along with his generation, fading out of human consciousness and into oblivion.

Callahan licked his lips and tasted death. His memories cascaded to the surface, rising like bubbles in a glass, reflections of one life nearing its inevitable end. Something happens when a person faces death, when the simple prospect of another breath becomes a luxury.

What had his presence on earth wrought? What had he created that would last? What would be his legacy?

He spent his life searching. He searched for spiritual meaning, and never found it in church. He gladly paid for everything except false salvation.

He searched for satisfaction, and found it fleeting. Even business triumph exerted its own corrupting influence. His passion for business faded. His ego demanded more than additional zeroes on a net worth statement. Money was not enough. It would never be enough.

He kept searching for a legacy. He never found it. He never found it abroad. He never found it at home.

That's where I fucked up, he thought. *I fucked up with Shea, and I fucked up with Kristen. I even fucked up with Baines.*

Writhing on the floor, mouth parched, head throbbing, his face a disfigured horror show, John Christian Callahan had an epiphany. He was not about bone and muscle, cartilage and sinew, the stuff he could already feel beginning to deteriorate and rot. He was more than the sum of his damaged parts.

He traveled to Guatemala to find something extraordinary. What he found was every sand castle he ever constructed being washed away and dissolving back into the beach. He was on the brink of returning to the earth. In a few short days his flesh would be gone. His bones would fall apart. He'd be eaten by worms, crunched back into microscopic dust, and nothing whatsoever would remain of John Christian Callahan, esteemed entrepreneur from Birmingham, Alabama.

There's going to be one hell of an estate sale.

All would return to the ecosystem and the highest bidder. All but Kristen.

If there was a regret, it was Kristen, and the way he left things. He made a complete mess of their relationship, treated her like an errant employee. He deserved her wrath. It was Kristen, he realized, who offered his only salvation. Kristen was his legacy. She was the living essence of Callahan, bravely carrying the albatross of his DNA forward into the future, whether she liked it or not.

He owed Kristen more than he delivered. He wanted more than ever to see her again. That was his greatest regret about dying like this, as ghastly wreckage on a floor in Guatemala. He'd never see Kristen again. That realization pierced his soul like a blade, wrenching and twisting and stealing his hope for peace.

He had to see Kristen again. He had to make things right. He could not go out like this.

He contorted on the dirty floor like a wounded insect. He twisted in the darkness until his bound hands reached a physically improbable position—his front pocket.

Once again his mind was illuminated by brilliant blasts of pain. The pain shot throughout his aching body, sharper and brighter than before.

He slipped a hand into his pocket. The matches were still there, right where he'd left them. He had four. Why hadn't he taken more?

He fumbled, and with one trembling hand withdrew a match. He had to make it count.

THE LOST SPYDER

He stroked the match gently against the concrete wall. Nothing. He did so again. The match broke, snapping in half like a twig.

Damn it, that was clumsy. Hold your hands steady.

He withdrew another match, one of three remaining. He tried again, this time using more care.

Be gentle, old man. Be gentle.

The match lit. The welcome smell of burning carbon entered his nostrils. He held the flame directly to his wrist, scorching the rope, lighting its dry fibers on fire. The skin on his wrists, already a bloody mess, was singed by the flame. The rope burned like dry leaves. The bonds were thick and tight, and the fire burned bright. Callahan leaned forward on the cold floor, pressing his stomach into the dust and dirt, holding his bound hands aloft behind his back. He wrenched his wrists back and forth, the pain growing more unbearable by the second.

He looked up from the ground, the light from the small brush fire behind his back illuminating the room. At that moment, he realized that he wasn't alone.

Someone was there.

No—not someone—*something*.

It was the Spyder. The Porsche 550 Spyder. It stood facing him in the darkness, silent, like a sentinel. Like a gargoyle of aluminum and leather and steel. Like a friend.

Had it been with him all this time? Had it been standing in the darkness throughout his torture and travails? That would be a rich irony, and Callahan appreciated irony. He'd spent most of his life in pursuit of this car. He'd sacrificed so much to find it, to acquire it, and then to personally deliver it home. Now it accompanied him in his darkest hour, standing watch in the darkness. He wouldn't die alone, after all.

He twisted his wrists, and the bonds came loose. He wrenched free his right hand first. Then he swung around the left and swiftly wrangled it loose from the flaming piece of rope. He gently sat the burning mass on the floor, and nursed the flame.

He loosened the bonds around his feet, and was free again. This time he'd remain free, or die trying.

Looking up, he finally got a clear view of his prison.

It was a small room, a damp concrete dungeon that served as the basement of the house. Above his head were long planks of wood, cross boards that served as support for the hardwood floors above.

Behind the Porsche was a wooden garage door, one containing small windows that were opaque with dirt and dust. Callahan moved quietly to the door, nursing the burning rope like a lit candle. He scrubbed away dirt from a window with his palm, and looked outside.

Peering through the dirty glass, he saw the courtyard. Lying throughout the yard were the dogs. The mongrels were asleep. But they were too many, and they were too vicious. The courtyard was a dead end. He would have to go upstairs. His only escape route would be upstairs and through the gauntlet.

He turned back to the Porsche.

We're trapped together, he thought. *Trapped on death row.*

More than fifty years had passed, and the Spyder was new. It was the most amazing thing Callahan had ever seen. It was a miracle.

The fire was dying, so he removed his shirt and lit a sleeve in the burning rope. As tendrils of flame licked up the side of the shirt, he walked to the car and peered inside.

The Spyder was silver, a dull aluminum that somehow glowed white in the flickering flame of his torch. The wheels were uncovered, and shiny as mirrors. The seats and interior were finished in crimson leather. At the rear of the car, each fender boasted a crimson dart, racing stripes. In the flickering light, they reminded him of blood.

The car was immaculate. It sat there like a time capsule, a gift from the past. Damn thing still smelled new, he could swear it. The mythical lost Spyder was everything he'd expected. It was everything the old man prized and pursued throughout his six odd decades on the earth. The greatest conquest of John Christian Callahan's life. The ultimate acquisition in his pursuit of mechanical happiness.

He leaned over the Porsche. His body and mind were ravaged, but the Spyder was serene. He caressed the machine gently, as if it were a sacred animal, a divine beast of burden that served its master well.

Another scent wafted across his nostrils, this time something different than body odor and urine and perfume. The old man smelled gasoline.

There was no reason for the car to smell of gasoline. The engine had never been started. It was more than fifty-years-old and the damn thing had never been touched, didn't have a scratch on it. It was pristine, perfect, and immaculate. It was youth, preserved. It was entirely original, right down to the original shipping crate and that German's initials hand-carved inside the front fender. This car was the Sistine Chapel creation of Professor Porsche, the holy grail of Callahan's existence. This was the essence of life.

It smelled of gasoline? No. Surely the devils hadn't tried to start it. Surely they didn't do something so stupid. Surely they didn't intercept the most valuable Porsche in the world and treat it like a fucking golf cart.

He moved to the front of the car, leaned onto the hood and peered at the gas cap, inhaling sweet fumes of petroleum. The evidence was faint but noticeable. A deep indentation and scratch, some nine inches in length, in the general vicinity of the fuel portal.

He thought back to the mirror. Not long ago he'd stared into the mirror, and seen his own beaten and battered and bloody face staring back. He'd been beaten so severely that he was scarcely recognizable—yet he'd taken all of that in stride. His body started its decay long before Guatemala. The torture and beating and starvation only accelerated matters. His body was a living science experiment, and so long as the eyes were still functioning, he'd watch its decline with detached interest.

But the Spyder was different. This car was perfect. It was immortal. These devils did far worse than damage a car. They committed blasphemy. They were evil, and they had to be destroyed.

In this moment created by a seemingly interminable period of torture and depravity, Callahan knew what he had to do. He wouldn't die quietly in the cold darkness. He wouldn't die alone.

The light from his shirt flickered and finally went out. In the darkness, he scooped up the thin rope that had once bound his feet.

He went back to the Porsche and unscrewed the gas cap. Leaning over the hood, he carefully fed the rope into the tank. As the rope disappeared into the car's belly, his tortured wrists again began to bleed. Small drops of blood fell onto the rope, and were absorbed by its fibers. Callahan was scarcely aware of the bleeding, the drops of blood streaming across radiant silver paint. His obsession with the Spyder might have cost him his life, but the car would bring him death with dignity. It would provide comfort in the darkness.

He lay there in the deathly gloom, after feeding the rope into the Porsche

550 Spyder, and waited. Gasoline slowly crept up the rope and mixed with his blood. The rope became saturated with fuel. He held it to his torso like an umbilical cord, a communal connection to his past.

Was he crazy? Perhaps. He didn't know or care. He had never cared, least of all now. He knew what he was doing. He knew what he was doing was right.

At last, the tip of the rope smelled of gasoline. He fumbled with his pants pocket, and withdrew another match. He stretched the rope out from the gas port, so it ran down the hood of the car.

The lost Spyder was now his last hope.

It was the most beautiful bomb in the world.

The match was lit.

For a moment, he held the match aloft like a torch and time stood still. Two old friends had one final conversation.

The Spyder glowed in the flickering light with an aura all its own. It shimmered with a pale luminescence, like the moon on a cloudy night. The room was filled with dull light.

For that moment, the Spyder was alive. There was sentience emanating from the car. Sympathy, understanding—and forgiveness.

J.C. Callahan wasn't a humble man. But in this moment, standing at the gates of eternity, he was humble. Reflexively, he knelt before the car. Looking up, the headlights of the Spyder seemed like eyes gazing upon him.

Go ahead, the eyes said. Do it. You are forgiven.

Then the match went out. It singed the old man's fingertips and sizzled in the darkness.

So he went to the well once more. One match left.

Still kneeling on the floor, he gently scraped the match.

Last match was lit. It was now or never.

Ashes to ashes, rust to rust.

He put the match to the tip of the rope. At first the rope resisted, and then a small blue and amber tuft of flame leapt from its fibers. The flame blossomed and inched its way up the car's hood until it reached the gas port.

John Christian Callahan turned and faced the stairs.

He had seconds to act.

He was behind the stairway when the explosion came.

37

CHARLIE BYRD WAS ON THE STREET, no more than a block away, when he heard the explosion. He was walking north along *Calle de la Nobleza* with Kristen Callahan by his side. They were walking on the sidewalk beneath *Cerro de la Cruz*, the Hill of the Cross, toward the rundown house at the end of the avenue.

It was dusk, and a brief moment of calm had befallen Antigua, Guatemala. The city was enjoying the respite that exists when the day is done and nighttime not yet begun. The flamboyant celebrations of the afternoon had ended. The air assumed a crisp coolness announcing the arrival of night. Mayan locals were in their homes having dinner and preparing for the *Semana Santa* processions of the evening.

The explosion rang across the city with a muffled roar. It came from the north, in the direction of *Cerro de la Cruz*, and worked its way south, echoing throughout the valley. The sound lingered in Charlie Byrd's mind like the guttural cry of a beast, some animal from beyond the natural world. It reverberated, causing his skin to turn gooseflesh and the hairs on his neck to stand.

That wasn't natural, he thought. *Something just happened.*

His companion knew. The only offspring of John Christian Callahan knew the exact moment she heard the boom. She knew that her father was in Antigua, Guatemala, that he was without hope, and that he had somehow beaten this unnatural drum from the deep. He shattered the calm of the early evening to send a message. The old man's soul was there, riding every wave of the sonic rumble. It defied logic and reason, but she wasn't governed by logic and reason—she felt it in her bones.

They stood in the street, gawking at the spectacle. They were frozen in time, mouths agape, eyes wide open, attempting to process events that were unfolding a little too fast.

The ground shook. Glass shattered. There were shrill clattering noises, as wood and clay and metal all collapsed in coordinated violence. The world was knocked off its axis. It rocked to the left and to the right like a ship being tossed by a tempest. Nothing, not even the earth itself—especially not the earth itself—was secure.

Their legs felt weak and lost balance. Kristen Callahan stumbled and fell. She was caught in mid-air. Byrd held her tight in his arms, pulled her to his chest, as the very earth moved beneath them.

Then silence was restored. It was an eerie unnatural silence, a calm in the center of the storm.

Then another deep, guttural rumble, this one from the south. They turned and looked toward *Volcan Acatenango*, one of the three dormant volcanoes that loomed above Antigua like ancient gods, kings from a time that history had forgotten.

The volcano Acatenango was alive. The green mountain was alive and upon its crown danced apparitions of flame and soot and smoke. Clouds of white ash gushed into the sky like snow from hell itself.

Byrd looked north toward *Cerro de la Cruz*. The Hill of the Cross loomed on the horizon, shrouded by the last fleeting rays of the setting sun. They caught one last glimpse of the slender white crosses high upon the hill. Then the crosses were gone, obscured by black smoke. Great billowing unnatural clouds of smoke filled the sky. There was a fire just down the street, and from it roiling pus spewed into the sky.

The rumble of the earthquake subsided, and they regained their balance.

Then they were running, down the street, past yelping dogs and crying children and shrieking car alarms, skipping over puddles of broken glass. They ran toward the towering plume of black smoke.

They ran side by side. They could both sense that something remarkable had happened, something even more remarkable than another earthquake in Antigua Guatemala.

As they ran, ash began to fall. White ash rained from the sky. It fell softly all around, like snow. They ran through the snow toward a beckoning column of smoke and flame.

They arrived on *Calle de la Nobleza* in front of a great house. The structure was like many other neglected homes on the outskirts of Antigua. From the street it was an opaque mystery, an imposing fortress of boarded windows and walls of stone.

The house was on fire. But they could see no flame. They only saw smoke, murky clouds of black smoke billowing from its rancid underbelly, seeping from open windows into the sky.

John Christian Callahan was surrounded by flame.

The staircase shielded him from the brunt of the blast. He knelt behind that simple shield, and it saved his life. He felt the shock waves pass through him, and for a moment thought his heart had stopped. When only echoes of the roar remained, he realized it was still beating in his chest.

His heart was beating, but not pounding. There was no rush of adrenaline, no sense of fear nor panic, not even a real sense of hurry. He approached the situation deliberately, almost in a silky slow motion trance. He knew what he was doing. He knew what he was doing was right.

He emerged from behind the staircase. The dungeon that served as his personal hell was now alight with flame.

The Spyder was a funeral pyre. The car exploded with a force he didn't anticipate. It was split open like a sacrifice, like a sacred animal that was slain and roasted on a spit. It was a shell, a pristine silver shell with blood interior that melted and bubbled with flame.

Callahan felt the earth shake. Confused, he lost his balance and dropped to one knee.

Kneeling, he again felt fear and awe. The house shook to its foundation. A support beam broke loose and fell from the ceiling, crashing to the ground in a flowing cascade of dust. Something had happened, something he didn't understand.

From above, a thud and cry.

The Fat Man came tumbling down the stairs. His body rolled forward and down. Down, down, down . . . down the flimsy wooden steps and into the dungeon. It tumbled and fell from the apex to the floor, each twisting turn wreaking more grotesque violence upon the body. At last his head bounced off the concrete floor and he sank into a lifeless heap.

Callahan emerged from behind the stairwell, and examined the Fat Man's limp body. Again, no emotion, no sense of elation, pity, sadness or rage. The Fat Man was dead.

The flames grew brighter in the burning car, and he felt the heat bore into his battered skin. He looked up toward the light streaming from the top of the stairs.

Got to get out of here, he thought. *Got to get out of here now.*

Flames spread throughout the room, engulfing the ceiling. Brilliant waves of apricot flame licked the hardwood floors like an advancing ocean tide. The house was an inferno.

Callahan took one last lingering glance at the Spyder. The heat was intense, and he couldn't approach. The car slowly disappeared in an expanding fog of smoke and flame.

Run, the Spyder seemed to say. *Run from the abyss.*

Back to the stairs. Callahan began climbing the staircase. The steps, weakened by age and abuse, creaked during his ascent. On the third step, his foot broke the thin plank and slipped through. He caught his balance and continued climbing. Up the stairs, up, up, up toward the light.

When he reached the apex, the door was standing open.

The smoke grew thick and black as night, and it swirled around him like a whirlpool.

Don't breathe. This air is death.

He crouched low and worked along the hallway, moving through the blackness from memory, feeling the wall with his hands. His left hand felt cold metal. It was a candlestick, encased in wax drippings on the shelf. He snapped the brass out of its encasement and continued crawling down the hall. Into the foyer he went, toward the front door and the exit.

Still, nothing. He was standing at the precipice. He was at the gateway between abyss and absolution.

The knife came from behind.

He didn't hear it; he felt it. Felt it breaching the cloth on his back, passing through his thin skin, tearing away tissue and ramming into bone. It happened in a fraction of a second. But he felt every nuance of that instant.

The knife ground to a halt on his back, to the right of his spine. It dug a groove in his shoulder blade, and then bone won. The knife glanced away, and Callahan staggered forward.

He rolled to the ground, trying to escape death.

But The Man with the Scar was upon him. Rebuffed by the bone, the knife blade raised toward the sky like the sword of Damocles.

Callahan looked into the face of his captor. It was spectral and hollow, a distorted skull. Twisted and angry and colorless, except for the eyes and the scar. The yellow eyes now glowed as if on fire. The face of The Man with the Scar was distorted like a mask and the scar looked like flame, burning its image into his brain.

For a moment, time stopped and the knife hung in the air. Callahan recognized the blade, for it had cut his flesh before. It had given him a scar of his own. He could feel the wound throbbing on his cheek. This knife had taken his blood. It had taken his dignity. Now it was poised to take his life.

The blade began its descent, and Callahan instinctively raised his arm to block the impending blow.

He poured all of his remaining strength, rage, hope and fear into a twisted piece of brass. He slung the candlestick, and scored a glancing blow against the skull of his opponent before it slipped from his hand.

Two slippery, bloody metal objects flew across the foyer.

The candlestick disappeared into the smoke and landed with a dull thud. It was somewhere in the house, out of sight, buried in the smoke. It was no longer a factor.

The knife, however, clattered on the floorboard.

Both men made a grab for it. It slid away and Callahan kicked it into the void.

Weapons gone, Callahan turned to the only remaining tools—his hands. He reached up, grabbed The Man with the Scar by the throat, and squeezed. A strength entered his hands; he channeled every fiber of his being into the grasp. Let go, he knew, and it was the end.

The two foes twisted and reversed positions. Now Callahan was on top, choking the demon. His mind flashed back to Fort Rucker, back to Korea, back to the front. This wasn't his first struggle with death.

His blue eyes bored into the Man's flaming coals until those coals grew dim. Like a dying campfire, their flame trickled away into darkness. At last they were dull and lifeless. The Man with the Scar collapsed into a heap.

Callahan pulled himself to his feet, and looked down through swirling smoke at his vanquished foe. The old man had run a gauntlet toward the only absolution he knew.

He flung open the door and emerged into the night.

The exorcism was complete.

Callahan staggered through the door, his face and body blackened with soot, and onto *Calle de la Nobleza*.

He had won.

He staggered into the street, struggled for a deep breath of clear air, and sank to his knees.

When he looked up, he saw her.

She was standing across the street, looking at her father. When their eyes met, all grew quiet. The noise and pain and chaos simply melted away.

Was he insane? Was he hallucinating? Or was that his daughter standing across the street, standing in the middle of an ancient village in Central America, standing like she'd expected him all along?

She watched the scene unfold, mouth frozen agape with awe and horror. The haunted form that staggered from the building bore little resemblance to John Christian Callahan.

Then their eyes locked. Beneath the layers of soot and blood and filth were her father's unmistakable eyes. They were unchanged, sparkling from his face like nuggets of sapphire. His eyes peered into her soul, the way only her father's eyes could.

She ran to him. They embraced, and hot tears flowed down his cheeks, leaving pale streaks amidst layers of dark soot.

He looked into her eyes and saw his mother and grandparents and aunt and uncle and every other thing in the world he'd known that was truly good.

When the words finally came, they arrived in a torrent.

"I knew you'd come," he said. "I knew you'd find me."

She felt a flush of anger. She hadn't expected to feel anger, but there it was.

"Oh, Daddy," she said. "Why did you do it? Why didn't you tell me?"

She gripped her father and demanded again, her voice shaking. "Why? Why did you do it?"

Her voice faded as she sought the words.

Looking at this twisted wretch of a creature, this sad shell of a broken man, at last, she could only look at him and ask, "Why?"

John Christian Callahan was a pathetic creature now, shriveled before her in the street. He understood exactly what his daughter was asking.

"It was about the legacy," he said. "It was about . . . immortality."

"The legacy," she spat the words. She had heard him use the phrase a thousand times before. The legacy. What did it really mean?

His eyes turned skyward.

"The lost Spyder," he said, looking at the plume of smoke that blackened the sky. "The lost Spyder is gone."

White ash fell gently to the ground. They were sprinkled with a snowfall of white volcanic ash.

The old man looked at his daughter with the tear-laden eyes of a child.

"I need to ask something of you now," he said. "I need to ask your forgiveness."

"What?"

"I need your forgiveness."

"Daddy, I . . ."

"Please."

Something in his croaking voice demanded a response.

"I . . ." She stammered. It didn't feel real.

"I forgive you."

He smiled as he heard the words. He felt satisfied, as though he'd just consumed a fine meal. The pain in his broken body began to fade, and he felt a sense of warmth and comfort.

He smiled and said, "My daughter. You are my legacy."

She looked down at him, tears streaking her own cheeks.

His voice was failing. The blackness that filled the sky was drifting downward to consume his soul.

"You are my legacy," he said as his voice disappeared into the night.

Looking up into his daughter's eyes, soaking up his last vision on earth, the old man smiled. In his daughter's eyes he saw his wife. Shea Callahan was looking down at him and she, too, forgave.

His heart stopped beating, and his chest grew still. He closed his eyes.

It was, at last, time to rest.

John Christian Callahan died.

He died in his daughter's arms, on *Calle de la Nobleza* in Antigua Guatemala.

He didn't die alone.

Charlie Byrd dropped to his knees.

38

FOR GENERATIONS, ELMWOOD CEMETERY SERVED AS AN ESTEEMED FINAL RESTING PLACE FOR ALABAMIANS. The sprawling grounds were replete with oak and willow trees, and beds of flowers nestled alongside tombstones and crypts. The Birmingham cemetery was so large that it wasn't uncommon for locals to get lost in it. Scattered throughout were scores of ordinary folk, as well as the occasional celebrity.

No fewer than three Alabama governors were buried in Elmwood. Two United States senators. A Confederate general by the name of William Wirt Allen. Native son musicians like jazz legend Sun Ra.

Perhaps the most famous permanent resident of Elmwood was the former Alabama football coach, Paul "Bear" Bryant. His grave was marked by a simple rectangular plaque that made no mention of the man's achievement on the gridiron. Bear was modest in death, yet the mere sight of his gravestone brought mist to the eyes of many.

When Bear Bryant was laid to rest in 1983, the entire state showed up for the service. Truckers and doctors, young and old—half a million people stood along the highway to pay their respects, as the funeral procession lumbered its way from Tuscaloosa to Birmingham.

It thus seemed appropriate that John Christian Callahan join the ranks of

Southern nobility in the peaceful fields of Elmwood. Callahan didn't receive a royal sendoff—no citizens lined the highway—but the local media attention was comparable. On the appointed day of his funeral, a flock of media converged upon the scene. Helicopters provided coverage from above. Satellite vans were on the ground, beaming live footage from Birmingham to outer space, where it bounced back down to earth and around the globe.

There were many questions and precious few answers. One of Alabama's most distinguished—in other words, richest—citizens had reportedly died in Central America, and the cause was baffling. Rumors escaped Guatemala. But rumors didn't travel well, and they were inconclusive.

There was a kidnapping, that much was certain. There was an earthquake; that was indisputable. There had been some sort of monetary transaction, the nature and legality of which were of some debate. The rumors didn't add up, and the media came to Elmwood seeking answers.

Their cameras were trained on a petite young woman, the apparent heir to the considerable Callahan fortune, who stood graveside. Her face was shrouded in an opaque black veil, black being the proper color of mourning. Though they couldn't see her face, her precise manner and the unusually lengthy funeral ceremony told them a lot—perhaps too much.

Indeed, it was the extreme length of the ceremony that was notable. This was the hottest day of the year to date, and the Alabama humidity was thick as turtle soup. Those few individuals who attended the funeral were drenched in their own perspiration. They were standing in Elmwood, broiling in the sun, listening to a particularly long-winded man of the cloth drone on about *Ecclesiastes* like he was being paid by the hour.

Most prominent amongst them was Brett Lancaster, the dogged reporter from *The Birmingham News*. Lancaster too wore black, and his dark attire exacerbated his beet-red complexion. It was cruel, he later said, the length of this particular graveside service. Attendees withered in the relentless heat. But the equally relentless Lancaster was determined to get his story. In hindsight, he was also intrigued by the conspicuous absence of a certain Charles Mortimer Byrd.

ง∽๛

Meanwhile, some twelve miles away, the spiritual rebirth of John Christian Callahan took place far from Elmwood Cemetery. Nothing about the ceremony was traditional. It happened on that other sacred ground in the Callahan world order—the racetrack. The man was reborn in the ebony asphalt of Barber Motorsports Park.

By any estimation, this invitation-only ceremony drew a small turnout. On this day, the Barber Park was calm, closed to the public. The track was even more peaceful than Elmwood.

There were but a few friends in attendance, and they stood on the tarmac of the racing paddock with proper funereal respect. Blake Williams was present, as were Stanley Griggs and a motley assortment of local Porsche aficionados. These were Southern gentlemen with well documented addictions to motorsport. They wore stoic expressions masking the emotions that roiled beneath. They came to the track to pay their respects. Mainly, they came because they were invited, and they were intensely curious. No one dared refuse a personal invitation from John Christian Callahan—especially since the man was rumored to be dead.

Charlie Byrd, eschewing his typical aversion to formal wear on this particular occasion, was also present. Byrd went against his instincts and wore a tie; he regretted the decision.

Kristen Callahan, the real Kristen Callahan and not the imposter going through the motions in Elmwood Cemetery, was also present.

She didn't wear black. The only offspring of John Christian Callahan wore a rainbow ensemble that captured every color of springtime. The outfit reminded Charlie Byrd of an *alfombra*, a collage of red and yellow and green that somehow turned one's thoughts away from death and back toward life.

Then there was Baines Jackson, the longtime Callahan employee whose steady loyalty had made the difference. Jackson stood alongside Kristen Callahan, his face a portrait of serenity, looking more like a grandfather than a family manservant.

But undoubtedly the most surprising attendee was the man himself, John Christian Callahan stood in the parking lot, in front of the paddock garage, of his own accord. He stood before the crowd and delivered his own version of an epitaph, turning the concept squarely on its head.

He looked like a man who had risen from the dead. His torso was bandaged, but he was standing—and that in itself was an achievement.

The wound that blemished his face was on the mend, but leaving behind a pronounced scar. The cheek wasn't bandaged. It was healing in the open air, free for all to see.

Callahan's remarks were few. He would no longer romanticize his life; nor would he publicly elaborate on his return from the dead.

Like all talented public speakers, he began with a joke.

"I've taken a few steps to ensure our privacy today," he said. "I'm sure that tomorrow's papers will be filled with interesting news."

There was laughter amongst the crowd. The head fake was vintage Callahan. He wasn't only alive, he was operating in fine form.

"This ceremony represents change," he said. "I'm a changed man. I've been changed by violence and I've been changed by regret. I've been changed by what happened in Guatemala, and I can assure you those changes will be lasting and permanent."

Murmurs of approval rippled throughout the crowd. These men—notably, they were all men—knew Callahan and loved him despite his faults. They shared little with him but one common passion. He was an eccentric, they understood, and eccentric men deserved their indulgences.

"I have three people to thank for that change, and for my second chance."

He gestured toward his daughter and Baines Jackson. "The first two you already know," he said. "You all know Kristen. And I'd especially like to thank Baines for his many years of loyal . . . friendship."

Kristen Callahan slid her arm around the butler's lower back, and gave him a squeeze. It was the first time she'd ever heard her father call Baines a friend. She liked the sound of it.

The speaker next turned to Charlie Byrd.

"The third person is also joining us today. The fellow back there in the tie."

An emphasis on the word "tie" evoked laughter from the crowd. Byrd felt all eyes turning to him. His face flushed at the attention. For perhaps the first time in his life, he was overdressed.

Callahan turned serious and continued.

"Now some may ask why I went to Guatemala, why I risked everything chasing a legend. They might as well ask me why I breathe. Or why I dream."

As Callahan spoke, he pulled out a silk handkerchief and dabbed perspiration from his brow. It was such a warm day that every delicate caress of wind was a blessing.

"They say youth is wasted on the young."

More nods of understanding.

"I've tried to make sense of what happened in Guatemala," he said. "I've tried to make sense of what happened there, and what really motivated me to do what I did. Most importantly, what did I learn?"

The men were attentive, focused. *The Spyder.* He was talking about the Porsche. They were like young boys in school, and the teacher had broached a favorite subject.

"I suppose," he said, "I was chasing the past. Youth. Immortality. Hell, call it what you want."

The statement lingered in the air. These men were dreamers, too.

"I was trying to turn back the clock," he said. "But the lost Spyder is gone. And so is my wife."

He turned and faced the garage.

"But gentlemen," he said.

The garage door rose, revealing it contents.

Callahan raised his hand and beckoned the men inside the air-conditioned bay. They followed eagerly, surrounding the centerpiece attraction with the gleeful enthusiasm of children.

Byrd recognized the car immediately.

It was the Porsche 550 Spyder, the one he'd seen in Callahan's underground garage.

But the car was no longer damaged. The effects of the long ago wreck had been erased. The car no longer bore a scratch, nor a drop of Shea Callahan's dried blood. It no longer loomed like an ancient relic from a tragic past. It was fully restored, and its paint and leather shined.

"Gentlemen," Callahan said as he opened a bottle of champagne. "This old bastard is still very much alive."

Charlie Byrd watched the scene unfold with bemusement. Callahan had finished his brief oration to the gathered crowd, but there remained more questions than answers. Perhaps that was to be expected. Just as no man's life could be summarized in a single telling, no man's rebirth could be explained in a simple speech, no matter how heartfelt the words.

Byrd's eyes drifted from the car to the sole woman looking at it. Kristen

Callahan bent over and peered into the cockpit of the Porsche. The interior metal was clean and polished as fine silverware, the leather restored to its original suppleness. She looked into the car one final time. Then she abruptly walked away from the 550 Spyder and away from her father's ceremony. She left the men behind, laughing and drinking their champagne and wondering what the hell else old Callahan had up his sleeve. She walked away and climbed a short flight of stairs above the paddock to the observation deck overlooking Barber Motorsports Park.

She stood on the rooftop deck beneath a row of motionless white flags, holding her transparent plastic cup of champagne. She stood alone, looking out over the Park. All was now in full bloom. The Park was a veritable ocean of green turf, rolling hills with crests of blooming flowers, all wrapped together by a winding black ribbon of asphalt.

Charlie Byrd shifted in his one and only suit. He didn't enjoy his brief moment at the center of attention, having every eye trained upon him. These social events fit Byrd as naturally as neckties. There were always clumsy moments when he felt an utter loss for words. He never knew what to say at times such as these, so Byrd generally said nothing. He'd mumble a few obligatory comments and be on his way. He'd be the first to flee the room, hop in his Bronco, loosen his tie, and flip on the radio. He would reestablish emotional distance.

This event was different. He didn't really know John Christian Callahan, and felt little emotion for the man. In Byrd's eyes, Callahan did something foolish, and he paid for it with his life.

But Callahan was also lucky, because Charlie Byrd saved that life. He'd been there on the street in Antigua when the man's heart stopped beating.

Byrd saw him die right in front of his eyes, in the contradictory chaos of sacred and profane that was Guatemala. Byrd saw him die and he heard his final words. Witnessing that exchange, the final embrace of daughter and father, Charlie Byrd dropped to his knees and brought John Christian Callahan back from the dead. He used the techniques he learned years earlier, the same skills that a CPR doll named Annie taught every kid in an Alabama high school. He pounded on the man's chest and breathed air into his mouth. After what seemed an eternity, he felt him shudder and cough and spring back to life.

THE LOST SPYDER

Charlie Byrd didn't know Callahan, but he brought him back from the dead. Brought him back for what purpose? How had the man changed?

Perhaps she would know. His daughter was standing along on the rooftop deck above.

At this moment, standing in an ill-fitting suit in the Alabama sun, Byrd didn't realize the extent to which he himself had transformed in Germany and in Guatemala. The changes were there, subtle but fundamental. The old Charlie Byrd, upon seeing this woman standing alone, might have turned and walked away. He might have climbed into his Ford Bronco and disappeared, only to reemerge once the standard emotional barriers were resurrected.

This time Byrd wouldn't walk away.

He joined Kristen Callahan on the rooftop observation deck. She was leaning forward against the guardrail, and he could just glimpse the tattoo peeking from the small of her back.

Hearing footsteps, she turned and welcomed his arrival.

"Charlie Byrd," she said with a smile. "See? You are the man of my dreams."

She embraced him, a lingering embrace that allowed Byrd to again feel her soft curves and smell her delicate auburn hair. Byrd smelled flowers in her hair, and he saw the musical jangle of her earrings. For a moment, his mind flashed back to bedrooms in Germany and Guatemala, back even to their first meeting at the track when she had introduced him to the modern definition of a thrill ride. With this woman he had dabbled in taboo by mixing business with pleasure. He had gotten involved. Somehow their relationship had survived.

She released and stepped back to take in the view. They were standing alone, holding plastic cups of champagne that seemed equally out of place as Charlie Byrd.

"Thank you for coming," she said. Then without a trace of a smile she added, "You were clearly not meant to wear a tie."

He smiled and felt his stomach clench into a familiar awkward knot. Their time together had been thrilling, but Byrd often felt uncomfortable, like he was out of his element. If the foundation of their relationship had a core weakness, it was this divide between her expectations and his reality.

"I'm sorry about this suit," he said. "I use it for Moot Court."

She stifled a laugh. It was most certainly a breach of etiquette to laugh at a man's clothing, but Byrd's ubiquitous law student costume demanded nothing less.

"I'm just giving you a hard time, " she smiled. "But you can afford a new suit. Come to think of it, you can afford a new truck. You happy with your pay?"

Happy? Happy was an understatement. Hell, it wasn't even the right category of emotion. Charlie Byrd wasn't happy; he was astonished. Thanks to the gratitude and generosity of John Christian Callahan, Byrd's money troubles were a thing of the past.

"Let's just say it was more than enough. The fine folks at Birmingham School of Law will be happy. But," he said, "I ain't selling my truck."

Laughter floated upward from the garage bay, laughter unrelated to Byrd's remark. Then they heard the source of the commotion. The Porsche 550 Spyder was cranked. It roared to life with a metallic growl, and the engine barked loud enough to shake the ground. It was a primal noise that echoed throughout the area, momentarily drowning their conversation. They stood on the rooftop together, leaning against the guard rail, listening to the engine blast its signature music from the paddock garage.

That sound made Byrd's arms turn gooseflesh. It seemed to confirm, to shout to the heavens with authority—yes, the old man and the old Spyder were still very much alive.

A voice came from behind.

"Hey there, little lady."

It was John Christian Callahan. The man himself had followed them onto the rooftop deck. He advanced from the opposite direction, having taken the plexiglass elevator. He was walking stiffly, and with a slight limp. His face looked beaten and skinned, like he'd just returned from some sort of mountaineering expedition gone awry. But that same face was grinning nevertheless. He nodded to the detective.

"Mr. Byrd," he said. "Thank you for coming."

The detective shifted in his suit. Although Charlie Byrd was not easily intimidated, Callahan exuded alpha dog charisma in spades. The man was less predictable than the weather, and his penchant for drama was unsettling. He wielded his own unique brand of personal magnetism. He could attract or repel depending on shifts in its polarity.

He embraced his daughter. He then gently tapped his own side, and the healing wound beneath.

"It hurts to hug," he said. "But today I'm just happy to be feeling anything at all."

They exchanged pleasantries, taking in the view from the rooftop deck, listening to the steady mechanical clatter of the vintage car below. Much to the delight of the assembled throng, the engine was performing like a champ.

"She sounds good, doesn't she?"

"Yes sir," Byrd replied, "she sure does."

Byrd tugged at his necktie. It was hot atop the roof of the paddock area, and the heat exacerbated his discomfort.

"Sir, I'd just like to thank you one more time," he said.

Callahan raised his hand.

"Please," he replied. "I'm the one who should be thanking you."

"That's right," Kristen said. "None of this would've been possible without Charlie."

"In other words," Callahan said, "feel free to remove the fucking tie."

Byrd laughed and accepted the man's offer, jerking off his tie with vigor. He drained the rest of the champagne from his plastic cup, and took a lingering glance at the woman by his side. She was watching the 550 Spyder as it crawled and sputtered its way towards the racetrack. Her emerald eyes sparkled in the sunlight. He'd been through hell with this woman, he'd made love to this woman, and yet she was still a mystery. At that moment, Charlie Byrd resolved to explore the mystery. To hell with emotional distance. To hell with tattoos and bumper stickers, fantastic dreams and astrological bullshit. She was no longer a client; she was a lover and a friend. She had a mentally unbalanced father, perhaps, but Byrd wouldn't let that small detail derail their relationship.

"If you'll excuse me," Byrd said, "I'm going to grab some more champagne. Can I bring you anything?"

His offer was declined, but Callahan made a suggestion.

"Tell Baines you want to try the ninety-six *Clos d'Ambonnay*," Callahan said. "You'll like it."

"Yes, sir," Byrd said. "I'll give it a shot."

He went down the stairwell, leaving father and daughter alone on the rooftop.

༄༅

J.C. and Kristen Callahan stood side-by-side, looking out over the track. The Spyder was now on the racing tarmac, spitting and churning out its mechanical song, as Stanley Griggs gleefully piloted the car in perhaps the most memorable test lap of his life.

"Why aren't you driving?" she said. "You should be out there."

"I figured Stanley would get a kick out of it," he replied. "Besides, I'm still a little stiff."

She nodded.

"How are you doing?"

"I'm standing," he said. "I'm walking. Doctors predict a strong recovery. All but the face."

He ran his finger lightly along the surface of his face, tracing the knife incision. The wound was healing well in the open air.

"Your face? Surely they can fix that."

He nodded.

"Yeah, they could fix it. But I think I may keep the scar. As a reminder."

His daughter nodded. It was a surprising revelation, but she didn't let the surprise show.

"Okay, so you're physically fine. But . . . I mean, how are you really doing?"

"You know what?" he replied. "For someone who was dead not long ago, I'm doing alright."

"How long did they have you?" she asked.

"Three days, three nights. I took the long way down to Guatemala, then spent some time as a tourist in Antigua. They grabbed me as I was leaving. Not long after Baines called you."

His voice trailed away as his mind fell into the same tired feedback loop. He'd been consumed by these thoughts and emotions for days. The guilt. The anger. The shock. He'd gambled everything, and damn near lost it. But he'd gotten everything back, and it was standing by his side, walking around with his DNA.

His daughter stared straight ahead at the track. Now the Spyder was on the far end of the race course, barely visible from their vantage point.

"I've gone over everything a thousand times," she said. "If only we had gotten to Guatemala sooner. If only we had moved more quickly. We could have gotten you out of that Hell."

He put his hand on hers.

"You can't do that to yourself. Honey, after all we've been through, I'm impressed that you came looking at all, and that you didn't dead end in Germany. Anyway," he added, "I have my own theories about the whole thing."

"Oh really?" She raised her eyebrows. "Care to share?"

Callahan steeled himself for the exchange. He feared few things in life, but dealing with Kristen was one of them. He feared his own propensity for saying the wrong thing, of making some verbal gaffe that would mar the occasion. He'd been guilty of it so many times with his daughter. He'd done it with everyone at one time or another. J.C. Callahan had tossed so many verbal grenades that people instinctively flinched when he opened his mouth.

"I've been thinking," he said. "I know you like it when I've been thinking."

Beneath the thick layers of Southern posturing and male ego, J.C. Callahan was a father who wanted nothing more than to reach his daughter.

"Go ahead," she said. "I'm all ears."

"I've had almost seven decades on the planet," he said. "That's more than a lot of people get. Probably more than I deserve. It's been a hell of a ride, and it's going to end someday. What happened in Guatemala was my fault, but . . ."

He paused, doubting himself. It was hard to say. But he had to say it.

"But?"

"I think things in Guatemala were *meant* to happen the way they did. I went looking for a lost treasure. But I was the one who was lost. When you go through what happened to me down there, you learn about yourself. Looking back at my life, I gained the world. But I nearly lost my soul."

She said nothing, but pondered the one conclusion she hadn't expected from her father.

He continued. "Looking back, I made some mistakes along the way, and I don't just mean with the damned car. I mean with you, and with your mother. With lots of other folks too, but it all starts and ends with you. I loved your mother with all of my heart. And I love you. I'm sorry that I haven't done a good job of showing it. I promise to do better."

Her eyes welled with tears, but she did not speak.

"So here's what I think," he continued, "I think we were all meant to be there on that street in Guatemala, at precisely that time. What happened to us was pre-ordained, fate. Out of our hands. Nothing we could've done to stop it."

More silence as she considered her father's words.

"We did what we were supposed to do," he continued. "We got together one final time. You talk about Charlie Byrd saving me. I remember what you said to me, there in the street. I think you saved me. All Byrd did was get my heart beating again."

At that comment, a single tear rolled down her cheek. She wiped it away with an open palm.

Callahan paused. Had he said the wrong thing?

"No, I'm okay," she said. "Go on. I want to hear this."

"Remember what I said about a legacy. Right before I passed out. You are my legacy."

It was unlike J.C. Callahan to talk this way, but his own internal debate and discussion was bubbling forth. Callahan had relived Guatemala a thousand times in his mind, and he attempted to draw conclusions. This, he realized, was the true prize, the real buried treasure he brought home from Guatemala. He was, at last, changed.

"It's like Antigua," he said. "Most things in the world crumble. But some things last. That's what it's really all about."

She smiled, and the smile was natural and genuine.

"Spoken like a true fatalist," she said. "Pretty impressive coming from you."

He gripped her hand firmly and added, "Thank you. You've given me a second chance, and I'm going to make the most of it. I promise you. I have changed. Things are going to be different between us. I'm going to be different."

Callahan felt a tightness in his throat. He'd actually said what he came to say to his daughter, and hadn't caused an uproar. He no longer felt like a bull in a china shop. For once, J.C. Callahan said the right thing.

"One thing I can't figure out," she said.

"What?"

"The funeral today in Elmwood Cemetery. Is it an empty casket?"

"I'm surprised you have to ask."

"I read about it this morning. It's all over the radio and TV. There's a huge service today in Elmwood. Going on right now. So who's in the casket?"

His voice beamed.

"I'm officially burying my past," he said. "It deserves a proper burial, don't you think?"

So it came to be that, on the day John Christian Callahan turned the ignition on his new life, the charred remains of the lost Porsche 550 Spyder were buried alongside Alabama royalty in Elmwood.

The thought of the media throng scampering to record every element of that service brought a broad smile to Callahan's face. It was, he concluded, poetic justice.

She burst into laughter.

"Oh, that's good. The lost Spyder is in Elmwood," she laughed. "You really are crazy, you know that?

"We Callahans are not crazy, honey," he replied. "We're eccentric."

She laughed again, this time a hearty release. Beneath them the revived 550 Spyder was providing plenty of eye candy. The aluminum chariot was now darting along the near side of the track, springing from corner to corner just like it did in the old days.

"I finally get it," she said. "I get the whole car thing."

"Oh?"

"I get what it's really all about."

He narrowed his eyes.

"And?"

"It's about being alive."

He smiled.

"That's as good an explanation as any."

Beneath them, Stanley Griggs piloted the Porsche 550 Spyder off the racetrack into the paddock area. Griggs eagerly waved as the car rolled past. The inaugural journey had been a success.

"What about the rest of your collection?" she asked. "What's happening with your garage queens?"

His voice turned resolute. Callahan had spent most of his life believing that the strong should eat the weak. This philosophy he had gotten wrong. It was far better, he realized, for the strong to protect and shepherd the weak.

"This is only the beginning," he said. "The garage queens are going to do something. They're going to do something good."

She smiled and gave her father a long hug. For a moment, she was his little girl again.

"I love you, Daddy," she said.

He looked into her eyes, and caught a glimpse of his wife. Shea Callahan was looking back at him, and she was smiling.

"I love you too, honey," he said. "I love you with all of my heart."

He turned and scanned the heavens. The wind was sweeping cotton across the celestial sphere, casting moving shadows on the ground. Callahan shielded his eyes from the harsh sunlight with his hand. He watched the clouds march in formation, an evolving menagerie of random wispy shapes.

One cloud caught his eye. He saw it twisting in the sky above the Park. He stared at it with wonder.

The apparition was gone almost as soon as it appeared. But for one brief moment, gazing into the Alabama sky, John Christian Callahan found himself looking at an ephemeral white carnation.

Then the flower was gone.

THE LOST SPYDER

C.S. Michael
The Lost Spyder

A native of Alabama, C.S. "Sean" Michael is the author of The Lost Spyder. He was educated at Birmingham-Southern College and the University of North Carolina at Chapel Hill School of Law. More importantly, he has piloted a Porsche around a race track, appeared in a *Business Week* cover story, been photographed by *National Geographic* dancing in Czechoslovakia, directed short films in Hollywood, drank cognac in the former Soviet republic of Transdniestria, tasted wine in Moldova, sampled herring in Sweden, hosted a party at the Playboy Mansion, lived in Greenwich Village, sat behind Dave Letterman's desk, publicly recited Russian poetry, watched ancient religious parades in Guatemala, piloted go-carts in Uraguay, told jokes onstage at LA's Comedy Store, watched wild grizzly bears fight in Montana, climbed volcanoes in El Salvador, played videogames in Japan, RV camped in Argentina, and most recently hauled an Airstream travel trailer throughout the lower 48 states. When not on a walkabout, he and his wife Kristy divide their time between Alabama and the Florida Gulf Coast.

The Lost Spyder is his first novel.

Made in the USA
Lexington, KY
11 November 2011